Echo FT 6—
Scan

PRAISE FOR

Wedding Season

"Full of crackling dialogue and astute asides, *Wedding Season* is a witty romp through the Manhattan social maze."
—Lucinda Rosenfeld, author of *What She Saw . . .* and *Why She Went Home*

"*Wedding Season* will appeal to commitment-phobes and marriage addicts alike. . . . A fun, bittersweet twist on the typical romantic comedy."
—Plum Sykes, author of *Bergdorf Blondes*

"With *Wedding Season,* Darcy Cosper takes on the puzzle of love with such sweet, sly, lusty, whole-hearted brilliance, the eternal questions seem newly sprung and deeply, beautifully answered. Noel Coward would blush with pleasure."
—Mary-Beth Hughes, author of *Wavemaker II*

"I adored *Wedding Season.* Not only is it a delight to read, with some of the sweetest smart-talking characters I've encountered in a long while, it contains wonderful insights about the institution of marriage that are so revelatory I had to read them aloud to my One and Only. It's very alive, very funny, and yet quite serious at its core."
—Lisa Lerner, author of *Just Like Beauty*

"Long after Darcy Cosper's sure-handed *Wedding Season* has its irresistible way with you, you remember her people—particularly the cantankerous, vulnerable, hyper-smart Joy Silverman. Cosper has a faultless ear for their talk and a sharp comic eye for their vagaries. But what ultimately sets *Wedding Season* apart from other contemporary novels of urban manners is her tough-minded affection for Joy and her lovingly, anxiously bonded group of friends, so soon to part, as they navigate their seductive, scary passages from full-of-beans young adulthood to fully adult life."

—David Gates, author of *Jernigan*, *Preston Falls*, and *The Wonders of the Invisible World*

"With eloquent humor, Darcy Cosper's refreshing *Wedding Season* dares to challenge the conventions of matrimony that still prevail in an era where women are free to vote and marry other women and (gasp!) not marry at all. An engaging meditation on life and love, independence and vulnerability, *Wedding Season* defies expectations and does so with humor and heart. Darcy Cosper's debut is entertaining and insightful, funny and bittersweet, and best of all, honest."

—Elizabeth Crane, author of *When the Messenger Is Hot: Stories*

"Everybody is doing it in this book—getting married, that is. *Wedding Season* is a glorious depiction of the battle between the sexes (and the same sexes); it is a gem of a novel, sparkling with heart and wit and humor."

—Jonathan Ames, author of *What's Not to Love?*

"*Wedding Season* is super funny with a dizzying confetti-toss of characters. Just when you think you'd heard it all about single girls and their marriage anxiety, Darcy Cosper comes along and, with high energy humor, intensity, and some serious thinking, reaches deep into the subject of modern love."

—Mike Albo, author of *Hornito: My Lie Life* and *The Underminer*

Wedding Season

THREE RIVERS PRESS • NEW YORK

Wedding Season

. . .

DARCY COSPER

Grateful acknowledgment is made to the following for permission to reprint
previously published material:

ALFRED A. KNOPF: Excerpt from *Collected Poems* by Frank O'Hara.
Copyright © 1971 by Maureen Granville-Smith, Administratrix of the
Estate of Frank O'Hara. Reprinted by permission of Alfred A. Knopf,
a division of Random House, Inc.

HOUGHTON MIFFLIN COMPANY: Excerpt from "Wait" from *Mortal Acts,
Mortal Words* by Galway Kinnell. Copyright © 1980 by Galway Kinnell.
All rights reserved. Reprinted by permission of Houghton Mifflin Company.

PFD: Excerpt from "Post Modernism: Adventures in Etiquette" by
Julian Barnes (*The New Yorker*, April 12, 1999). 75(7): 102–103, 105–106,
108–109. Reprinted by permission of PFD on behalf of the author.

Published by Three Rivers Press, New York, New York.
Member of the Crown Publishing Group, a division of Random House, Inc.
www.crownpublishing.com

THREE RIVERS PRESS is a registered trademark and the Three Rivers Press
colophon is a trademark of Random House, Inc.

Printed in the United States of America

Designed by Barbara M. Bachman

Library of Congress Cataloging-in-Publication Data
Cosper, Darcy.
Wedding Season / by Darcy Cosper.—1st ed.
1. Weddings—Fiction. 2. Single women—Fiction.
3. Mate selection—Fiction.
I. Title.
PS3603.O865W43   2004
813'.6—dc22   2003027921
ISBN 1-4000-5145-2

10 9 8 7 6 5 4 3 2

FIRST EDITION

For their faith, this book is dedicated

to Elizabeth Mermaid Sheinkman

and to that most honest and honorable of men,

my father.

*Etiquette is not about life but about creating a
simulacrum of life; and manuals of etiquette, even in
their democratised, multiple-choice manifestations,
have a similar essential unreality.*
The *Book of Life, being non-fictional,
always ends in death, whereas the* Book of Etiquette,
*being pastoral or romance, ends in marriage.
For all its appearance of diurnal helpfulness, its underlying
function is to offer an ideal vision of the world.*

— *Julian Barnes*

Olivia: *Are you a comedian?*
Viola: *No, my profound heart: and yet, by the
very fangs of malice I swear, I am not that I play.*

—*William Shakespeare,*
TWELFTH NIGHT

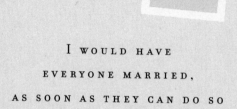

1.

I WOULD HAVE
EVERYONE MARRIED,
AS SOON AS THEY CAN DO SO
TO ADVANTAGE.

—*Jane Austen,*
MANSFIELD PARK

THIS CAN'T BE TRUE.

But, of course, it is. And I am, therefore, by various connections, alliances, and accidents, happy and not, for one reason or another, hereby obligated to attend seventeen weddings in the next six months.

How I've managed to avoid confronting such a state of affairs, what with save-the-date cards and engagement party announcements and solicitations for bridal shower gifts fluttering down on me for months, a blizzard of tastefully engraved handmade paper collecting in heavy cream-colored drifts around the apartment—well, it's a testament to something. My capacity for denial, probably.

See, most rituals I hate. Which is not to say that I'm not a creature of habit, because I am, in the most profound of ways; I am a walking antonym for spontaneity. This, however, should not be confused with an affection for ceremony, and particularly not for the wedding ceremony.

This afternoon was given over to one of the few rituals I don't mind: the biannual transfer of my upcoming social and professional appointments from many, many small scraps of paper to the laminated six-month calendar that I keep on the wall above my desk at work, and which I have dragged home for this purpose. It usually gives me a sort of thrill, a bracing sense of victory over the forces of chaos. Not today, though. Today my study became the site of a psychic massacre, as I plucked wedding invitation after wedding invitation from the piles of paper around my desk, and felt my anxiety mount in spectacularly direct proportion to the number of ceremonies I have promised to attend.

"Goddamn," I tell the air around my desk.

"Goddamn," I tell Francis, the elderly and long-suffering dachshund asleep on my left foot.

"Goddamn, goddamn, goddamn," I tell the nearby photographs of my mother, my father, and my younger brother, Josh, whose third, second, and first marriages, respectively, are among those requiring my attendance. I blow a kiss at the photo of my elder brother, James, who in addition to being gay is also a certified, off-the-chart commitment-phobe, and unlikely to get hitched any time soon. I'm very fond of James.

"Goddamn," I add one more time, loudly, for good measure.

"Oh, don't stop." Gabriel pokes his head into the study. "I love it when you talk dirty, Joy. Don't stop." He has smudges on his face and a feather duster in his back pocket.

"Are you aware that we have seventeen weddings to go to between now and mid-September?" I wave a handful of the offending invitations at him.

"I hadn't counted, but it makes sense." Gabe slouches against the door frame.

"Beg to differ. It's totally senseless."

"Probably just a by-product of everyone you know turning thirty. Same thing happened to me a couple of years ago."

"To this extent?"

"Well, no. Seventeen? No." Gabe shrugs. "Something like five in a year. Guess that's not quite the same, is it?"

"Not quite."

"Hey, maybe someone dosed the national water supply." He laughs. "A nation of brides. You remember that Cheever story where there's a costume party, and people are supposed to dress as they wish they were, and all the women come in their wedding dresses, and all the men come in their old football uniforms?"

"Gabe, I'm going to throw up."

"Don't do that. The bathroom is spotless." He assumes the Olympic victory pose, chest thrust out, arms raised above his head. "And the kitchen. I even defrosted the freezer."

"Truly uncommon valor. May I take you out for dinner?"

"Hero sandwiches? Veal medallions? Army bratwurst?" Gabe has an unredeemable fondness for puns, and the more like blunt instruments they are, the more pleased with himself he becomes.

"Not if you keep that up."

"Anyway, it's Girls' Night," he says. On cue, the phone rings, and I pick up.

"Hello, Henry," I say into the receiver.

"Hello, smartass," she answers. Henry is my best friend. By the grace of whatever forces govern student housing, she was assigned as my roommate freshman year at college, and my life hasn't been the same since. Henry, or Hank, if you prefer, is short and shorter for Henrietta, god forgive her parents, who must have named her with some kind of eerie prescience about and totem against her magnificent beauty—though ostensibly it was after a great-grandmother. Henry: six feet, one inch in stockings, with a body that would make *Sports Illustrated* swimsuit models gnash their little capped teeth in envy. Bales of blonde hair, Aegean eyes, an elegant nose, just slightly and winsomely too small for her face. A faint Louisiana accent, which she trots out at full strength for special occasions. Et cetera. And, to the everlasting chagrin of red-blooded boys worldwide, she's a lesbian.

"Want to meet me early for a drink?" Henry asks.

"No."

"That's my girl!" she yells.

"I'll be there in half an hour." I hold the phone away from my ear.

"Give Pretty Boy my best," Henry says, and hangs up. Really, she likes Gabe well enough. And it's a fact that Gabe is possessed of those fine-boned, patrician good looks only minutely removed from overt prettiness by a square jaw and a jaunty, assured, I-just-finished-my-rowing-practice glow of testosterone. However, the first time we met, Hank introduced herself to me as, quote, swamp trash hauled dripping from the Louisiana bayou by a state scholarship fund and the kindness of strangers, unquote. So it's not a wild leap to say that class resentment may be the basis of a tiny grudge she bears my boyfriend, whose family, through absolutely no fault of his own, is listed in the Social Register.

"Hank sends her love," I tell Gabe, who is perched on the edge of my desk, flipping through the stack of invitations. "This is going to be a season in hell."

"Nah, it'll be fine." He looks at my calendar. "Inconvenient, is all."

"And annoying. And expensive."

"Don't worry about that, Red. You can leave the wedding gifts to me. Just think of the dancing. We haven't gone dancing for months."

"Think of all the people asking when we plan to tie the knot."

"Opportunity for witty remarks." Gabe pushes his hair out of his eyes, languid and unperturbed. "Bon mot body building. We'll find so many different variations on 'when hell freezes over'."

"Thereby exposing ourselves to impertinent personal questions, peer pressure, and misguided ridicule."

"You're funny. Hey, I know what." Gabe snaps his fingers. "We'll make a documentary out of it."

"*Lifestyles of the White and Foolish?*"

"A sort of Wildlife Safari nature special. *Mating Rituals of the American Upper-Middle Class.* You can be the fearless anthropologist, and I'll be the trusty cinematographer." He hoists an imaginary camera onto his shoulder and zooms in on my face. "Here we see the intrepid Adventurer Silverman approaching that most dangerous of all connubial creatures, the mother of the bride. She's made contact! Note the Adventurer's mode of engagement here: downcast eyes, limp-wristed handshake, demure manner, all deployed to communicate passive acceptance of authority and avoid being set up with one of the bride's horrible medical student cousins." Gabe sets down the invisible camera. "In the end, I'll be attacked and devoured by a rabid band of bridesmaids and you'll have to forge on bravely without me. Ah, look at that. I got a smile."

"Gabe, you're an angel."

"I love you, too." He assumes the Olympic victory pose again. "So, will you do that swearing thing some more when you get back from dinner?"

GABE AND I MET, as it happens, at a wedding.

It was the first I'd attended for one of my peers, and I went not so much out of affection for the couple as out of a slightly morbid curiosity. The invitation, issued by a semi-friend of mine from college, was printed in an ersatz Art Deco typeface; guests were instructed to dress for the occasion in "croquet formal." Thus I found myself, along with Henry and our friend Joan, on a brilliant afternoon in mid-

September, in the nether regions of Long Island. We had traveled by rental car, getting lost twice, to an estate landscaped within an inch of its green life and featuring a built-to-order, very loosely Tudor-esque mansion. There we joined the crowds strewn across these rolling acres—several hundred guests attired in white and off-white and ivory, adorned with straw hats and fedoras and cunning chapeaux with little veils, endlessly refilling fluted glasses at the champagne fountains and picking over mile-long buffet tables. To me we looked like nothing so much as a herd of escapees from an insane asylum with a semiformal dress code.

In a show of good sportsmanship, my friends and I had bent to the sartorial dictates and arrayed ourselves in white tea dresses; bonhomie ended when the bride, who had majored in theater, attempted to recruit us for the post-ceremony croquet tournament. We retreated to a small table in the dappled shade of several old trees, where we had an excellent view of an eighteen-piece swing band performing under a white-canopied tent the size of a city block.

"We are one giant fashion faux pas," Joan said, sighing. "Three weeks past Labor Day, and nothing but white shoes as far as the eye can see."

"Sweetheart, you can hardly see the end of your cigarette." Henry patted Joan's shoulder. "There are champagne bubbles coming out your ears."

Joan gave her a wicked grin, peered at the few drops of champagne remaining in her glass, and emptied them onto Henry's blonde coiffure. I heard a loud crack and watched a croquet ball roll by us.

"What country, friends, is this?" I asked.

"Who cares? Get a load of the natives." Joan nodded in the direction of the tent. "Hunk of burning love at twenty paces."

We looked. Walking toward us was a tall, slender man in

a pale linen suit, carrying a pair of empty champagne glasses. His nearly black hair curled in a forelock that fell across long-lashed, dark blue eyes. His mouth looked like an overripe valentine. As he passed near our table, he saw the three of us staring and paused.

"A little more champagne?" The vision gathered up our glasses and headed off without waiting for an answer. We stared after him.

"Good God." Joan shook her head. "I could impale myself on those cheekbones and die happy."

"He's a prop," I told them. "He came with the floral arrangements."

"You really think a boy in a three-piece suit is playing for your team?" Henry asked. "That hunk of burning love is pure, one hundred percent USDA fairy. Big fag. Bet you money."

"He just hasn't found the right woman yet." Joan mock-sobbed, dabbing at her eyes with the hem of her dress.

"Nice undies," Henry said; Joan lifted her skirt higher, swishing it back and forth like a Moulin Rouge dancer.

"Steady, there," I told her. "The cheekbones are back."

The vision was nearing our table, managing five full champagne glasses with remarkable grace.

"Well, thanks." Henry's bayou accent made a surprise guest appearance. "That was sure nice of you."

"You're welcome." He had a furry, warm, tenor voice, and very white, slightly crooked teeth. I don't generally have an irrational weakness for male beauty, but the total effect of this young man made me want to wrap my arms around a stack of school books, swing back and forth, and dig the dainty toe of one saddle shoe into the gravel of a high school parking lot.

"And you are?" Joan raised her glass unsteadily.

"Gabe. Gabriel Winslow."

"Of *course* he is," Joan murmured to me.

"Charmed." Henry kicked Joan under the table. "I'm Hank, and this is Joan. And Joy."

Gabe nodded to them, and turned to me.

"Foxtrot?"

"Gesundheit," I told him, extending a cocktail napkin.

"Listen," Gabe said. "I have to deliver a glass of this swill to the mother of the groom. But I'll lose my mind if I have to hear any more stories about her brilliant son, so I need an alibi. That's where you come in."

Joan and Henry were grinning and bobbing like toy ducks in a carnival shooting gallery.

"You're taking the fate of your feet into your own hands," I said. Gabe laughed and offered me his arm.

"I promise to have her back before midnight." He gave the girls a little bow. As we walked toward the tent, I looked back over my shoulder and saw them doing their best Lenny and Squiggy impression: pelvis-thrusting, wrist-biting shimmies around the table.

SOME OF MY FRIENDS say you can tell everything you need to know about a prospective beau from a kiss. I say dance with him. Gabriel deeply endeared himself to me in this way: After a couple of not too awkward turns around the floor, he stopped and smiled at me. I'm on the tall side, so our eyes were almost level.

"I think I know what our problem is." He pulled my right hand around to the small of his back. "You should be leading. I'll follow you."

Now let me be clear. This was not about gender politics, per se. What I liked about Gabe's gesture had to do with how it was unconscious, not a showy inversion of roles intended as comment on my character, or a demonstration of how profoundly comfortable he was with his masculinity. It simply meant nothing to him one way or another who did the leading, so long as the dancing was good. And as it happens, the dancing was good.

As the festivities drew to a close, Gabriel and I sat alone at a table under the big top, picking over the remains of what had been a very large slice of chocolate wedding cake and watching girls gather for the ceremonial toss of the bridal bouquet.

"Aren't you going to go fight the good fight?" Gabe nodded toward the lacy white mob knotting together on the dance floor.

"I'm allergic."

"To flowers?"

"To marriage."

"Ah," Gabe said. "You don't want to get married?" A funny half-smile dimpled his face.

"No. And specifically, no." I eyed him with suspicion, bracing myself for the usual queries, the predictable patient scorn, but they were not forthcoming.

"Never cared much for weddings myself." Gabe leaned back in his chair and looked intently at me. "Never saw the point of marriage, really."

Now, this exchange may not strike the average Jane as the quintessence of romance, but it was an aphrodisiac for me. Gabe and I stared at each other for a few long moments, during which I felt as though my chest were filling with helium. It was terribly cinematic. There was a thud behind us, and we turned to see that the bouquet had hit the floor. Several women dove for it. Gabe stood and held his hand out to me.

"Would you like to take a turn around the grounds and discuss the possibility of forming an allergen-free colony with me?"

"That sounds like an excellent idea," I told him, and put my hand in his.

And it was.

GABE AND I HAVE been dating for a year and a half now. It's my first real relationship; I once had a boyfriend for two years—the first and last time, until Gabe, that I was in love—but that was in high school. I didn't really date much during college, in part because there was a supreme dearth of straight men at Vassar, and I wasn't about to jockey with a thousand crazed undergraduate girls for some lousy keg-party—ignited two-week romance. I did have a couple of postmixer flings with well-meaning young men from nearby colleges. And for a brief shining moment I contemplated cultivating a crush on my Victorian Lit professor, but everybody I knew had a crush on a professor, which made the whole enterprise seem unattractively redundant and, as my father is a Nineteenth-century Lit professor, unpardonably Oedipal.

Also, there was the one summer that I spent entangled, albeit platonically, with a junior partner in the law firm where my mother had arranged an internship for me. He was just a few years my senior; he was bright, funny, and a relentless flirt. However, Mr. Junior Partner was engaged to be married, and there was no way I was going to play the concubine or trollop or what-have-you—not with my supervisor, not with an acquaintance of my family, and not with someone named Bryce, for heaven's sake. Of course he attempted to persuade me a number of times, and at first it took every filament of moral fiber I had to resist. Toward the end, though, the temptation was mitigated by the fact that transgression for its own sake has never held that much appeal for me, and also by what a cliché it all seemed—illicit workplace liaison, older man/younger woman, and so forth. These misgivings were confirmed by my father, who, when I discussed the situation with him, laughed and told me it was just a crisis of originality, and that I deserved better (though by better I didn't know if he meant a man who was actually available, or a situation less predictable).

When I graduated from college and moved back to Manhattan, I humored my parents and went on a couple of dates arranged by family friends, of which less than nothing came. After a few years, my friends began to despair of what they considered my premature spinsterhood. For a period of time they threw eligible men into my path at every conceivable opportunity; as often as not the men would ask me out, and I would agree, sometimes simply because it was easier and less embarrassing than declining. We'd go out once or twice and that, usually, would be the end of that. A few times things progressed—or at least continued. One fall I dated this very soft-spoken, eerily well-dressed computer programmer whom my older brother James introduced me to (after making a pass at him and finding out he was straight). For a couple of months I went out with a jocular, deliberately eccentric guy who worked as a deejay for a local public radio station and owned three dogs as large and hirsute as Shetland ponies. I was avidly pursued by and for a brief period succumbed to a sculptor a decade my senior, with a picturesque loft, a mind-boggling libido, and a troublesome pair of ex-wives. And so on. In the end, whoever it was, we always broke up. Because I, in the Gospel According to the Exes, am: edgy, intense, hard, too cynical, too analytical, too defended. Or they found me reserved, secretive, elusive, emotionally unavailable—they couldn't understand me, couldn't get to know me, I wouldn't let them *in*. Or I didn't take anything seriously, I made a joke out of everything, I was flip, glib, too clever by half, I didn't really listen (which is what my mother always said about my father; go figure). All of which I interpret as their sense that I was not sufficiently vulnerable, fragile, pliable, woundable, to meet the standards of the Eternal Feminine Principle. Either that, or I'm some delightful mix of the very worst qualities of both my parents, and woe to all comers.

Gabe was not of this opinion, apparently. He called me the day after the wedding, and we had our first official date a couple of days later. From the very beginning it was easy between us, easy to be together, easy to proceed. We dated for well over a month before we spent the night together; there didn't seem to be any rush. It felt as if we had all the time in the world. It still feels that way. It's like everything has been all settled for us via some prearrangement or osmosis, and we're simply getting on with the matter of spending our lives together.

I don't think my affection for Gabe takes much explaining. He's the kind of man almost anyone would like. What he sees in me is something more of a mystery. I know he's partial to redheads, which I have in my favor. He appreciates my sense of humor, and I put up with his awful puns. Beyond that, I just thank my lucky stars and don't ask too many questions, for fear of jinxing it. Gabe and I just fit. For example: We've never been big talkers about The Relationship, by some apparently mutual, tacit agreement. Which is not to say we don't talk. We talk constantly about anything else—books and movies, politics and art, the news, our families, our work, quotidian stuff. We banter. We gossip. We chat, as Henry says. She means it as a pejorative, but this is precisely what I want—someone to chat with.

Also, we don't fight. We've had a couple of very mild

squabbles; easygoing as Gabe is, he can also be outrageously stubborn on occasion (he's an oldest child, the beloved only son, and accustomed to getting his own way). The closest we've ever been to an argument was over our plans for Labor Day weekend last year. He wanted me to go sailing with his family and I resisted, because being around his family makes me uncomfortable; their formality and their coolness keep me constantly on guard. Also, I don't think they're terribly keen on me. So when this Labor Day plan was proposed, Gabe and I had words over it. He won. We went. I can't say that I had the time of my life, but it turns out Gabe had planned the whole thing so he could have a suitably atmospheric setting in which to propose cohabitation. Two weeks later, I moved into his apartment.

Apart from that incident, Gabe and I have had only one major disagreement, and it was about manners. It took place on Valentine's Day (of course—who ever gets through Valentine's Day unscathed?) at this very fancy restaurant Gabe had selected for a romantic dinner. It was one of those places where the tables are set with napkins folded like prizewinning origami and nineteen different utensils for each course; I guess the whole atmosphere and the ritual aspect of the evening had me a little tense. The fight began when I picked up a fork with which to consume my appetizer, and Gabe told me it was the wrong one, and I snapped at him. Who cares, I argued, whether I eat my salad with the salad fork or the oyster fork or the butter tongs? I chew with my mouth closed and beyond that it's a pack of classicist bunk. Gabe told me—not gently, and I can hardly blame him, since I had taken a fairly antagonistic tone—that I was quite wrong; at the table, in the drawing room, in the office, in the barracks, manners are gestures of respect. Feh, I said, they're useless silly conventions intended to enforce social order and social distinctions. Not so, Gabe insisted, hushing me; by adhering to the behaviors assigned to denote politeness in any given culture or society, one demonstrates regard for one's fellows. Exactly, I said, you sublimate and efface yourself and become a subservient clone. And on we went. There was no shouting or anything, but it felt like a serious event. We never really resolved it, either. What finally happened was that Gabe pulled a small gift-wrapped box from his pocket and asked whether, as I disliked social rituals so much, he should just return my Valentine's gift, since he didn't want to insult my value system. He waved the box at me and we both started laughing in a nervous, embarrassed way, and then with relief, and we went on with dinner as if nothing had happened. My gift, by the way, was a watch that had belonged to Gabe's grandmother. It's delicate and elegant and feminine—in short, very nice and nothing I would ever choose for myself. I wear it almost every day, though. What it represents is more important than what it looks like.

The fact that Gabe's little jewelry box might have contained something quite different—a certain item that most young women rabidly desire—didn't cross my mind until I spoke with Henry the next day and she brought it, not without considerable mockery, to my attention. I don't know why she was surprised. Things like that never register with me. They're just not on my radar, for one very good reason: I don't believe in marriage. I don't want to get married. Yes, Gabe seems to be my ideal mate. Some days I'm still taken aback by how much I like him. And yes, I hope to continue on with him, ad infinitum, until we're doddering and drooling and infirm and incontinent, and I believe this hope is mutual. But I don't want to marry him.

It seems silly that I should have to explain or justify my resistance to marriage at this late date in history, but I usually do. Part of it can be explained by the fact that I, like everyone else, fancy myself an independent thinker. Social conventions, the weight of those expectations and assumptions, give me a kind of metaphysical claustrophobia. They make me feel squashed and breathless, flattened out like a paper doll. Why do that to a relationship? Everything else in my life is institutionalized anyway; why should I voluntarily offer up to the preconceptions of church, state, and society one element that isn't?

Also, and more to the point, I have no empirical evidence that marriage is really all useful or effective these days, that it does anything good for relationships and the people in them. To the contrary, from the moment divorce became relatively legally simple a few decades back, all over the country it's been sayonara, sayonara, sayonara. Who even needs statistics to make the point? How many happily married people do *you* know, honestly? I know of almost none—neither in my generation nor in our parents'. They're either newlyweds, grumpy and/or discontented and/or unfaithful, or divorced. Which makes a pretty strong statement about the efficacy of modern wedlock.

The reasons people get married in this era—in the last fifty to seventy-five years, say—are fundamentally different from the reasons for which marriage was conceived and which it served for the last twenty-odd centuries. So why bother? Getting married these days is like, I don't know—using leeches or bloodletting to correct an imbalance of the humors, instead of taking a rational twenty-first-century antibiotic.

To forgo marriage seems so clearly the sensible, the intuitive, the obvious option that I really don't understand why people react with such disbelief to my position. But they do, and since being treated like a reactionary crank whenever the subject comes up is irritating, I prefer to avoid the issue.

That, apparently, is not possible.

I ARRIVE AT PANTHEON before Henry. The restaurant is quiet, just a few customers at the tables for an early Sunday dinner. Waiters cluster and lean against the banquettes, murmuring to one another at the back of the dim, dozing, lofty room. Luke, my favorite bartender, is on duty.

"Hey, little gal. You're a sight for sore eyes." He comes from behind the bar to hug me. His flat, soft Oklahoma accent, flaxen hair, and ever so slightly hayseed manner always make me picture him as one of those wholesome, broad-shouldered, lightly freckled soda fountain attendants featured in Norman Rockwell posters. He's also extremely tall, and as always, his embrace lifts me half a foot off the floor. "What's shaking, Joy?"

"The foundations of contemporary society," I tell him, my legs dangling.

"Bad day?" He returns me to earth and slips back behind the bar. "Tell the bartender your troubles."

"My troubles." I watch him uncork a bottle of wine, the tips of his long fingers permanently stained by oil paints. "Well, I have seventeen weddings to attend between now and September."

"Aw, you're making that up. April fool, right?"

"I wish." I accept the glass of wine he offers, and toast him.

"Well, that's just a hell of a thing. You of all people. How'd that happen? Hello, Blondie."

"Hello, barkeep." Henry slides onto the stool next to me, flicks her fingers dismissively at Luke, and kisses me on the cheek. "Why so glum, chum?" She takes off her coat and throws it over the stool beside her. She's wearing a yellow T-shirt that reads *Slippery When Wet*.

"She has to go to seventeen weddings between now and the end of September." Luke sets up Henry's usual, a dirty gin martini with four olives.

"Including mine," Henry chortles.

"Including hers. Henry loves weddings. I'll get no sympathy from her."

"That's great," Luke tells Henry. "Congratulations."

"You get all decked out, drink free booze, and watch people French kiss in front of an audience." Henry lifts her glass to us. "What's not to like?"

"Magical thinking on an epic scale?" I put a finger to my chin. "Let's see, now: shameless kowtowing to outdated traditions. A total lack of imagination and foresight. Mass delusion, did I mention that? Oh, and perjury."

"Whatever." Henry rolls her eyes at me, unfazed. She doesn't take it personally. We've been through all this before.

"Perjury?" Luke scratches his jaw. "How do you mean?"

"The usual. Lying under oath. Anyone who gets married knows the divorce rate is higher than fifty percent. The occurrence of adultery is even higher, of course. So these people vow until death do us part, forsaking all others, and so on—knowing full well these are promises that they have less than a fifty percent chance of keeping. In essence, they're willfully lying to their lucky new spouses, and to themselves."

"That is a staggering leap in logic, Jojo." Henry sloshes down the dregs of her martini. "I applaud your bold disregard for nuance. Barkeep! Another round for me and this, this, this *ridiculous* creature I call my best friend."

"Who's the lucky girl?" Luke asks Henry.

"Delia Banks. You remember her?"

"It would be a miracle if he did, you slut," I tell her.

"No, no, I do," Luke says. "Pretty African-American girl. The composer, right?"

"Yes! And Luke, guess who's going to be my best man?" Henry turns a beatific smile on me.

"You're kidding, right?" I shake my head at her.

"Not kidding." Henry gets down on her knees and grabs my hand. "Little bundle of Joy, please, please be my best man? I can't get married without you." She covers my hand with kisses. "You can't say no to me anyway. You've already agreed to be a bridesmaid for everyone else."

"Henry, I'd be honored. Please get up now. You're making a scene."

"It's what I do best!" Henry hops up and throws her arms around me.

"Hello, darlings!" Joan, who has appeared beside us, takes off her coat and makes kissing faces in our direction. "Don't want to get lipstick on you, girls. Luke, darling, be a doll and make me a Manhattan. What's new, all?"

"Joy is going to be Henry's best man," Luke says. Joan laughs her hoarse laugh and pulls up a bar stool. She's a classic Tough Broad, raven-haired and hourglass-shaped and possessed of this very 1940s quality that she plays up to great effect. Joan is not an especially good-looking woman, but by sheer force of will, and that preternatural sexual confidence usually seen only in European women, she's brought the world around to a general consensus about her desirability. She carries an air of sexual allure around with her like a formidable designer handbag with which she might whack anyone at any time. We met when I was in law school and she and Henry were working together as editorial assistants at some fashion magazine. (This was before Henry quit to become a Latin teacher, of all things, at a private high school in the West Village.) Joan kept her shoulder—and her sharp tongue, and her ferocious ambition—to the squeaky wheel of journalistic endeavor, and now works as the executive editor at *X Machina*, an online magazine of literary erotica.

"I can hardly wait to hear your wedding toast." Joan lights a cigarette and gives me her wicked grin. Her incisors stick out a little, and they give her smile a predatory aspect.

"Oh. God." I feel myself go pale. I am very much less than fond of public speaking. Very much less. In a subzero kind of way. In my family I'm known as Silent Silverman. To see me with my friends you might not guess it, but I'm shy. Or socially anxious. Whatever. I get pathologically self-conscious and awkward in the company of people I don't know well, or in situations where attention is focused on me, or at large public functions. Weddings, for example. "Henry, I can't—"

"No backsies, Joy. You promised."

"Oh, sweets," Joan says. "You'll be marvelous. Cheer up. Watch me tie the cherry stem into a knot with my tongue. You always like that."

Someone grabs me around the waist, and I turn to see Miel, and Maud skipping up behind her. Miel is a wispy girl, slender and small with a narrow, sallow pixie face and pale, lank red hair. She's an artist, the very picture of an artist, in fact: fey and dreamy, with a tubercular-orphan quality that makes us covetous and protective of her. Maud calls herself our diversity quota girl; she's Korean—second-generation Korean-American, I think. She's round and cheerful and sanguine as a farm wife in a Victorian novel, part hip-hop tomboy and part Hello Kitty kitsch princess. Tonight she has a dozen rhinestone barrettes holding her hair so that it sticks out in little tufts, and when she speaks, the tufts quiver like antennae.

"Where's our table?" Maud pulls at one of my curls. "I'm starving."

"Where's Erica?" asks Miel.

"Maybe she and Brian decided to elope." Joan smirks. The idea of Erica—that quintessential Upper East Side debutante currently making her modest entrance—on the connubial lam is unlikely and amusing. Erica roomed with me and Henry our first year at Vassar; the other girls on our floor called us The Odd Triple, which was apt. Henry, being Henry, adored Erica, and made us a team for the year. I was more ambivalent; it wasn't until several years after graduation and a good year after the founding of our girls' night that I was able to take Erica on her own terms. Finally, Erica was just so obliviously and unapologetically and sweetly her blonde, blithe, sweater set—wearing, single-strand-of-pearls self that to judge her for it seemed to miss the point completely, and I gave in to just liking her. She surprised me by becoming a very successful literary agent at a large commercial firm, and has since used her contacts to incredibly kind and generous ends for many of her friends, including me. Erica is simply a happy girl, and perhaps the only perfectly self-accepting person I know. Tonight, however, she is the locus of my anxiety and irritation, for the simple and only reason that she is the first wedding on my list; next weekend I will be her bridesmaid.

Erica, who has been in consultation with the maître d', waves us toward a table. The girls collect their coats and march. Henry brings up the rear, singing "Here Comes the Bride" loudly enough for the other customers to take notice, swiveling their heads around and peering at the group. I raise my hands helplessly to Luke, who laughs.

"I remember the first time you came in here." He touches my wrist with one finger.

"That was almost six years ago. You've been here too long."

"*You've* been here too long. Find another goshdarn bar. And keep those ladies quiet, will you?"

My table has just erupted into squealing laughter. I nod at him and go to join my noisy, my old, my dear old friends, with whom I've been coming to this goshdarn bar once a month for almost six years. Which is kind of nice.

ERICA IS SANDWICHED between Joan and Henry on one side of the table, flushed and giggling. Maud and Miel shift over to make room for me, and Miel knocks over a full water glass. No one misses a beat; we just grab napkins and keep talking. Miel is as dependable as a national park geyser in this respect, guaranteed to make at least one mess per meal, and on the scale of things, this is minor. Once, getting up to go to the bathroom, she knocked over the entire table. Henry always says that what Miel lacks in coordination, she makes up for in clumsiness.

Erica reveals to me the source of their uproar a moment before; she holds up a cat's-cradle tangle of leopard-print string that, after close inspection, Maud swears to be a negligee. The outfit seems tame compared to what they'll dredge up for Joan, but it's entertaining to think of Erica working it on her sturdy fiancé, who wouldn't even consent to live with her until they married.

"But wait, there's more!" Maud hands over a little gift bag. Erica digs into the tissue paper, comes up with a pair of leopard-print thigh-high stockings, and flushes ever pinker with excitement.

"Model it for us," Henry says. Erica giggles. Our waiter comes to the table and eyes the stockings without expression.

"Let me guess," he says. "Bridal shower."

We nod. Erica giggles.

"Congratulations," the waiter tells her wearily. "Want to hear the specials?"

AFTER THE ORDERS have been placed and the drinks have been handed around, our conversation makes its inevitable turn to the wedding. Or, I should say, to the weddings, plural, because each and every one of the women at this table, except for me, is wearing an engagement ring. Every one of them figures among the brides who comprise my seventeen.

Erica will marry Brian, just the kind of boy you'd expect her to marry, a ruddy-complexioned, hale and hearty, solid and good-natured entertainment lawyer, whom she'd known for all of three months before he proposed. You just know when you meet the right person, she told us when she announced the engagement. You just know. You just *know*.

Maud will marry Tyler, a lean, Scottish-born and broody-melancholy hipster in his early forties, who happens to be the lead singer of a quite successful rock band known as The False Gods. They've been a couple for more than ten years; they met while Maud was interning on a documentary project about the band. At the time Tyler was in the midst of a divorce that subsequently turned nasty and got quite a bit of public attention, which is at least in part why he and Maud waited this long before making it legal.

Miel will marry sweet Max, who resembles, in temperament as in appearance, an angel just out of bed. He worships Miel, which alone would be enough to make me like him, were he not so likable anyway, in the manner of an especially tender and well-behaved child. Max is a friend of Gabe's from the Yale art department—he now owns a small art gallery—and he and Miel met through us, when Gabe and I had been dating for just a couple of months. Because of this connection, after Max and Miel became engaged Gabe and I were treated to a flurry of insinuation and speculation regarding our plans for the future, which we did our best to ignore. Gabe asked me to move in with him a few weeks later. Coincidence, inspiration, or peer pressure? I'll never know.

Joan will marry Bickford, who is, I'm sorry to say, known at large as Bix; he is this generation's first-born of the St. James clan, as in the St. James Foundation, the St. James Collection on loan to the Guggenheim, the St. James Auditorium, and so on. Bix is the family's requisite wayward son, a dilettante, a bon vivant, a maker of very, very bad independent films, and quite able to keep pace with Joan, who fell from an exceptional career as a man-eating femme fatale into his dissolute arms. Gabe has known Bix for years—they attended boarding school together in Massachusetts—and does not like him at all. I just find him kind of ridiculous; Henry finds him amusing, Maud irritating, and Erica horrifying. Miel's too oblivious to have an opinion on him, which may be why she and Max double-date with them so often; the rest of us are usually at pains to avoid socializing with Joan and Bix as a couple. It's a little awkward, but in any circle of friends, a complication of this sort is more likely than not to arise. I feel lucky that out of so many potentially disastrous unions it's just this one instance that has rated any friction.

Last but not least, Henry will marry the lovely Delia, native of Chicago, who is, among other things, an experimental composer trained at Juilliard and now the leader of the twenty-one-girl a cappella chorus Mercy Fuck. To the great delight of denizens of the downtown music scene, the band opens unannounced at a variety of weird little rock clubs, performing the most elaborate vocal arrangements of power ballads from the late 1970s. I personally am partial to their Gregorian-chant–inspired version of Foreigner's

"Waiting for a Girl Like You." Henry and Delia met at a lesbian bar where Mercy Fuck was performing, and Delia came on to Henry by serenading her with "My Girl." She climbed on the tables and everything. Henry was smitten. She still is. They've been together for several years, a first in the annals of Henry's romantic life, and as far as I know Henry has observed absolute sexual monogamy throughout—also a first. I think Henry's crazy New Orleans family was actually more freaked out about her dating a black woman than they were about her dating women *en général*. They seem to have recovered, from what Henry tells me—or, at least, they're too soused to stay mad. Members of Delia's family, on the other hand, continue to stay mad. Whether their parents and siblings and so on will attend the wedding is still very much up in the air.

OUR DINNER ARRIVES, and Maud begins telling us about the latest project taken on by Some Nerve, her film company; it's a documentary about pre- to postop transsexual men.

"We're trying to get one of the subjects to let us film the operation." She bounces up and down on the springy banquette, and her little antennae of hair bounce with her. "How cool would that be?"

"You're a brave woman, Maud. Godspeed." I do a quick mental calculation about where video-documented castration might register into my scale of coolness and draw a blank. I empathize with transsexuals; I am a straight girl trapped in the body of a straight girl. There's no corrective operation for it that I know of. The best I can hope for is a change in the zeitgeist; short of that I'm left squirming around in the world like a restless child in the back seat on a long car trip.

"So, darlings." Joan looks around at us with a portentous expression. "This is our last night together as single girls."

"Hey, Luke!" Henry hoists herself up and yells over the banquettes. "Bring over a bottle of champagne!"

I slouch down low on the banquette, until I'm bent double, almost horizontal, halfway off my seat and nearly out of sight. Assuming this position is a deeply immature habit that I've never managed to outgrow. I'm in very close touch with my inner adolescent—and her posture is just terrible.

"Resistance is futile, Joy," Henry says, kicking at me. "All roads lead to this place. You'll be a common-law bride in five years anyway."

"Common-law marriage doesn't exist in New York." I try to sit up, slip on the slippery banquette leather, and land on the floor underneath the table. "And neither does no-fault divorce. Did you know that?"

The lower portion of Luke appears next to me, and Joan sticks her head under the table.

"If you want the champagne, you have to come out of your secret fort," she tells me.

"What's the password?"

"I do," she answers, and disappears. I briefly consider the possibility of remaining under this table until everyone I know is married. I hear a crash, and champagne drips down my shirt; Miel has knocked over her glass. I crawl toward Luke's feet and out from under the table.

"Thanks for joining us." Henry hands me a glass.

"Sorry I'm late." I take my seat. "The traffic was hell."

"Jojo, just be happy for us," Miel whispers to me. "We're happy for you."

"I'm happy that you're happy," I whisper back. "I really am."

"To the blushing bride!" Henry winks at Erica, and we clink our glasses together.

"Cheers, sweetheart," Joan says. "This time next week you'll be Mrs. Erica Fiske!"

"No," Erica shakes her head gently. "I'm keeping my name."

"You are?" asks Joan. "Why?"

"Honey, are you joking?" Maud turns on her. "This is the twenty-first century. Who the hell still takes her husband's name?"

"I'm going to." Joan lifts her chin. Maud and I gape at her.

"So am I," Henry tells us. "We're going to hyphenate."

"But when you have children," Erica furrows her brow, "the long, hyphenated names, they'd be so hard to learn how to spell."

"Joan, I can't believe you're taking Bix's name." Maud slaps the table. "You're supposed to be a feminist."

"And I can't believe we're having this conversation again. Tell me," Joan says narrowing her eyes at Maud, "how exactly is it a more feminist act to keep my father's name than to take my husband's?"

"But it's your name now," Maud says.

"I didn't choose that name. Now I do get to choose. It seems like a positive political action to me, that I exercise the right to make my own decision about who will be my family."

"Blah blah blah." Henry makes a face at Joan. "Why doesn't Bix take your name? Oh, I guess it'll probably come in handy to be a St. James."

Joan pretends to ignore the comment, but I see her suppress a smile.

"Max and I are picking out a new last name for us to share. We're getting ours changed legally." Miel sloshes champagne on me. "But I'm keeping my name professionally."

"I guess that's mainly why I'm doing it." Erica hands me a napkin. "I'm known as Erica Stevenson in the industry. And I like my family name. Fiske isn't very pretty, is it?"

"See, now, Miel's choice, to me, is an interesting creative alternative," Maud says. "Taking your husband's name is so traditional, it just has all this historical baggage associated with it that I can't imagine you'd want to deal with."

I bite my lip and start sliding down the banquette again.

"So does marriage." Henry kicks me under the table until I sit up straight. "But that fact is not stopping any of us from tying the knot. As the lovely Joy Silverman would probably declare flat out if she weren't such a passive-aggressive freak."

"The great crusader!" Maud pokes my ribs.

"Listen to you, Little Miss Ideology." Joan lights another cigarette and waves it at Maud. "We're the ones with all the political opinions. When have you ever heard Joy take sides on any other issue?"

"Ask her about lawyers," Henry says. "She has very strong opinions about lawyers."

"You all just go on about your business," I tell them. "I didn't say a thing."

This is not, strictly speaking, true. Over the years I have said a great deal on this particular subject to these particular women, some of whom—Joan and Miel, actually—were basically in agreement with me. To my credit, be it ever so slight, I have kept my opinions to myself since they began announcing their engagements.

"Leave Joy alone, you guys." Erica smiles at me. "She's being very good about all this."

"Good about what?" A pretty, petite blonde appears beside our table and addresses Joan. "Have you been good, Joanie? That's not like you."

After a moment I recognize the blonde as Ora Mitelman.

Ora was a discovery of Joan's, in the latter's capacity as editor of *X Machina*. She's a writer, and Joan was the first to publish her work—a serialized group of lyrical, tragic reminiscences on her poetically unhappy childhood as the product of a turbulent marriage between a free-spirited debutante-heiress and a moderately famous Abstract Expressionist painter, and the melancholy yet bodice-ripping tales of her sexual coming of age as a sensitive and therefore tormented and therefore drugged-up and medicated adolescent in New York's mondes, beau and demi both. The series, which ran under the title "Spirit & Flesh," was picked up by a prestigious publishing house and released, several years back, in the form of a memoir by the same name.

The book made Ora a darling of the media. She did a national book tour, appeared on high-profile talk shows and was fawned over by their hosts, and was commissioned by magazine after magazine to write essays as a spokesmodel for her generation. For a time it was all but impossible to pick up a piece of printed matter without seeing her lovely face—those bottomless green eyes, those delicately molded lips, the Pre-Raphaelite gush of curls—paired with a manifesto about the death of love and the bitter emptiness of modern coitus and the deep, desperate grief of girls everywhere in regard to same. Meanwhile, she continued her column in *X Machina*, cataloging the endless stream of empty, meaningless sexual forays in which she engaged in her thankless, fruitless search for true love.

This quest, which given its impressively exhaustive nature should by rights have provided Ora not a single spare moment, did somehow leave her with enough time to write a novel, published earlier this spring. Entitled *The Sadness of Sex*, the book details a privileged young woman's poetically unhappy childhood as the product of a turbulent marriage between a free-spirited debutante-heiress and a moderately famous Abstract Expressionist painter, and the melancholy yet bodice-ripping tales of the heroine's sexual coming of age, et cetera. I waited for someone, anyone, to cry foul, but the sensible shriek was never heard. The media went into its frenzy. The world continued revolving on its axis.

"Ora, darling!" Joan stands and leans over Henry to embrace her. "What are you doing here?"

"Having dinner with my agents. So good to see you, Joanie! You look gorgeous, as always."

"And you. When did you get back in town?" Joan asks. "I thought you were still on the book tour."

"It's over at last, thank goodness," Ora tells Joan. "I'm just exhausted. I got back a couple of days ago. I'll be in and out of town this summer—but I'll be here for your wedding, of course. I wouldn't dream of missing that! And who are these lovely ladies?"

Henry makes a face at me. To say that she dislikes Ora would be an understatement; the tender moniker she has bestowed on our authoress is 'Tis-Pity-She's-A-Whore. We've both met Ora several times at events with Joan, and found that she seemed to speak at length only with the male persuasion, granting any woman to whom she was introduced only a graceful nod and lowering of the lashes in acknowledgment, before the visiting audience was dismissed and she returned to bright and animated conversation with whichever potential Mr. Right she happened to be investigating. I am not remotely surprised that she doesn't remember me.

Joan introduces us one by one, and explains the occasion for our gathering.

"How sweet!" Ora trills. "You come here every month? How funny! I haven't been here for years and years, not since I was a mad little thing in the bad old days. Who knew people still came to Pantheon!"

"It's making a comeback, apparently," Joan says.

"My goodness, with bartenders like that, I should think so." Ora smiles around at us. "Isn't he delicious? I know I'll be coming back soon!"

I look at Henry, who makes a low but distinct growling noise in the back of her throat.

"And will you all be getting together to fete our Joanie next month for her wedding? I'd just love to join you if I'm in town! I so love spending time with girls. Isn't it the best?" Ora says.

Maud rolls her eyes at Miel, who looks puzzled.

"Darling, I'd love that," Joan tells Ora. "I'll call and give you the details."

"Wonderful! You must! Then I'll see you all next month. I have to dash, honey. Great to meet you, ladies!" She waggles her fingers at us and trips off across the dining room.

"Isn't she adorable?" Joan beams. "What a doll."

"She's sure something." Henry nods.

"You guys, hey, you guys, let's take a picture." Miel rummages frantically through her purse and pulls out a little camera. "To commemorate our last single night."

"Luke!" Henry yells. "Come be our photographer!"

Luke lopes over and Miel gives him the camera. Henry grabs my hand across the table, and I turn to survey them, the brides-to-be, my old, my dear old friends.

"Smile," Luke calls, and I look, we lift our glasses, and the light blinds us.

IT'S A MILD MIDNIGHT and I'm walking home, having waved and kissed and bundled the other girls into cabs and watched them disappear into the dark. The buds on the trees are swelling, and a few stars strain through Manhattan's luminous halo to make themselves known. On the corner across from the building where I live with Gabe there is a Unitarian church, a dark, neo-Gothic number; we can see it from our kitchen and on Sunday mornings sometimes we have breakfast by the window to watch the hats and the children climbing on the iron fence and the kisses of peace traded on the front steps. As I pass tonight it occurs to me that we'll soon be seeing a parade of weddings there, too. Resistance is futile, I think to myself. Beside the church's front door is a glass case holding a sign, black felt with movable white letters, like the menus in diners that feature blue-plate specials. Tonight the sign announces that the theme of this morning's sermon was the power of loyal friendship. Below this is a quotation from the Book of Ruth: "Whither thou goest, I will go; whither thou stayest I will stay; your people will be my people, and your God, my God." I turn and look up toward my apartment. The light in the bedroom is on, and I see Gabriel's silhouette. He's at the window; he's waiting for me.

Monday, April 2, 200—

I ARRIVE AT WORK at a reasonable hour—that is, a not unreasonable hour, for a Monday morning. My company's office occupies the top floor of a very narrow brownstone building on Greenwich Avenue. We have decent views but pay daily for the privilege with a breathtaking march up several flights of steep and crooked stairs, through dim, grimy hallways, past the suites of our fellow tenants: a real estate broker, a small socialist press, a psychologist, and, in the ground-floor storefront, a New Age bookstore. At the uppermost landing is the entrance to our quarters. The front door has a cracked, frosted piece of glass set into it, upon which my partner, Charles Vernon, in the spirit of the genre, hired a graphic designer friend to paint the name of our company, Invisible Inc., with the words HACKS AT LARGE below it, and a very nice illustration of an old Underwood typewriter.

Invisible Inc. is a slightly odd proposition, a loose consolidation of writers founded one evening a few years ago. Charles and I met while working as content providers on a project developing toddler-friendly software content for Baby's First Palm Pilot. We bonded as fellow dropouts, he out of a doctoral program in philosophy and I out of law school. One day we went out after work and were discussing the dubious pleasures of the freelance life and the difficulties of navigating the commercial world solo. It began as a joke, the notion that we could pool our resources and form a merry band of ghostwriters and copy slaves to feed the maw of the market and its appetite for a well-turned phrase. But by evening's end we had signed declarations of intent on a cocktail napkin, toasted to Necessity, the cunning, desperate mother of invention, and not even formidable hangovers the following day could convince us of the follies of an enterprise so born.

And here we are, four years later. Our hunch paid off and the captains of industry embraced us: a collective of poly-specialized scribes for hire, easy to track down, more reliably talented than temps, asking lower fees than recruitment agencies. We provide an uncomplicated relationship. We're on call, we do the job right and get out, we're available without rancor or complication whenever our services are required. We've done everything: billboards and brochures, grants and guerrilla marketing projects, autobiographies and ad campaigns, photo captions and political speeches and pornography, leaflets and love letters. Our work is everywhere—simple, nameless, blameless. Occasionally someone calls with a legitimate journalism assignment, and occasionally we'll take it, but most of our staff have grown so accustomed to and fond of anonymity that they'll furnish the pieces with anagrammatic bylines. This pleases me; it seems proof that we're offering a valuable service not only to our corporate clients but also to the strange flotsam of humanity that drift through our doors to offer their writerly talents in exchange for a little filthy lucre, a little camaraderie scarce and avidly sought among our breed of semiprofessionals: grad students moonlighting, novelists with writer's block, journalists looking for an income supplement, and so on. A few have stayed, our little brood of invisibles.

No matter how early I make it to the office, Pete is already here, as he is this morning, stuffing a filter into the coffee maker. He ducks his head in greeting and gives me his sweet, sheepish smile. Pete has been with us for over three years; he came as an undergrad and remained after being granted his degree in medieval literature (he did a thesis on something about the troubadours). He still has the look of a child about him, the child you don't set a play date with. He's pale and thin, with straggly brown hair that hangs over his face and large dark animal eyes. Tattoos peek from under his garments, a perpetual outfit of solid black and T-shirts featuring the names and slogans of fearsome-sounding punk groups, including his own band, Road Rage. He is a soft-spoken, tender-hearted, and unfailingly polite young man, specializing here as our Cyrano, writing love letters and poetry for the romantically challenged. He has also consulted several times on marriage proposals, all of which were accepted. Naturally, then, he has very little personal success with women.

Our office is just a couple of rooms filled with desks and file cabinets and battered couches that we found on the street; there's a large main work area up front, and the office I share with Charles is in a smaller room at the rear. Charles has a framed vintage poster for *The Sweet Smell of Success* above his desk, and a photograph of Nietzsche; I have my calendar. My desk is next to the windows at the back of the building, which offer a view of our neighbors in their bathrooms and kitchens, engaged in the serious business of daily life. The fire escape across from our own serves as a balcony for Miss Trixie, a drag queen of some local renown. From time to time, when she hasn't been up all night performing,

Trixie and Charles and I will take our morning coffee together and converse over the dank gully between our buildings like country gossips at a picket fence. This morning, though, the only sign of our lady is a row of fishnet stockings in shocking neon colors, doing a breezy, ghostly cancan on the clothesline.

As I SETTLE at my desk, Charles drags himself into view and leans heavily, dramatically against the door frame that separates the two rooms. He's an odd-looking man, in a compelling way: pale brown hair, dark olive skin, and light hazel eyes that could put a snake charmer into a trance. On the short side but sans Napoléon complex. His features are perfect, but slightly askew, as if he had slept on them funny and everything got a little bit rearranged. As usual he's dressed to kill, but this morning he looks like he's been backed over by a gallon of vodka. Pete slips a cup of coffee into his hand and puts another on my desk. I thank him, and he eyes Charles sympathetically.

"Want some aspirin?" Pete ducks his head.

"Don't speak." Charles places a hand over Pete's mouth. "It does me harm."

Pete bobs and departs.

"You are setting a very bad example for our employees," I tell Charles, who lowers himself into our prized leatherette recliner, trying to move his head as little as possible. He takes a swallow of coffee.

"Good morning, Vern." He tries a smile on me, which turns into a wince, and puts his face back into the coffee cup.

"Good morning to you, Vern. You look like hell. Have a nice weekend?"

"Please kill me now."

"Nope. You have a client meeting today. Nice suit, by the way. And here come the troops." Noises from the next room indicate that the rest of our staff is arriving. "Vern, how about you suffer in silence, and I handle the assignment meeting?"

"Bless you. Job book's over there," he gestures to his desk with his empty cup. "Try to get all of your notes on the same piece of paper, not sixteen Post-its, okay? Refill, please?"

"Waitressing. Not in my job description." I pluck the assignment book from his desk and head into the front room.

MY FLOCK OF BARTLEBYS is settling at our proud alternative to a conference table: a lovely pink 1950s Formica kitchenette set with matching chairs. Besides Pete, there's Myrna, a Rubenesque, very serious young woman with a mass of dark curly hair and pretty blue eyes set so wide that it seems as though she can look in both directions at once, like a guppy. She has ghostwritten autobiographies, political manifestos, and speeches for some of the nation's most prominent politicians, but she likes the variety here. And Damon, beloved by advertising agencies and PR firms city-wide for his pithy copy. Damon's a lanky, hunky ex-surfer with sun-streaked blond locks and a sloth-like Super Dude manner so convincing that I routinely forget he's actually very bright. He has a background in science, went to grad school for sociology—unlike Charles and me, he actually completed a postgraduate degree, and then, just like Charles and me, found himself with absolutely no idea of what to do next. So here he is, and has been for the last three years. Finally, there's Tulley, a tiny, perky, pink-cheeked English girl with a high and tiny voice, chestnut hair that she usually wears in two shiny braids, sparkly eyes the color of maple syrup, and a predilection for profanity that would put a long-shoreman to shame. She's a diplomat's daughter, speaks seven or eight languages fluently, and has a degree in international finance or something like that, but she was bored out of her mind in the corporate world, and someone referred her to us a couple of years ago. She handles translations, helps out with accounting, and does most of our pornography, including her regular assignment writing the so-called letters from readers for a nudie magazine called *BabyDoll*.

IN THE FRONT ROOM, Damon is stooping around the table, pouring coffee for everyone.

"Hey, boss," he greets me with his trademark hair flip, a world-class move that would, I'm sure, cause a swooning epidemic if deployed in the vicinity of any American high school. The other Invisibles turn from their conversations to wave and nod greetings.

"Damon, could you do me a huge favor and go give Vern a warm-up?"

He lopes off, and I put another filter in the coffee maker.

"Everyone survive the weekend?" I ask over my shoulder. A collective grumbling is my answer. Damon comes back into the room and hands me the coffee pot.

"I think Charles is dead," he tells me, as we sit down at the table.

"We'll make funeral arrangements after the meeting. Status updates, please." I feel, as I always do when I preside over these meetings, like an imposter. The idea that I'm the head of a company—that I'm a grown-up, that I have any legitimate claims to authority—seems patently absurd to me. I'm certain that at any moment someone will discover I'm merely posing as an adult, and expose me for the fraud that I am. Also, as I've said, I loathe being the center of attention; it makes me extremely nervous.

"The *BabyDoll* letters are done," Tulley says. "Could you please have Charles tell the editor that we're going to drop the account if he doesn't stop asking me to dinner? And someone from another skin mag got my name and called to ask if I'd do a sex advice column."

"That was *Cosmo*," Pete reminds her.

"I'll do it," Damon says. "Could be cool."

"Could be actionable." Tulley shakes her head. "False pretenses."

"Right." I wave my hands. "Okay. Focus, please."

"I'm nearly finished with the materials for the day spa," Myrna announces. "They've extended an offer of complementary oxygen therapy facials to all our staff members."

"I've always wanted to try one of those." Pete brightens at this news. "Oh, and remember Hector? He wants something new."

"What does he want? An anniversary poem?" I ask. Hector was one of the marriages assisted by Pete's literary talents.

"Sort of. He wants some kind of love letter for his mistress."

"That lout," Myrna snaps. "He was married just a year ago. This is insupportable. Joy, we can't possibly be party to his dalliances."

"Hey, who are we to judge?" Damon flips his hair. "We're just the writers, guy, not the Moral Majority."

"Enough," I tell Damon and Myrna, who are glowering at each other. "Pete, let's talk about this later today." I run my finger along a column in the assignment book. "Damon, we have a screenplay that needs overhauling. Myrna, someone from City Hall needs a speech for some celebrity fund-raiser. I'll give you the notes when we're done here. Pete, Tulley, Charles is meeting with the people from Modern Love Press in an hour. They want us to help produce this new twentysomething romance series. I'll put you guys on that if it comes through."

Pete and Tulley give each other high fives across the table.

"All set?" I stand, and the group begins to shuffle up. "I'm going to check on Vern."

CHARLES IS LOLLING in the recliner with one hand to his brow.

"Hey." I slap lightly at his face. "Rise and shine."

He bats my hands away and glares.

"What did you do to deserve this?" I settle at my desk.

"The road to romance is paved with good intentions and many martinis." Charles closes his eyes. "I took Derek out for dinner. And drinks. And drinks. Did I mention drinks?"

"Get lucky?"

"Not even a good-night kiss." Charles sighs.

"Are you sure he's gay?"

"I'm beginning to wonder."

"Wonder on your way uptown. You have half an hour to get to Modern Love."

"Anything fun come up at the meeting?" Charles struggles to his feet.

"Porno. Adultery. A little infighting."

"I love this job." He straightens his tie. "You'll have to fill me in when I get back."

"Good luck," I tell him. He waves and heads out the door.

———

MY PHONE RINGS.

"Good morning, baby girl," my older brother James says when I pick up.

"Good morning, big girl."

"Can we have lunch this week? We need to get a present for Charlotte."

Charlotte is our favorite aunt, my mother's younger sister. She's getting married later this month—for the first time, at the age of forty-eight, and to the very lucky Burke Ingerson, a man fourteen years her junior. Both my family and Burke's are more than a little upset about the whole thing. The wedding should be interesting.

"I thought we were going to get them a gift certificate for sex toys."

"Joy. That was a joke. Mom would have an aneurysm."

"And this is a problem for you?"

"We don't need to add to the misery, baby. She's already in such a tizzy about the whole thing."

"Only because Bachelor Number Three isn't as young and handsome as Burke. Why should I humor her competitive streak?"

"Baby." James puts on his stern eldest brother voice. "I'm trying to be a good boy for once. How about if we make nice? For the sake of novelty."

"Oh, fine. But I can't do it this week. I'm booked." I wave through the window to Miss Trixie, who is on the fire escape, reeling in her stockings and singing "Happy Birthday, Mr. President."

"You busy professional. Next Monday?"

"Nope. What about Tuesday?" I look up at my calendar.

"Mmm. No. I have student meetings all day." James is an

associate professor at NYU; he followed our father's footsteps to the shady groves of academe.

"Wednesday?"

"Next Wednesday. That's perfect," he says. There's a silence, and I can picture him writing it down in his beautiful leather-bound teacher's agenda, in his beautiful handwriting. I scratch a note onto the back of a receipt and tape it to the calendar. "I'll call you that morning," he says. "Love you, baby girl."

"You, too." I set the phone down gently, and look out the window.

FROM TIME OUT of mind, or at least since my parents' divorce, the family assumption was that I'd become a lawyer, like my mother. There was no apparent reason for this beyond parental vanity; I was a shy child, and possessed nothing particular in the way of character or aptitude—except bookishness and a kind of adolescent moral rigidity—that would have made it an obvious career choice. But by the time I was in college, a future defending the spirit and letter of the law was beyond questions of desire, beyond questions of any kind. It had been assumed for so long as to become doctrine, an article of absolute faith. After the implosion of my mother's second marriage, she decided, possibly out of sheer perversity, to specialize in divorce law. She began to make a name for herself by winning high-profile cases and obscenely large settlements for the ex-wives of wealthy men, and by the time I got to law school even my fellow students knew her as Goldfinger. I had a legacy to uphold.

I received my undergrad degree in prelaw with an English Lit minor to keep all the parental units happy, after which I was accepted by Columbia University's law school.

But from that point things went downhill with a certainty equal and opposite to all hopes and expectations that had come before. After my first year, in particular, I had something like a crisis of faith. My aforementioned moral rigidity, and perhaps some feeling of self-importance—which were initially nurtured on the bracing rigors of law school and throve on ethics classes and tomes of theory—had begun to dissipate. The sense that I was aligning myself with the Good and the True slipped away. My studies became haunted by the specter of subjectivity: There is no Good, no True, and as far as the truth, the whole truth, and nothing but the truth is concerned, in any given instance each of us has only a *version* of what we believe to be true, and each version is merely a question of perspective. As this notion took hold, the idea of representing under oath another person's truth began to seem like not such a fabulous idea. It sat badly with me. I started to lose sleep over it. One of these sleepless nights, deep into the spring semester of my second year, I was in the library studying. I went to the bathroom to splash water on my face and found, scrawled in fat black strokes across the mirror above the sinks, the *cri de coeur* of some fellow-sufferer: "Only when we realize that there is no eternal, unchanging truth or absolute truth can we arouse in ourselves a sense of intellectual responsibility." I read the scrawl once, eyed my reflection through the text, read it again, and then bent over and threw up into a sink.

I suppose I should have seen this as a bad sign. But I pushed on through that term to the bitter end, and bitter it was, though amusing, in retrospect. The professor of my trial advocacy class set up a mock courtroom situation as our final exam. Each of us was assigned a hypothetical case that we had to win twice—first as the prosecution and then as the defense—in order to get a passing grade. For a week in the last humid days of May, I sat by day on the jury, watching my classmates shift sides with the effortless flexibility of Chinese acrobats, and by night at my window, staring out past my haggard reflection at the parades of drunk, more or less innocent undergraduates rollicking down the street toward one another's narrow dormitory beds. I was sleep-deprived and ill-prepared when my number came up, and went to class that day looking only slightly less miserable than I felt. And there, mere minutes into my trial, I paused, looked around at the woman who was acting as my client; at my professor, who was presiding as judge; at the jury of my peers—and fainted onto the floor of the classroom.

I thought it ranked pretty high in the annals of court-room drama. But after meetings with various advisers and teachers, and a significantly less than stellar report card, the heads of my department suggested, reasonably enough, that it might be inadvisable for me to forge ahead toward a law career. So I fled from the halls of truth and justice. My mother threw fits and claimed a broken heart; I think it was something more along the lines of profound humiliation, but either way I could do nothing to remedy the situation.

Back in the real world, without the maternal legacy or familial expectation to guide me, I wandered vaguely for a couple of months, a shade in the American purgatory of the unemployed, trying to find some professional direction. Henry got me what was supposed to be temporary employment while I uncovered my true calling: I took a position writing headlines, photo captions, blurbs, and such at the magazine where she and Joan worked at the time. But the path of least resistance has a gravitational pull of its own, and down that path I continued as circumstance became habit, habit became experience, and experience became profession. And here I am.

———

"Joy." Myrna's head appears around the door frame. "May I have a word?"

"Just one?" I wave her in.

"Hector wants us to woo his mistress. This is not good business."

"No?"

"Doesn't it seem rather shady to you?"

"Compared to what? Helping crisis management firms do spin control on felonious movie stars? Writing naughty letters for porno magazines? How about those politicians you write speeches for? Not exactly spotless little lambs."

"There's something about the individual versus the institution that seems more dubious to me this morning." Myrna wraps a strand of hair around her finger.

"Persuading the anonymous masses is more comfortable, of course." I push the assignment book around on the desk. "Look. We're in business, Myrna. We don't represent our clients, per se. We don't speak for them. All we're doing is giving them more eloquent ways of saying what they're going to say anyhow."

"But shouldn't we attempt to maintain some modicum of personal integrity?" Myrna starts on another strand of hair, twisting it so tightly around her fingers that the tips turn purple.

"Sure. You think that infidelity is wrong. So don't do it. You can't take on the sins of every philanderer in the city. And Hector will be cheating on his wife whether or not we write the letter."

"Aiding and abetting. Knowledge of a crime. You attended law school." One section of Myrna's hair is now standing nearly on end.

"Dropped out of law school. We're not really in criminal

territory here. The stakes aren't quite as high as you're making them out to be."

"For whom, exactly, are they not high?" Myrna looks out the window and sighs. "Don't you have a personal philosophy about lying?"

"Yes, I do, about not making promises that I can't keep, not misrepresenting myself, not deceiving people in that way. But it's personal. I certainly can't impose it on my clients. The entire advertising industry would become obsolete." I wait for a laugh. I don't get one. "It's not like we're condoning what they're doing, or participating in it. We're just hack writers. Says so right on the front door."

"I suspect this conversation is in vain." Myrna releases her hair and spreads her arms wide, martyred. "You're determined to take the assignment, aren't you, Joy?"

"I don't know. Probably." I let out a sigh. "If we turned away every job that seemed morally questionable to one of you, we'd be out of business."

"Very well." Myrna gets up and heads for the door. "I have registered my opinion."

"Duly noted." I watch as she stomps out. "Thanks. Myrna?" I make a screaming Munch face at the place where she was standing and pick up the phone, which is ringing again. It's Charles, calling from a taxi.

"We are going to make *so much* fucking money off of Modern Love," his voice crackles through the cell phone. I think briefly of Myrna, and of my mother, and of the prostitutes who show up at dusk in the meatpacking district ten blocks or so from our office. "We are the proud producers of the *Extreme Romance* series, baby," Charles laughs. "Love for a new generation of glamour slackers. An eco-tourism installment. Radical disc jockeys in Eastern Europe. A love affair on snowboards. The turbulent passions of a couple opening a trend-spotting company in Iceland."

"They're only about ten years behind the curve," I tell him. "It could be worse."

"Oh, fine. What would you propose? Something a little more timeless?"

A story about a woman who has to attend seventeen weddings in six months, I think to myself. A bildungsroman. A picaresque. A comedy of errors. There are no original plots.

AFTER THE USUAL postwork debriefing at our kitchen table, Gabe and I decide to have dinner at Café Paradiso, a restaurant on a little street off Washington Square Park. It's one of our favorites, both for historical reasons (we had one of our early dates here) and because it's nearly perfect: nice but not too nice, quiet but not too quiet, and the food is good, but not too good. I don't have a particularly refined palate, and anything gourmet is pretty much wasted on me. Fine dining makes me feel guilty and skittish, and foodies—those people who get completely obsessed and collect olive oils infused with saffron and talk about heirloom tomatoes and moan ecstatically about the hints and tensions of this or that ingredient in what is, as far as I can ascertain, a tasty but ordinary entrée—suffice it to say that I don't understand them. The first couple times we went out, Gabe took me to dinner at these incredible, multi-star-reviewed, celebrity-chef restaurants, and I was concerned that he might be one of the gourmet evangelists. In reality, he was just trying to be nice, and to impress me, I guess; after a few dates, he figured it out and brought me to Paradiso. I think that was the night I really fell for him.

Tonight Gio, a rotund waiter who has developed a slightly proprietary relation to us, seats us at a table in a bay window overlooking the street; we order and watch him wobble back to the kitchen.

"Mom called today," Gabe tells me. "She wants to know if we've decided about spending Labor Day with them. Are you up for it? They'd really like to spend some more time with you."

"Labor Day? It's not even Memorial Day yet." Somehow I doubt very much that Gabe's family wants to spend more time with me. Or if they do, it's probably just to confirm their suspicions that I am not the girl for their beloved only son, and to demonstrate as much to him.

"You know my mother," Gabe says. "She's big on advance planning."

"Will we be on the boat again?"

"Nope. Maine. My uncle's place. I think it'll be nice."

"Ah." Funny how the way Gabe says it, his uncle's place sounds like some sweet little ramshackle cabin, when it is, in fact, a compound that occupies an entire island. I mean, a small island, but still. I really have to get over my Winslow phobia, sooner rather than later. As Gabe's spousal equivalent, it's likely I'll be seeing quite a lot of them; although he resists certain of their values and demands, Gabe is deeply, surprisingly family-oriented.

"Hey." Gabe snaps his fingers. "Speaking of schedules. When you have a second, could you get me the dates and details for all these weddings? Is it really seventeen?"

"It really is. Three this month, four in May, four in June—one of those I'm going as arm candy with Charles and you don't have to come. But Max and Miel. And my brother's wedding. And your sister's wedding."

"Little Mo. I still can't believe it." Gabe's youngest sister, Maureen, goes by Mo; the other, Christina, a tall, lumpen young woman who shares her father's tendency to speak without moving his lips, is known to the family as Teeny.

"Believe it," I tell him. "Then three in July, two in August. And Henry in September, if we're still alive."

"Don't worry, Red. Maybe some of them will get jitters and pick fights and call the ceremonies off."

"God, are you ever romantic. One of the many things I love about you."

"It's the Connubial Summer Tour, USA. We should have roadies." Gabe laughs. The little oil-burning candle on our table flickers and goes out. Gio, noticing, waddles tableside.

"Look," he tells us. "This candle has gone out."

We exchange glances and nod at him.

"Oh, no," Gio says. "You do not understand. Look, all this oil, it is gone. The candle has burned here for eleven years. No candle has ever finished since I have been working in this place." He gives us an important smile. "Tonight I will light a new candle for the first time. This is an occasion. Marco, look! A candle has gone out."

"A candle has gone out," I tell Gabe. Marco, the elderly host, comes to our table. Together he and Gio examine the candle as reverently as if it were a holy relic.

"We light a new candle for you, my friends." Marco regards us with a benevolent smile as Gio waddles away. "You must celebrate with us. I bring you wine." He leaves, and returns with two brimming glasses. Gio waddles back, cradling a new candle in his hands, sets it gently on the table, and pulls a book of matches from his pocket.

"Raise your glasses," Marco exhorts, and we obey. Gio strikes a match and touches it to the new wick. It sparks, crackles, and then the flame steadies and rises.

"To those things that burn long!" Marco makes a triumphant sort of flourish. Gabe and I toast him. Marco claps a hand to each of our shoulders and returns to the bar.

"What was that all about?" I ask Gabe, when the Italians are out of earshot. "Vatican nostalgia?"

"Longing," he says. "Mortality, maybe. The comfort of continuity."

"What do you want to be doing in eleven years?" I whisk my finger back and forth through the candle's flame.

"I don't know." He gives me a lazy smile, and puts his hand over mine to stop me from fidgeting. "This. Something like this."

"I'll pencil you in," I tell him.

THE DAY OF ERICA'S WEDDING, I loll around the apartment, trying to pretend I have nothing more strenuous in store for me than reviewing the outline for "Mountain of Desire," the snowboarding installment of the *Extreme Romance* series. Gabe comes and goes industriously, picking up his suit from the cleaner's, getting a shoe shine. He pauses in the apartment between errands and watches me shuffle from room to room.

At noon Henry calls. She is in a spitefully good mood. When I answer the phone she is singing "Going to the Chapel" at full volume and off-key.

"Henry, stop or I'll hang up."

"Come on, my little bridesmaid!" Henry drawls. "All the Veuve Clicquot in the world awaits your ruby lips, and all you have to do to earn it is take a little teeny walk down a little teeny aisle. You're still in your pajamas, aren't you, Joy?"

"Um." I stalk toward the bathroom, shedding pajamas as I go, the cordless phone cradled between my shoulder and cheek. "No."

"Good. Because I'm about to walk out the door and hail a cab. I'll be outside your building in five minutes." She hangs up.

I stand naked before the bathroom mirror and take inventory: item, two lips, indifferent red; item, two gray eyes with lids on them. One jaw line, squarish; one forehead of average height and width. Hair: by virtue of my apathy, medium length; by the dictates of my father's DNA, wildly curling and of a very dark rust color known in polite society as auburn. Physique: on the tall side, angular to bony, no cleavage to speak of, knees still knobby, elbows still lightly scarred from excessive tomboy activity in my callow youth; overall pale and very freckled. Nothing new. Not much to brag about, but not much to complain about, either.

Calculating for Henry Standard Time, I estimate that I have fifteen minutes to spare. I get into the shower, where I remain, thinking of nothing and humming advertising jingles to get "Going to the Chapel" out of my head. At last, I hear the front door shut. Gabe calls my name, and I turn off the water, cursing quietly. I dress at a leisurely pace, collect the garment bag that holds my bridesmaid's dress, and shuffle into the living room, where Gabe lolls on the sofa with the dog, reading the newspaper.

"There was a message from Henry on the machine." He looks up. "I think her exact words were 'Stop dawdling in the goddamn shower or you're going to make us late.'"

"Thank you." I sit down next to Gabe. He puts an arm around me and continues to read. Francis licks sympathetically at my hand. "This is going to be a shameless orgy of conventionality," I tell them.

"Don't you start, Red." Gabe gives me a little push off the sofa. "I'll see you at the church at four."

Gabe may be on my side when it comes to marriage, but in other ways he can be quite traditional. His adherence to social customs, and his occasional impatience with my critiques of and resistance to same, is largely a function of his upbringing—his breeding, as his mother might say.

Growing up in New York, I had wealthy friends, but I didn't believe in the existence of people like Gabe's family

until I went to college and met some of my friends' families:
America's version of the aristocracy, the Pips and Serenas
and Edmunds, with their summers abroad and colonial win-
ters in the tropics, their stables and tennis courts and mari-
nas, family jewels and heirloom china and New England
estates. The Winslows are of that variety, the rich who are
different from you and me. His mother, a Mayflower-family
descendant, has never held a job. His father, following in the
footsteps of his father before him, was president of some
bank before retiring at the age of forty-five. Gabe's youngest
sister is getting married this summer, at the age of twenty-
three, to a banker. Her marriage announcement will read
something like: "Until recently, Mrs. So and So was an executive assistant at the Ladies' Aid Society," which means that
she will not malign her husband's ability to provide by con-
tinuing on in the workforce.

The Winslows are regular attendees of charity balls and
society teas. They are museum donors and country club
members. They are Episcopalians. Several generations of
Harvard men were grossly affronted when Gabe chose Yale
instead; aunts and cousins were shocked, shocked, when he
didn't pledge a fraternity. And most devastating of all, he
dropped his poly-sci major to study photography. The family
might never recover from this blow.

I think Gabe's parents are a little horrified by me,
though of course they're much too well-mannered to ever let
on, at least in any direct sort of way. I just have a hunch. My
background must seem terribly "bohemian" to them. Both
of my parents come from working-class backgrounds; both
are first-generation college graduates. As I mentioned
before, my mother is a divorce lawyer, twice-divorced. My
father is in academe, which has some redeeming dignity to
it, but he doesn't really treat it as a gentleman's profession,
the way a gentleman should. I don't know how much of this

Gabe's family actually knows, but sometimes it seems they just sense it. Their radar identifies me as other, not quite nice, not ladylike—Not Our Kind, Dear.

That's the family, though, not Gabe. As far as I can tell, he's his own man—as much as anyone can be. He seems to like me despite my inappropriateness. For all I know, he could like me *because* of it; he's never smoked, he doesn't have any tattoos, and while Yale may not be Harvard, it's not the Hell's Angels, either. It may be, then, that I am Gabe's rebellion, which I find funny and weirdly gratifying. Compared to my flamboyant, fantastic friends, I know I seem quite average, so the idea that to Gabe I appear eccentric, offbeat, attractively odd, is flattering. Gabe makes me feel unique, and (ironically) who doesn't like that?

I WAIT ON the sidewalk for fully five minutes before Henry pulls up in a taxi. She is wearing a black T-shirt with red lettering that reads *Come to Where the Flavor Is*. I climb in next to her, and no sooner have I closed the car door than she begins to sing "Going to the Chapel" again.

"Don't make me hurt you," I tell her. Henry is silent for a moment, and then starts in on "Get Me to the Church on Time." I punch her arm, and we proceed to sing every wedding-related song we can think of on our way up to Erica's parents' apartment. When we get out of the cab, humming "We've Only Just Begun," the driver gives us a look of pure hatred and screeches away down Fifth Avenue.

A maid shows us into the apartment. The other brides-maids have already arrived, and the living room is a frenzy of blonde. Arrayed across the tasteful sofa sets are Erica's three sisters, blonde; one childhood friend, very blonde; and the maid of honor, Melody, a peroxide-blonde actress whose wedding we will be attending later this summer. Erica's mother, an angular, face-lifted blonde, strides through the apartment, talking soothingly into her cell phone. Erica, blonde and pink-cheeked as a china shepherdess, comes out of the bathroom and runs to us squealing with pleasure, wearing nothing but a lacy ivory garter belt and her string of pearls. She reminds me, in a nice way, of a little pink piglet. I decide against passing on this observation and hug her back, murmuring vague flattering things toward the little pink ear that is crushed against my face. We round the room, exchanging tiny air-kisses as we go.

"Girls, into your dresses, please. The stylists are on their way." Mrs. Stevenson sweeps through the room clapping her fine-boned hands together like a headmistress directing a spring pageant. The flock of bridesmaids churns in her wake. I bob along, a dark decoy on a sea of blonde.

The Stevensons' master bedroom is outfitted with a massive picture window that overlooks Central Park, and a bed approximately the size of an Olympic swimming pool. I put my face close to the window, fogging a patch of the glass with my breath, and look out over the park to the distant buildings on the other side. I wonder briefly about how many other apartments up and down this avenue enclose how many other brides, how many hysterical, half-naked bridal entourages, at this very moment.

One of Erica's sisters, coming in with the bridal gown, claps her hands in perfect imitation of her mother, and we all turn obediently to the serious business of primping. Out froth the bridesmaids' dresses, which struck me from the very beginning as a dubious proposition and seem even more so en masse. They are elaborate affairs, consisting of long, tangerine-orange satin sheaths—which are viciously fitted and produce a lot of stomach sucking and groaning and assistance with zippers—and creamy chiffon overslips with Empire waists and puffy cap sleeves. Fully arrayed, we look like a chorus of Greek maidens from a *Disney on Ice* spectacular. I am staring blankly into a full-length mirror when Henry comes up behind me.

"I am Creamsicle Girl," she whispers to me, and strikes a runway pose. Melody, who is standing nearby, overhears and snorts.

"I was just thinking I look like one of those Christmas oranges wrapped in tissue paper," she says, sotto voce. "You know, my bridesmaids are going to be in orange, too, and I'm wondering now if it's just too cruel." Henry grabs Melody's hand and twirls her around the room, singing, "Orange you lovely, orange you wonderful," to the tune of an old Stevie Wonder song, until Erica emerges from the dressing room in her gown, and everything stops.

There is an involuntary moment of silence in the presence of The Dress, The Bride. Even I am not immune, though I can't ascertain whether my personal hush is a response to the iconic image or group-think or simply to Erica, who looks beautiful and, clichés notwithstanding, radiant.

Before I have time to sort it out, the moment passes, and we proceed to spontaneously enact the ritual reserved for such occasions, and probably performed through the ages by our ancestral mothers: We surge forward, emitting those little pitched, chirping sighs as we swarm around Erica. Her sisters fuss over her like rodents over a store of acorns, fluffing the long train of her skirt, and then there's a knock on the door and yes, everyone's decent, and in come Hair and Assistant Hair and Makeup, plucked by Erica's mother from some elite salon where a haircut would cost my weight in narcotics. The style crew pounce and circle around Erica, cooing and squealing, just as we had done a moment earlier. I wonder briefly if folk dancing had its origins in this impulse.

"Who's ready to be beautiful?" asks Hair, a gaunt, pony-tailed man, turning from Erica and beaming at us. Assistant Hair and Makeup, two lithe young women in stretchy black pants and enormous sneakers, begin unpacking little metallic cases and setting up their glamour altars. Two of the Stevenson sisters wave their hands and flutter forward. Hair pounces on Henry, and reaching up, runs his hands through her blonde mane.

"Darling," he says to her, "this is fabulous, fabulous hair. Where did you get this fabulous hair?"

"Black market," Henry tells him.

"Serge is going to do fabulous things with this hair. How do you feel about an updo, darling?"

"Serge," says Henry, "I feel just fabulous about it."

"Fabulous!" enthuses Serge. "Erica," he calls over his shoulder, "come over when your war paint's on, darling. And you, sit that shapely behind down right here." He draws a chair up in front of the window seat for Henry, and she sits her shapely behind down, tossing her head and sweeping dramatically at her skirt like a concert pianist. Serge rummages through the case Assistant Hair has set up for him, and gets to work. Henry makes faces at me. One Stevenson sister, whose hair has become an elaborate mass of loops, seed pearls, and tiny white flowers, cedes her place to another sister, whose mouth sports a hideous orange-red lipstick. I watch as Makeup takes Erica's face in her hands and turns her head this way and that, gentle as a lover.

I find myself remembering an afternoon last fall at my mother's apartment on the Upper West Side, where I grew up; she lives in Connecticut with her fiancé now, and they keep the place as a pied-à-terre. Gabe and I had gone up to water the plants and collect the mail, and for some reason I wound up looking through the white leatherette, silver-filigreed photo albums of my parents' wedding. There they were in black and white, forever younger than I as they came down the aisle, their faces lit up with bright unquestioning faith. Gabe found me on the floor of the living room, staring out the window with an album in my lap open to the photo of their first dance. We'd just moved in together, Gabe and I, and he didn't say anything. He sat down on the floor next to me and took my hand. After a while, we stood up and put the albums back on the shelf, locked the door behind us, and went home in silence.

HENRY'S VOICE rouses me. She's standing in front of me with a vampire grin, patting at her hair.

"What do you think, Joy? The bridesmaid that ate New York!" Her way-the-hell-up-do brings Henry's total height to nearly seven feet.

"Fabulous," I tell her.

"Where's that gorgeous bride?" coos Serge.

"Your turn, sweetie," Assistant Hair calls to me. Melody looks earnestly at Makeup, who is giving her face a blankly searching appraisal. "Do you have any non-orange lipstick?" Melody asks.

"We're working with a concept, sweetie," Makeup instructs her. "Our concept is orange."

When we emerge from the bridal boudoir, bedecked and be-flowered and besmirched, Mrs. Stevenson is directing the rearrangement of furniture with a photographer and his assistant. Henry makes obscene shapes at me with her shiny orange mouth while Erica's oldest sister hands out the bridesmaids' bouquets, neat little bundles of peach-colored freesia bound in an elaborate crosshatched pattern with straw twine. Erica gets a bundle of white freesia the circumference of my thigh. The photographer's assistant pushes us into position for group shots while the photographer flirts with Makeup. We pose and simper for the camera: bridesmaids only, bridesmaids clustered around bride, bride with sisters, and so on. The photographer positions Erica by the window, winsome in the afternoon light. Assistant Hair runs in to adjust her veil.

"My underwear is riding up my butt," the lovely bride says through a clenched smile, and the photographer snaps the shot. Mrs. Stevenson claps her hands and the maid weeps and we're hustled out the door and downstairs to the waiting limousine.

THE PHOTOGRAPHER MAKES it to the church before us and takes pictures like mad, clicking and hunching as we climb out of the limo one after another, clowns at a wedding-themed circus. It's a mild, sunny day, and the people out walking pause to watch us as we help Erica out of the car and loop her train over her arm.

"Oh, my god," Erica says to me and Henry, as we walk toward the church's front steps with the photographer trotting along beside us. "I'm getting married." She stops on the bottom step and draws a breath. "Could someone make the photographer stop? I feel like I'm in a fashion shoot."

"You're a model bride, baby." Henry waves the photographer away and puts her arm around Erica's white waist.

"Where's my mother? Where's Melody?" Erica sounds plaintive.

"Right here, gorgeous." Melody comes to take her hand. "Look at your adorable attendants." She points to where the Stevenson blondes stand, in the great shadowy curve of the church's entrance, with Erica's tiny blonde niece and nephew, who are dressed, respectively, as miniature bridesmaid and groomsman.

"Look at our escorts," I tell her, as the full-size groomsmen fill the doorway, waving to us. "It's just like *Seven Brides for Seven Brothers*. Wait until you see our musical number."

Erica gets a laugh out, and we pat her encouragingly. Mrs. Stevenson appears, clapping her hands.

"Everybody ready? Boys, get inside and take your places. Girls, remember your order? Let's line up, please."

"There's my girl." Mr. Stevenson comes down the church steps. "Don't you all look lovely," he says to us. "We've got a full house, sweetheart. May I have the honor?" He offers her his arm, and Erica takes it; the organ music begins, and we move in our bridesmaidly regiment toward the doorway. Through the high, dark wood arch that stands at the entrance to the aisle, I can see hundreds of faces in the garlanded pews turn expectantly in our direction, and far up at the altar, Brian and his groomsmen are lined up like toy soldiers beside the priest. Erica's eldest sister and the toddlers go first, and little murmuring cries rise up from the guests and echo in the church's stony heights. Standing in front of me, Melody counts to ten, mouthing the numbers and nodding her head, then steps into the aisle. Watching her move away, I feel slightly ill. I stare at her retreating back until I feel Henry's hands on my waist, giving me a little push forward, and I begin my long march down the aisle.

There's a cinematic trick that you see a lot in movies, which I think involves the camera rotating on some kind of rolling platform, so the actor seems to remain in place while the world spins around him. I guess it's intended to communicate a sense of confusion, disbelief, shock. That's how I feel now: disconnected, as if I'm floating down the aisle, the upturned faces passing away beside me. I'm a wolf in bridesmaid's clothing, I think; I have no right to be here, acting as a representative of something I condemn. My head feels absurdly light, and for a moment it seems certain that I'm going to faint. Then I catch sight of Gabriel in the crowd, smiling at me, and remember a moment at my mother's wedding to Bachelor Number Two. As she walked down the aisle, James turned and whispered to me, "If this is the happiest day of their lives, isn't it all downhill from here?" I nearly laugh, and Gabe sees it and winks. The pews stop sliding around, and I nod at Brian and take my place on the bride's side of the altar and watch Henry and her hair approach. She gives Brian a big, hammy wink and sashays up next to me. The remaining bridesmaids take their places. The music stops. There's a moment of silence before the "Wedding March" begins, and everyone rises, rustling and whispering, for The Dress, The Bride.

Erica and her father come down the aisle toward us like a dream, a dramatic reenactment of a wedding. Each step, every sideways glance and inclination of the head and glinting tear, seems perfectly matched to some Platonic ideal, a perfect correspondence to the gestures of every bride on her father's arm, kissing him good-bye, taking the hand of her groom, throughout the ages, forever and ever, amen. The reverend begins his dearly beloveds.

Traditions, I tell myself, keep us safely in the sweet embrace of the familiar; they are narrative touchstones that anchor us in the stories we've learned to tell about ourselves. Maybe I should be happy for my friends who find in these moments what they need to live, I think, as Brian fumbles to put the wedding band on Erica's finger. Maybe I should be. But I'm not. I mean, I'm happy that they're happy. But I want something more for them, something finer, newer, more visionary, broad and brave and pure. What that would be, though, I have absolutely no idea.

"I now pronounce you husband and wife," the reverend says. "You may kiss the bride."

Brian lifts Erica's veil. She is facing away from me, so I can't see her expression, but I can imagine it: the happiest china shepherdess in the whole world. They kiss, and everyone applauds, and the current of sound carries us from our places and back up the aisle. I take the arm of my groomsman, Gary, a solid, football-shoulders type who went to school with Brian in Virginia. Several paces in front of us, Henry and the blonde bouffant tower above her groomsman.

"Hey, young lady," Gary says to me. "You sure look pretty." There are tears running down his face.

"You look pretty, too." I give his arm a squeeze.

"That was so nice I'm ready to run out right now and get hitched myself," he murmurs as we pass the laden pews on our way to the church's entrance. "What do you say, Joy?"

"Gary, I'm flattered. But how about if you just save a dance for me instead?"

"I'll do that." Gary kisses my cheek, and we follow the newlyweds out of the cathedral's cool dusk and down the church steps into the bright day.

Wednesday, April 11, 200—

I'm in the office, looking over one of Tulley and Pete's drafts for Modern Love—a love affair between a full-breasted young federal agent and the strappingly handsome computer hacker she's been assigned to arrest—when the phone rings and I jump, accidentally sending a squiggle of red ink across several perfectly acceptable paragraphs. I guess I'm a little wound up.

"Hi, baby girl." It's James. "Still up for lunch?"

"Yes, please. Had any divine inspiration about Charlotte's wedding present?"

"Since you mention it, an angel came to me last night and said unto me, 'Thou shalt honor the bridal registry.' "

"Well, that solves that. Did the angel tell you where they're registered?"

"The usual fetish shops. Kitchen fetish, bathroom fetish. Charlotte's a fag."

"Because she shops the same places that you do, James?"

"Because she shops at the same places my boyfriends do. Professors can't afford to sleep on seven-hundred-thread-count sheets, darling."

"You sleep on them for free, don't you?"

"Nothing's free. Speaking of which, how's your poor little rich boy?"

"Gabriel is fine. I hate it when you call him that." I

crumple a piece of paper and toss it recklessly toward a recycling bin across the room. The ball of paper makes it in. Charles, at his desk, applauds.

"Why do you hate it, baby? Grandma always says it's as easy to love a rich man as it is to love a poor man. We're just proving her point."

"Gabe is not rich."

"He has a trust fund, Joy. His parents live in tasteful splendor in Beacon Hill when they're not summering in understated shabby chic splendor on Nantucket or wintering at some posh resort on St. John."

This I cannot deny.

"Gabe's *family* is rich," I tell James. "Gabe, as you know, works for a living."

"I know, darling." James takes a pacifying tone. "He's a very talented photographer. I'm not attacking his character. I'm delighting in your luck."

"You're an old-fashioned tart, James."

"Introduce me," Charles stage-whispers. "I love a tart."

"Like hell I will."

"What?" says James.

"Not you," I tell him. "Where shall we meet?"

"Let's go to Boîte. It's right around the corner from one of the places where Charlotte registered. One o'clock?"

"That den of celebrity? We'll never get in."

"I slept with the owner."

"God, James. You probably did it just so you could get a table."

"That's not such a terrible motive, is it?"

"I've heard worse, I guess. One o'clock, then." I set the phone down, and Charles gives me the evil eye.

"Why don't you ever invite your brother over to see the office, Vern?"

"Because. Were the two of you to ever be in the same

room, I am convinced that it would result in some kind of natural disaster, and I don't want to be held responsible."

"Some people call that good chemistry. We might be perfect for each other. Would you rather be responsible for keeping me apart from the love of my life?"

"Nice try, Vern, but no dice. You know I don't believe in fate."

"But observe your metaphor, dear. Dice. Luck. You contradict yourself."

"Not at all." I push the *Love Bytes* manuscript around on my desk. "Fate assumes an outside force of some intelligence or a fixed structure that determines our lives, something we can't avoid or change. Luck is the name we give chance when it works dramatically for or against us. Chance is an observable universal law. Fate isn't."

"Some people could argue with you, Vern," Charles says. He shoots for the wastebasket and misses.

"Some people believe in the infallibility of the pope," I say. "That's the difference between science and religion. Certain things exist whether or not we believe in them. Others exist only by our faith. Like Tinkerbell. Do you believe in fairies, Vern? Clap your hands if you do."

"And you know how to tell the difference?" Charles claps vigorously.

"Hector called again." Pete knocks on the door frame and shuffles in. "He wants to know if we're going to do that letter to his mistress or not."

Charles and I exchange glances. I nod.

"You sure?" Charles asks me.

"Why wouldn't I be? Go for it," I tell Pete. "We've never done infidelity before."

Pete grins significantly at us from underneath his hair.

"She means as an organization, you little hack," Charles

says, trying to sound stern. "It'll be a learning experience. Get to work."

Pete bobs and shuffles out. A moment later Myrna sticks her head into our office.

"If a spurned wife brings charges against us, I sincerely hope that I will have the good grace not to say I told you so. But I doubt it very much."

"You don't suppose Myrna's father cheated on her mother, do you?" Charles asks after she has disappeared, widening his eyes and putting one finger under his chin, an ersatz ingenue.

"Shut up, Vern. Personal anguish isn't always at the heart of an ethical position."

"Not always." Charles looks at me hard. "But often, don't you think, dear?"

AT A QUARTER TO ONE I leave the office and head downtown on foot. It's a clear, cool spring day, the sky pale blue and the sunlight a watery gold on the streets and crowds. I cross through Washington Square Park, passing the corner where old men pair up at stone tables to play chess, with small groups of acolytes, still as statues, gathered around them. The park is full of tableaux like this—lovers on the benches, knots of college students tightening around earnest young men who strum guitars. Near the center of the park, a couple on Rollerblades are skating their hearts out in a fantastic duet around the broad circle of the empty fountain. I move through the shadows of the hulkingly ugly buildings of the university where James works and onto the busy sidewalks of Soho, weaving between laden shoppers and aspiring models, past shiny boutiques where bright dresses and trinkets fill the windows, tempting passersby. I turn onto a side street and nearly walk past the entrance to Boîte, the door to which is marked only by a tiny engraving of a female figure, holding in her hand a box from which a mysterious ether drifts. The door is locked. I search for and find a small buzzer to the left of the door, press, and wait. I think briefly of the Prohibition era, and the strange pleasures of exclusivity, which have never held much charm for me. The door is opened by a neat young woman in black who eyes me silently.

"I'm with James Silverman," I tell her, and she waves me in. I follow her up a narrow set of stairs to a waterfall of velvet curtains. We push through them into a large, high-ceilinged room with a wall of windows at one end. The decor is minimalist opium den crossed with 1940s grand hotel lobby. Tall frondy plants in giant urns cast shadows on the flocked metallic wallpaper. Black velvet couches, strewn with tiny embroidered throw pillows, cluster around low, faux-Oriental tables, at which diners are forced to hunch and lurch over their meals. Along one wall stretches a long bar, painted black and lacquered to a frightening brilliance. At the center of the room are a cluster of round banquettes elevated on daises and generously draped in canopies of sheer gold fabric.

My silent escort points, and at the far side of the room, crowded with people who all look vaguely familiar, I see my brother waving at me. I often forget how oddly handsome he is—we're both tall and slender and topped with our father's dark red hair, but James is more elegantly arranged all around. He looks like a dethroned Russian prince. I weave between the tables toward him, noting several minor celebrities along the way.

"This is hideous." I fall into a club chair across from him.

"I know." James preens and looks around. "Isn't it divine? Bad taste is in again."

"Dare I ask about the food?"

"French-Japanese fusion. It's awful. Look, there's the editor of *Vanity Fair*."

"You're an academic. You're not supposed to care about the things of this world. You're supposed to live the life of the mind."

"Darling, I teach American Studies. One has to keep up. Look, there's that director everyone is calling the next Orson Welles. Isn't he cute?"

While James is craning his neck around, I puff out my cheeks, cross my eyes, and stick the tip of my tongue out at him. He turns back, and I drop the face. He narrows his eyes at me.

"You were making the baboon face," he accuses.

"No, I wasn't."

"Yes, you were. You always make it when I'm being shallow."

"I'd have to be making it constantly."

"I recommend that you try the *cervelles de veau* sushi rolls," James tells me severely from behind his menu. "The Cornish game hen skewers braised in sake are not completely dreadful. They come with sweet little shallots."

"Actually, I'm suddenly not so hungry."

"Just get the vegetables Provençal tempura," James says, and nods to a vicious-looking waiter. He slinks over, and James orders for both of us. When the waiter has gone, James turns to me. "Now, darling. Something obviously has you in a snit. Don't bother denying it. Tell big brother what's on your mind."

"You're so sensitive. Weddings are on my mind, is what."

"God, I know. What a nightmare. Charlotte, Mom, Dad, and Josh. They must have arranged it out of spite."

"That's not the half of it. Charlotte will be the third of seventeen for me."

"All this year?" James gasps.

"Between now and September. All of the girls, Gabe's sister, one I promised to attend with Charles. A few others."

"What were you thinking, Joy? You hate weddings."

"I do, yes."

"Just cancel for some of them."

"I can't. I've already promised I'd be there."

"Oh, yes." James rolls his eyes. "And Joy Silverman never goes back on a promise. Never breaks her word."

"Why do you still make fun of me about that? As principles go, it's not such a ridiculous one to have."

"The best of positions become useless when they cease to make you happy. Right now your precious integrity is making you miserable."

"On the contrary. Principles don't mean anything if you abandon them when they become inconvenient or uncomfortable."

"So you've said. Countless times."

"I don't know why it bothers you so much." I peer out the window. In the loft across the street, a nearly naked man, sagging into his late middle age, is rubbing paint onto a giant canvas with his bare hands.

"Rigor depresses me." James raises his glass of mineral water. "Cheers. You know, this really is a Freudian sickness."

"How do you mean, Professor?"

"Don't you remember when all of this started?" James squints at me. I shake my head. "When you vowed never to break a promise? No? Of course you don't. How perfect."

"You're so awful when you try to be knowing. Just tell me."

"It was just a couple of months after Dad moved out." James swirls water around in his glass. "He was supposed to come and take us to the zoo. It was a Saturday, I believe. It was spring. You must have been nine or ten. You don't remember this?"

I shake my head. James imitates me, making a faux-naïf expression as he shakes his head, his dark hair lashing over one eye.

"He didn't come. He'd promised, and he just never showed up. Mom was furious. She told us that he had done it on purpose, to teach us a lesson. To teach us that you couldn't count on anyone, and that promises meant nothing. You were sitting on the floor of the living room, very quiet. Then you stood up and announced to us that you would never break a promise, and you'd never make a promise you couldn't keep. And Mom laughed at you, and then she started crying, and went into her bedroom, and stayed there for the rest of the day. I can't believe you don't remember."

"I can't believe you do. I think you're making it up. You've been sitting in on too many of those freshman psychology classes."

"Your denial is embarrassing." James glares at the waiter, who has returned with our meal. "Look, there's Donald Trump's new girlfriend."

MY BROTHERS AND I grew up in New York City. Our family lived in an apartment on the Upper West Side, a nice big prewar place with too many little rooms and not enough closets, a creaky old elevator and a creaky old doorman, not too far north of Lincoln Center, and just off Central Park. All three of us kids attended some freaky experimental grade school that was part of the education program at the university where my dad was a professor. Starting in middle school we commuted to a private day school downtown, also of the alternative variety. We spent the Jewish holidays with my father's parents, who lived out on Long Island along with most of the sprawling Silverman clan. The other holidays we spent with my Granny Celeste, a lapsed Catholic from a small town in southern France. My mother's father died before I was born; Gran jokes that her cooking did him in, that he, a first-generation American, born to English immigrants, wasn't man enough to eat like the French.

Anyway, after not quite sixteen years of marriage, my parents separated and then divorced—irreconcilable differences, they said. My father moved out and took a studio closer to the university, a one-room apartment so small that we couldn't even spend the night with him there. Instead, we lived with my mother, who was granted uncontested custody of us, and had outings once or twice a month with Daddy, for whom my brothers and I had a definite preference. He was a clever, easygoing, unflappable man who seemed amused by everything. He was always laughing, always making these dry, droll, deadpan asides to us, delivered with knowing looks and conspiratorial winks. He reminded me of James Bond or Cary Grant in the old movies I saw on television, suave and cavalier, able to master any situation with cool charm and a witty comeback. When my mother or James, who both tended toward the high-strung, voluble end of the spectrum, got worked up about something, my father would chuckle, flexing his hands out in front of him as if he were smoothing wrinkles in the air, and say, "Water off a duck's back, sweetheart." Once, in response to the duck comment, James quacked at him and my father laughed for five minutes straight; after the divorce, whenever my mother got into

one of her fits of temper (which was often), James and Josh
and I would make quacking noises at one another and usually ended up giggling helplessly while Mom yelled at us.
Daddy, by contrast, was rarely angry or impatient—though I
can see now that this was in part because he left all house-
hold and child-rearing responsibilities to my mother and
secured the Good Cop position for himself in perpetuity. At
the time, though, he was our uncontested, adored favorite,
and in particular during the first few years following their
divorce we looked forward to his visits with the manic anticipation most kids reserve for school vacations. I honestly
don't remember the particular afternoon James mentioned,
but I can imagine how wounded I would have been if he had
failed to show up.

About three years after the divorce my mother got
married again, to a man named Chet, a golf pro she met at
someone's country club during a weekend outing in the
Hamptons. My brothers and I were not thrilled. Daddy, of
course, thought it was hilarious. By that point James and I
were a little too old to see Chet as anything but an interloper
and a buffoon, which he kind of was, in a handsome, harmless sort of way. Only Josh, eleven at the time, was of an age
to feasibly consider him a stepfather, and Josh didn't. He
was one of those old-soul kids who did everything correctly
and quietly and called no attention to himself and was thus
left to his own devices, which was precisely his plan.
Meanwhile, I brooded in my room, and James made noisy
trouble; he was coming out around that time, and he demon-
strated his feelings about my mother's marriage by staging a
make-out session with a busboy at the wedding reception—
on the dance floor, in full view of my mother and Chet and
both extended families. James has never been all that interested in subtlety. He and Henry love each other.

Anyway, things were fine for about two years, and then

they weren't. Mom and Chet started bickering—about the usual things that aren't the real things: who gets home when, who takes responsibility for what, who coaches too many pretty young divorcées on their putting techniques. And so on. James went off to college and, after much heated debate between my parents, Josh went to boarding school. Which meant that I was alone for the final two and really bad years of Mom's marriage to Chet, and alone with her after their separation. I spent an inordinate amount of time being forced to listen, late into the night, to her kitchen-table tirades, during which I silently swore to myself I would grow up to be nothing remotely resembling her. If someone wants to psychoanalyze me, there are probably worse places to start.

I read somewhere that if you can't be a positive example, you'll just have to serve as a terrible warning, and my mother was great for that. I mean, I love her. I do. And I know she's had a hard time. She grew up believing that marriage and motherhood were a woman's highest calling. Then the world as she knew it was shaken and stirred by big bad Betty Friedan and Simone de Beauvoir, just a little too late for her to really join the revolution. She's done the best she could, and I admire her for it. But as far as role models go, well— she tends to the irrational, the emotive, the clingy, the hysterical. In short, my mother is the stereotypical female, and nothing I ever wanted or want to emulate.

JAMES AND I finish lunch and are on our way out of the restaurant when I hear a voice call my name. I turn to see Luke, the bartender from Pantheon, leaning from one of the raised, lamé-swathed banquettes at the center of the room. I wave and he beckons me over.

"Hey, gal." He hops out of the tent and kisses my cheek.

"Hey, yourself. What's a nice guy like you doing in a dump like this?"

"Having lunch with—"

"Luke, who are your friends?" Ora Mitelman pushes aside the gold drapery and gives me an acute and very unconvincing smile.

Luke introduces me as an "old friend." I introduce James to both of them. I don't bother reminding Ora that we've met. And met. And met. I suspect she'll remember me now that I'm the "old friend" of a new conquest. There's never been anything more than the bar between me and Luke, but I don't go out of my way to correct what is clearly her misconception; I do go out of my way to tender Luke a very affectionate farewell. I'm not usually like this, but Ora rubs me the wrong way. She's such a *girl*.

James and I walk to Salle de Bain, where Charlotte and Burke have graced the bridal registry with their soon-to-be hyphenated names. The store is a half-block-long shrine to pewter and bath linens, lit entirely with beeswax candles that glimmer in the reflection of a hundred gilt-framed mirrors and illuminate a thousand bottles of overpriced, exotically scented bath salts.

"It's like something out of the Brontë sisters by way of Southeast Asia," James whispers to me, in the cathedral hush of the entrance. "Very luxe-sinister."

"I hear their blood-of-virgins bubble bath is very popular," I whisper back. "Why are we whispering?"

"Welcome to Salle de Bain," a fey blonde in a white dress whispers to us. "Can I help you?"

"Bridal registry!" James shouts. I choke. The girl gives us a cool look.

"You'd like to register?"

"Yes!" James shouts.

"No," I tell her. James drops to his knees before me and

covers my hand with kisses. "There are certain conventions even I won't flout," I inform the salesgirl, and attempt to retrieve my hand. "Marrying my gay brother is at the top of the list. James, get up."

"You're no fun." He stands and dusts off his pants.

"Charlotte Blake," I tell the blonde. "Will you show us what she's registered for, please?" She huffs off. James plucks three satin-wrapped lavender sachets from a large basket and juggles them. I ignore him and inspect a nearby shelf of certified organic bath oils. The salesgirl returns with a large, leather-covered book. James catches the sachets neatly in one hand and returns them to the basket.

"Is that the *Book of Souls*?" he inquires politely. She gives him a blank look, and begins flipping through the pages.

"Blake." Her voice drips contempt. "Charlotte. Yes. Towels, Turkish velour, bath sheet, standard, hand, guest, washcloth. Sheets, Sea Island cotton, king. Sheets, cashmere, king. French swansdown pillows, king. Throw pillows, ivory damask-covered. Shower curtain in sterling mesh. Bath accessories, pewter. Soap dish, toothbrush holder, lipstick organizer, tissue box cover, toothpaste tube cover, bath stop, doorstop, candelabra set. Frankincense- and myrrh-infused beeswax candles, three dozen. Electric towel-warming rack. Steam-free in-shower shaving mirror with matching silver shaving dish and silver shaving brush with hand-gathered pashmina bristles."

"How about the matching set of eunuch servants?" James asks.

"We'll take the towel rack," I tell the salesgirl.

"I'll have to see if we have any left in stock," she says icily, and marches off with the book under her arm.

"I wanted to get the candelabras." James pouts.

"Behave, or I'll make you charge this to your account and

then you'll be locked up in debtors' prison." I march to the register.

"You may very well end up there yourself," James says, "with seventeen wedding gifts to purchase. And presents for bridal showers. And god knows how many bridesmaid's ensembles with dyed-to-match shoes."

"Thank you for reminding me. What would I do without you?"

When the salesgirl returns I hand her my credit card and she rings up the towel rack.

"Didn't you want the pewter vibrator?" James leans over my shoulder to look at the receipt. "Six hundred dollars? Are you insane?"

"Charlotte's our favorite aunt, remember?" I sign the slip and push it back across the counter. "Ante up."

"She *was* our favorite aunt."

"Love is not love which alters when it alteration finds," I tell him. The salesgirl hands me a large bag made of hand-made paper with thick, silky handles.

"Where your treasure is, there will your heart be also," James quotes back, as we leave the store. "Paper, scissors, rock. Bible trumps Shakespeare, my darling."

AFTER AN UNEVENTFUL afternoon at the office, I get caught in a spring thunderstorm's downpour on my way home, and arrive at the apartment drenched. I kick off my shoes by the front door, noting that the living room is newly immaculate. Gabe, hunched on the couch with Francis, glances up as I come in, then returns to his book, something about the history of zines.

"Hi," I tell him.

"Don't drip on the floor. I just washed it."

This bodes nothing good; when Gabe is in a bad mood, he cleans. In fact, he cleans constantly, but in particular when he's angry or anxious; he claims it's therapeutic. My predilection to clutter makes him insane. I shake my wet coat out in the hall and hang it in the closet.

"Hi." I sit on the couch beside him.

"Did you know," he says, not looking up, "that the printing press was first used in North America in January 1631?"

"No, actually, I didn't know that." I wait. He says nothing and continues glaring at the book. "Gabe? How was your day?"

"Great, just great." He rapidly turns a couple of pages. "The lab ruined two rolls of film. The *Times* magazine photo editor is going on maternity leave and her replacement has an IQ in the negative integers. And my mother insists that I come up to Boston to get fitted for a suit for Christina's wedding. Apparently there is not a single decent tailor in New York. It was a tremendous day, thanks." He stares balefully at his book. I lean at him until my face is directly under his. He blinks.

"Hi," I say. "Let's take a bath."

"I don't want to take a bath."

"Yes, you do." I remove the book from his hands and push him off the couch. "I'm freezing, and I want a bath, and I need someone to wash my back. You go run the water and I'll make tea."

He sulks at me for a moment, then stomps off toward the bathroom. I go to the kitchen, put a kettle on, and arrange a tray with teapot and cups. I add a plate of the truly disgusting ginger biscuits that Gabe developed a taste for as a child, pour the water, and carry the tray into the steamy bathroom, where the bath is nearly full, and Gabe is slouched, fully clothed, on the edge of the tub, grimly sprinkling in bath salts. I set the tea tray on the floor and turn to him.

"Up." I pull him to his feet. "Get undressed."

"I don't want a bath."

"You do. But even if you don't, you're going to have one." I begin unbuttoning his shirt, and he stands quietly, watching me.

"Those two rolls of film had some really good shots on them," he says at last, and sighs.

"They always do." I slide the shirt off his shoulders. "I'm sorry you lost them."

"I hate that goddamn lab." He unbuttons his pants.

"Let's sue." I drape his clothes over the toilet, watch him get into the tub, and hand him a cup of tea. "Criminal neglect. Gross incompetence. I'll see if my mother has some free time."

"I was thinking more along the lines of Molotov cocktails. Assassins. Good old-fashioned execution."

"We can do that." I strip off the last of my clothes and climb into the tub behind him. "Henry will pay a visit and talk them to death." Gabe laughs. I put my legs around his waist and he leans back against me. "What do you want to do tonight?" I ask. "How about if I take you for dinner at Paradiso?"

"No. I'm not fit for public consumption. I'll end up being rude to the waiters."

"Maybe a movie? We could see something with no plot and lots of explosions."

"Let's stay home," Gabe says. "Order Chinese and play Scrabble and make out on the couch."

"We did that last night. And the night before."

"God, you're right. Note to self: Must be less predictable. Let's order Thai and play Monopoly and make out on the kitchen table."

"I love the way your mind works," I tell him. "Hand me the loofah, will you?"

"ONCE MORE UNTO the breach, dear friends." Gabriel straightens his tie in the bathroom mirror and sighs. It's Saturday evening, and we're dressing for wedding number two. "Couldn't we just stay home and log on to their website?"

Yes, it's true. This evening's ceremony will be broadcast on the Internet. Meg, the bride du jour, worked for me at Invisible; I referred her to Joan, and she's now a junior erotica editor at *X Machina*. She met Joe, her husband-to-be, online in the www.xmachina.com chat room. Very shortly after they began dating, before they'd even met in the flesh, Meg and Joe started up a website on which they kept, and still keep, parallel diaries of their relationship. And it is here, amid the pixilated tales of their first phone sex encounters and so forth, that their wedding will be uploaded, live, for all to see.

"This one won't be such an orgy of conventionality, now, will it?" Gabe's mirror image looks back at me.

"I'm afraid not." I stand behind him and rest my chin on his shoulder. Our faces waver together in reflection. "Oh, Gabe. I'm sorry. I shouldn't have said yes—"

"Hush. It's fine. I mean, of course I'd rather not go. But." He shrugs. "Duty calls."

"Zip me?" I ask. Gabriel turns and closes the zipper to my dress. He puts his hands on my shoulders and turns me to face him.

"You look beautiful, Red." He pushes a strand of hair away from my forehead. "May I have this dance?"

"With pleasure." I place my hand in his and we sway around the bedroom and into the living room, with Gabe humming in my ear. We are circling the coffee table when I feel his hands move up my back, and he tugs the zipper of my dress down again.

"Oops. Sorry about that." He slips his hands inside the dress, and continues to dance, his fingers brushing the bare skin of my waist.

"What do you think you're doing?"

"Nothing." His lips move against my neck, and his hands slide over my hips. "Just dancing. You're a great dancer."

"I'm not going to be dancing for much longer—you're making my knees weak."

"You're not wearing underwear."

"Yes, I am." I laugh.

"Not anymore." He lifts up the skirt of my dress, hooks his thumbs into the waistband of my underpants, and eases them down. He leans to kiss me, looking smug as hell.

"Gabe," I say through the kiss. "We're going to be late." Like I care, at this point. He straightens and pulls away.

"That would be terrible," he says. And picks me up in his arms, and carries me into the bedroom.

GABE AND I HAVE, I think, a pretty average sex life. A few times a week, nothing fancy, and no discussion about it, which is just right for me. I'm not a prude; I don't have any hang-ups about sex. I like it. But I like to have it, rather than talk about it. Talking about it seems weird and beside the point. Joan and Henry love sex. They *love* it. But I think even more than that, they love to *talk* about sex. Loudly. In public places. I don't understand their obsession with it, or their fondness for chatting about it. It doesn't bother me, particularly; I'm not embarrassed or squeamish or anything. I just don't really have much to add to those discussions, or any pleasure to gain from them. Sex is sex. It's fun. It's fine. End of story.

GABE IS STILL humming as we climb out of our cab and onto a grimy street in the meatpacking district. In the pale, rank twilight, the litter-strewn, industrial block swarms with couples in fancy outfits, picking their way down the cobblestone street past warehouses and storefronts with names like Joe's Hamburger Quality Chopped Beef, interspersed with a few desperately chic stores and bars. A clutch of transvestite prostitutes looks on from the corner. One entrance is lit up and a red carpet lures and leads us in. We follow a laughing bunch of very young men and women into the building, and stand with them beside the door to a freight elevator.

"An industrial-strength wedding," Gabe whispers. I punch him in the arm. "Ow. I wouldn't steak my life on it. I didn't know you were going to grill me." The elevator arrives, an operator in black tie waves us in, the great steel doors slam closed on us, and we creak and rattle perilously upward. I examine something on the floor that looks like a bloodstain. Gabe makes quiet mooing noises. Two or three of the other couples look around and titter nervously. At last the elevator grinds to a halt, and the doors open onto a vast, open loft space, ringed with windows and filled with music and bodies and the burbling of voices. Gabe and I exchange glances.

"What a meat market," he tells me solemnly. "Don't be cowed by it, though."

I laugh, take Gabe's hand, and together we plunge into the chattering crowd. The contrast between the street below and this shiny, flawless white space with its gleaming hardwood floors is fantastic; waiting at the bar I overhear someone telling someone else that it's a photography studio.

"Gabe, look." I point to the windows. "You can see the river."

"And New Jersey." Gabe guides me up to the bar and waves at a server. "But what the hell is that?" Against one wall are two giant screens, filled with scenes of parties that aren't this one.

"They're videoconferencing San Francisco and Seattle," the bartender says bitterly. "Friends who couldn't make it out here for the happy occasion." He hands us glasses of champagne. "There are computers set up over there, if you want to join the live chat. Though there seem to be quite a few people in line ahead of you." He sneers in the direction of one corner, where a crowd clusters around glowing monitors set up on pedestals.

"Do you suppose I could check e-mail?" Gabe clinks his glass against mine.

"Can I disapprove of a tradition and its perversion at the same time?" I ask him.

"Hello, children." Joan's face appears inches from mine. She kisses my cheek. "You made it at last! We'd given you up for dead."

"Hullo, Joy! Hullo, Gabriel!" Bickford St. James delivers a hearty smack to the small of Gabriel's back, and the latter chokes on his drink. Bix reminds me of something I read once about a mark of the aristocracy being their carelessness of dress. Tonight he is wearing what looks to be a very fine and expensive suit that's been crumpled in the dusty back corner of a closet for several months. His sky-blue silk tie, which dangles loosely from his unbuttoned collar, has a cigarette burn at the bottom edge, and his pale brown hair sticks up in all directions, but his eyes are wide and bright, his skin as flushed and pure as a child's. He's already drunk. He wrings Gabe's hand in a long handshake, and turns to kiss me.

"Joy, you look stunning this evening. How are you? Good, good." He turns to Joan. "A drink, dearest?"

"Several, please, dearest."

Bix elbows his way toward the bar, and Joan slips one arm around me and the other around Gabe.

"So," she says, "it sounds like you two were discussing the happy couple's very modern arrangement?"

"We were discussing their hardware, if that's what you mean," I answer.

"No, dear, I was talking about their software." Joan smirks. "They have an open relationship. They're going to have an open marriage."

I blink at her, but before I can say anything, noisy clinking on glasses draws the attention of the crowd to one end of the room.

"Let's get started," a man standing on a chair exhorts the crowd. "Grab your seats!"

The guests bump around against one another and herd toward the round tables that line the room. Joan hails Bix and the four of us find a table and sit down. Across the room, at another table, I see Pete and Tulley waving to me. On the video screens, the ghostly distant crowds cluster close, waiting with us.

"That's the CEO of Joe's company." Joan indicates the

dreadlocked, goateed white boy standing between the two computer-topped pedestals. "He got a marriage license on the Internet so he could perform the ceremony."

Bix reaches into his pocket and pulls out a pair of old-style 3-D glasses, paper frames with red and green plastic lenses. He puts them on and turns to us.

"I want the full effect," he says.

"Hush," Joan hisses. "It's starting."

The room dims and fills with the unmelodious strains of techno music. One spotlight creates an aisle of light from the CEO and the computers to the opposite end of the room, where Meg and Joe emerge together. Meg is wearing a white leather bustier and a long tulle skirt spangled with shiny sequins. Joe is wearing black tie and tails. They are both wearing top hats, white and black respectively.

"Oh, my," Joan whispers. "They'll never get anyone else to fuck them looking like that."

I feel Gabe's hand tighten on mine. His expression is pained.

"Want to try the glasses?" Bix offers them to me. I decline. Meg and Joe have reached the CEO. The music fades.

"Dear friends," the CEO's voice cracks. He clears his throat. "Dear friends, you here in New York, in Seattle, in San Francisco, and those of you joining us from all over the world on the Web, we're here to celebrate as two amazing people get together to celebrate their unique and special union together, and share this amazing moment with all of us."

Gabe shifts in his seat and presses his knuckles against his mouth.

"The great poet Anaïs Nin," the CEO continues, "once said, 'Each friend represents a world in us, a world possibly not born until they arrive, and it is only by this meeting that a new world is born.' Meg and Joe made worlds like this for each other on the lucky day that they met, and today they come here to merge those worlds into one big world that they will share with each other, and that they will open wide to the friends, new and old, who represent more worlds to explore and enjoy."

"That's a fancy way of saying they're going to fuck around all they want," Joan leans across Gabe's lap and whispers to us. Gabe puts a finger to his lips and shakes his head at her.

"Here are the rings you have chosen to represent your vows," says the CEO.

Joe takes one of the rings from him, turns to face Meg, and takes her hands. "Meg," he recites, "I trust in your love for me, and mine for you. I believe in you, and don't need to possess you. This ring represents my love for you, not my ownership of you, and I want you to wear it knowing that." He slips the ring onto her finger.

Meg takes the other ring from the CEO and repeats the speech to Joe.

"Joe," asks the CEO, "do you promise to love this woman with all the love in your heart, and strive to make her happy?"

"I do," says Joe.

"And do you, Meg, promise to love this man with all the love in your heart, and strive to make him happy?"

"I do," says Meg.

"Richard Lovelace wrote, 'If I have freedom in my love, and in my soul am free, angels alone that soar above enjoy such liberty,' " the CEO drones. "Meg and Joe promise each other freedom and love. They celebrate and entrust to each other their bodies and hearts and souls, not to claim, but to care for and treasure and adore in love and freedom, and we who are gathered here to witness their union rejoice in it with them. Meg and Joe, I now pronounce you life partners. You may kiss each other."

Meg and Joe throw their arms around each other and engage in a long, deep kiss, and Joe bends Meg back so far that her top hat falls to the ground. The crowd erupts into applause and laughter, and from the speakers I can hear the tinny cheers from our videoconferenced companions in distant cities. I wonder about the people out in the world, sitting alone in front of their computer screens, looking on, and what they might be thinking of this. Meg and Joe are still kissing, and our fellow guests are giving them a standing ovation. The music comes on again, and Gabe lifts me to my feet.

"Yes," he says, under his breath.

"Yes, what?"

"Yes, you certainly can disapprove of both a tradition and its perversion. And yes, let's go get a drink."

"Just what I was thinking." Bix tucks the 3-D glasses into his breast pocket. "Great minds, huh?" He claps Gabe on the back. Gabe coughs.

"But don't you boys want to line up to fuck the bride?" asks Joan. Gabe flinches.

"Joan." I feel ill. "Enough, already."

"Oh, come on, Joy," Joan snaps. "Lighten up."

"We'll go fetch those drinks," says Bix. "Come on, Gabe."

"That was just a bit much," I tell Joan, sinking back into my seat as the boys depart. She sits down next to me and looks at me irritably.

"Darling. You of all people, with your famous opinions on marriage. You're not usually so anemic."

"One of my famous opinions against marriage, if you recall, is that monogamy is a rather unlikely proposition. So on some level, it would be my position that Meg and Joe are to be commended for understanding that."

"You're defending this spectacle?" Joan's smile is fixed and stiff.

"No. But I do wonder—maybe this open marriage business has you concerned about Bickford's ability to sleep exclusively with you for the next half-century. Which is why you're acting this way."

"And how exactly am I acting?" Joan glares. I bite my lip and wish I'd kept quiet. She opens her mouth, reconsiders, then starts giggling. "Darling, I'm so sorry. I'm all wound up. I'm absolutely on the verge. Bix and I had—oh, the most awful fight on our way over here." She takes my hand. Her laughter has become slightly hysterical. "Sometimes I think you may be right about marriage, after all. I'll probably lose my mind and be locked away before I get our damn wedding planned. Oh, god. I need a drink. I'm going to go find Bix. Forgive me?"

I nod, and she sweeps away, hiking up the bodice of her strapless dress, the red satin sweeping the floor behind her.

"That was a dramatic exit." Gabriel emerges from the crowd, hands me a fresh glass of champagne, and watches Joan disappear into the crowd.

"They're Joan's specialty." I take a sip of the champagne. "Thank you. Well, that ceremony was—"

"Unusual, yes." Gabe obviously doesn't want to discuss it any further. I'm not surprised. Raised as he was in the If-You-Can't-Say-Something-Nice-Nod-Politely-And-Change-The-Subject tradition, Gabe is generally disinclined to talk about anything he finds genuinely offensive or affronting. "Ah, familiar faces." He waves to Tulley, who is skipping toward us with Pete in tow.

"Hello, boss! Hello, Gabriel," Tulley calls.

We rise to greet them. Gabe extends his hand to Pete, who takes it shyly, ducking his head. Tulley pulls me down until I'm almost doubled over so she can reach to kiss me on both cheeks, then fusses over wiping off the lipstick marks she has left.

"What did you think of the ceremony, Joy?" She twinkles. Tulley actually can twinkle. It's the weirdest thing.

"I think our master of ceremonies should have availed himself of your services, Tull."

"I didn't think it was too bloody bad. Very original, wasn't it?" Tulley gives me a bright smile. I can't be sure if she's joking.

"You're our foremost authority on romantic tracts," Gabriel addresses Pete. "What did you think?"

Pete blushes at the compliment and bobs his head.

"I think it's kind of cool, I guess," he says. "For them. But I, ah. I guess I'm kind of old-fashioned."

"So only angels above should enjoy adultery?" Tulley snags two beef carpaccio canapés from the tray of a passing server, and hands one to Pete.

"Well, you know." Pete bobs. "That's not really what Lovelace was talking about, exactly, I think, in that poem, I think. He was kind of talking about how his love for this girl and being loved by her made him free. I think. In a larger sense, I guess. Spiritually free." He puts the bloody sliver of meat into his mouth and chews thoughtfully.

"Well, there's the rub," says Gabe.

"So you're all old-fashioned about this." Tulley twinkles. "You think their arrangement is immoral?"

"It's not about morality. It just raises questions," Gabe says.

"Such as?" Tulley puts her hands on her hips and lifts her little chin.

"The nature and purpose of marriage. Forsaking all others. These two whom God has joined let no man put asunder, and so on."

"Why not reinvent the bloody institution?"

"Why not dispense with it entirely?" I ask. "If one wants freedom."

"Why throw the baby out with the fucking bathwater?" Tulley tries to look austere, then lapses into giggles.

"I can kind of see," Pete says, "how you would want to get married, even if you didn't want all the stuff that comes along with it. Everybody gets married. It would be hard not to." Pete's brow furrows. "People want to get married, and the world wants people to get married. And, um, the way that the world thinks about love makes it hard to prove that you're really together in a real way, I think, even to each other, right? Unless you get married."

"I love this song." Tulley leaps up. "Pete, let's go dance!" She pulls at his arm. "We'll talk to you old traditionalists later!"

"He's really very eloquent in print," I tell Gabe as they disappear into the crowd.

"Traditional," Gabe says. "First time I've been called that for not planning to get married."

"I think she meant literal, really, not traditional," I answer. Gabe blinks, this slow-motion, feline, half-in-a-trance blinking thing he does when he's processing something.

"Huh. I suppose she may have something there." He looks at me blankly for a moment, then blinks again, shakes his head slightly as if to clear it. "Want to dance?"

"Yes. Right out the door and all the way home."

IN THE LATE AFTERNOON, Charles and I are pushing things around on our desks, pretending to be productive, when Damon lopes in.

"That's the ninth revise on the screenplay." He drops a pile of papers on my desk. "Can you look it over? And then let's never work for them again."

"The glamour of Hollywood," Charles protests.

"The money of Hollywood, is what he means," I tell Damon. "Is it that bad?"

"The wealthy wayward son of a powerful, presidentially ambitious senator," Damon tells us, putting on the sun- glasses Charles has left on my desk. "Boy falls in love with and is transformed into good person by sensitive girl from the wrong side of the tracks or, in this case, the art world." Damon dances around the room, flailing his long arms. "Our heroine is an artiste. Through a strange series of events, the wayward son discovers that the girl of his dreams is in fact his half-sister, who his father abandoned as an infant after his mother and her lover were killed in a car crash when our hero was a wee child. Scandal is brought to light by son's for- mer friend turned evil gossip columnist for city paper. Ambitions laid to waste. Lovers torn asunder. All ends in disaster and tears." He bows deeply. "I tried to get them to throw some vampires in there. Hot vampire chicks. Vampires are big this year. But no go."

"I think it sounds fabulous," Charles declares. "Very Greek tragedy. I can hardly wait to read the novelization."

"Guy, I hate to tell you, but it's already an adaptation."

"All the better." Charles waves his pen at Damon. "A novelization of an adaptation is so, so . . . post-post-something!"

"Vern, you're so literary," I tell him. "Maybe you should go to Hollywood."

"They could do a box set!" Charles claps his hands. "The novel, the screenplay, the novelization, plus a tell-all, behind-the-scenes, making-of documentary DVD. And—"

"Just get the thing out of here," says Damon. "I'll see you next week." He waves and strolls out.

"My sunglasses!" Charles yelps. The sunglasses come sailing back through the door and land on my desk. "Our babies." Charles sighs. "So multitalented."

"Yoo-hoo! Girls!" Miss Trixie's voice echoes across the courtyard through our open windows. She's standing on her balcony waving to us. Charles and I get up and clamber out onto the fire escape. "Hello, darlings!" Trixie hoists a martini shaker at us. "Ready for a little drinkie?"

"Yes!" Charles cheers.

"Vern, it's four-thirty."

"It's always cocktail hour somewhere in the world, sweets," Trixie says. She's wearing pink capri pants with matching pink shoes and a yellow halter top. Miss Trixie is a rather tall, athletic-looking man, broad-shouldered and slim-waisted, like a member of a high school swimming team. The effect is an odd one; I'm always amazed at how the practiced grace of her gestures distracts the eye from and denies her physique. She's a master illusionist.

"You're looking very springy," I tell her, as she leans daintily across the dim canyon between our buildings to hand Charles a pink drink in a plastic champagne glass.

"An old queen has to keep up appearances, sweetie. Cosmopolitan?"

"Don't you have to go to a bachelorette party tonight?" Charles asks me. "Better pace yourself."

"Just a thimbleful," says Trixie, pouring. She performs a neat little arabesque to deliver the glass, then raises hers to us.

"To you, girls. Divine neighbors." We stretch out over the void to touch glasses. "I want to invite you both to a Miss Trixie extravaganza," she tells us. "I have a new show premiering in a couple of weeks, and our little friend Delia and her girls are opening for me."

"Henry's girlfriend?" asks Charles.

"Fiancée," I correct.

"The very one. The second week in May we have our gala opening at the club. You'll be my guests."

"Put us in the front row," says Charles. "We'll throw bouquets of snapdragons and kiss the hem of your gown."

"And what are you two working on these days?" Trixie asks.

"Today, a bad screenplay," I tell her. "And some bad romance novels."

"Screenplay? Is there a part for me?" Trixie vamps. "I've always wanted to be in pictures."

"You can play the ingenue, gorgeous," Charles says. "You reform a bad man."

"Only in the movies," Trixie sighs. "And my ingenue days are long gone. I'm only good for a Norma Desmond role. Ready for my close-up—but for God's sake, not so damn close!" She strikes a pose, leaning on the rail of her balcony. "Now I have to get ready for rehearsal. You two be good little girls, and I'll throw over some invitations for the Trixie-Fest next week."

We hand our glasses back to her, and she disappears through the narrow French doors and into the mysteries of her boudoir. I lean back on our rusty fire escape and push my face into a shaft of sunlight. Charles surveys the narrow canal of air below us, the quiet, dingy backs of the buildings across the way.

"All this could be yours, my dear!" He spreads his arms wide.

"I always knew you were the devil." I struggle over the windowsill and back into the office.

"Speaking of soul-selling." Charles clambers in behind me. "Interesting new job opp. Someone from your friend Erica's agency called us. They want to start a corporate sponsorship program for young writers and artists. Commercial patrons for individuals—like the Medicis, they said. Isn't that precious? And they're interested in having us help develop it."

"This job gets weirder by the minute."

"They're sending the materials over for us to look at. If you approve I'll meet with them in a couple of weeks."

"Okay. It seems a little off our normal beat, but what the hell."

"We're expanding our skill sets," he tells me. "We're thinking laterally. Maybe we can throw some vampires in there. I hear vampires are hot this year."

A COUPLE OF hours later, Henry comes to pick me up; we are going to Aunt Charlotte's bachelorette party together. The office is swooning in pale, dusty sunlight, and quiet as a church. Most of the staff have departed. Besides Charles and me, only Tulley remains in the front room, seated at the conference table with her laptop computer, squinting and reading softly aloud her latest masterpiece for *BabyDoll*. I'm standing by the front windows with a sheaf of papers in my hand, watching the street below. It's a mild day in the city, though not actually warm, but everyone seems to have removed as much clothing as possible. It's as though they can't bear to wait a moment longer for spring to begin and believe that by disrobing they can will the temperature to rise. I hear footsteps on the stairs, and a minute later, Henry pushes our door open.

"I'm stuck." Tulley looks up. "What's a good synonym for jism?"

"Spooge is one of my personal favorites." Henry waves at me.

"Want a job?" Charles calls from the back office.

"How about it, Hank?" I leave the window and come to kiss her. "Want to become invisible? Tulley will share assignments with you, won't you, Tull?"

"And leave off teaching *The Iliad* to those little hormone-addled darlings at Greeley? How could I?" Henry pretends to weep at the thought of it. "It's been hilarious lately. The seniors must have been fucking like rabbits all through spring break. I can't make it through a sentence without one of them sussing out a double entendre and setting the rest off."

"Maybe they're just quicker than we are," Tulley suggests.

"It's kind of amazing that the mere suggestion of sex is so powerful for them," Charles says, wandering into the front room. "I remember it like it was yesterday."

"That's because it *was* yesterday, Vern."

"You're the one editing the trashy romance novels, Vern." He points to the manuscript in my hand.

"That's *my* trashy romance novel you're talking about," Tulley scolds.

"Pete did this one," I tell her. "It's the bankers in Hong Kong installment. Young futures trader falls for beautiful daughter of Chinese mobster. Very Oriental."

"Put down the exotica," Henry says through the police megaphone of her cupped hands. "Let's go get a drink. Want to come, guys?"

"I have a date," Charles says.

"I have a date," Tulley says at the same time.

"I didn't know you two were dating." Henry giggles. "That's great."

"Office romances allowed only in our trashy romance novels," I say.

"I'm having dinner with the owner of Boîte." Charles waves dismissively at us.

"My brother knows him," I mention to no one in particular. "How about you, Tull?"

"Um." Tulley looks sheepish. "That editor at *BabyDoll.*"

"That's interesting." I squint at her. "You know we can't do anything about sexual harassment off the job, right? Can we, Vern?"

"Tulley's a professional." Charles winks at Tulley. "She doesn't mix business and pleasure."

"Working for you, Charles," Tulley says, curtsying, "business *is* pleasure."

"And working for *BabyDoll*, pleasure is your business." Charles tips an imaginary hat at her.

"Oh, my god, *stop*. Death by witticisms." Henry stands and stretches. "Come on, Jojo. Let's motor."

I collect my things and follow Henry down the stairs. The door to the Socialist press on the floor below Invisible is open. As we pass, the sounds of a passionate argument are audible. Someone pounds a table. A woman coming up the stairs flattens against the wall to let us through, then slips into the psychologist's suite. Out on the sidewalk, I take a deep gulp of the early evening air.

"Oh, no." Henry angles her head in the direction of a petite blonde exiting the New Age bookstore. "Don't look! Too late. She saw us. Better go say hello."

Here's a weird thing about Henry: For all her rowdy bitchiness, she has this stringent (though erratic) sense of etiquette; she'll show up late to a dinner party with an extra guest or two, but she'll always write a lovely thank-you note, for example. Which is why she insists on dragging me over to make small talk with Ora Mitelman, whom she obviously hates. Maybe it's a Southern thing; I don't know.

"Hello, Joy." Ora clutches a lavender paper bag emblazoned with the Crystal Visions bookstore's logo, some kind of giant mandala, which she is holding so that the mandala is positioned directly over her pelvis. "And, Harriet, is it?"

"Henry, it's Henry."

"Henry." Ora holds up her cheek to be kissed. Henry obliges, barely.

"How'd the shopping go?" Henry nods at Ora's bag.

"A gift for a couple of friends who just became engaged." Ora holds it out for inspection.

"*A Gathering of Spirits*," Henry reads from the cover of the book. " 'A collection of multicultural marriage rites, rituals, and vows.' That sounds so . . . inspiring."

"I hope so." Ora tucks the book under her arm. "It must be such a challenge to write the ceremony oneself. But my friends really feel that it's the right thing to do. They want the wedding to represent who they truly are."

"Well. I think that's just great," Henry tells her. "Don't you, Joy?"

I nod.

"Listen, we have to run, but it was great to see you!"

"Yes, and I'll see you girls at Joan's bachelorette dinner, if not before." Ora directs a gracious smile into the middle distance behind us.

"We're looking forward to it. Aren't we, Joy?" Henry bares all her teeth at me. "Taxi!"

"ARE YOU SURE we have time for a drink?" I ask, as the cab pulls up outside Pantheon. The yellow neon sign over the entrance burns a halo into the gray twilight.

"There is always time, little missy." Henry hands the driver his fare. "Always time for a gathering of spirits. And the party is close by. Out!" She pushes me out of the cab, slams the door, and with her hands on my shoulders, marches me ahead of her into the bar.

Pantheon is already crowded with young professionals, sharp-eyed women hiking up their skirts to perch on the bar stools and young, very young men in several-thousand-dollar suits. Their smooth, elastic faces and bright, blank stares give them the appearance of unfinished sculptures, and they elbow one another in silence and move aside for Henry, a tribute she accepts with the oblivious entitlement of the organically gorgeous. Luke has seen us coming in and is chilling a martini glass and opening a bottle of wine by the time we take our seats. He leans over the bar to kiss my cheek.

"Where's mine?" Henry pouts.

"You can have extra olives." Luke swirls his martini shaker.

"Fantastic." Henry watches him pour. "She's not even your girlfriend, and you won't cheat on her. We should stuff you and put you in a diorama in the Museum of Natural History."

"Maybe you should stuff me instead." I put my head

down on the bar. "A rare specimen for inspiring such loyalty."

"My, my." Henry fishes an olive out of her martini. "Barkeep, tell that girl in the red sweater I want to buy her a drink." Luke and I look down the bar.

"The one with the Brooks Brothers model attached to her mouth?" I ask. The woman in question, a spunky sit-com type with a wheat-colored ponytail swishing across her back, is nuzzling giddily with one of the young suits who checked Henry out when we came in.

"Damn. He beat me to the draw."

"Aren't you getting married in a couple of months?" Luke asks her.

"What's your point?" Henry sucks gin off her fingers.

"Look, there's Donald Trump's new girlfriend." I gesture vaguely in the direction of the entrance.

"To the best of my knowledge, most girls stop sending drinks to strangers when they're planning to get hitched, is my point," Luke says.

"There are two categories of flirtation." Henry drains her glass. "As a means to an end, and as an end in itself."

"What's *your* point?" Luke laughs, but it's unconvincing. I look from one to the other, trying to figure out what's happening.

"That there's a difference between me buying a drink for a pretty girl because I feel like flirting, and buying a drink for her as a first step toward fucking her."

"And your fiancée is okay with that distinction?" Luke presses both hands on the bar, ignoring a customer who waves a handful of money at him.

"What's it to you whether she is or isn't, Luke?" Henry asks sweetly.

"Wow, look at the time." I poke her. "We should go soon."

"Was your heart broken by some siren who couldn't keep her hands in her pockets, Luke? Is that it?" Henry's smile is seraphic. Luke opens his mouth to answer, gives me a stricken look, and moves down the bar to take an order.

"Hank, what are you up to?"

"What?" Henry looks innocent. "The barkeep and I are just having a little conversation."

"You're goading him. For no reason. What has Luke ever done to you besides get you drunk on the house?"

"Little bundle of Joy." Henry sighs. "That barkeep is in love with you and it's so pathetic I can't help tormenting him a little."

"Not one part of that sentence made anything remotely like sense."

"I hear the weather in the state of denial is really nice." Henry waves at the sweater girl, whose new boyfriend gives us a curious stare. "When did you buy property there?"

"Did you set fire to insects for fun when you were little? Go wait outside. I'm going to say good-bye to Luke. Go." I give her a push toward the door. She laughs and ambles away.

"Are you leaving?" Luke returns to my end of the bar.

"We have a party. Hey, Luke. I'm sorry about that."

"Naw, don't worry. I'm fine. She was only playing." He's a terrible liar. "And you just put that away. It's on me." He pushes my hand, and the twenty-dollar bill in it, back toward me. "See you soon?" I nod and turn to wriggle out through the increasingly dense crowd. At the front door, I look back over my shoulder. Luke is watching me go; he gives a wave and a half-smile.

As I emerge onto the sidewalk, Henry pounces on me and showers me with kisses.

"Get off." I push her away. "You're a bitch."

"I'm not bad, I'm just drawn that way," she vamps. "Oh, lord. Duck!" She grabs my arm and yanks me behind a couple of large potted shrubs that stand at the restaurant's entrance.

"*Ow*, Henry. What the hell?"

"It's *her* again."

"Who?" I peek from behind one shrub to see Ora Mitelman breezing through Pantheon's front doors, golden curls and gauzy skirts aloft. "Ugh. Is she stalking us?"

"She's at Pantheon all the goddamn time now." Henry sighs. "I ran into her here a couple of nights ago. She called me Henley. Come on, toots. Let's go party with Aunt Charlotte!" She takes my hand and skips down the street, singing "Going to the Chapel" and dragging me along behind her.

HENRY AND I used to stay with Charlotte when we were in college; we'd come into the city on the weekends and sleep in her guest room. It was an arrangement infinitely preferable to staying with my mother for a number of reasons, our postadolescent vanity not the least of them. As she always had with me and my brothers, Charlotte treated us like adults; she played generously along with our delusional visions of ourselves as terribly sophisticated creatures, listened attentively to self-enraptured monologues about our academic adventures and romantic travesties, and let us come and go as we pleased. She led what seemed to us a very glamorous life: She worked as a fiction editor at a prestigious publishing house, attended parties every night, knew famous authors, and received flowers and phone calls from men whose handsome faces adorned the backs of books that we had heard about. More often than not, on the weekends we stayed with Charlotte, we would arrive home in the small hours to find her still awake, sitting on the couch in a black cocktail dress, picking Chinese food out of paper cartons with her fingers and flipping through an obscure literary quarterly. It was rapture. For girls who feared the ordinary, she was an icon of adulthood sweeter and finer than anything we'd ever laid eyes on.

Moreover, Charlotte was for me proof positive of a viable alternative to the conventional strictures of marriage and motherhood; though they seemed to have failed every other female role model I had, these conventions still appeared, to my bafflement, to be the prime mover of the herds of fresh-faced and otherwise independent-minded college girls with whom I daily trekked from classroom to dining hall to dormitory lounge. They had ambitious career plans and took lovers in the same casual spirit with which they shopped for summer sandals. At the same time they wanted romance with all the trimmings; they accepted Jane Austen's novels at face value, wept openly over made-for-television movies in which love conquered all, and returned from family weddings with starry eyes and total recall about the details of the bridal accessories. I was increasingly puzzled by this; increasingly, my peers began to seem very misguided.

It may have been merely a question of influence. My father dated so many women from so many walks of life that during one period I ran into them almost weekly on the streets of Manhattan, and struggled to remember their names as I answered their polite questions about my life, their elaborately casual inquiries about Dad (whose charm I had begun to find less charming, more ridiculous). I was fresh from my mother's second divorce, her tirades about the inherent evils of men, her newfound calling as divorce specialist to the stars. I knew almost no one whose parents were still married, and of those only two or three couples that had claims to anything resembling conjugal bliss. It was during this period that I began to consider marriage an absurd position, a grand delusion, a deeply stupid thing.

Still, it was what people believed in and what they did;
Charlotte served as an excellent lesson that there was
another way to live, and I became quite attached to her as a
symbol of that alternative. Naturally, then, I was a little disappointed when she announced her engagement, thereby
depriving me of my icon, my patron saint of alternate reali-
ties. On the other hand, she's marrying a guy almost fifteen
years her junior whom she met when he was hired as her
editorial assistant. This departs from the predictable just
enough to appease me.

IN FRONT OF a restaurant on a little side street, Henry
stops so suddenly that I slam into her and nearly knock both
of us over.

"Take it easy, cowboy." Henry prances ahead of me
through the big glass doors into the foyer. "We're here with
the Blake party," she tells the man at the front desk, who
exchanges a smirk with the coat check girl and points to a set
of stairs curving down into darkness. As we descend, the
sound of women's voices rises to meet us and echoes off the
stone walls. Candles flicker in the dim below.

"I didn't know this place had a torture chamber." Henry
gropes her way down the last stairs. "I would have come here
before."

"Apply for a job, Hank. You're eminently qualified."

"Joy? Is that you?" A figure pauses silhouetted in the
archway before us, and stumbles forward. "Honey, you made
it!" My aunt's best friend, a tall, slender blonde in her early
fifties, emerges from the dark and flings herself on me.

"Hi, Francine." I hug her back. "Remember Henry? You
met at Charlotte's birthday party a couple of years ago. And
at the engagement party."

"Yes, of course!" Francine reaches over and pets Henry's

face. "So nice to see you again! We're so glad you could come, both of you." She puts an arm around each of our waists and pulls us in close.

"Wow," Henry whispers to me. "Eau de Jack Daniel's. We have some catching up to do."

"You're just in time." Francine's voice is conspiratorial; the effect is only slightly thrown off by her slurring. She leans on me and gives a big wink. "We brought some friends for Charlotte. Some *friends*. They're getting ready right now." She nods in the direction of the rest rooms and nods at us, and for no apparent reason, keeps nodding. "Charlotte doesn't know. It's a surprise. Joy, baby!" With some effort, she focuses on my nose, swaying lightly. "I remember you when you were just a little, little, little baby girl, baby. Let's go get you a drink before the show starts."

Francine takes our hands and tows us along behind her through the medieval-looking stone archway and into a shadowy banquet hall where, seated at a long table, several dozen women of a certain age are chattering and giggling like adolescent girls.

"Charlotte, Charlotte," Francine shrieks. "Look what I found!"

My aunt is seated at the center of the table surrounded by several women whom I recognize vaguely from her engagement party. She rises in her chair and waves her arms at us as we approach. I'm often taken by surprise by how much Charlotte and my mother resemble each other. They're both fair-skinned and fine-boned, with wavy, pale brown hair, heart-shaped faces, and eyes an astonishing shade of hazel; Charlotte's features, though, are softer, and overall she has a less sharp, angular aspect than Mom.

"Hello, girls!" Charlotte smiles at Henry and takes my hand. "I'm so glad you're here. You're our only family representation, kiddo. Your mother declined to join us this evening. Oh, and Dora, Burke's sister." She indicates a woman about our age, an evil-looking brunette at the far end of the table.

"Dora Ingerson?" Henry peers through the dim. "I know her. She worked at the magazine with me." Henry waves, and the brunette waves back. "What a bitch. I'll go say hello."

"Joy, let me move over so you can sit next to your aunt." The portly, henna-haired woman on Charlotte's right heaves out of her chair. "How are you, dear?" She looks distractedly around the room.

"Maggie Bean," Charlotte whispers into my ear.

"I'm fine, Maggie. Nice to see you again. And you?"

"Oh, good. And you? You're looking pretty tonight." She pats my cheek. "You girls talk. I'm off to the ladies' room." Maggie waddles off into the dark.

"I met her at your engagement party?" I lower myself into the seat she's vacated, which is still warm.

"One of the most powerful women in the literary world, believe it or not. An agent. We've worked together for years. And she introduced me to Burke. Her son went to school with him, and Maggie sent him to me for the assistant job." Charlotte gives me a little smile. "Look. The girls are back."

Henry and Francine weave toward us, both giggling and spilling cocktails as they proceed across the room.

"Joy, why didn't you tell me you knew a floral designer?" Henry slaps the side of my head, sloshing part of her drink down my back. "Francine is going to do the flowers for my wedding. She did the arrangements tonight. Aren't they gorgeous?"

"You girls will have to come down to the shop and talk bouquet design with me next week." Francine smiles modestly and reaches over to fondle the centerpiece in front of

Charlotte, a vaguely pornographic-looking topiary sculpted from sweet pea blossoms and ivy. "A September wedding is such a nice challenge. Not that I won't love doing yours, Charlotte. I think it's time for a toast, don't you, Henrietta?" Francine climbs unsteadily onto an empty chair and Henry clinks a fork noisily against her martini glass. The chattering buzz of the room quiets, and the several dozen women of a certain age turn their eyes toward us.

"Ladies, thank you for coming." Francine wobbles dangerously on the chair. She puts a hand on Henry's shoulder. "Ladies," Francine continues, "why are we here? Because. Because our friend Charlotte has robbed the cradle, that's why. God bless her!" Cheers and applause from the crowd.

"Nice work," Henry tells Charlotte.

"No, no, no." Francine waves her arms. "Seriously, now, we're here because our dear friend Charlotte has found true love." More cheers. "With an infant," Francine slurs. Louder cheers. "Maggie Bean, this is all your fault." Francine raises her glass in Maggie's general direction. "Could you find an assistant for me, too, please?"

"And for me," a pretty woman in her early sixties calls out.

"Maura, you're already married," Francine giggles.

"Twice," says Maura.

"Good help is the secret to every successful marriage," says the woman sitting to Charlotte's left.

"Now, girls," Francine continues. "Our friend Charlotte has had a good run. She pursued her work and made her way as a single woman in the city while most of us were getting married. And divorced. And married and divorced again. God bless her. She was a rebel. She was a career girl. She got to sleep with all the men we didn't. And we were sick with jealousy, weren't we, ladies? But now. Now! She's been brought down by a mere child. See how the mighty have fallen." The crowd roars. "See how the mighty have fallen, ladies. A toast. To Charlotte! We love you, honey."

"To Charlotte!" The women around the table clink their glasses together with great enthusiasm; at the other end of the table they do it with such enthusiasm, in fact, that some- one breaks a glass. I watch Charlotte laughing back at her friends as they wave their glasses at her, and wonder to myself, is this what Charlotte has had to put up with for the last two decades out of wedlock? Is this what waits for me? The subtle jibes, the tiresome loving concern, the passive- aggressively manifested resentments and fears of women who pity or envy me for what I won't do? Maybe it's a gener- ational thing. It occurs to me that Charlotte may be getting married less because she wants to be married and more because she's too exhausted by what is involved in not being married.

"Oh, my." Francine points theatrically as she climbs down from her chair. "Oh, my. Look at that. What could they be doing here?" Emerging through the dim archway are three large, plastically handsome men, one dressed as a policeman, another as a priest, and a third in a business suit, carrying a briefcase.

"Oh, Francine." Charlotte laughs as music begins to play and the men come slinking around the table. "You really shouldn't have."

"My god, it's like a borscht belt joke." Henry elbows me. "Did you hear the one about the cop, the priest, and the lawyer?"

"What's the punch line?" I ask, but Henry doesn't answer. The other guests are, for the most part, on their feet instantly, whistling and clapping. A few titter and bury their faces in one another's shoulders, a few others remain seated and apparently oblivious, engrossed in their conversations. Francine and Henry howl with glee and press dollar bills into the hands of the women around them. The dancers have arrived next to us, and begin to circle around me with big, fixed grins, stagy and lascivious.

"Wrong girl," I inform the priest, pushing him and the cop toward Charlotte. The men lift her onto their shoulders, carry her across the room, and seat her on top of the bar. Marvin Gaye's "Sexual Healing" moans out of the speakers at top volume, and the men line up and begin their bump and grind of the seven veils. Henry elbows me and nods in the direction of the doorway, where several of the restaurant's waitstaff cluster in the shadow of the stone arch. The guests have gathered around the men in a wide semicircle, waving bills and screaming with delight as articles of clothing are removed and come flying into their midst.

"They take their clothes off," Henry tells me. "That's the punch line. Wow, look at his ass."

"I've heard that joke before," I say. "It was on an episode of *The Honeymooners*, wasn't it?" But she's run off to tuck a tip into the priest's G-string.

Sunday, April 29, 200—

ON THE BRIGHT SUNDAY of Charlotte and Burke's wedding, I spend the first hour of the morning in bed with the covers pulled over my face while Gabe tries valiantly to coax me into action.

"I'm spending quality time with my hangover," I growl through the sheets, when he tries to bribe me with coffee.

"Tell your hangover you need to reschedule." He sits down on the edge of the bed. I reach my hand out from underneath the blankets for the coffee cup. "Not until you're actually vertical," Gabe says, moving it out of range. I pull my hand back in and burrow deeper. "Joy, we have to be at the wedding in two hours. Less."

"What wedding?"

"The one we had a rehearsal dinner for last night, remember? Come on. If we survived that, we can manage this. Get up." Gabriel puts his head under the blankets and looks at me.

"I don't think the dress I was going to wear today is really suitable." I roll on my side to face him. "Do you happen to know where I can pick up one of those lab suits doctors wear to work with the flesh-eating virus that liquefies you from the inside out?"

"Red." Gabe climbs in beside me, pulls the covers over both of our heads, and lies on his side, facing me. "You *could*

let a wedding make you crazy, but don't, okay? I'd miss you if
I had to send you to the loony bin."

"Even if I survive this one, there are fourteen more left."

"You have an excellent sense of humor. Or you used to.
That should help."

"I seem to be missing the joke."

"Apparently." A rare and, I know, perfectly understand-
able note of impatience has crept into Gabe's voice.

"The last time I checked, you weren't such a raging fan
of the marriage ceremony, either, Mr. Winslow."

"Look. None of these ceremonies is my wedding or
yours, right? There are other things I'd rather be doing with
my weekends, too, but I'm fairly certain marriage isn't con-
tagious."

"That can't be right. It's clearly a virus, and it's spread-
ing. Like the flesh-eating disease."

"But we've been inoculated, okay? We're immune."
Gabe throws the covers back and sits up. "Here. Take your
medicine." He hands me the coffee, goes to the bathroom,
and comes back with a bottle of aspirin. He shakes a couple
of them into my hand, and as I chase them down with a swallow of coffee, he makes the sign of the cross over me and
intones, "Body of Christ, blood of Christ." Then he starts
doing a bayou voodoo queen dance around the bed, moaning
a gibberish chant and waving his hands over the body of the
novice prone on the altar.

MY HEADACHE HAS subsided to a comparatively agreeable dull thudding by the time we arrive at The Original
Hotel and are swept through the lobby on a tide of guests to
the grand ballroom where the wedding ceremony will take
place. This venue represents an Ingerson family defeat;
Burke's parents lobbied hard for a ceremony in Philadelphia

and then, when Burke held fast to Manhattan, pleaded for a nice Presbyterian chapel uptown. But Charlotte, bless her secular heart, refused, and though the stand involved a number of lengthy phone calls and brunches ranging from the terse to the histrionic, the happy couple won out. They placated Burke's parents with The Original, which belongs to an old friend of the Ingerson family, and left catering and the guest list—which thereby grew to three times the suggested length—in the hands of his mother, if only to keep her distracted from the fact that the ceremony would be performed by a justice of the peace.

We were out to dinner with Charlotte one night a couple of months ago, when she and Burke were still in the thick of wedding day logistics, and Charlotte, in one of her rare moments of anger, wished marital strife and swift divorce upon the Ingersons: "Then his mother could plan her own damn wedding all over again, which is obviously what she wants to do," she snapped at me and Gabriel. At that time a number of my friends were engaged in similar wrestling matches with their families, and Charlotte's remark struck me as quite correct. Why else would individuals who were involved, really, only peripherally in the ultimate point of the wedding ceremony—that is to say, *the marriage*—care so much and battle so fiercely over its particulars, but that they saw it as some grand opportunity for a personal do-over?

THE ORIGINAL BALLROOM is stuffed with huge, aggressive arrangements of orange tulips—it looks like Francine and her floral minions were on Dexedrine when they got together to do the flowers—and lined with row upon row of flimsy, ribbon-bedecked white chairs. The room is already swarming with guests in Waspishly tasteful spring finery who ricochet toward and away from one another like charged

ions. The high arc of air under the vaulted ceiling trembles
with the shrill cries of recognition from women who haven't
seen one another for ten years and would happily have gone
another decade unseen; the booming and backslapping of
the husbands; the shrieking laughter of children who climb
on chairs and chase one another in circles around the elevated platform that will shortly serve as an altar for the ceremony. It looks like the opening scene of some pastoral
operetta. I hear my mother keening my name and look
plaintively at Gabriel, who tows me toward the heaving
bosom of my family.

Along with Bachelor Number Three (aka Mom's fiancé),
my younger brother Josh and his Nice-Jewish-Girl
betrothed, Ruth, are already in their seats of honor, the
advance guard, waving at us. My mother stands in the aisle
beside them fluttering her hands; her face contorts as we
approach.

"Honey," she says, coming forward with her hands outstretched, "*what* are you wearing?"

For a moment I think I might be having one of those
nightmares where I turn up at school stark naked.

"Claire, you look lovely," Gabe intercepts.

"Thank you, Gabriel." My mother pecks him on the
cheek. "Joy, what on earth are you doing in *black*? You know
you're *never* to wear such dark colors to a wedding. A *spring*
wedding, too. An *afternoon* wedding!" My mother talks in
italics; I can almost see the little curls and loops etching the
air as she speaks.

"Hi, Mom. Nice to see you, too." I put my hand on her
shoulder. "This is New York. We wear black to everything.
And I don't think Charlotte cares too much what we're wearing, as long as we're here, right?"

"But what will the *Ingersons* think? They'll think I didn't
know how to bring you up. And it makes you look so *sallow*."

She reaches up and pushes my hair away from my face. "Why don't you borrow my blusher and run to the powder room, honey? Just a little color."

"I think James has taken care of that," Gabriel says, and we turn to see my brother come mincing toward us, resplendent in a bright pink suit with a chartreuse cravat and very loud, heavily embroidered waistcoat. My mother pales.

"Hello, baby girl!" James lifts me in his arms and twirls around. "Look at you, all dolled up."

"Look who's talking, big girl. I thought we were going to play nice."

"Did I say that?" James puts me down. "I don't recall saying that. Temporary insanity, your honor. Hi, gorgeous," he says, bowing low over my mother's hand and pressing his lips to the sizable diamond of her engagement ring.

"Oh, Jamie," my mother says. "*Jamie*. Oh, for heaven's sake. Everyone is *looking* at you."

James turns to the crowd of guests behind us and gives a big beauty-queen wave.

"Jamie, stop! Sit *down*. Let's just sit down." Mom tugs at his arm and he lets her drag him into a seat in the front row. She's trying to maintain her ire, but as usual it's not working. When it comes to Mom, James can and always has been able to get away with anything. Josh is the model son, has done and been everything standard-issue parents wish for, and he's certainly held up as the shining example. But in the end, James is the beloved. As the firstborn, and the obvious candidate for the office of family black sheep, he was supposed to have blazed the trail for me, getting the first and worst of parental anxieties, severities, projections, displacements, and doing the basic breaking-in from which most second siblings benefit. Alas, that is not what happened. To his credit, James doesn't take particular advantage of Mom's doting on him. He likes to bait her, but it's not out of malice.

I think he feels a genuine compassion for her, which I can't quite bring myself to share.

"I'm going to the bathroom," I tell no one in particular.

"Honey, take my blusher." My mother reaches into her purse and retrieves a compact, which she hands to me. "Hurry, though."

"You wouldn't want to miss the ceremony," Gabe adds, straight-faced, as he settles into the chair next to James.

"Don't tempt me," I hiss, and march away. Passing a group of guests who are bent together and bobbing their heads like nuns at prayer, I catch fragments of a joyously horrified conversation: "Fourteen years . . . her assistant . . . his mother . . . shush, hush!"

A couple of heads swivel in my direction. I lift my chin and, hurrying past, slam directly into Mrs. Ingerson, the mother of the groom, who reels backward into her husband. Mr. Ingerson steadies her as I apologize, and leans over to kiss my cheek.

"Well, well," he says. "Well, well, well."

"Well," Mrs. Ingerson adds. "Well, *Joy*."

"Fancy running into you here," I say, and immediately regret it. They blink at me. "You both look very nice," I tell them. They smile and nod.

"*You* look very nice," Mrs. Ingerson smiles. "Though you're a little *pale*, dear. Is it too warm in here? Farley, do you think it's too *warm* in here? Joy, you can't *imagine* how nice it is in Philadelphia this time of year. We got married there, in the *sweetest* little church, didn't we darling?" Her smile stretches out until her whole face trembles, and for a moment I imagine that she's going to burst into a bright cloud of dust, which will hang in the air for a moment before it falls shimmering into a pile at our feet.

"Well, well." Mr. Ingerson pats her hand, and we stumble into a conversational black hole, staring blankly and nodding stupidly at one another. I clear my throat.

"The room looks very nice," I say. "The tulips are really something."

"I guess you and your young man will be walking down the aisle one of these days now, won't you?" Mrs. Ingerson beams at me.

"Oh, yes," I tell her. "Absolutely. During the winter season in Hades, I think." Their automaton smiles confirm that they have missed this completely. I feel immensely cheered up. "Will you excuse me, please, Mrs. Ingerson, Mr. Ingerson? I was just on my way to the powder room."

"Would you like to borrow my blusher?" Mrs. Ingerson asks. "You look *terribly* pale, dear. Though maybe it's just that dark color you're wearing."

"Drink a glass of water," Mr. Ingerson calls after me. "Wouldn't do to have you fainting during the ceremony, would it?"

I consider this possibility as I skirt a group of small children using their plump little hands as automatic weapons in what appears to be a complete massacre near the ballroom's entrance. One girl, a gawky kid who looks to be about seven, turns her index fingers on me and makes vicious machine-gun noises, her face contorted into a bloodthirsty scowl. I clutch at my gut, stumble against the door frame, and slump down on the carpeted floor of the hallway, moaning. I open one eye a fraction to see the girl standing over me, giggling.

"Hey, lady," she says. "It's not loaded."

"That's what you think," I tell her. "It's okay, though. Consider it a mercy killing."

"What's that?" The girl sticks her machine-gun finger into a sizable gap between a couple of teeth that haven't quite finished coming in.

"It means you did me a favor." I prop myself up on one elbow. "I was going to have to go put on makeup, but now that I'm dead there's no point, is there?"

"You're not dead," the girl points out. "You're breathing."

"Oh, well. I guess I'll have to go put on makeup after all."

"Can I have some?" The girl watches me sideways as I stand up and dust myself off.

"Sure. Come to the bathroom with me." I offer her my mother's blusher compact. "You can do mine, too."

"Your backside is dirty," she notifies me, as she trails me down the hall.

"Good," I tell her. "What's your name?"

"Fred."

"Fred?"

"It's really Frederika but I hate that so you call me Fred, okay?" The girl says this all in one breath, then eyes me to see how it will go over.

"I'll call you Fred. And you call me Mickey the Fin, okay?"

"That's not your real name." Fred giggles.

"It is today." I hold open the door to the ladies' lounge. "You get started with that stuff while I go to the bathroom, and then you can put some on me."

"Okay, Mickey the Fin," Fred climbs up onto one of the chairs arranged before a long mirror and counter designed to accommodate mass primping. I push through the swinging door into the bathroom, and several women at the sinks stop their conversation and turn to look at me. I ignore them and head for the stalls. From behind the door, I can hear their conversation resume, the voices overlapping like a cross-tide of little waves.

"Well, I don't care what the Ingersons say," one of them

shrills. "They're in love, and I say good on her. I'd trade places with her in a minute."

"They're right. He'll live to regret it. It's not like she's going to start having children at her age."

"Not everyone has to have kids."

"Look who's talking. Your kids are everything to you."

"Love isn't everything, either. And he's breaking his parents' hearts."

"If we'd all got married to please our parents, where do you suppose we'd be now?"

"Better off, probably."

As I come out, the conversation stops again, and the women watch my reflection in the mirror as I leave. Back in the ladies' lounge, Fred has succeeded in applying a great deal of rouge to her small cheeks, in big pink circles.

"How do I look, Mickey?" She squirms around and lifts her face for inspection.

"Fabulous. You look like my gorgeous friend Miss Trixie." I sit down in the chair next to her. "Do mine just like that, please."

Fred kneels in her chair, facing me, and begins the application with a serious expression. The bathroom door swings open and the women from the sinks emerge.

"Fred!" One of them, a woman about my mother's age, in a slim black dress, crosses to us as the other women leave.

"Grandma Fred! Look what me and Mickey are doing! Grandma, this is Mickey the Fin."

"Hello, Mickey. Don't you both look lovely?" The woman gives me a big, beaming smile and lifts Fred up in her arms.

"Grandma, I'm not done yet," Fred scolds.

"I see that. Mickey looks a little uneven."

"You don't know the half of it," I tell Grandma Fred. "Fred, come finish me."

"Will she do mine, too?" a familiar voice asks, and I turn to see Henry leaning against the doorway in a skintight powder blue dress, grinning like a lunatic.

"When I'm finished with Mickey." Fred takes my face in her little hands. "Hold still, Mickey." Turning to Henry, she asks, "Who are you?"

"They call me Henry."

"I'm Fred. This is Grandma Fred, and this is Mickey the Fin."

"Mickey and I go way back, Fred. This is your namesake?" she asks the older woman.

"Granddaughter. Frederika the Younger. My daughter couldn't let a terrible name just die the quiet death it deserved."

"I got Henrietta. Our crosses to bear."

"The sins of the fathers, no? Or the mothers, as the case may be," Grandma Fred says.

"Your turn," says Fred, pointing to Henry. "You want to be next, Grandma?"

"You bet, kiddo. I always knew you had an artistic streak," she says, admiring Fred's handiwork: extra large, very irregular ovals slanting across my face.

"Groom's side?" I ask her.

"I'm Burke's aunt. His mother's reprobate sister."

"The best kind." Henry smiles as Fred steadies her face with one paw against Henry's high, fair forehead.

"And you're Charlotte's people, correct?" Grandma Fred asks me.

"Niece. Her sister's daughter." I check my watch. "Fred, you'd better work fast."

"I like Charlotte so much." Grandma Fred strokes her namesake's hair. "She's a great lady."

I meet her eyes in the mirror, and she means it.

"I like her pretty well, myself."

"Me, too," Henry vamps at her reflection. She has long, dark slashes of pink running from either ear almost to the corners of her mouth. "This might be the only moment in the entire day that anyone agrees on anything. Except for the wedding vows, of course." She gives the junior beautician a noisy kiss. "Fred, I look divine! You're a genius."

"You now, Grandma." Fred the elder sits obediently in front of the child. Alas, Fred has time only to complete one of the matriarch's cheeks before a woman who looks to be just a couple of years my senior bursts into the ladies' lounge, the very picture of frantic.

"Frederika!" She sighs, catching sight of the little girl, and then says, high-pitched, "Mother! Frederika! What on *earth* are you doing?"

"Mommy," little Fred says, guilty and pretending not to be.

"Moira," big Fred says, at the same time, and in precisely the same tone.

"Oh, my god." Mommy/Moira takes us all in.

"Hi, there," Henry grins, extending a hand. "Your lovely daughter was giving us last-minute beauty treatments. I didn't have time to get to the salon this morning."

"Mother, you're *supposed* to keep her *out* of trouble," the woman says, ignoring Henry. She digs angrily into her purse and pulls out a packet of antibacterial wipes. "Frederika, come here. Mother, really. The *ceremony* is about to start. What are people going to *think* if they see her like this? And you! *Here*." She takes a break from her vigorous scrubbing of the cheeks of a whimpering Fred the Younger, and viciously extends a towelette to Fred the Elder.

"It was just lovely to meet you all." Henry deepens her swamp-trash drawl and takes my arm. "Freddy, thank you so much for doing our makeup. We love it." She throws Moira a steely glare and drags me out of the bathroom.

"Good-bye, Mickey the Fin," I hear little Fred call after us.

Bursting out into the hallway, we meet my aunt, who is walking toward the entrance to the ballroom with Francine, the former clad in a slim, white dress and the latter in an enormous bridesmaid's pouf of golden-orange organza and silk. My aunt's face lights up at the sight of us, and then, registering our cosmetic aberrations, she does a double take worthy of a place in the Slapstick Hall of Fame and breaks into laughter.

"There's a renegade beauty school student in there," Henry says. "Watch your backs. She's armed and dangerous."

"I wish you'd sent her up to the bridal suite." Charlotte hugs me sideways.

"Are we missing your wedding?" I ask.

"Can't start without the bride," Francine points out. "They can just wait until she's good and ready."

"You look pretty great." Henry brushes her fingers over the fabric of Charlotte's dress. "White! I didn't know you'd been saving yourself for marriage, Auntie Cee."

"Neither did I." Charlotte watches the two Freds scurry past us in the wake of Mommy/Moira. Fred the Elder winks and blows a kiss to the bride. Fred the Younger gives us a little surreptitious wave. Watching her skinny back retreat, I suddenly want to shanghai the girl, hail a taxi, and direct it to take us to some remote hamlet in the rural Midwest, where we will start a beauty parlor and live in a state of grace, giving the elderly women of the town makeovers and eating banana pancakes for every meal.

"There goes your inner child," Henry tells me.

"And you girls should follow along," Francine says. "You can only keep a man waiting for so long. This day had to come, Charlotte." She giggles. My aunt giggles.

"Right-o." Henry grabs my hand. "Resistance is futile. See you girls out there. If Joy's mom doesn't kill us first."

And ask not for whom the wedding bells toll, I think to myself, as Hank tows me along toward the ballroom, Charlotte's laughter ringing down the hallway behind us.

Sunday, May 6, 200–

I T ' S   T H E   F I R S T   S U N D A Y   E V E N I N G of the month, and so, as is the monthly custom in this country, I leave Gabe to his own devices—perusing contact sheets from a series of shoots he did this week, Hot Young Novelists in their own outfits and natural habitats, for a glossy city weekly—and head down to Pantheon to carouse with my girlfriends. Leaving my apartment building I note, according to the Unitarian church's blue-plate-special board, that today's sermon was on tolerance and forgiveness; the featured scripture is that old favorite, "Let he who is without sin cast the first stone." I think of the meek pastor whom I often see lingering on the steps on Sunday mornings, bidding adieus to the congregation, and wonder what he might have on his conscience.

F O R   O N C E , I am not the first to arrive. Ora Mitelman is seated at the bar, smiling up at Luke. He sees me come in and waves, but for perhaps the first time in the history of our acquaintance he doesn't leave the bar to welcome me. Ora twists around on her bar stool.

"Hello, Joy." She lowers the thick fronds of her lashes at me. "What a coincidence. What brings you here?"

"I'm here for dinner with Joan and our friends. As are you, I believe."

"Yes, I am," Ora coos. "What a nice surprise to see you. Do you come here often?"

"Joy's a regular." Luke hands me a glass of wine.

"Oh, you're a barfly!" Ora smiles. "I envy you, Joy, I really do. I don't get out much these days." She gives a martyr's smile and flutters her hands.

"Really? How strange. Because I see your picture in the 'Night Life' column all the time. Just today, you were in—"

"You looked great," Luke cuts me off. "That film premiere party. You photograph so well."

"Oh, no." Ora shakes her head prettily. "Well, thank you. I was hoping no one would see that. My publicist makes me go to these things. He says it's good for the book, and what can I do?" She sighs.

"It must be exhausting." Luke touches her wrist with one finger.

"It really is." Ora sinks a little on her bar stool, weary with the thought of it, then turns to me. "Joy, I just had an idea. I know the nicest boy. Maybe you'd like to meet him. We used to date, but he wasn't right for me. A lawyer, a little conservative. He might be perfect for you. He's really very sweet."

"Thanks so much for thinking of me." I swallow half my glass of wine. "But I'm seeing someone."

"You are?" Ora's eyes widen. "I'm surprised."

"Why?" Luke laughs. "Joy's a catch! Aren't you, little gal?"

"Of course she is." Ora gives him an icy smile. "But she just *seems* single somehow, don't you think?"

A bloodcurdling howl comes from the entrance, and Henry rushes in and flings herself upon me, pretending to weep with joy. Emblazoned on her T-shirt are the words *What Would Joan Jett Do?*

"Honey, baby, angel, darling! Let me look at you! My god, how you've grown! It's been so long, darling!"

It's been eighteen hours; Gabe and I had dinner with Henry and Delia last night, and we accompanied Henry to see Mercy Fuck perform at Miss Trixie's show on Friday. Henry crushes me to her chest. Over my shoulder, she acknowledges our companions, then goes back to mauling me.

"Honey, bunny, lovely, sweetheart! Look at you!" She scrunches up her face and pinches my cheeks.

"Hi, Hank. How was your day?"

"Well!" Henry flings herself down on the stool beside me. "Barkeep!"

"What are you drinking, Henrietta?" Luke asks, though Henry always has the same thing, and he knows exactly what it is.

"A lot. I am drinking a lot. Of the *usual*, Luke. The USE-YOU-WELL. You're not angry with me over our little debate the other night, are you, my darling, darling barkeep?"

Luke turns away without speaking and mixes Henry's martini.

"What debate?" Ora asks.

"Ah-HA! Funny you should ask, Ora." Henry pronounces the name absurdly, emphasizing and drawing out the second syllable like a sigh. "That's a very, very interesting question. Isn't it, Joy?" She lifts the drink that Luke has just set in front of her. "Ladies and gentlemen—present company excluded, of course—a toast to our resident celebrity! Pictured with Bobby De Niro in today's 'Night Life' column! The new Dorothy Parker-meets-Marguerite Duras! The next Anaïs Nin! The female Erica Jong! To your book, Ora! To your triumph!"

Ora, who isn't clear about Henry's intent, smiles tentatively and lowers her lashes. I, who am quite clear about it, feel my spirits rise, and clink my glass against Henry's. Luke, who is also in the know, gives Henry the evil eye.

"We were debating, little Miss Mitelman," Henry says, pausing to slurp her martini, "a topic near and dear to your heart: flirtation and fidelity." Henry puts on a whining English accent. "The relation of the lover to the beloved. Ends and means. A whole happy host of false oppositions. It was simply delightful! I'm so terribly, terribly sorry you missed it." Henry leaps up and trots to greet Joan and Miel, who have just come into the restaurant.

"What is she talking about?" Ora turns to me.

"Henry has an unconventional definition of romantic fidelity." I glance at Luke, who is apparently enraptured by Ora's profile. "She believes you can be faithful without necessarily being monogamous. Or rather, that sexual drift is basically inevitable, and that it's not useful to condemn or suppress it."

"Well." Ora smiles. "I certainly agree with her on that last point. Until you meet the person who's meant for you, you're going to be restless, because you're incomplete. You're still looking for the love of your life. God knows I've had plenty of married men pursue me. And I've pursued them, too. Nothing wrong with that, if there's a chance that we're meant to be together." She lowers her lashes at me. Luke frowns.

"I don't think that was quite Henry's point," I tell her, but she has turned away to kiss Joan, first one cheek, then the other. Henry, who is standing beside me and has apparently overheard Ora's proclamation, makes a gagging noise.

"You'd better fucking believe it's not what I meant," she whispers. "Boy, it's a good thing Erica's not coming tonight. She'd be having fits. 'Tis-Pity-She's-A-Whore has reached new depths in the Hank opinion polls. Though there's apparently not a consensus on this point." She jerks her head toward Luke, who is staring at Ora with an addled expression. "You've been displaced in his big lunky heart, Joy," she hisses into my ear as I wave over Ora's head to Joan. "No more bartender pining after you."

"I'm crushed," I tell her.

Henry gives me an acute once-over and raises an eyebrow, but makes no comment, for which I am grateful. I wave a hand in front of Luke's eyes and ask him for another drink. Miel sidles up to me and leans the bird-frail bones of her little rib cage sideways into my lap.

"Hi," I tell her.

"Hello, Joyful." She looks up at me. "How are you?"

"Oh, you know. Fine. Want a drink?"

"Yes, please." She twists around in my lap. "Luke, may I have—Luke?"

THINGS DO NOT improve over dinner. Joan, who is in a state of near hysteria over her imminent nuptials, drinks several cocktails in rapid succession and strips down to naked id, talking loudly and viciously about her future husband and his various shortcomings in this last week of preparations; she convulses with braying laughter one moment and is overcome by misty-eyed sentimentality the next. Maud, usually the stalwart, cheerful anchor of our group, is in a dark mood; a major chunk of funding for her company's film has been pulled as the result of a rift between her and one of her coproducers. Miel is even more abstracted than usual, and when she knocks a glass of something over and floods the table, I find myself fantasizing about shaking her violently by her little shoulders and shouting, "Earth to fairy princess!" into her little pink ears.

"So, Ora." Henry gives a bright, welcoming smile, propping her elbows on the table and making a show of chewing with her mouth open. "Did I overhear you saying that you have a taste for chasing married men? Tell me about that. As soon-to-be married women, I'm sure we're all very interested. Useful to know what to look out for."

"I didn't say that." Ora turns from her conversation with Joan. "I don't get my thrills from breaking up marriages."

"Though you've broken up a few," Henry says, "if I recall correctly. I mean, according to your memoir."

"That was in the novel." Joan tries to focus on Henry. "It's fiction. It was, wasn't it, Ora, my sweetheart?"

"What I meant is that I don't go for men simply *because* they're married. That would be horrible. But when two people feel a powerful connection to each other, I believe the mandate to explore those feelings overrules everything else."

We stare at Ora.

"I'm not going to throw away a chance to find the love of my life just because circumstances conspired to attach him to somebody else before fate brought us together," she says. "So he's married. Or has a girlfriend. What does that mean, anyway?"

"That's what Joy thinks, too, don't you honey?" Joan slurs. "Joy doesn't believe in marriage. She thinks the connection should be enough."

"I'm in total agreement." Ora nods at me.

I glare at Joan, but she's waving at Luke for another cocktail.

"And if the connection isn't there," Ora continues, "then we're not really breaching anything, or violating anything, or doing anything wrong. We're really doing what's right, by doing everything in our power to find our true loves. Because what else is life about?" She looks to me for acknowledgment, and I am so stupefied that I nod at her.

"You really don't feel bad at all about the women you might hurt?" Miel sounds mournful.

"No. I'm really doing them a favor, if you think about it." Ora leans a cheek into one hand. "I mean, if the man this woman is with is truly meant to be with me, they'll never really be happy together, because some part of his heart will always be yearning after the sense of completeness that he could only find with me."

"Oh, come on!" Henry says. "You really believe there's only one person in the world that baby Cupid has intended just for you? Give me a break."

"I do believe it." Ora glares back at Henry. "And I know if I just keep looking, I'll find him. This man I met this past week—he just might be the one. There was this incredibly powerful energy between us the minute he walked into my apartment."

"The plumber?" Henry says. "The UPS guy?"

"A photographer, actually." Ora tosses her hair. "This very beautiful man who came to photograph me for *City* magazine. I think maybe he was already interested in me, because he insisted on coming to do the shoot in my apartment. He said it was what the magazine wanted, but I think it was really what *he* wanted."

"Very sweet." Joan strokes Ora's hair. "All the boys love Ora."

"And how, exactly, would you describe this very powerful energy?" Henry asks.

"I can't put it into words," Ora says. "It was just this *force*."

"How do you know he felt it, and not just you?" I ask, all casual-like.

"Oh, Joy. You can tell, can't you? When there's that spark? When you connect with someone right away, from the moment you lay eyes on each other?"

This, to me, sounds like your boring basic sexual attraction, but an image flickers across my mind, of Gabe with his hands full of champagne glasses, crossing a broad lawn in Long Island on an early autumn afternoon, and I feel ill.

"He was so attentive, and such a brilliant, profound, charming man. He's got broad shoulders and beautiful wavy dark hair. And so clever," Ora continues, dreamy-eyed. "I love a man who makes me laugh; it's the most important thing. He stayed for hours, to get the right shot, he said! He was *very* flirtatious, very chivalrous. *And* he didn't mention that he had a girlfriend until the very end. I asked him for his card. I told him that maybe I'd have him do my new author photo!" She lowers her lashes at us.

"So you'll be seeing him again?" Henry smirks.

"I'll make sure of it. We're supposed to get together this week so I can see how the pictures came out. And I'll bet you anything, ladies, that he won't be with that girlfriend of his for long." She flashes a triumphant smile.

"And who is this Romeo?" Henry asks. "What's his name?"

I'm surprised she hasn't figured it out yet.

"His name is Gabe." Ora smiles. "Gabriel Winslow."

Silence, thorough and awful, arrives at the table.

"Oh, Christ," Henry says, after a long moment. Maud coughs nervously, and Miel looks from one face to the next, panic-stricken. I discover that I am shaking rather violently, though whether from anger, fear, or some more elusive emotion, I am not certain.

"Ora." Joan suddenly approximates sobriety. "Honey, that's *Joy's* boyfriend. Joy is the girlfriend."

"Oh." Ora's smile fades. "Oh. Well."

"So, Ora." I knot my hands together in my lap to keep them from trembling and clear my throat. "Are you going to do me that favor you mentioned earlier, and take Gabe off my hands, since we're clearly not meant to be together? I mean, we're living together, but I know that shouldn't stand in the way of true love. We're not even married, after all."

Ora opens her mouth, closes it, opens it, closes it again. She looks like a carp drowning in air.

"You'd better hurry up and *get* him to marry you," she finally says. "Or *someone's* going to steal him from you, even if it's not me."

This offends me on so many levels I can hardly think straight. There are a thousand things I want to say, but I hear them in my head and know what they are: stupid defenses, hollow jibes, the taunts of the playground, the petty melo-dramatics of soap operas and pulp romances, the motives and moments to be expected of girls, girls, girls. I struggle with myself. I lose.

"According to your theory," I tell Ora, "marrying him won't be any use. And according to my theory, if he can be stolen by a nymphomaniac with a trust fund and a dye job who plagiarizes her own memoir, he's probably not worth marrying, is he?"

Ora flinches, and for a moment I'm full of righteous tri-umph. It doesn't last long.

"If he can be stolen," she says coolly, "then *you're* the one who's not worth marrying, aren't you?"

"Maybe I'm worth *not* marrying," I hear my voice rise, "because, like my boyfriend, I'm not some idiot so obsessed with the *idea* of love that I need some stupid institution to shore up my relationship."

"Oh, I see. Of course. But did you ever think maybe he hasn't asked you to marry him because he doesn't *want* to?" Ora's voice is sweet and smooth as taffy. "And your stupid ideas just make it easier for him to wait and amuse himself until someone worth marrying comes along."

"That's quite enough," Henry says, standing up and

looking down at Ora. "It's been a pleasure having you as our guest, but we don't want to keep you from your next appointment. Have a lovely night." She gestures at the door. Ora turns to Joan for help, but Joan has fallen gently, drunkenly asleep. Ora snatches up her purse, gives me and Henry a long baleful look, and stalks to the bar. After a brief exchange with Luke, she leaves the restaurant, tossing her hair back and lifting her chin like a czarina on parade. We watch in silence as the glass doors swing shut behind her.

"Holy fuck." Henry drops back into her seat. "You two deserve Emmys for that fucking performance. Best catfight in a nighttime drama. What do you think, ladies?" She turns to Maud, who struggles into her jacket as Miel attempts to revive Joan, without success.

"I think that I've had a hell of a day." Maud glares into the middle distance. "And since I'm one of those idiots who needs a stupid institution to shore up my relationship and I'm in the middle of planning a stupid wedding, I'm going home now. Excuse me, Joy. I need to get out."

"Maud, no—"

"What?" She looks at me fiercely. "What?"

"I didn't mean *you*. I'm sorry."

"Get up, Joy. I need to go."

"Maud, please. Please. You know what I believe."

"I knew you didn't want to get married. I didn't know you thought your friends were idiots for doing what *we* believe in. Let me out."

I slide out of the banquette and let her climb out. Henry gives her a hug and whispers something in her ear. Maud nods.

"Want to share a cab?" she asks Miel, who stands on tiptoe to kiss Henry, and then comes to me.

"Don't worry," Miel breathes into my neck, her slender hands on my shoulders. "It's just a bad night. I'll talk to

Maud, okay? And I'm so sorry about that girl being so mean." She straightens up, gives my forehead a little pat, and follows Maud, who is heading briskly for the door. I sit down and put my head on the table.

"How to win friends and influence people, by Joy Silverman," Henry says. "Iconoclasm is a thankless profession, isn't it, honey?"

"Henry, do you love me?" I lift my head and look at her.

"Yes, you idiot. I love you. Now, let's wake Joan up and get her home. Damn," she adds. "We got stuck with the check."

WHEN I GET HOME, the apartment is quiet and dark.

"In here," Gabe's voice comes from the bedroom. Francis waddles out to meet me, wags his tail in the dim of the foyer, and trails me down the hall. Gabe is in bed, the duvet tucked around his waist, reading glasses sliding down his nose, and a biography of Guy Burgess facedown on his bare chest. "Hey, Red. You're home early. How was dinner?"

"Fine." I can't look at him. I kick off my shoes and slink into the bathroom. "How was your night?"

"Uneventful. My parents called. They both send their regards."

"Thanks." I give my teeth an unusually thorough brushing, splash some water on my face, and put on Gabe's striped pajama top, which hangs on the back of the bathroom door. I avoid my reflection in the mirror.

"What took you so long?" Gabe asks when I come back into the bedroom. "I missed you. Get over here." He holds the blankets up for me, and I crawl in next to him. He wraps an arm around my waist, pulls me onto his chest, kisses my neck, and reaches over to set his book and glasses on the nightstand. "So, how are the girls? Any news?"

What a question. Let's see. Well, Gabe, Joan will probably require heavy-duty animal tranquilizers to get through her wedding without murdering her groom, I behaved like Joan Crawford, Maud is no longer speaking to me, and Henry almost beat up our special dinner guest. And are you planning to leave me for Ora Mitelman?

I can't do it. I just can't. Naturally, I want to ask. But more than even the worst answer I might receive, I am afraid of becoming the kind of woman who would ask that kind of question. A woman like my mother, who toward the end of their marriage waited up nights for my father when he stayed out late, and pounced on him as he came in the door, dive-bombing him like a flock of querulous birds. I would listen from behind my bedroom door to their arguments, which made me think of the ones I saw men and women have in the movies. As in the movies, the fights were almost identical from night to night. Night after night, they ended with the same scene: My mother ran weeping down the hall to their bedroom and slammed the door, while my father stood looking after her, smiling wryly. And every night, shaking his head and chuckling, he would comment to some invisible audience, "Women!" It was as though they were fighting by agreement, accepting out of sheer exhaustion the roles assigned to them, and playing out a scenario with only one possible outcome. It seemed to me that if only they could change something, some little thing, if one of them could just manage to alter a line of dialogue or a gesture, then another story, some other version of their lives might suddenly open up and unfold before them, an undiscovered country.

No, I promise myself. Absolutely not. You will not ask Gabe about her. You will not do anything of the kind, you will not say anything of the kind. Not for any reason, not ever. Not on your life.

2.

You must lie upon the
daisies and discourse in
novel phrases of your
complicated state of mind,
The meaning doesn't matter
if it's only idle chatter
of a transcendental kind.

—*W. S. Gilbert*,
PATIENCE

Wednesday, May 9, 200—

IT'S LATE AFTERNOON and I'm in the office, answering e-mail while Charles paces in circles around my desk and gives me the weekly status report of standing and incoming jobs. All over the office the windows are open wide to let in the late spring air, and the whole staff is a little giddy; periodically I hear bursts of hysterical laughter from the front room.

"The Jehovah's Witnesses' website is done," Charles tells me, "and they want to retain us for ongoing work, but I spoke with Jones and he said we should drop it."

"Why?" I ask. Jones is our lawyer.

"He says the company has high lawsuit potential, and it'd be better to distance ourselves from it now."

"What, someone's going to sue if the Apocalypse doesn't come on schedule?"

"Littering fines from all those flyers, maybe? Oh, also on the litigious front, *BabyDoll* is dropping their account. I got a call on Monday from the editor's secretary." Charles slurps the dregs of his coffee. "I guess Tulley's date with him didn't go as he had hoped."

"I guess not. Well, good riddance. We've got plenty of work." I wave through the window to Miss Trixie, attired in a minuscule yellow bikini and giant dark sunglasses, who has pulled a lawn chair out onto her fire escape and is preparing to sun herself.

"Hollywood was very happy with the rewrite Damon did on *The Senator's Son*, and they want to retain him in case anything comes up." Charles perches on the edge of my desk. "Hey, you'll like this. I got a call from a company called the Transgression Enterprise. They're doing this new retail chain based on the seven deadly sins."

"Is there anything in this great green world that can't be commodified?"

"Apparently not. Vanity is going to be a spa—they've recruited some of the nation's top plastic surgeons and lipo specialists for it. Lust is a cocktail lounge and dance club, with on-site matchmakers and private rooms. All very sophisticated and upscale, they promise me."

"Better get that in writing."

"Anger's a rage therapy facility. Boxing gym and primal scream sessions on one side, yoga and meditation workshops on the other. Gluttony's a prix-fixe restaurant with a ten-course-meal minimum, and Greed's custom jewelry—nothing less than five carats—but the client's thinking about repositioning the store as 'Rapacious.' Sounds better, doesn't it?"

"Very wily of them. What's Sloth?"

"A resort on a private island. With a ratio of something like eight employees to every guest. Rickshaws. All service is room service. Stuff like that."

"And Envy?"

"A clothing boutique—one-of-a-kind items and limited editions only. They'll start the whole thing in Los Angeles, naturally, then bring it to New York next year. They want us to write all the peripherals and brainstorm a PR campaign. And they're offering a pile of money. The wages of sin!"

"It sounds amusing, I guess. Give the sins to Damon?" I delete several e-mails promising that I can get rich working part-time from my home.

"Sure," Charles says. "And Tulley—her mother was a devout Catholic, she has all this doctrine memorized from childhood. She can help out with the research."

"Did we hear anything about the Extreme Romance business?"

"They loved the last installments. *Loved* them. They're commissioning a dozen more, and they also want to discuss developing a line of erotica."

"Great." I delete a pyramid scheme, a promotion for a cybervirus detector, and an e-mail entitled "Top 20 Lies Men Tell." "We'll have Petey keep on with the love, and I'll call Joan about the sex. Maybe we can do some cross-branding with *X Machina*."

"Clever girl. Speaking of which, Talent Agency's corporate sponsorship program. It's looking really good for us."

"What's that?" I ask, distracted, noticing that an e-mail from Maud has just arrived.

"The thing I told you about a couple of weeks ago." Charles gets up and starts pacing again. "Erica's agency is developing a program to broker individual sponsorships between their hot young artist clients and big corporations. The Medici Project. I took a meeting, and they really want us on board from the ground up. Huge commission—website, ad campaign, events, the works. They're going to hire an ad agency, but they want us to be the creative leads, coordinating with their strategic planners and marketing department. We may have to bring on a couple of additional people if we take it. Hello? Vern?"

Charles's voice comes to me faintly through a sudden wave of nausea. I've opened Maud's e-mail, expecting to find one of the information queries she usually sends out when she's doing research on a new film, and have found something quite different.

> *Joy,*
>
> *We've been friends for a long time now. You know I value your friendship and your ideas about the world, which often get me to think about my own, and challenge me to figure out what I believe. I know that when you said what you said at dinner the other night you were angry, and didn't mean it the way it came out. And I know that whole thing with Joan's friend must have been awful for you, and I'm sorry for that. But I've thought a lot about it since then, and I keep coming back to the same thing. It's hard for me to say, but given how you feel about marriage, I just can't have you as a bridesmaid. Of course I want you to be there when Tyler and I get married because I want to be surrounded that day by all the people I love, and I love you. But I hope you'll understand that it just doesn't feel right for me to have you as a part of the wedding ceremony. If you need to talk about this with me, we can get together—just call.*
>
> *Truly,*
> *Maud*

"Joy, are you okay? What is it?" Charles circles the desk and puts his hands on my shoulders. "You look like someone died. Oh, damn, I'm sorry. No one died, did they?"

"Nope." I put my head down on the desk. "Nothing like that. It's okay."

"What happened? Did you get bad news?"

"Maud's angry at me." I lift my head. "She recused me of bridesmaid duties."

Charles looks at me, agog, and then begins to laugh.

"Vern, you brilliant little thing! How did you engineer that?"

"It's not funny."

"Of course it is! You were joking about how to get out of service just last week, remember? Burning your brides-maid's draft card, fleeing to Canada?"

"I didn't do this on purpose, Vern."

"Well, look, she's not mad at you." Charles reads the e-mail over my shoulder. "You haven't been disinvited to the wedding or anything catastrophic. It's the best possible scenario. Or did you want to be disinvited?"

"You're not listening. I feel bad about this."

"Honey, I *am* listening, I just don't understand. I know you've been going crazy with this wedding marathon, and just a couple of weeks ago you were chafing at the girdle to me over how many of them you had to be in." He sits on the edge of my desk and gives me a stern look. "Now you're out of one, and there's no irreparable harm done between you and Maud, as far as I can tell from the e-mail. Just get her an extra nice present, and go to the wedding wearing something besides another horrible orange bridesmaid's dress. It's not like you don't have any others to wear this summer. So what's the problem?"

"I don't know." I sigh and put my head back down on the desk. "I feel left out, I guess."

"But out of something you don't want to be included in anyway."

"Right, okay. But I'm being punished for my position, which seems unfair."

"I don't know about that, Vern. It doesn't sound like

Maud's punishing you. You have the courage of your convictions, and she has hers. You can't expect to believe something counter to the norm—or anything at all, really—and not have to deal with the consequences. You know what Saki says, don't you? 'Never be a pioneer. It's the early Christian who gets the fattest lion.'"

The phone rings, and I pick up to hear my father's voice singing Beethoven's "Ode to Joy."

"Hi, Daddy." I raise my eyebrows at Charles.

"Hello, sweetheart," my father says. "How's my little capitalist?"

"Exploiting the proles, as usual. How's life on the mesa?"

"Ah, the mesa." He chuckles. "A dry heat. Kiddo, it's fine. Everything's fine."

Last year my father took a sabbatical from Columbia and moved to New Mexico to live amid the New Age prayer beads and southwestern kitsch of Santa Fe with his fiancée, Desiree, an interior decorator who applies a concoction of feng shui and ostensibly Native American design principles to the homes of wealthy urban expats living in the Southwest. How a man like Daddy could fall for a woman like her is perplexing, but there it is: love, the eternal mystery—or the perennial hoax. And, frankly, my father no longer seems to me the cool and clever hero he once appeared to be. I have begun to suspect, in fact, that he is a perfectly ordinary, average, predictable man.

"Sweetheart, listen," my father says. "We've had a little change in plans for the wedding."

"What's up?" I allow myself the brief, bright hope that Dad is calling off the ceremony and ditching Desiree.

"Well, we've had to change the date. Do you have a calendar nearby?"

"Yes." I eye the calendar over my desk, oracle of my season's agony.

"We're switching the ceremony from that first Saturday in July to the afternoon of Sunday the twenty-second."

"Daddy. You can't. That's the same weekend as—" I stop to draw breath. "That's one day after Mom's wedding."

"It is?"

"Daddy. You knew that. Josh told me you guys coordinated it. Him, then you, then Mom. Why you all had to do it in a month and a half I'll never understand."

"They fuck you up, your mum and dad, they may not mean to, but they do," my father quotes.

"Yeah, well. Mom's ceremony is on the evening of the twenty-first. The evening. As in probably up until midnight."

"Honey, I guess it just slipped my mind. I didn't exactly have your mother's wedding in my date book. But we've already switched everything. It's too late to change back."

"Oh, Dad. Why did you change it in the first place?"

"Joy, I know this won't make sense to you. Nor does it, particularly, to me. But—the things we do for love. Desiree's . . . well, her astrologer advised against it. The date. Extremely inauspicious, apparently. Star-crossed." He chuckles.

"Ha, ha," I tell him. "Ho, ho. How about if your loving children just astrally project themselves to your wedding, then?"

"I'd recommend the red-eye."

"Better," I tell him. "I've sold my soul to Extreme Romance and the Transgression Enterprise anyway. There's nothing to project with."

"Beg pardon?"

"Never mind, Dad. Never mind. We'll figure it out."

"What was that all about?" Charles asks, as I set the phone down.

"That was the fattest lion," I tell him.

"Joy Naomi Silverman!" I hear Henry howl from the front room. "I know you're in there! The mountain has come to Muhammad!"

"*That* would be the fattest lion, actually," Charles stage-whispers.

"Henry." I get up from my chair as she flings herself through the door and onto our leatherette recliner. "Come on in. Have a seat."

"Holy toledo, girl, your desk is a disaster. This area should be condemned. Charles." Henry narrows her eyes at him. "Did this young lady get the several messages I left for her, or did she not?"

"I delivered them personally." Charles begins to edge out of the room. "I'll just be leaving the two of you alone, now."

"Oh, Vern, you can stay. Stay." He doesn't. "Well, Hank. What a nice surprise. What brings you here?" I know very well what brings her here: I have not spoken with Henry since Sunday—the night of the Ora debacle—though not through any fault of hers. She's left multiple messages for me at home, on my voice mail at the office, and with various members of the staff here. I have failed to return her calls.

" 'Fess up, Jojo. What's going on?"

"Oh, you know. The usual. Really busy here. Just working on—"

"Uh-uh. No. The last time you went incommunicado on me was when you got the honorable discharge from law school. I don't buy it. What's going on?"

"Hank, nothing. Everything's fine. Maud asked me to step down as bridesmaid, but whatever."

"She did? Wow. Bold move. Is she that mad?"

"No, I don't think so. She says she just feels weird having me in the wedding, seeing how I'm anti-marriage and all."

"You okay with that?"

"I see her point, if that's what you mean. I'll just sulk about if for a couple of days, and then I'll be okay."

"That's my girl." Henry claps her hands together lightly. "And what about Gabe? Did you talk to him? What did he say?"

"Talk to him about what?" I begin to type an e-mail, addressed to myself, which reads: *help I'm trapped in a fortune cookie factory.* "Oh, the thing with what's-her-name. No. No, I decided not to."

"You decided not to." Henry gives me her X-ray-vision look. "Any particular reason?"

"Just seemed like a bad idea." This is, strictly speaking, the truth. "My dad always says, don't go looking for trouble . . ."

"Because you're certain to find it." Henry rolls her eyes. "Yeah, yeah, yeah. I know. But—"

"I appreciate your concern, Henry. Thank you. And don't worry, okay? I've got it under control."

"But—"

"No buts. End of discussion."

"*But* out, is what you're saying?" Henry laughs. "Kiss your *but*?"

"You sound like Gabe. Hey, Hank, are *you* having an affair with my boyfriend?"

"Eeeew. What a totally hideous thought. No offense."

"Right, okay. None taken. You skanky bitch."

This sends Henry off into a gale of laughter. When she recovers, panting for breath, she turns to me.

"Listen, I have to run. I still haven't got a wedding present for Joan. Or Maud. Or Miel. I'm on a mad bridal scavenger hunt. Want to come?"

"Gosh, that sounds like loads of fun, but I think I'll pass."

"Call me tonight, okay?" Henry stands and stretches.

"Okay."

"You promise?" She gives me a wink.

"Yes, Henrietta. I promise." I wave and she flounces out, blowing kisses to the Invisible staff in the front room.

May into June 200—

A MONTH GOES BY IN a white blur of weddings.

Joan and Bix are married in an old prewar building downtown, in a ballroom lined on three sides with arched windows that reach from the polished wood floor to the twenty-foot ceiling, and through which the upper reaches of the Manhattan skyline look close enough to touch. The couple exchanges vows as the sun sets and the city recedes into gray twilight, reemerging slowly from the darkness as a crazy skeleton of itself etched in bright lights. The bridesmaids, including me, wear strange, stiff, architectural dresses made of deep red-orange fabric. Joan is unusually calm throughout the evening; when I comment on it, she opens her clutch and shows me a sleek little pillbox—platinum, engraved with her initials, a gift from her new husband—containing enough Vicodin to tranquilize the population of Lower Manhattan. A semifamous actor, several times a nominee for awards at independent film festivals, gives a wedding toast so long that guests begin departing and the groom's father has to intercede. As if by divine intervention, Ora Mitelman is called out of town for an appearance on a television talk show, and is thus unable to attend.

My friend Chloé—half-Dutch, half-Italian, raised in Belgium, and schooled in France and England before coming to the States for law school, where we met—marries her

Argentine fiancé, Ricardo, in a very formal ceremony at a Catholic church. The wedding is attended by people from no fewer than seventeen countries; the reception is held at Ricardo's restaurant (wildly popular last year when it opened, but declining in favor since a celebrity diner was stricken with a terrible case of food poisoning on a night when both a noted food critic and a gossip columnist were present). There are a great many clumsy attempts at tango made by the American guests; there are an abundance of loud, laughing, weeping, gesticulating toasts given in broken English; there are a staggering number of relatives; there are orange bridesmaids' dresses. There is some tension over the attendance of some half-sibling who is the out-of-wedlock child of someone's father's mistress, but no one, as far as I know, gets food poisoning.

Maud and Tyler are married at the home of a friend, a parking-lot-size loft in Tribeca. Someone leaks the location to the press, and the street has to be barricaded off to keep out paparazzi and weeping teenage girls, fans of the False Gods, Tyler's band; police and bodyguards escort Tyler's band members and celebrity guests through the fray. I bring a framed Nan Goldin print of a transsexual as a peace offering. Maud cuts in on Gabe and asks me to dance with her. I wear a non-orange dress. The space is lit exclusively by hundreds of candles, and the catering staff spends a lot of time replenishing the candelabras and scraping up spilled wax. I had thought myself more than happy to attend as a civilian rather than as a member of the wedding, but seated at the table next to the orange-clad bridesmaids for the wedding dinner, watching them laugh and talk, I find myself curiously lonely. When Maud throws her bouquet, a white globe of gardenias the precise size of a volleyball, it bounces off a bridesmaid's head before landing in Henry's outstretched hands. I am briefly disappointed she doesn't spike it.

Ian and Brad, the former a heartbreaker ex-boyfriend of Charles, have a commitment ceremony in the Hamptons. I attend as moral support. A gay priest officiates. The two grooms wear white. Nobody wears orange. The guests seem to be mostly ex-boyfriends of one groom or the other; this group turns out to include my brother James. He and Charles meet at last, and it's immediately evident that I'm in for extensive precourtship questioning on both sides. I am rounded up with the other dozen women in attendance for what the wedding planner calls a "fag hag portrait." I watch as the afternoon light fades and in the twilight a hundred men in summer suits dance cheek-to-cheek on the wide lawn.

Miel and Max are married on a bright morning in a sculpture garden on the roof of an industrial building occupied by art galleries and artists' studios on the west side of Manhattan, overlooking the Hudson. Max's mother, a judge from Kentucky, conducts the ceremony, which is interrupted throughout by the honking of car horns from a traffic jam on the West Side Highway below. There are perhaps thirty guests. Miel is barefoot. I wear an apricot-colored bridesmaid's dress. The cake, designed by one of the couple's artist friends, is nearly seven feet tall and topped by specially made marzipan figurines of the bride and groom. These rather remarkable likenesses are set aside for safekeeping and subsequently consumed by two of Miel's young nephews.

THERE ARE BRIDAL SHOWERS, bachelorette parties, rehearsal dinners, white tulle, white flowers, mountains of silver and white wrapping paper. There are white ribbons, white rice, white doves, white cake frosting on fingers and lips, white lies. My mind gives in to the white, goes blank. I lose track of days. I have inadvertently memorized the pre-amble to the wedding ceremony. I can't concentrate at work; I find myself staring out the window, thinking about the songs chosen for first dances: Cole Porter, Burt Bacharach, love, yours, you, us, ours, two, one, forever, always. And no matter what the song, it always goes like this. The couple joins hands at the center of the dance floor, at the center of a ring of guests; as everyone looks on they circle slowly, smil-ing into each other's eyes, suspended and revolving in the empty space; they part and dance with their parents; mem-bers of the wedding party join. And gradually, couple by couple, guests fill the dance floor, until we are all there, all participants, all implicated.

I make Gabe lead every time.

My brother's wedding is held in Gramercy Park, a private park occupying a single block in downtown Manhattan, laid out in the English style, bounded by a high iron fence. The park is accessible only to those lucky few who reside in the fine old buildings on the surrounding streets and are provided with the keys to this little green kingdom. I think my mother blackmailed someone to get us in here.

It's a hot, humid day, and the lush green square is swimming in full afternoon sunlight, the trees and flower beds opulent, the shade offering little in the way of shelter or relief. James and I, posted like lawn jockeys beside the vast iron gates at the park's entrance, direct a parade of perspiring guests to their seats. We pass his handkerchief back and forth until it is uselessly damp with sweat.

"It was like Invasion of the Body Snatchers up there," I say, as James attempts to wring out the handkerchief. "Someone replaced Mom and Daddy with pleasant, well-adjusted human beings." At the prewedding reception for the families of the happy couple, my parents were not only cordial but actually warm to each other, and to their disbelieving offspring. Mom even complimented me on my dress. I'm still in shock about it.

"They're on their best behavior for the blessed day,"

James says. "Or maybe they're both feeling so good about Josh marrying a nice normal lady they've forgotten that they hate each other. Don't worry, baby girl. It won't last. Hello, there," he tells a fat couple in straw hats who have arrived at the gates, puffing and beaming. "Take the path around there to the seats."

"Oh, my," the woman gasps at me. "It's so hot out today."

"So, what do you think of me and Charles?" James watches the fat couple as they trundle away.

"I'm not going to answer that question. I don't think anything about it. I don't want to know anything about it. I'm Switzerland. And you—don't ask, don't tell."

"I never kiss and tell."

"Since when? Hello, welcome," I address a man with an infant in his arms, trailed by a glamorous young woman wearing an outrageously patterned, extremely short dress, her face obscured by a huge, flower-laden hat. A child clutches each of her hands.

"Joy!" The woman looks up, and I recognize Abby, a cousin on my father's side. We used to spend time together at my grandparents' house when we were little, and went out sometimes when we were in high school. She's a couple of years older than I, and she was a wild girl, a troublemaking teenager. I had my first drink with her, went to my first dance club with her, stayed out past my curfew for the first time with her. Of course, she drove her parents and mine to distraction. Of course, I adored her. We lost touch after high school; she ran off to Europe and lived for years in Prague, having affairs with impoverished counts, vacationing with reputed Mafiosi and porn stars, and occasionally sending me postcards from Venice or Paris or Amsterdam. A few years back she returned to the States, having eloped with an American businessman she met there, and moved to the fancy Chicago suburb where he resided. I've met him only once, when she was pregnant with her first child and they came to New York for a holiday.

"James, Joy, you remember Richard," Abby says. The man with the infant nods and smiles at us. "And this is Max, and Zoe." She lifts the fat little paws of each toddler in turn. "And that handsome creature is Morris, our latest effort. My god, it's been years. How great to see you guys!"

"This one was still in the oven the last time we saw you." James solemnly shakes Max's hand as I wave and point to another group of guests down the path.

"He's almost four now," Abby tells James.

"You've been busy." I kiss her cheek.

"Lucky streak," Richard says. "Though I think we're done for the time being."

"Damn right," Abby says. "Poor Zoe—the only girl, and the middle child. Just like you, Joy."

James laughs and pretends to lunge at me, his face contorted into a menacing scowl. Zoe shrieks with laughter, and he turns on her instead and tickles her.

"Looks like she'll do just fine," I tell the placid parents. "You'd better go get seats while there's still shade to be had."

"Joy, come find me at the reception," Abby says. "I want to hear everything."

Richard, in whose mouth the infant Morris has lodged one tiny hand, nods to us as they pass into the park.

James and I take turns wiping Abby's bright orange lipstick traces from our cheeks with the handkerchief. James looks at his watch.

"That must be nearly everybody."

"Ceremony's supposed to start in about five minutes." I peer out of the gates and see a familiar figure coming down the sidewalk. "James. Oh, my god. You invited Charles?"

James bats his lashes at me demurely.

"You did. James, this is my business partner we're talking about, here. If you break his heart—"

"I'm subjecting him to the family, baby girl. You must therefore conclude that my intention is not to break his heart."

"It never is, and you always do."

"Shut up. Hello, gorgeous!" James waves to Charles.

"Hello, gorgeous and gorgeous." Charles kisses my cheek. I raise an eyebrow at him and he giggles nervously. "Surprise, Joy!"

"Hello, Vern."

"Glad to see me?" Charles loops his arm through my brother's. I roll my eyes as they kiss, and march ahead of them along the gravel path, wishing there were some agnostic version of the sign of the cross that I could make to protect myself against—whatever.

THE WEDDING IS actually quite beautiful, not to mention brief—a mercy for the two-hundred-odd guests who sit fanning themselves and mopping their brows in the full afternoon sun before the chuppah under which Josh and Ruth take their vows. An old friend of Ruth's family, a woman named Mina, is the rabbi, and though there are flower girls and bridesmaids and attendants in great abundance, the ceremony itself is a simple one. My little brother, serious and calm, declares his eternal devotion to Ruth, and her to him—and I find that I believe them. Why not? I ask myself, as they exchange rings. Here are two people who actually seem built to live this way, able to keep these promises. Why not? As they turn to face us, husband and wife, my mother weeps loudly into her handkerchief. My father puts his arm around his fiancée. James and Charles whistle and clap. I look at Gabe, who looks farther out into the park with a dazed expression.

AFTER THE CEREMONY, the guests march across the street and into a fancy old social club where the reception is being held. Gabe and I, with James and Charles, pick up our seating assignments and hunt down our table, where the rabbi and her husband are already seated. Abby is at the next table, and I am introducing Gabriel to her when I hear James, who had been checking the remaining place cards, let out a groan. Gabe excuses himself and goes in search of the bathrooms.

"Abby," James hisses. "Quick, trade me one of your place cards."

"You don't want them." Abby laughs. "It's my parents and my grandmother."

"We'll take the grandmother. She'll love it. The rabbi is here. Hurry!"

"James, what are you doing?" I ask.

"Ora Mitelman." James hastily restores the place card to the right of Gabe's seat, as the young lady in question arrives at our table.

"Ora. What are you doing here?" My tone is not precisely welcoming.

"Lovely to see you, too, Joy. Ruth and I went to school together, as it happens. Hello, gentlemen."

"Ora Mitelman." Charles extends his hand to her. "I was just this very morning reading that great piece on you in *City* magazine. I'm Charles Vernon, Joy's business partner."

"How nice." Ora beams at him, all graciousness. "And you must be Joy's brother." She looks to James, who gives her a cold smile. He is the one person, besides Henry, with whom I have discussed my altercation with Ora. "You look so alike!" Ora tells him, whether oblivious to or ignoring his chill response, I can't be sure.

"We've met." James turns from her.

"Charles, you must save me a dance this evening." Ora smiles sweetly.

"With pleasure." Charles looks from her to James and me.

"Ora!" says Gabriel, who has just returned to the table. I can't read the tone of his voice.

"What is going on?" Charles whispers to James, just over my shoulder.

"Gabriel, how nice to see you." Ora takes his hand and proffers her cheek, which he kisses.

"Nothing," James whispers back. "You don't even want to know."

"Our article turned out so beautifully, didn't it? Thank you so much." Ora has yet to release Gabe's hand.

"But Charles, my love," James whispers, "if you dance with the bitch I'll never speak to you again."

"Glad you liked it," Gabe tells Ora. "Do you know Joy Silverman, Josh's sister?"

"We've met." I beg your pardon—did he just introduce me as Josh's sister?

"Temper, temper," Charles whispers to James.

"Joy and I know each other through Joan." Ora smiles at Gabe. "And Ruth is an old friend of mine. When I made the connection and realized that Josh was Joy's brother and that you'd be here, I asked specially to be seated with you all." She turns her sparkling smile on me.

"This is the tip of the iceberg, darling," James hisses at Charles. "Trust me."

"Have you met Charles and James?" Gabe asks. The boys give Ora tight smiles. Gabe holds a chair for Ora, then for me, and sits down between us. I take a moment to bestow a silent curse of eternal suffering on whoever was in charge of the seating arrangements.

"Mina," Ora says, inclining her head to the rabbi, "the ceremony was wonderful."

"Thank you, Ora. You remember my husband, Jacob?"

"Of course. Lovely to see you again, Jacob. Gabe, didn't you just love the ceremony?"

"Abby," I whisper over the back of my chair. "Let me trade places with someone. Zoe, come here."

"Leave my daughter out of this," Abby tells me, grinning. "What the hell is going on?"

"See the blonde? She's after my boyfriend."

"Ah. Well, you can't do much about that, can you?" Abby says. "She chases, and he'll either let himself be caught, or not."

I gape at Abby. She shrugs.

"Look, I speak from experience. As a former chaser of other women's men."

"Thanks. Very helpful."

"Yeah, well. Sorry about that. You could always marry him," she adds, as Richard sits down beside her. "Makes it a little harder for them to get away. Isn't that right, my darling?"

"Whatever you say, my own." Richard relieves Zoe of the fistfuls of silverware she has been collecting. "Max, you're not quite old enough to appreciate the subtle charms of Chardonnay. Please put Mommy's glass down. What are we talking about, again?"

"Nothing," I tell him. "Nothing worth further discussion. Max, hand that glass over here."

Dinner is distinctly less than pleasant. The final guest at our table is a distant cousin of ours, a young woman who has just graduated from college with a major in creative writing.

She has apparently read both of Ora's books several times, and spends the entirety of the meal fawning from her seat between James and Charles. This necessitates that Charles, by virtue of his position between her and Ora, participate at least nominally in the homage. Ora accepts these attentions with elaborate graciousness, meanwhile directing little asides, in a hushed and intimate tone, to Gabe. He shifts in his chair toward her by degrees in response to these attentions, like a flower following the sun, until his back is to me. Watching them, I feel as if I had been removed to a very high altitude and were looking on through the thin air down to some scene taking place far below me. James makes all efforts, within the realm of the reasonably polite, to reorient the dynamic of the table away from Ora, but she's too good for him. At last, he glares ferociously at Charles and turns his attentions to the rabbi and her husband.

"You must have presided over thousands of weddings at this point," James says to Mina as the waiters hand dinner plates around.

"Not quite." Mina laughs. "But a few. I lost count after a hundred. I do about ten a year, I think. More this year, for some reason. People seem to have the marrying bug this year."

"How do you do it, Rabbi?" James asks. "You must get so bored with doing the same thing, month after month, bride after groom."

"Oh, no, not at all," Mina says. "Far from it. But remember, much of religion is about just that—repetition. You read the same texts hundreds or thousands of times, you say the same prayers day in and day out, you celebrate the same holidays year after year. The idea is that meaning accrues and deepens, rather than diminishing. That's how rituals function. It's why they work, if they do. And marriages, for that matter."

I look over at Gabe, who is nodding and smiling at Ora as she addresses the doting graduate.

"But weddings," James says. "Other people's weddings. It doesn't get tedious, at all?"

"Not really. Each couple is different, so in many ways it doesn't feel like a repetition. The newness of their experience, that's what keeps the desire for union and the belief in it fresh for people. But it's the sameness of the weddings that I like, actually."

"I don't know if all those couples you've united would like hearing they're all the same to you." James drains his glass.

"Too bad for them." Mina laughs. "What could possibly be less original than falling in love or getting married? There's no reason that weddings should be or feel original, because marriage isn't about novelty. Quite the opposite. Like any tradition, religious or otherwise, marriage is about continuity. And the pleasures of repetition. Same person beside you day after day when you wake up, when you fall asleep." She nudges her husband. "I haven't found myself bored yet. Have you, Jacob?"

"No," he answers. "But it's only been, what, twenty-three years? There's still plenty of time for me to bore you, Rabbi."

"Ladies and gentlemen." Ruth's father stands with his wife at the microphone in the empty space of the dance floor, with the band behind them. Ousted from his place, the band leader shifts sheepishly off to one side, hands folded and eyes downcast. "Ladies and gentlemen, may I have your attention, please?"

"Hey." Gabe turns to me. "How are you holding up, Red?"

"Fine," I whisper back, not looking at him. "Hush."

"Thank you," Ruth's father says. "Thank you all so much for coming to be with us today, and being part of it. And today, we want to give special thanks to Josh's grandparents, Morris and Eleanor Silverman, who, I think we can all agree, are a model of what a marriage can and should be. Josh tells me they have been an inspiration to him all his life. And yesterday, they celebrated their sixtieth anniversary. Eleanor and Morris, please come up here." My grandparents, my dad's mother and father, whom I adore, stand as the guests applaud and make their way to the front of the room, where they exchange kisses and embraces with Ruth's parents. Waiters begin handing around glasses of champagne to the guests. Papa offers Nana the microphone, but she laughs, says something to him, and pushes it back into his hands.

"Friends," Papa tells the room, "as my dear wife has just pointed out, my whole life I've been holding forth to my family, and she sees no reason I should stop now. And this, I say to you, is the key to a lasting marriage: a spouse who knows and forgives your foibles. It's easy to love strengths. But, Ruth and Josh, for you, I wish that you should learn to love the worst in each other, too—pride and anger, vanity, fear."

I glance over at Gabe. He is leaning in to Ora, who whispers something to him. He nods, and I look away.

"Such faults, you must work to overcome in yourselves," Papa continues. "But treasure them in each other, if you can. These failings, they're part of the people we love. They make us human, and the more they are loved, the more you look on them with compassion and patience, the less they nip at your heels and make problems in your life together. I don't mean you should put up with any serious trouble, God forbid, and Ruth, if Josh misbehaves, you call me over—I'm old-fashioned. I believe in a good spanking." He pauses for the room's wave of laughter. Nana shakes her finger at Josh, who is seated at a table next to the dance floor, and he mock-cowers behind the wide folds of Ruth's dress.

"Do you love my foibles?" Gabe's voice is low; his lips brush against my ear.

"I didn't know you had any." I watch Ora watching us.

"Love really is blind, isn't it?" He slips an arm around my shoulders. "Thank god for that."

"I trust and hope," my grandfather continues, "that I'll never get such a call. Josh and Ruth, I can only wish that you are as lucky and happy in marriage as I have been, and continue to be, with this wonderful woman who has stayed with me, in spite of all my failings, for sixty years." Papa reaches out and takes Nana's hand, and raises a glass with his other hand. "We wish you a lifetime of love and understanding. My friends, to Josh and Ruth."

"To Josh and Ruth," the room cries, glasses aloft.

"To Josh and Ruth," the guests at my table tell one another, and Gabe touches his glass to mine.

"And now," says the band leader, restored to his rightful position, "the new Silvermans have requested that their grandparents share the first dance. Ladies and gentlemen, it is my great pleasure to present Josh and Ruth Silverman, and Morris and Eleanor Silverman."

He turns and waves to the band, and the opening notes of "My One and Only Love" are heard. The guests murmur with pleasure and smile at their seatmates. The two couples move into each other's arms and out onto the dance floor. At our table, my little cousin sighs and leans her chin on her arms. Jacob takes Mina's hand and kisses it. James grins at Charles, who actually blushes.

"How sweet." Ora smiles radiantly at Gabe. He doesn't answer. He's looking at me. Ruth leaves Josh to dance with my father, and Josh dances with my mother. When they separate to collect Ruth's parents, I watch as my parents stand facing each other, hesitating, until my mother laughs and says something to my father, and he holds his arms out to her and they begin to dance.

"Come on, then." Gabe stands and takes my hand. "Time to dance, my one and only."

IT'S A TORPID MIDAFTERNOON, a bona fide dog day. Charles and I are at the Invisible conference table, going over assignments, when we hear stomping up the stairs, accompanied by a loud and tuneless rendition of "Love and Marriage." A few moments later our front door swings open and Henry skips into the office. She is wearing a very tight green T-shirt that reads *It's not a bald spot. It's a solar panel for a sex machine.*

"Like a horse and carriage," Henry announces. "Hi, guys."

Tulley and Pete, seated at the other end of the conference table, look up from their latest Extreme Romance manuscript and applaud.

"Could a Juilliard graduate really find love with the tone-deaf?" Charles kisses Henry's hand.

"Miracles happen. Want to come try on wedding dresses with me and Joyless?"

"Ivory isn't my color," says Charles.

"Don't be so traditional, Vern." I shake my head. "All the girls are wearing orange to their weddings this year."

"Right," Tulley says. "Orange is the new white."

"Then what's the new orange?" Pete asks.

"Up, up, and away, Jojo." Henry lifts me out of my chair and I follow her out the door and down the stairs. A man with a tear-stained face nearly knocks me down as he leaves the psychologist's suite. He brushes past me and hurries ahead of us. His silhouette lingers for a moment in the bright arch of the front entrance and vanishes.

WE TAKE A TAXI to the dressmaker's shop, which is on a dirty street on the Lower East Side. I look at the boarded-up storefront, and raise an eyebrow at Henry.

"O ye of little faith," Henry says to me. "Just wait." She rings a buzzer beside the graffiti-covered door and waits. The door opens, and a young woman beckons us in. We pass through a dark lobby and into a large room where bolts and bolts of fabric in rich, shining colors are piled high against the gold-painted walls. For a moment I think I've stumbled into Ali Baba's cave of treasure. I blink. Henry grins at me triumphantly.

Standing at the center of the room is a beautiful, ageless woman with deep-set black eyes, dark hair pinned up on top of her head, and a cigarette dangling from her lips. She advances on us.

"Veruka?" Henry extends her hand.

"Yes, it is me," the harpy says in a very thick Russian accent, ignoring Henry's hand. "You are Henry." She's not asking. "An odd name for such a pretty girl as you. And who is this?" She peers in my direction; I have instinctively moved slightly behind Henry.

"This is Joy," Henry says. "One of my attendants."

"You are from Odessa," Veruka tells me. She's not asking.

"My father's family, a couple generations back." I peek around Henry.

"Yes. I also am from Odessa. It is in the eyes. Good. Very good." She claps her hands. "Magdalena!" she calls, and the young woman who let us in rematerializes. "Please to measure the girls, dear," Veruka instructs her. "Off, off," she says to us. "You take clothes now off so we can see."

"Just her," I tell Veruka.

"Wrong," says Henry through the T-shirt that is halfway over her head. "I'm buying you a dress."

"No, you're not."

"Yes, I am." Henry, topless, glares at me.

"No, you're not. I don't want a dress. Hank, you know I hate dressing up."

"Off, off!" says Veruka sternly, tugging at my shirt.

"What did you think you were going to wear to my wedding?" asks Henry.

"I thought you'd spare me another insane ball gown. How about black tie? I am your best man, aren't I?"

"Yes," Henry says. Magdalena's hands appear from behind her, straining to get the measuring tape around her breasts. "And as such you'll do as we say. Now strip!"

I strip. Magdalena entwines me in her yellow measuring tape.

"Please to put these on." Veruka hands us thickly embroidered Chinese robes. "Let us now look at the dresses, yes?" With one hand on each of our backs and a fresh cigarette clenched in her teeth, she marches us to the far side of the room, where rows of soiled white sample dresses dangle like grimy angels on the metal racks. Veruka looks Henry up and down, and begins pushing through the dresses.

"You have the big bosoms," she says with her back to us. "We will show these off, I think. Ahh." She lets out an ecstatic breath, pulls a dress off the rack, and shoves it into Henry's hands. "You are a size ten." She's not asking. Henry takes off her robe and starts to step into the dress. "No, no!" shrieks Veruka. "No, no, no. You must to put it on in there." She points to a curtained cubicle behind the racks. "You put on, then you come out and we see."

Henry shrugs and strides away, the dress a superhero cape flung over her shoulders and flapping behind her.

"It is the magic," Veruka says to me, smoke drifting into her eyes, hand on hip. "We must not see her put the dress on. We must only see it on, so. Ah, yes, like so. You see?"

A bride appears around the corner of the dress rack. She is wearing a gown that grazes the floor at the bottom and her nipples at the top, with a long billowing stretch of white in between.

"This is fucking beautiful," says the bride to her reflection. "What do you think? Joy? Hello?"

"Henry," I say.

"What?"

"Henry."

"What?"

"Is very nice, no?" Veruka reaches a hand around Henry's waist to tighten the fabric slightly.

"Is very nice, yes," I tell Henry.

"Is perfect," says Veruka. "I know. You will take?"

"I will take," Henry agrees.

"You don't want to try on any others, just to be sure?" I ask. Veruka looks at me disapprovingly.

"No. Why you try another? Is perfect. I know. When you find perfection, you do not try further. You rejoice."

"I'm rejoicing," says Henry.

"Very good." Veruka beams at her. "Magdalena! Pins, please." Magdalena trots over carrying a red velvet pin cushion in one hand and fabric swatches in the other. "Take in, here, here," Veruka says to Magdalena, jabbing her cigarette at the bodice seams. "Now. Let us look at fabric."

"I like this." Henry strokes the dress.

"No, no. Is all wrong. Here." Veruka holds an ivory square out to Henry. "Is what you want." Henry rubs the scrap of cloth against her cheek. Her face is suddenly gentle, simple. She looks very far away. For some reason this makes me feel like crying.

"Yes," Henry says dreamily. "Yes."

"Now." Veruka turns on me with ferocious intent. I briefly consider asking her to marry my father. "Now is your turn."

I look pleadingly at Henry, who ignores me. Veruka runs her hands swiftly along the rack, looking not at the dresses, but at me.

"Size four," she says, and pulls out a dress, not taking her eyes from me. "This pattern will be very good for you." She puts the dress into my hands. "Go."

I go. In the dim of the small curtained cubicle, I take off my robe and look askance at the dress, which I have hung on a hook. It's a full-length affair, white smudged by the hands of a hundred, a thousand prospective brides before me who have undressed in this little room, living out a dream that may very well have haunted them from earliest girlhood: The Dream of the Dress. I never had it. Naked, I slip the dress off the hanger and step into the acres of cool, slippery fabric, sliding the bodice over my hips, reaching around myself to close its long zipper. There's no mirror, but I can feel that the dress fits as if it were made for me alone, the heavy, silky cloth lifting me, bearing me up, defining precisely the space that I occupy.

As I turn and push the curtain aside, its long train whispers on the floor behind me. Henry begins singing "Here Comes the Bride," then stops, and her eyes widen. Veruka, a fresh cigarette drooping from her lips, nods without expression as I cross to them. I catch a peripheral glimpse of a figure moving through the mirrors, but do not turn to face it.

"Wow," says Henry. "Maybe you should get married instead of me."

"We will make without train, to be sure. Leetle shorter,

yes? Just below knee." Veruka tugs at the skirt. She puts her hands on my hips and turns me to my reflection. The train of the dress swirls on the floor, ascending into a narrow, unadorned sheath of white held up by thin, delicate straps. I look into the eyes of The Bride. From a great distance, from some other place, she looks back. I blink. And it's just me, in a dingy white dress, Henry behind me smiling like a kid in a Jell-O commercial, and Veruka squinting through her cigarette smoke.

"What color you want?" Veruka asks Henry. "Everybody this season, orange, orange. You want orange?"

"Henry," I beg. "Not orange."

"Orange," Henry grins fiendishly at me. "Oh, very orange."

IT'S JUST AFTER ten o'clock, and I'm not particularly tired, but I climb into bed, turn out the lights, stare into the dark. For the past couple of nights, I've worked late and come home to an empty nest; on Monday Gabe caught a shuttle flight up to Boston, to be with his family during the preparations for his little sister's wedding. I will fly up on Friday afternoon to join him for the rehearsal dinner, and the wedding on Saturday.

It's been odd with him gone. I'd always thought of myself as an independent, resourceful person, but the evenings without him have been aimless and vacant, and I've turned in early just to avoid the sudden large quiet of the apartment, which makes me vaguely anxious.

I am just tipping over the edge of sleep when the phone rings. It's Gabe.

"Hey, Red."

"Hi." I pull the phone under the covers with me. "I'm glad you called."

"You sound sleepy. What are you doing?"

"Just getting ready for bed. How was your day?"

"I wish I were there to tuck you in. What are you wearing?"

"Your pajama top. As usual. Sorry I missed your call this afternoon. I went to look at wedding dresses with Henry."

"Oh, to be a fly on the wall for that scene. How was it?"

"Hysterical. The dressmaker is this brutish, gorgeous Russian woman, kind of a cross between Sophia Loren and General Patton. I want her to marry Daddy. She ordered us around, barking commands, and Hank turned into this docile little puppy. I've never seen her so obedient."

"Good lord. I think she *should* marry your father. Let's invite her to crash his wedding. Sounds like she could take Desiree down."

"No contest. She could take both of them down without putting out her cigarette." Now that I think of it, Veruka would make a marvelous bodyguard. I wish I could get her to be my escort for the Winslow wedding.

"So was the expedition a success?" Gabe's voice trembles with laughter.

"Yup. Veruka—that's the dressmaker—pulled a dress off this rack of maybe a hundred dresses, without even looking, and it was perfect on Hank. Really beautiful, actually." I have a vision of Henry in her gown, her face soft and remote, and then of the white, strange figure I saw when I turned to face myself in the mirror. Something in me unlatches and pulls.

"Gabe?"

"I'm here."

"I miss you."

"You, too. It'll be nice to have you here. But you're really better off not here, just now. The Winslow women are on a rampage. I'd bet on my mother in the ring with your dressmaker, at least this week. You should have heard her on the phone with the florist today. Mom put the fear of God into them."

Of this I have no doubt. Where Gabe is concerned, Mrs. Winslow personifies tender indulgence, but she's one of those incredibly poised society matrons who can ice you with a glance.

"Ah," Gabe says. "And there she is. Hi, Mom."

I hear Mrs. Winslow's voice in the background.

"Joy, Mom says hello. She's looking forward to seeing you. I need to go—there's some family conference happening downstairs."

"Talk to you tomorrow?"

"Of course. Sleep tight." He hangs up. I hold the receiver against my ear for another few moments, listening to the silence.

"I love you, too," I tell the empty room.

Saturday, June 30, 200—

I WAKE UP IN A BED and breakfast in upstate New York, with sun streaming through the open windows, and Gabe whistling in the bathroom. For a moment I'm lost in a sleepy sense of absurd well-being, the way I used to feel as a child opening my eyes on the first day of summer vacation, all those golden days of nothing unfurling before me. I pull the covers over my head and watch the light filter through the blossom-print duvet, a little Eden—until the awful memory of last night slaps me awake.

I MAY BE SUFFERING post-traumatic stress syndrome from the Winslow wedding last weekend. It looked like any other understated and overpriced wedding, except bigger. That is, if you didn't know that the well-mannered, badly dressed, overbred, gin-preserved, dour-faced guests crowding Trinity Church were Kennedy cousins and Rockefeller offspring, titled Europeans and Fortune 100 scions. When I arrived in Boston last Friday afternoon, Gabe presented me with a gift from the family: a dress to wear to the wedding. It was this gauzy, floaty, floral number selected by his mother, probably hideously expensive, and about as much to my taste as mud wrestling. I joined the charade that this was a marvelously thoughtful gesture and not a catty insult (as was obvious to everyone but Gabe), and wore the damn thing with what little poise I could muster; I looked like something out of a 1970s feminine hygiene commercial.

And, of course, everyone I met—at the rehearsal dinner, the wedding, the reception, the postwedding breakfast on Sunday morning—asked when Gabe and I planned to be married. That is, everyone except his immediate family. They were very polite, of course. They always are. But at the rehearsal dinner, apropos of nothing, Teeny gave me a long discourse on the value of family traditions, and how important it was to the Winslows that she and Mo had both married a certain kind of man—by which she meant blue-blooded Yankees with an exhaustive knowledge of silverware for all occasions. And at the reception, Gabe's mother introduced him, in my presence, to a suitable young lady—Serena Horseface or something like that, a Wellesley graduate recently relocated to New York to take her master's degree in education. I stood by with mounting blood pressure as Mrs. Winslow encouraged Gabe to look her up. After she had departed, Gabe's mother said: "Such a lovely, accomplished girl. I simply adore her family. And so pretty, don't you think, Gabriel? So feminine."

IN THE WAKE of all that, we left the city yesterday in Gabe's old convertible with the top down, singing loudly to radio stations that would flicker in and fade as we drove north. It was late afternoon by the time we arrived in the small, bucolic town where the parents of the groom du jour, my high school friend Ben Rushfield, have a sprawling old summer house on a dozen wild, green, and wooded acres nestled into the famous local hills. I misplaced my virginity here, once upon a long-ago summer when the Rushfields invited a half-dozen of Ben's classmates up for a lazy, impossibly happy week of country living—which, for my part, included a long-planned and quite romantic sexual initiation courtesy of Christopher Adams, Ben's best friend and the love of my high school life.

By the time Gabriel and I checked into our aggressively charming and rustic little inn, located just off the hamlet's aggressively charming and rustic little Main Street, both of us were irritable from a long drive made longer by my navigation errors. Even Gabe's inexhaustible good humor had reached its limit. We dressed for dinner, moving around one another at elaborately wide, cold distances in the ruffled, pine-furniture-stuffed room, and drove to the Rushfields' house in silence.

As we rolled to a stop at the end of the long driveway, several people tumbled out of the door of the old house and down the steps toward us. Ben pounced on me as I climbed from the car and bear-hugged me as best he could, being several inches shorter than I am. Behind us, his little sister bounced on her toes as she introduced herself to Gabe and chattered at us as we crossed from the lawn into the cool shade of the house.

Though I knew that Christopher (who goes by Topher) would be there, acting as Ben's best man, it still gave me a shock when he came out of the kitchen, wiping his hands on a towel and waving to us. We hadn't seen each other for maybe five years, since he abandoned a Ph.D. in eighteenth-century poetry, was hired as a writer by an entertainment company, and moved to Los Angeles.

"Hello, you." Topher leaned to kiss my cheek, and I felt myself blushing.

"Topher, this is Gabe." This must be what people refer to as regression, I thought: I suddenly felt all of sixteen years old.

"The famous Topher." Gabe shook his hand. "At last we meet."

"Evelyn, come on out here," Topher called back into the kitchen. "There's someone I want you to meet."

I could practically hear an aria swelling up as a seraphically lovely young woman appeared beside him, with a radiant and exquisitely drawn face and tawny hair spilling over her shoulders. The smile that she bore toward me faded and then blossomed again as she saw Gabriel, and she ran to him laughing and threw herself into his open arms. Topher and I looked from them to each other, and then Topher pointed, laughing, at Gabe.

"You're that Gabriel!" he said, as I told Topher, "She's that Evelyn," and Evelyn, turning between the two men, asked, "This is Joy?"

"What's going on here?" asked Marilyn, Ben's bride-to-be, coming down the stairs.

"Your wedding has just turned into a French farce, I think." I gave Marilyn a kiss. "It looks like my high school sweetheart is now the boyfriend of my boyfriend's high school sweetheart."

"What?" Marilyn squinted at me. "Oh, right. Topher and Evelyn. They're engaged, actually." She patted my shoulder. Evelyn laughed a tinkling laugh and came to take my hand between both of hers.

"I'm so glad to meet you." She gave me the apple-blossom smile, and then put one hand on Topher's shoulder and the other on Gabe's chest. "It feels like fate, doesn't it?"

"Thank you." I took the sweating glass of lemonade that Ben offered. "Rushfield, was this a little surprise you were waiting to spring on us?"

"Nope." He shook his head. "I never put two and two together."

———

THERE ARE NO single people here, I thought as we sat down to dinner, and an image floated through my head of the assembled couples marching in neat animal pairs onto an ark. Ben's parents held court at one end of a long table, Marilyn's at the other, flanked by complete sets of grandparents (one widowed and remarried). A couple of high school friends, and a handful of people I'd never met, mostly from Ben and Marilyn's graduate program, all married or engaged. Even Ben's little sister had a boyfriend, who was seated to my left, a handsome boy who still had about him the sweet, brutish look of a high school jock popular enough to be nice to everyone. He told me he was twenty-three, and the matron of honor, a very pregnant woman in her late thirties seated on my other side, overheard and whispered to me, "No one should be allowed to be twenty-three."

Across from me, Evelyn sat laughing and luminous between Topher and Gabe, who both attended to her as if under a spell. I watched as Gabe leaned close and whispered to Evelyn; she drew back to look at him with her large soft eyes, her gaze serious and liquid, and put one slim hand against his cheek. I turned away, and when I turned back, Gabe was looking at me, his cheeks flushed. He gave a crooked smile and raised his half-empty glass to me. Topher stood to pour wine for the people sitting across from him. I noticed the curve of his neck, brown against the white linen of his shirt collar, and suddenly remembered resting my head in that hollow during a slow song at some formal dance, laughing together afterward over the limp orchid of my corsage, which we'd crushed by holding each other so tightly.

———

AFTER DINNER a few of us decided to take a swim. In the cool midnight we wandered down a long slope to the pond, our faces pale in the light of an almost-full moon. Watching Gabe's silhouette advance in front of me, I stumbled, and Topher, beside me, put a steadying hand on the small of my back.

"Oops." He slipped an arm around my waist. "You okay?"

"I'm okay." I leaned into the warmth of his body as we passed several white tents set up for the wedding dinner.

"Look at this place. Hasn't changed, has it? You remember our summer up here?"

"Of course I do." I blushed into the dark. "The age of innocence."

"Something like that." His arm tightened around my waist. "I'm glad Evie's getting to see it. Isn't she great?"

I felt myself tense, and I moved away, slipping from the curve of his arm.

"Gabe seems to think so," I said.

"Come on, you're not jealous? That's not like you."

"How could I be jealous? I'm out in the moonlight, arm in arm with her fiancé."

"Gabe seems like a solid citizen," Topher said. "You're living together?"

"Since last fall."

"You talking about getting married?"

"God, no. You know how I feel about marriage."

"Still?" he said, and laughed. "I thought you'd grow out of that."

"I've grown into it. It's an ingrown idea."

"Don't get uppity with me, Silverman. I knew you when you were in braces," he said. "I took you to the prom. I know all your secrets." He peered down at me through the dark. "You're a romantic."

We had reached the water's edge, where clothes were strewn on the damp grass. In the shallows, Ben's sister and her boyfriend were splashing at each other and howling with laughter. Beyond them, Gabe's narrow body flashed through the water as he raced Ben out to the raft where Marilyn and Evelyn sat, naked and shining in the moonlight.

" 'In the sun that is young once only, time let me play and be golden in the mercy of his means,' " Topher recited. "I cried when I read that in freshman English. I was such a sensitive little lad. Is that why you liked me, Joy?" He stripped off his shirt.

"No. I liked you because you were a babe. And I loved your fade-away shot."

Naked except for his boxers, Topher tossed an imaginary basketball into the air, and jumped to land ankle-deep in the pond.

"Christ in hell, that's cold." He stepped back to the bank and stripped off the underwear. "Hurry up. I'll race you to the raft," Topher said. I sneaked a glance at his so-familiar naked body—the muscular shoulders and back sloping down to a lower region that I still found embarrassingly attractive. I looked away as he waded back into the water swearing, and plunged headfirst into the shallows. A moment later Ben's sister shrieked and fell backward, and Topher surfaced beside her, one of her ankles in his hand, water streaming from his dark hair. As I undressed, I looked back up the hill to the house. Lights were on in all the windows, and shadows moved across the porch. I could hear music faintly through the open door, and bursts of laughter floated across the lawn. I dove.

I hit the water, and the several glasses of wine I'd consumed hit me. I swam dizzily in the general direction of the

178 · *Darcy Cosper*

raft, with Topher a few strokes ahead and the group on the raft yelling and clapping for us. Topher reached it first, took the hand that Ben offered him, then yanked him into the water with a colossal splash. Some other man leaped in after them, followed by Marilyn's sister, and they chased one another around the raft, churning the water and shouting into the night. I hauled myself up onto the raft and lay panting on my back beside Gabe, who put one cold hand on my wet shoulder as he talked with Evelyn, seated on his other side with her arms wrapped around her knees. I closed my eyes and felt the raft spinning beneath me. I opened them, and the raft stopped spinning, but the thick band of stars above us began a blurring spiral.

"Gabe, I think I'm drunk," I told him, as the swimmers struggled back onto the raft in a damp tangle of naked limbs.

"I think I also am drunk," Gabe said, and he and Evelyn laughed together.

"I think I need to go home," I said. Topher flung himself down beside us.

"New York? Did you forget something?" Gabe asked. Evelyn laughed again and stroked Christopher's hair.

"The hotel. I need to go back to the hotel."

"You need to go right now? We're still swimming."

"I need to go now." I hadn't needed to leave quite so urgently thirty seconds ago, but the more Gabe resisted, the more annoying I found the situation generally and his proximity to Evelyn specifically.

"I'm in no shape to drive, Joy. Can you wait? Could you just take a nap on the couch?"

"The hotel," I told him.

"If you really need to go, I can drive you," Topher said. "I wouldn't be long," he told Evelyn, and she nodded.

"Is that okay, Joy?" Gabe patted my arm. "I'll be there in an hour or so."

I shook my head gravely, not looking at him, and lowered myself into the water. Topher slid in beside me.

BY THE TIME we had dried off and dressed, I had mostly sobered up, but I didn't say so to Topher. We climbed into his car, drove slowly down the bumpy road to the highway, and turned toward town. The windows were open and the radio played some song about summer. Topher hummed along, and I turned to watch his profile and faintly remembered having made the same drive with him fifteen years earlier, half my life ago.

"How did you and Evelyn meet?" I asked. "How do people meet in L.A.?"

"Some party. Mutual friends. Same way they do in New York."

"When was that?"

"In September it'll be two years."

"Same as me and Gabe. We met at a wedding."

"Don't tell me you're not a romantic." Topher laughed.

"I never said I wasn't. Just that I don't want to get married. When did you know you wanted to marry Evelyn?"

"Honestly? I still don't know for sure." Topher glanced into the rearview mirror, then sideways at me. "It seems impossible you could ever really know for certain that you'll be able to spend the rest of your life with a particular person."

"Then why get married?"

"She wants to, which is reasonable, given cultural pressures and biological clocks and all. And if you *can't* ever know for certain, why not try? I like Evelyn, I like spending time with her. I don't get bored. It's pretty unlikely that some perfect mate is going to come along and make me more certain."

"Fine, but that doesn't really answer the question."

"I've never been married before. I'm curious to see how it'll change things," Topher said, signaling a turn at an utterly deserted intersection. "Society responds pretty strongly to participation in the institution, and those responses are bound to shift our experience of the relationship."

"Pretty fancy talk for a sitcom writer," I said, as we passed the gas station and town market, both closed. "You'll forgive me if I say your views on marriage don't sound particularly romantic in any traditional sense."

"Ah, but I never said I was a romantic. I only said that you were."

We pulled into the shadows behind the little hotel and parked the car. The engine shuddered and quieted.

"It's good to see you, Joy." Topher turned and drew me into his arms. I rested my cheek against the warm familiar curve of his neck, conscious of a vague sadness. I sighed and Topher pulled back and looked at me; his face was inches away, and without thinking I slipped my hand around the back of his head and tugged a little to bring his mouth onto mine. He kissed me back, lightly, and I pressed closer to him.

"Hey." He pushed me away gently, then reached to smooth my hair.

"What?" I leaned in for another kiss.

"This isn't the best time to get nostalgic, Joy." Less gently than before, he put me back into my seat.

I crossed my arms and stared out the windshield to the dark windows of my empty room. "Why not? When do we get nostalgic, then?" I heard myself say this as if from a great distance. "What are nights like this for? Do you really think Gabe isn't getting nostalgic out there on the lake with Evelyn?"

Topher was silent. I opened the car door but didn't make a move to climb out.

"That's a specious argument if I've ever heard one," he finally said, turning from me and twisting the key in the ignition. "Your jealousy doesn't require that there be anything to substantiate it. Go to bed, Joy. It won't feel like this tomorrow."

HE WAS RIGHT. It feels much worse.

Gabe comes out of the bathroom and sees me peering from the bed. He is wearing frayed sweatpants, his hair stands on end, a toothbrush sticks out of his mouth, and he is obviously the most fabulous and desirable man in all of creation. Never underestimate the powers of guilt to shed new light on a situation, I tell myself, resisting an urge to fling myself on him and gibber incoherently.

"Morning," he tells me, through a mouthful of toothpaste. "I feel like hell. Hey, you were out cold when I got back last night. How are you feeling?"

How am I feeling? I have no idea, actually. The question is absurd. I never know how I'm feeling. I think of the look on Topher's face as I climbed out of his car last night, and then of a photograph Gabe showed me shortly after we'd moved in together, a picture that he'd taken of Evelyn years earlier, and then of Gabe's naked leg resting against hers on the raft, and I think, nothing could be less interesting to me than how I'm feeling. I feel like screaming at the top of my lungs. I feel like I'm going to pieces. I feel like I do right before a sneeze—that frantic, discombobulated, debilitating tension, overwhelming and unbearable, that precedes an explosion. No wonder I don't pay attention to my feelings. I can't imagine why other people are so keen to get in touch with them.

"Fine," I tell Gabe. "I feel fine. But I haven't moved yet."

"You have nothing to lose but your balance." Gabe returns to the bathroom, and I hear him spit into the sink. "And your dignity," he adds.

I pull the covers back over my head. Peekaboo, I think. Where's Joy? Where did Joy go?

BY TWO O'CLOCK I am dutifully arrayed and arraigned on the Rushfields' broad lawn, chatting with distant relatives of the happy couple. I have planted a chaste kiss on Topher's cheek, returned Evelyn's embrace, admired half a dozen toddlers in their finery, squeezed Ben's hand as he passed, complimented the dresses of mothers of both bride and groom, petted three dogs, posed for photographs with a group of high school classmates, nibbled hors d'oeuvres, tucked behind my ear the flower offered to me by Ben's sister, mounted the creaking stairs to deliver a pitcher of lemonade and murmur niceties into the gabled bedroom where Marilyn was dressing with a flock of women around her. I have been gracious and charmed and charming, penitent and proper, I have been agreeable, sensible, helpful. The afternoon feels as frictionless as the atmosphere of some distant and perfect planet: everyone well groomed, good-natured, the conversations proceeding like easy minuets, the steps pleasantly known, gracefully executed. The sky is a pale, miraculous blue, the roses are in full and righteous bloom, the air is sweet with pollen and lilting voices. Even the weather gives benediction, and who am I to question what seems so fair and flawless, so functional? I give in. I drink iced tea, exchange bright, benign observations with those to whom we are introduced, and shush any critical thoughts that float into my head, as if they were naughty children. After an hour or so, I realize that I'm actually having a fine time. I'm fine. I'm so fine that when Gabriel departs from a little knot of guests in which we have become ensconced and the woman standing beside me asks when the two of us are getting married, I give her a winning smile and say nothing at all. As word goes around that the ceremony is beginning, I take Gabriel's arm and move toward the white chairs set in the shade of a big green-and-white striped awning, feeling something almost like pleasant anticipation. Look, I want to tell him, look at your virtuous and good, your beautifully behaved, outlandishly normal girlfriend, your altogether suitable beloved. You can take me anywhere. Whither thou goest, I will go.

The justice of the peace, a small woman in her late forties with a shock of dark, silver-streaked hair and a wry expression, appears at the front of the crowd, and Ben and Topher come to stand on one side of her, Marilyn's sister on the other. We rustle expectantly, and after a long minute, without cue or music, Marilyn comes out of the house. She's wearing a simple white summer dress made of a light fabric that flutters at her ankles, and a small bouquet dangles from one hand. She takes the porch steps two at a time to meet her mother and father, who wait for her on the lawn. At the bottom of the stairs she takes their hands, and together they cross toward us. When they reach the head of the aisle, she kisses both of them and practically skips toward the altar. Ben apparently can't keep still; he takes several steps up the aisle toward her, reaching out his hand for hers, and the justice laughs.

"I've known Ben since he was a kid," she tells the guests. "He's always been eager to get things done. So I won't keep him waiting. Dearly beloved," she says, over a ripple of laughter, "we are gathered here today to witness the marriage of these two wonderful young people. We'll begin with the readings. Lila?"

Marilyn's sister steps forward.

"This is a selection from the seventeenth-century *Book of Common Prayer*," Lila announces. "The marriage vows. 'Matrimony is an honourable estate, instituted of God in the time of man's innocency, signifying unto us the mystical union that is betwixt Christ and his Church; and therefore is not by any to be enterprised, nor taken in hand, unadvisedly, lightly, or wantonly, to satisfy men's carnal lusts and appetites, like brute beasts that have no understanding; but reverently, discreetly, advisedly, soberly, and in the fear of God; duly considering the causes for which Matrimony was ordained. First, It was ordained for the procreation of children, to be brought up in the fear and nurture of the Lord, and to the praise of His holy Name. Secondly, It was ordained for a remedy against sin, and to avoid fornication; that such persons as have not the gift of continency might marry, and keep themselves undefiled members of Christ's body. Thirdly, It was ordained for the mutual society, help, and comfort, that the one ought to have of the other, both in prosperity and adversity. O God, who by thy mighty power hast made all things of nothing; who also didst appoint, that out of man, created after thine own image and similitude, woman should take her beginning; and, knitting them together, didst teach that it should never be lawful to put asunder those whom thou by Matrimony hadst made one, look mercifully upon these thy servants.' "

Lila gives the largely secular and very stunned assembly a crooked smile and retreats. The wedding proceeds.

As the vows are made, the rings offered and accepted, I am surprised to feel tears stinging to my eyes. I'm not generally given to emotional outbursts of any kind. I don't like to make a scene, and growing up with two brothers, a father who teased us constantly, and a mother whose weeping fits confused and embarrassed me, I learned not to cry. I never cry. Ever. But I'm crying now, and I can't seem to stop. The bride and groom turn to face us, beaming, and the guests rise, smiling back. Sobs beat against my rib cage. Ben and Marilyn pass down the aisle and the guests leave their places to greet, press, murmur, wish, and I push past bodies in the row beside me and walk swiftly toward the apple trees on the far side of the house. Out of sight of the striped awning and the smiling faces, I slip off my shoes, leave them in the grass, and break into a run for the little orchard. The grass underneath the trees is lush and warm from the afternoon sun, and light filters in shifting green shadows through the bright leaves. I stop and lean against the low branch of one old tree, my breath coming in ragged sighs, then hitch up the skirt of my dress and climb the tree to a cleft where two branches meet and the leaves are thick around me. I sit with my legs dangling, my shins scraped, one knee bleeding a little, my arms wrapped around the tree's trunk, and weep the way girls do in movies when their hearts are breaking.

I'm not sure how much time has passed when I hear Gabriel call my name. I consider climbing higher into the branches and out of sight, but before I can move, he appears at the base of the tree, carrying my shoes in one hand.

"Joy, what the hell?" He peers up through the branches at me, scowling. "Why are you causing such a scene? You're acting like— You're crying?" Gabe has never seen me cry before. "Are you okay?"

I press my face against the tree as if it could save me and whisper no, no, no into the rough dusty bark.

"Red, what's wrong?" Gabe puts my shoes down and moves closer.

"I don't know." It comes out in a sob. I really don't know.

"Can I come up?" Gabe puts his hands on the low branches.

"No." My voice trembles. "No, I'm coming down. I'm sorry." I shift off my branch and lower myself toward him. When I'm close enough, he reaches for my waist and lifts me down, sets me on the ground. "I'm sorry," I tell him again.

"Hey, you're the apple of my eye." He brushes twigs from my hair. "We'll get to the root of the problem. You just can't see the forest for the trees. Maybe we just need to branch out a little, turn over a new leaf."

I laugh, and open my mouth, hoping some rational explanation will emerge. Instead, I begin to cry again. He puts his arms around me, and I sob into his shoulder.

"Don't leave me," I hear myself plead, over and over again, hardly aware that I am the one saying it. "Don't ever leave me. Promise you won't ever leave me."

ON THE NIGHT BEFORE my thirtieth birthday my family holds a dinner in my honor at my mother's apartment uptown. Mom and Bachelor Number Three, Charlotte and Burke, James and Charles, Josh and Ruth—we haven't been here all together for a long time, and the collective presence of my family has an alchemical effect on the familiar rooms. The atmosphere seems dense with memory—though maybe it's just the inadequacy of the ancient air-conditioning. We gather in the dining room, which smells faintly of dust and disuse. The walls are still covered with the ill-advised wallpaper that my mother applied during her post-second-divorce decorating frenzy. We sit in the same chairs in which I've been seated for meals since my legs were too short to reach the ground, around the same long dining table at which I did my homework, ate two dozen Thanksgiving dinners, listened as my parents informed me and my brothers of their plans to divorce.

Everyone is in high, manic spirits. It's not the usual forced gaiety of family gatherings, but the near-hysteria of overstimulated children. Josh and Ruth have just returned from their honeymoon, a safari at some luxury eco-resort in South Africa. They're tan, chipper, and alight with the self-satisfied nuclear-fusion glow of well-matched codependents. Burke and Charlotte hold hands under the table.

Charles and James, now apparently inseparable, have attended commitment ceremonies for ex-boyfriends two weekends in a row, and make use of the first-person plural as often as possible. After dinner, my mother and the fiancé, who are getting married next weekend, burst from the kitchen wearing party hats and giggling, and sing me the birthday song performed with Motown choreography. Ruth brings out a birthday cake with what looks like the full thirty candles, and everyone claps.

After we are all settled with coffee and cake, Josh pulls out several fat envelopes of pictures from their wedding. There seem to be hundreds of photos, and I have stopped paying attention when one stops me cold: a black-and-white photograph of Ora and Gabe dancing together. He seems to be holding her very close. She looks so small, her head tilting back to look up at him with a come-hither smile (though he's already as hither as one can come).

"When was this one taken?" I pass Gabe the offending article.

"Oh," he says, after an unacceptably long pause. "It must have been when you were saying good-bye to Abby and Richard and the kids." He hands it to James, who gives me a look behind Gabe's shoulder, shakes his head at me, and tucks the photo under the cushion of his chair.

"These are just *lovely*," my mother says. "There are some *adorable* shots of you kids."

"There are," Ruth tells her. "Gabe, did you see that one of you dancing with . . ."

"I am *inspired*!" James shouts, all joviality. "Charles and I may just have to elope."

Charles blushes and grins. My mother beams.

"Don't you two *dare* elope." She shakes her finger at them. "I will not be deprived of the pleasure of seeing my firstborn son tie the knot. It's a mother's privilege. A reward for all that I *suffered* bringing you up, you *rotten* boy."

"I'm sure I don't know what she's talking about," James declares. "I was a perfect angel. I never caused her a moment of trouble."

Josh chokes theatrically on his dessert. Charles raises an eyebrow.

"Don't worry, Mom," James says. "You can pick out my wedding dress. And you can give me away."

"Isn't he a good boy?" my mother says to Bachelor Number Three. "Now, if only *Joy* would let Gabriel make an honest woman of her, I could die happy."

"Mom, please." I hide my face in my coffee cup. "It's my birthday. Please."

"She may already be too honest for her own good, Claire," Gabe tells my mother.

"Gabriel, you are a darling," my mother answers. "You'd *better* marry him, Joy, or some other girl will *snap* him right up. You'll lose him."

"I could lose him just as easily, married or not." I'm trying to keep my voice light. I can't look at Gabe.

"Don't be *naive*, Joy." My mother laughs. "Marriage changes things. That commitment *matters*."

"Right." I set my cup down hard. "It mattered so much for all your clients. And for you and Dad. And for you and Chet. I'm sure it's really going to work out well for you this time, too. Good thinking, Mom."

A silence slams around the table.

"Joy," Josh says. I turn to James for help. He looks away. Bachelor Number Three puts his hand on my mother's shoulder. I wait for Gabe's touch, but it doesn't come.

"It *did* work out, Joy," my mother says at last. Her voice is trembling, but her gaze is level. "Not forever, but for a

while it *did* work out. And I *truly* believe the marriage mattered—it matters to me. It *does* make a difference. It *changes*
things. *Why* would I get married again if I *didn't* believe—"
She breaks off and gets to her feet. Her napkin clings for a
moment to the place that had been her lap, then slides to the
floor. "You are a *nasty*, judgmental, narrow-minded child,
and I am *ashamed* of you." She turns and half-runs toward
the master bedroom at the rear of the apartment, where, as I
know from long experience, she will fling herself down on
the bed and weep. I hear the sharp tap of her footsteps fading away down the hall.

"Joy. I think you should go," Josh says. His voice is soft
with fury.

No one looks at me. Before I can think to protest, Gabe
has pushed his chair back and risen.

"Come on, Joy. Josh is right. Please give our apologies to
Claire for leaving without saying good-bye." Gabe offers
Bachelor Number Three his hand, then walks away without
looking back.

"It's okay, Joy," James tells me. "I'll call you."

I raise my hands helplessly to my family—a surrender, I
give up, I am disarmed—and follow Gabe's swiftly retreating
back to the door.

IN THE TAXI DOWNTOWN, Gabe sits as far away from me
as he possibly can, looking out the window. After twenty
blocks of silence, I put my hand on his shoulder, and he
shakes it off.

"You're angry?"

"I am very angry. You were unspeakably, unconscionably
rude to your whole family." Gabe is still looking out the window. "And I'm beginning to think your mother is right."

"That marriage is a necessary evil?" I try to laugh.

"That you are judgmental and narrow-minded."

"What?" I feel as though the wind has been knocked out of me. "Because I don't want to get married?"

"No, Joy. Because you are unwilling to understand why anyone else would want to get married."

"That's not fair. I do understand. I understand very well, and I think they're wrong."

"That's not really your call, is it?" Gabe turns from the window and looks at me. "You have your own reasons for not wanting to get married. I thought you were reconsidering, but apparently I was wrong." He sighs. "Look. Obviously you're at liberty to be guided by your own beliefs. But it's not your place to impose them on the rest of the world."

"Now wait. Wait." I take a slow breath and try to steady my voice. "What do you mean, *my* beliefs? I thought we were in this together. I thought we were in agreement about marriage being pointless and problematic and just a bad idea all around."

"I don't think I ever said that, Joy. I'd never personally seen the point of it—for me. That's all. I wouldn't presume to make decisions about it for anyone else. And I certainly wouldn't throw temper tantrums and abuse people just because they disagreed with me. That's not what ideals are for." He opens the door of the taxi, which has stopped in front of our building, climbs out, pushes money through the front window to the driver, and heads for our front door. I stare after him, and consider directing the car to Henry's place, so I can throw myself on her doorstep, or to Pantheon so I can throw myself on Luke's mercy, or to the West Side piers, so I can throw myself into the river. Instead, I climb out, close the door, watch the taxi drive away, and from the curb look up at our windows, where the lights have just gone on. Whither thou goest, I think to myself. I'm losing you, I think to myself. I don't have my keys, I think to myself, and I ring our buzzer.

"Who is it?" Gabe's voice, metallic and thin, comes through the intercom.

"It's me. I don't have my keys."

"Is that Joy?"

"Please buzz me up."

"Joy Silverman?"

"Gabe, come on."

"The Joy Silverman I used to know and love, or the new take-no-prisoners Joy Silverman?"

"Let me in."

"I can't open the door to just any stranger on the street. Is this the Joy who is funny and smart and principled but open-minded? Or the one who misplaced her sense of humor somewhere between here and the Bloomingdale's bridal registry counter?"

"This is the Joy who is getting cold and impatient on the doorstep. Buzz me in."

"Sorry. Wrong apartment." The intercom crackles and goes dead. I stare at it blankly. I lean my head against the front door for what seems like a long time and think about crying. I am suddenly very, very tired.

I press the buzzer.

"Who is it?"

"This is the Joy who wants to apologize for having been a pain in the ass."

"Who?"

"The Joy who will be on her very best behavior for the rest of the decade."

Silence.

"For the rest of the century."

More silence. He drives a hard bargain, this man.

"The one who promises to attend every wedding for the rest of the summer with an open mind."

Still more silence.

"The one who believes in you more than anything else she believes in." There is no answer. "Gabe? Are you there?"

"Hey, Red?"

"Yes?"

The intercom crackles.

"Will you marry me?"

I burst into tears. The door buzzes open.

Saturday, July 14, 200—

AFTER BREAKFAST IN BED and stern encouragement from Gabe, I lock myself in the study with the phone and, feeling equal parts irritation and terror, dial my mother's phone number. She answers with the famous telephone voice—light, fruity, fluting—that resembles her natural speaking voice not even remotely.

"Hi, Mom. It's me."

"Oh. Joy."

I can picture her flipping through the pages of the Neurotic's Manual of Retribution and Guilt.

"I *really* can't talk right now. I'm quite busy. I *must* run."

"Mom, Mom, please don't hang up. I'm calling to apologize."

"Oh, Joy. Never *mind.*" She lets out a slow, weary sigh. "It's *done.* Let's just forget about it."

I mentally take my hat off to her: a bold selection of the brave martyr role.

"Mom, no. I owe you an apology. I was very rude to you, and I was wrong to say what I did. I'm so sorry."

"All right, Joy." Her voice, though warmer now, still thrums with that wounded-but-resigned tone. "Your apology is accepted."

"Thank you, Mom. I appreciate that." I wait. I know I'm not getting off this easily.

"Yes, well. Don't worry about *me*." She shifts to a brisk, businesslike tone. "But you positively *shocked* Ruth. And you made Howie feel just *terrible*. *He's* the one you should really apologize to." Howie is Bachelor Number Three.

"I know, Mom. I'm sorry. I will." Ah, the proxy guilt trip. Always effective, but for my mother it's too mild to be anything but a feint. I brace myself for the real attack.

"You were *awfully* touchy last night, you know. I know birthdays can be stressful, especially at *your* age. But honestly, Joy, I don't *understand* how such a logical girl as you can still be so *unreasonable* about marriage. It's not like joining a religious cult. It's just *marriage*. You and Gabe are practically married *already*."

I know it would probably be best to just wave the white flag and offer my mother the spoils of her victory—but I can't do it.

"That's true, Mom. We are practically married. So why bother with the formalities?"

"*Because*, honey. Because it's *different*. That's what I was *trying* to tell you last night, Joy. It *is*." I hear something shift in her tone, the fight slipping out of it, the tone more naked. It makes me feel reproached and culpable, strangely angry, helpless in the face of this ridiculous space between us.

"But how, Mom? How is it different?"

"If you don't—" Her voice catches. "If you don't think there's any *difference*, if there's no difference to you one way or the other, why don't you just get married and make me happy, Joy?" She's crying. I marvel at how much all of this means to her, how she's propped up in the world by this belief, this faith, as much as I am by my own.

"Mom, please don't cry, okay? Listen, I'll think about it, okay? Mom?"

"Okay, honey. Okay." She blows her nose. "You do whatever you need to do, though, Joy. Oh, I *know* you will anyway.

You've *always* been such a stubborn, strong-willed girl. Remember, honey, I just want you to be happy. I just want you to do what makes you *happy*." She has recovered the brisk voice, now cut with a dash of torpid melancholy. It makes me want to laugh and cry at the same time.

"I know you do. I love you, Mom."

"I love you, too, Joy. You *know* I do. And *happy* birthday, honey."

LATER, IN THE fading heat of the dreamy midsummer twilight, Gabe and I leave the apartment and walk to Café Paradiso for a quiet birthday dinner.

When we arrive, Gabe holds the door to the restaurant open for me and smiles like the Cheshire cat.

"What, Gabe?"

"Nothing. Reservation for Silverman?"

The host beckons us toward the rear. We follow him through the nearly empty main dining room and up a flight of stairs. Gabe glances back and gives me the grin again.

"Why are you smiling like that?"

"You look lovely."

"Why are they putting us up here?"

"It's quieter," he says.

The host opens a door at the landing, stands aside to let us pass, and a tremendous cry goes up: "SURPRISE!"

I turn to walk out and slam into Gabe, who turns me back around and pushes me through the door and into a large room where a crowd of my friends is laughing and clapping and whistling. On a small stage at the front of the room, Miss Trixie, in a sequined gown and a blonde wig, leans on a piano complete with accompanist in black tie.

"Gabe," I say, "what have you done?"

"I thought it would be a good idea for you to start getting over your phobia about ceremonies." Gabe rests his hand on the small of my back. "Smile. Greet your public."

Miss Trixie nods to the pianist and begins singing "I Wanna Be Loved by You."

"Gabe?"

"Yes, Red?"

"I meant thank you."

Henry gallops toward us. She gives me a crushing hug.

"I suspect you had a hand in this spectacle," I tell her.

"Moi?" Henry asks. "Perish the thought. I know you hate surprises. And birthdays. And birthday parties. Why would I do a thing like that?"

"Because you're evil."

"Come sit, birthday girl." Henry takes my hand.

As she leads us through the crowd, people call greetings, smile and wave, stand to kiss me. All of my girlfriends are here with their new spouses. So are the members of Delia's band Mercy Fuck, the entire staff of Invisible Inc., past and present, and a dozen old friends and colleagues I haven't seen for ages. How did Gabe track all of them down? Aunt Charlotte and Burke are here, seated with Josh and Ruth and, to my great relief, my mother and Howie. Mom gives me a small smile and waggles her fingers at us.

By the time we make it to the head table in front of the stage, Miss Trixie has finished her song.

"Happy thirtieth, gorgeous," she says, bending down to kiss me. "God, thirty. I remember it well . . . well, not really. Actually, not at all."

"You don't look a day over," I tell her.

"A day over forty-five, you mean. But you lie divinely. What would you like to hear?"

"Cry Me a River?"

"Bitch." She turns and whispers to the pianist, and he starts in on "The Lady Is a Tramp." I salute Trixie and sit down between Gabe and Henry.

"You're old now," Henry says.

"Ancient," says Delia, who is on her other side. "Thirty, and what have you done with your life?"

"You have a crap job," Charles tells me from across the table.

"Family hates you," James says.

"Friends don't understand you." Maud gives me a sly smile.

"No property, no savings," Bix says.

"No husband, no children." Erica giggles.

"No talents," Miel says.

"No manners." Gabe hands me a glass of champagne.

"And you can't dress to save your life," Joan says.

"To Joy Silverman!" Henry grabs my arm to stop me from sliding down in my seat, and raises her glass. "A complete disaster." My friends clink their glasses together. "Oh, my god," Henry says. "She's getting misty-eyed."

AFTER DESSERT, Henry gets up on stage and takes the microphone.

"Hey, you all," she tells the room. "It's time for presents. Invisible kids, you first."

Charles gets up and heads for the stage, carrying a package under his arm. Pete, Tulley, Damon, and Myrna struggle forward through the crowd and clamber up beside him.

"First," Charles says, "some poetry."

"I'm not doing this unless she promises not to fire us," Tulley says.

"You have my word," I tell her as they gather around Charles.

"We work with a woman named Joy," Tulley recites. "Her integrity one can't destroy. She won't compromise, and she never tells lies, and she never will marry that boy!"

I glance at Gabe, who takes my hand.

"She's all that you'd want in a boss." Damon tosses his hair back. "Though we operate at a loss."

"Not true, Mom," I call to her. "We're turning a profit. Don't worry."

"But she has to confess that her desk is a mess," chants Myrna, "and her file drawers are covered with moss."

"Scraps of paper and Post-its abound, her notations are scattered around." Pete plays a little air guitar. "Appointments get tossed, assignments get lost, and some of them never get found."

"So we have developed a ploy, and we hope that it will not annoy." Charles holds up the box, and opens it. "For we think Joy will find, if she opens her mind, that it's a most useful new toy!"

Tulley reaches into the box and holds aloft, for all to see, a tiny, gleaming Palm Pilot. The crowd applauds.

"We're going to pass this around the room," Charles says, "and you can help our fearless leader to join our century by entering your contact information. Happy birthday, Joy."

"You're all fired," I tell them, as James climbs onto the stage and takes the microphone from Charles.

"I'm up here on behalf of Joy's long-suffering family," James says. A couple of sympathetic murmurs are heard. "Thank you," he continues. "You can imagine the horror. Joy has always been—how shall I put this?—firm in her beliefs. Which is an admirable quality, of course, but has sometimes put her and those who love her in difficult positions. She will never make a promise she can't keep. She will never tell a lie. This makes her a loyal friend, an honorable businesswoman, and a colossal pain in the ass. And, as we have finally come to accept, she will never get married. So we've decided to dispense with the dowry and send her on a non-honeymoon." James holds up an envelope. "From your long-suffering, loving family, an all-expenses-paid vacation for two to Aruba. Happy birthday, baby girl."

I try to smile as James makes his way through the applauding guests to the table and hands me the envelope.

"Well." Joan has taken the microphone. "It seems that great minds do think alike, James. Joy has attended many bridal showers this year, and purchased many items of lingerie for her friends, and we have despaired of ever being able to return the favor. Since she seems intractable on this point, we decided there was no reason to wait."

My girlfriends begin pulling from beneath our table, and piling into my lap, an array of dainty boxes and bags embossed with the names of fancy lingerie stores.

"So now," Joan says, "you have an untrousseau for your nonhoneymoon. Don't open those packages here, as there may be minors present." Laughter and applause. I cringe. Gabe squeezes my hand and stands up. "Gabriel, you can thank us later," Joan tells him, as he ascends to the stage.

"I'm sure I will," Gabe says. "But everybody, thank you for being here tonight. In particular I'd like to thank my partner in crime, Henry, for her contributions to the plot. And thanks to all of you for your remarkable discretion, which enabled us to throw a surprise party that was actually a surprise for perhaps the first time in recorded history—and certainly in the life of Nobel-winning gossip James Silverman. James, forgive me. You're a national resource."

"Get on with it, Winslow," James snaps over the laughter. "That's your mockery quota."

"Okay, okay." Gabe holds up his hands for silence. "I remember, when I turned thirty, it occurred to me that growing up wasn't really a matter of a dramatic or deliberate putting away of childish things so much as it was a recognition that certain changes were already taking place. I'd recently realized that certain of my opinions and views— some of which I thought would always be guiding principles—had shifted or faded, without my being conscious of it. And I wrestled with this for a while. First I'd assure myself it was a normal part of becoming an adult. Then I'd accuse myself of trying to justify the abdication of important beliefs that had just become inconvenient." Gabe stops and clears his throat. He looks at me, and I feel the heat rising in my cheeks.

"At one point," he continues, "a friend accused me of selling out because I'd begun to do editorial photography. And like a good artist, I stayed up for a couple of Sturm-und-Drang nights brooding about this, until it occurred to me that there was actually no problem. If I'd been acting contrary to my beliefs, that would have been a sellout. But my beliefs had *changed*. I had long since stopped thinking of commercial work as a crime against art.

"So our ideas, our values—they do change, they evolve. Even the ones we think are bedrock. It's just the way things go. And if they have changed, the loss of integrity comes when we fail to admit it." He stops and takes a breath. "It turns out the gift I've chosen for Joy is going to put your very thoughtful presents to an unexpected use."

"Oh, no," I say, and realize I've said it aloud. Charles and Delia give me puzzled looks.

"I'm afraid so." Gabe smiles down at me.

"What is going on?" asks Henry, grabbing my arm as I try to slide down in my chair again.

"And I suspect you'll be pleasantly surprised," Gabe tells the crowd, "as I was. As we were."

"Gabe, no," I whisper.

"Oh, my god," says Henry. "Oh, wow."

"Last night," Gabriel's gaze is on me, and his voice trembles slightly, "I asked Joy to marry me. And she said yes."

The room is suddenly and quite utterly silent. All heads turn in my direction. Gabe reaches into the breast pocket of his jacket and takes out what is, I know even before seeing it, an engagement ring.

"I couldn't be happier," he says, "and I want everyone to know it. And so, in front of God and everybody, I'm asking again." He moves to the edge of the stage and kneels down with the ring in his fingers. "Joy, will you marry me?"

I turn and see James and Charles staring at me wide-eyed, my girlfriends with maniacal grins on their faces. I look at Josh and Ruth beside him, her eyes full of tears, and my mother, with her breath held, a ravenous expression on her face and her hands clutched tightly to her chest. Miss Trixie, seated beside her, is in precisely the same posture. I look at Henry, who sits beside me, open-mouthed and blank-faced, and back again to Gabe's bright and expectant eyes. I did, as it happens, say yes last night—yes to him, yes to marriage. Still, I wasn't prepared for this, but it doesn't matter much now. What else can I say?

"Yes," I tell him. "Yes, I will. Yes."

Saturday, July 21, 200—

IT'S A HUMID SATURDAY AFTERNOON and I'm trudging up Central Park West through the heat, dragging my unwieldy garment bag along behind me. I've been carrying the damn things to weddings all summer, and I still haven't figured out how to do it gracefully. I sideswiped a toddler with it on the subway ride up. Unintentionally.

I climb the broad front steps of the brownstone where my mother's wedding will take place, the home of Gertrude Something-or-other, an early divorce client of Mom's with whom she later became friends. The house was part of the settlement she won for Gertrude; it seems to me like an inauspicious locale for a wedding. I ring the bell and wait. The massive front door swings open, and a tall woman in her early sixties with very red hair and a very small nose gives me a perplexed look, then clutches me to her chest.

"Joy! How nice to meet you at last." She releases me. "I'm Gertrude—oh, obviously! Come on in. Boy, don't you just look so much like your mother!"

I quash the urge to tell her she's delusional, and follow her into a pristine, lofty foyer where a grand marble staircase rises up to an atriumed mezzanine, on which it seems likely that Cary Grant or the Von Trapp family might appear at any moment. Gertrude springs uselessly up a few steps and calls to my mother while I stare around at the lavish fur-

niture and shake out my left hand, trying to restore the circulation cut off by the garment bag. A voice wends from a
distant upper floor, increasing in volume until my mother's
head appears from behind the mezzanine banister.

"Joy!" She brightens, looking down at me as if she'd only
just remembered she had a daughter. "Come on up. And
could you bring up the—oh, never mind. I already did.
Gertrude, when you—" She stops midsentence, peers at us
blankly, and whisks away like a windup toy. We stare at the
empty mezzanine. Gertrude opens an elegant pewter box on
a side table, pulls out a joint, and lights it.

"It's hard to believe that's the star attorney who kicked
my ex-husband's ass back and forth across the tri-state
area." She gasps through a lungful of smoke. "Want some?"
She waves the joint at me.

"No, thanks. But maybe blow it through the keyhole of
her dressing room."

"Great idea." She laughs out a great cloud of smoke at
me. "Well, guess you'd better go on up. Top of the stairs, take
a left, door at the end of the hall. I'll be there in a jiff—just
have to make sure the caterers are on track. Hey, take a look
at that rock!" She grabs my left hand, which I've managed to
revive, and raises my engagement ring to eye level, a maneu-
ver executed by approximately a million people in the past
week. All these heads bowed over my hand make me feel like
a princess returned from exile.

"Nice ice," Gertrude tells me. "You know what they say."

Actually, I don't. Diamonds are forever? A girl's best
friend?

"Clean it with a toothbrush and baking soda." Gertrude
drops my hand. "Once a month. And just a little water.
Works like a charm."

"Okay. Thanks." I head up the stairs, stopping midway to
do a little Ginger Rogers tap dance, and follow the descant of

women's voices to my destination. In the boudoir at the end of the hall my mother, clad in a lacy slip, paces staccato circles while Aunt Charlotte and Ruth watch her. As I come in, Charlotte winks and flutters her fingers at me from the chaise where she is stretched out, smoking a cigarette. Norah, my mother's oldest friend, attenuated as a greyhound, six-foot-two if she's an inch, and as English as she is tall, puts away her microscopic cell phone.

"They found the bouquet." Norah turns to my mother. "It was in the truck after all, but it got mixed up in someone else's order. They're bringing it over straightaway."

"We only have an hour." My mother stares vaguely at us. "An hour before the ceremony, right, Ruth? Where's my watch? Oh, here. Yes, an hour. Joy, honey, do you think I should wear my hair up, or down? I was planning on up." She sits down at a small dressing table, stands up, sits back down again. "But maybe down would be nice. What do you think?"

I open my mouth, and my mother shakes her head.

"Up. We said up and we'll do up. Norah, where are the bobby pins? Oh, they're in the bathroom. Will you—never mind, I'll—" She gets up again and walks into the master bathroom, pokes her head back in and looks at us, then retreats. Ruth catches my eye and giggles. Norah and Charlotte exchange glances and sigh.

"Has she always been like this?" Ruth asks.

"Always," Charlotte says. "We never made it to the first day of school on time—not once that I can remember. Joy, honey, you look great. Engagement suits you."

"That's right," Norah says. "Best wishes to you, love. Your mom told me. God, she's just thrilled."

"We all are." Ruth slips a timid hand onto my shoulder. "Did you see the beautiful ring Gabriel gave her?"

Norah bows over my hand. I resist the urge to curtsy.

"Joy's in the club now!" Charlotte sweeps over and laces her arms around me. "She's going to be an old married lady just like the rest of us!"

"Right," Norah says. "Have you got the handbook yet?"

"The what?"

"How to Be an Old Married Lady: An Instruction Manual," Norah says. "Everything you need to know. How to fight with your husband. How to commiserate with other wives. How to loathe your in-laws. Chapter seventeen, how to stay in your bathrobe all day with your hair in curlers."

"Chapter twelve, how to associate only with other couples." Charlotte squeezes me. "I'll make you and Gabe come over and play bridge with me and Burke. We'll fix canapés and gossip in the kitchen while the boys drink Scotch."

"Chapter nineteen, family holidays," Ruth says. "We'll have big Thanksgivings with lots of kids running around and everyone slamming doors and bickering with everyone else."

"Your point being," I ask Norah, "that it's nothing like that?"

"Of course it is, sometimes." She smiles and puts a hand on my arm. "Stereotypes have to earn their keep, after all."

"Don't worry, Joy." Charlotte wanders back to the divan and lights another cigarette. "There aren't any rules. You just make it up as you go."

Is that possible, I wonder, to make it up as you go? After you've chosen to do something the way everyone else does? I hope it is. I can only hope that it is.

Wearing a suit of ivory-colored raw silk, her hair pinned up in a French twist, my mother returns from the bathroom as Gertrude comes in with a bottle of champagne and a handful of glasses. Mom picks up my hand and looks at my ring.

"I'm so glad you're here with us, darling." She gives me a distracted kiss on the cheek.

"Thanks, Mom." I kiss her back. "Me, too." I am, more or less.

"You aren't dressed yet." Gertrude examines me. "You'd better get a move on. The judge just arrived, and the guests will be here any sec now. Hustle, ladies!" She nudges me toward the bathroom, and I comply, dragging the prehensile garment bag and shutting the door behind me. It's a large, gleaming room, and every inch not tiled in marble is covered by mirrors; I am inescapably everywhere I look.

"Chin up," I tell my reflections, and we all take a deep breath. "This will all be over soon." I undress and step into the melon-orange shift my mother selected for the occasion. "Engagement suits you," I tell them. They look unconvinced. I slip into my shoes, dab on lipstick, and give one of the reflections a kiss. "Make it up as you go," I whisper to her, and go to join the other women.

My grandmother, the latest addition to our prenuptial coven, reaches up to pat my cheek as I join her on the divan.

"So." She peers up at me. "I hear you will be married to that nice young man." Her accent is still so French, I sometimes wonder if it's a put-on.

"It looks that way, Gran."

"You like him very much?"

"Yeah, I like him."

"Okay. Very good." She beams at me. "I hope you will be very happy. Enjoy, my dear. You want some advice?"

"Of course I do, Gran. What's your secret for a good marriage?"

"Don't cook with too much butter," Gran says. "Or he will get very fat and sweat like a beast, and wheeze like a steam engine when he climbs the stairs." She makes a little face.

"No butter. Got it. Thanks, Gran."

"Here." Gertrude hands around glasses of champagne. "Up on your tootsies, girls! Let's have a little toast for the bride."

We circle together, Norah with one arm around my mother's waist, Gran on her other side. Ruth smiles at me.

"To the bride!" Charlotte raises her glass. "Our lovely friend, my big sister. We wish you all the happiness in the world."

"To the bride," we repeat, and touch glasses.

"Thank you," my mother says. "Thank you so much. I can't believe it. I actually feel a little nervous!"

"Don't worry." Norah winks. "Third time's a charm."

"It had just *better* be." My mother laughs. "I'm getting too old for this."

"We are never to old for love, n'est-ce pas?" my grandmother says. I wonder briefly if she has a new boyfriend.

"What a pity," Gertrude says. "I was hoping to have it out of my system by now. Come on, ladies. It's time. Oh, the bouquet arrived. Ruth, will you bring it up to her? It's on the top shelf of the fridge, next to the lox."

DOWNSTAIRS, JOSH STANDS at the front door greeting the guests as they arrive, while James ferries them to the little rows of white chairs set up in Gertrude's vast high-ceilinged living room, before a wide set of French doors. Beyond, a narrow terrace overlooks the garden. In one corner, my mother's fiancé Howie huddles in consultation with his best man and the judge. I walk through the room to my seat in the front row, stopping to greet my mother's friends—many of whom I have known, as they are fond of reminding me, since before I could walk—and accepting their beaming congratulations on my engagement and their compliments on my ring. As I sit down, James prances over and gives me a kiss on the cheek.

"Hi, baby girl. God, that color is just awful on you. Cantaloupe. Jesus."

"Mom picked it out. But thanks."

"Admirable restraint with the guest list." He glances around the room. "I think it's only forty people all together."

"Fewer witnesses. Just in case."

"Oh, Mom. Bless her heart," James says. "She does still have one, doesn't she?"

"She's actually in pretty good form today." I straighten his tie.

"Joy, did you—oh, never mind." James makes his voice high and squeaky.

"Honey, will you find me the—no, it's right here." I giggle.

"Darling, where's my—oh, it's up my ass," James whispers. Gabriel sits down next to me, slightly out of breath, and reaches to shake my brother's hand.

"Our bags are all in the study," he tells us. "The car service is coming at nine, which will get us to the airport at ten. The plane's at a quarter to eleven. We get into New Mexico at around one tomorrow morning, and your father's sending a car to take us to a hotel for the night."

"You just know Daddy's hag arranged this out of pure spite." James snorts. "I'm going to un—feng shui their house while they're out. Oh, there's Charles. I'll be back." He trots away, waving to our future stepfather's children, our almost-siblings: a man about Josh's age from Howie's first marriage, a woman in her early twenties from his second. They smile at us as they take their seats beside their grandparents on the other side of the aisle.

"Thanks for taking care of the luggage," I tell Gabe. "I owe you."

"Just hold my hand when the plane takes off," he says. "We'll call it even."

I nod as my family begins to scramble for the seats beside us, while the judge, groom, and best man take their places at the provisional altar in front of us.

"Here we go again," James whispers, as Charles kisses the side of my head. Ruth punches James in the arm, and I laugh.

"Look out, brother," Josh tells James. "She's not as sweet as she looks."

"Thank god," James says. "She'd never be able to deal with you if she were."

"Hush, children." Charlotte, seated with Burke one row back, shakes a finger at us. "At least pretend you're adults."

James, Josh, and I look at one another and begin to shake with silent laughter. Our significant others are soon similarly taken, until the whole front row is pink-faced with the effort to suppress a bona fide fit of giggles. Predictably, it's no use. As soon as one of us pulls it together, gasping for breath, we hear the others snorting and are off again. Before long, I hear my step-siblings chortling across the aisle.

"Oh, god," James begs. "Please stop. Stop, stop, stop. The ceremony's starting."

Sporting her corsage like a military medal of honor, our grandmother marches down the aisle, takes her seat beside us, and gives a chilly sidelong glance—accompanied by the ferocious eyebrow-arch she reserves for very dire circumstances, which has its usual sobering effect.

"Please rise." The judge gives our row a stern look, and the guests shuffle to their feet and turn expectantly toward the entrance of the living room. Clutching her bouquet, my mother pauses under the arched doorway for a moment, and returns our gaze. I suddenly remember a photograph in my parents' wedding album, a picture of her posed before an arch of flowers, with the same half-smile on her young, young face, and the same tiny trembling vague fear behind it. I am struck by a ferocious urge to run to her and put my arms around her and keep her from harm forever. This is what she will feel when I walk down the aisle, as she is walking now, I think, and tears flood my eyes. I look over at Josh, and see that he is crying, too. So is James, whose hand I take. He doesn't turn his head to look at me, but he squeezes my fingers, and doesn't release them.

The ceremony that follows is short and simple. Do they take each other, to love, honor, and cherish, for better or worse, for richer or poorer, in sickness and in health? They do. I hear my mother vow, for the third time in her life, *until death do us part*, and wonder how it feels. My heart does a strange little mambo as I realize Gabe and I will be saying more or less the same words to each other in the not-too-distant future. The judge turns to the assembly.

"And do you, who have witnessed these vows, promise to do all that is in your power to uphold these two persons in marriage?"

We do—before I even have time to consider what that would involve. But, I tell myself, I do promise. Whatever it means.

As Mom walks back down the aisle on the arm of her new husband, all of her children are weeping openly. The guests get to their feet and follow the new couple out into the foyer. James mops his face with a handkerchief and hands it to me. It occurs to me that I have cried more this summer than in the last five years put together. Maybe it's because everyone else gets so emotional about weddings, and I've caught their histrionics, like a summer cold that's going around.

"What the hell is wrong with us?" James sniffs. "I've gone soft."

"We're getting old," Josh says, handing a handkerchief to Ruth.

"Early form of incontinence?" asks Charles.

We're under the influence of wedding season, I think to myself.

AFTER A LONG DINNER and an exhaustive, exhausting string of toasts, I am leaning over the back of my chair to talk with my new stepbrother when a doorbell rings in the distance, and Gabe looks at his watch.

"It's nine," he says. "I bet that's the car."

"Mom." James pushes back his chair. "We have to go now. Give me a kiss."

"Wait, wait, wait," my mother says, standing and wobbling slightly. She raises her glass. "My dear friends," she calls out. "May I have your attention, please? I want to propose a toast to my children. My sweet children."

"Thanks, Mom." Josh touches her shoulder. "We really have to go."

"Sit down," my mother says, swaying. "I'm toasting."

"She's toasted," Charles whispers to us. "I'll go get your bags."

"Where was I?" my mother asks. "Oh, yes. My dear, sweet children." She stops and smiles lazily at us, and suddenly her eyes well with tears. "It hasn't been easy for my kids," she tells her guests. "It hasn't been easy for any of our kids, has it? In my line of work, I see a lot of families going through very hard times. The divorce rate is great for my business, but I'd give anything to never see another divorce. There was a time when I thought none of my children would ever get married, and I could hardly blame them. How could we blame them? Look at us. We haven't made it look so good, have we? We haven't been very good examples." Her voice catches in a sob. "But we try. We do our best," she continues. "And look. Look at them now."

"Look at us running very late," James whispers, as Charles returns to the table. "We've really got to go."

"The driver is waiting," Charles whispers back. "He says traffic is really bad. You have to hurry."

"Look at my babies," my mother says, wiping tears from her face. "They didn't give up, in spite of everything. They had hope. And they found love, they found wonderful partners. Ruth, and Charles, and Gabriel—who could ask for better sons- and daughters-in-law, or better kids?" She hides her face in her hands. James taps his watch at me. I shake my head.

"Mom," Josh says quietly, "we really need to leave."

"They're the best kids in the world," my mother says, choked up. "The very best. And they're not afraid to love. They're taking chances. They're so brave and good. And I'm so proud of them. To my children. I love them so much."

"Help," I whisper to Gabe, and hand him a glass. "Say something."

Gabe takes the glass, and stands up.

"To Claire," Gabe says. "A woman among women, who, fortunately for Ruth, Charles, and me, brought three beautiful children into the world, and raised them to be the extraordinary people you see here before you today." He pauses for the guests' laughter. "To the bride and her lucky groom," he says, raising his glass. The rest of us grab glasses and hold them aloft.

"To the bride," we tell her. And, blowing kisses and waving, we flee.

Sunday, July 22, 200—

"YOU *HATE* MARRIAGE!" the bride screeches at me. "I *know* you. I know *all* about you, Joy!" My father's betrothed—a reputedly sweet-tempered New Age interior decorator, just four years my senior (or so she says)—flings herself back and forth in front of me, her bridal gown flouncing, her blonde pageboy flipping, her teeth gnashing, her face gone almost lilac with fury. "That's no reason to ruin *my* wedding! How dare you? How dare you do this to your father and me? How dare you do this to your family? How dare you act out your personal issues on me, on my wedding day?"

It is just after eleven in the morning, with an hour to go before the wedding ceremony begins.

AT THREE this morning, my brothers, Ruth, Gabriel, and I checked into the Santa Fe Grand Oasis Hotel and Golf Resort. In all our jet-lagged, under-rested glory, we rose at seven A.M. for a breakfast in the hotel restaurant with the happy couple's families; this was followed by a mercifully brief wedding rehearsal. Afterward I returned to my hotel room with Gabe and passed out.

I woke to a severe kink in my neck, a ringing phone, and the groggy revelation of my tardiness. Snatching up the garment bag that Gabe had packed for me, I raced, with my head tilted about thirty degrees to the left on my aching neck, to the room where Desiree and her other bridesmaids were dressing. So far, not so bad. Until I opened the garment bag and discovered that it contained: the wrong dress. The garment bags for my summer wedding duties had been hanging together in chronological order on one side of my closet, so they wouldn't get lonely. Knowing this, Gabe had packed the first in line. What he didn't know was that I hadn't vetted them. Instead of the jaundiced peach, puff-sleeved horror that Desiree had selected for her attendants, I found the sparkly electric orange, off-one-shoulder, disco-ruffled gown I didn't wear as Maud's bridesmaid. And Desiree, who needs seven puffy-peach-clad bridesmaids—no more and no less, corresponding to mystical strictures and numerological dictates the importance of which I am apparently too spiritually bankrupt to grasp—is not happy at all. Nor, for that matter, am I. As Desiree bellows like a drill sergeant in tulle about my passive-aggressive act of connubial sabotage, the six appropriately dressed bridesmaids cast baleful feline glares at me and do their ineffectual best to soothe the bride.

"No, I will NOT calm down!" Desiree shouts at her maid of honor. "She's wrecked my wedding! You can't *stand* the idea of Sheldon being happy, can you? You've just never dealt with your abandonment issues, and your life is full of negative energy, and this is how you've decided to take your revenge on your father. You should be ashamed of yourself."

"Um," I tell her, trying to get my head into an upright position, and failing. I wonder briefly if I'm delirious from sleep-deprivation, and hallucinating this whole business.

"Where is Marina?" Desiree whimpers. "Someone get her up here!"

Marina is a retired second-string movie actress who, after a highly publicized plastic-surgery fiasco and subsequent nervous breakdown, moved from Los Angeles to New Mexico. She is now a practicing shamaness and, as Desiree's primary spiritual adviser, she'll conduct the wedding ceremony. I met her at breakfast this morning; she called up the local spirits to bless the wedding breakfast, and burned wands of sage in the ballroom during the wedding rehearsal.

"Desiree, honey," the maid of honor says, "don't add to the bad vibes. Lie down. Let's just take some deep breaths and center ourselves. Kendra, do you have your healing stones?"

Desiree allows herself to be guided to the bed, and collapses in a great pouf of billowing white fabric. One of the bridesmaids arranges the skirt of Desiree's gown. Another sits beside her, opens a little fabric bag, and takes out a handful of shiny pebbles, which she arranges on Desiree's face and chest, humming quietly and whispering. If I weren't so tired, I'm relatively sure I'd laugh. Instead, I move toward the phone by the front door to call James, and Desiree sits bolt upright, scattering healing stones in all directions.

"Don't you move," she says. "You're not leaving this room."

"I was just going to make a phone call," I tell her. She looks at me severely, but sinks back onto the pillows under the hands of her attendants. I am reaching for the phone when I hear the lock click, and the door swings violently open, clocking me in the face. I fall over. Several bridesmaids shriek. Marina bursts into the room, her purple shamaness gown swirling around her like a minor tornado. She takes note of me: on the floor at her feet, clutching my face. She turns to Desiree, who is laughing and kicking at the bedclothes.

"What's going on?" Marina asks her.

"Instant karma," Desiree says. Her giggles edge toward hyperventilation.

"Drop dead," I contradict, and struggle to my feet.

"Desiree, breathe, for goddess's sake," says Marina. "Does anyone have any sage? I'm all out. We need to burn some sage and cleanse this space. Now, what seems to be the problem?"

I consider telling her that the problem, in my spiritually bankrupt opinion, is that my father is marrying a complete and certifiable psycho. Instead I test my face for swelling.

"And the dress is all wrong and she did it on purpose and it's going to throw the energy balance of the whole wedding off," Desiree keens as Marina massages her temples. "She's ruined everything! She's ruining my marriage! If we get divorced it'll be your fault, Joy! Do you hear me?"

"Desiree," Marina coos. "Honey, breathe deeply. Focus your energy. Open your heart and head chakras. Let the light in. Be the beautiful angel."

Desiree cries harder. Marina looks at me, her holy New Age eyes penetrating my being, her crystal and turquoise jewelry sparkling.

"You're going to have a hell of a black eye, kid," she tells me. I nod. Desiree wails. "Desi, pull it together," Marina says, and slaps her across the face with not insignificant force. It makes a deeply satisfying smack. I am suddenly deeply fond of Marina. "Holy shit, honey," the shamaness says to the suddenly quiet bride. "It's just a damn dress. It's just a ceremony. You know what *symbolic* means? All right, then. That's better. Now will someone please get this kid an ice pack for her shiner?"

IN MY SPARKLY orange disco dress, I march down the aisle with the other bridesmaids to the accompaniment of drums and wooden flutes. My head is stuck at a thirty-degree angle. My right eye swells shut and turns a glorious shade of purple that just about matches Marina's dress. The guests gape at me. Gabriel spots me and shakes his head. James gets one look and bursts out laughing. I wink at him with my good eye and peel off to take my place at one side of the chuppah where Marina presides. My father, next to her, trembles visibly. Beyond the massive picture windows, the resort's golf course sprawls, expensively green. Squinting, I can see where the finely mowed grass ends abruptly, like a child's drawing, and the apparently infinite desert begins. A couple of golf carts trundle past the window as the bride starts down the aisle. I utter a tiny prayer to no one in particular that the golfers have a good game. It would be too bad if someone's misadventures at the seventh hole threw the wedding's energy balance off any further.

"YOUR FACE LOOKS like it's going to putrefy." James joins Gabriel and me in the line of guests waiting to congratulate bride and groom.

"So does yours, James. But mine will heal." I put my head on Gabe's shoulder. I don't even have to tilt it, as it's still stuck at that angle.

"Ha fucking ha. What happened, exactly? Did the other bridesmaids fight you for that fabulous dress?"

"More or less. Let's just say that mistakes were made. Gabe, when we get back to New York, remind me to label the rest of the garment bags, okay?"

"Yes," Gabe says. "I'm really sorry, Red."

"Really not your fault. Ah, Desiree. Congratulations."

We have arrived in front of my father and his bride. I lean in to give Desiree a kiss on the cheek, and she catches the back of my head and holds my face close to her mouth.

"Joy, I'm so sorry about all that back there," she hisses, her breath stinging my wound. "I was a little nervous, right?

But listen, if you ever, ever, *ever* tell your father what happened, I'll totally *kill* you. Okay?"

"I'm sure you will," I say, looking sideways at my father. "And I think it's just wonderful. Really. Welcome to the family."

Dad turns a vast smile on us, which fades as he registers my black eye.

"What happened to you, sweetheart?"

"Oh, I, um. Bumped it on a . . . thing." I attempt ease and goodwill. "But it's fine, Dad. And congratulations, both of you. Look, here's James and Gabe and—"

"You poor thing." Desiree oozes maternal concern at me. "And what's wrong with your neck?"

"Slept on it funny. It seems to be kind of stuck like this, actually."

"Hold still." Desiree tosses her veil efficiently over her shoulders and reaches for me. Before I can move out of range, she places a hand on either side of my face and gives my head a sudden and brutal snap to the left. "There," she tells me. "That should do it."

I tip my head experimentally back and forth, and find I have regained a full range of motion.

"A woman among women, is my bride," my father says as he turns to the guests behind us. "She has chiropractic training."

"I know jujitsu, too." Desiree gives us a feisty wink. "Black belt! See you at the reception, guys!"

"Let's go get you some ice for that eye." Gabe takes my arm.

"Screw the ice." James takes my other arm as we walk toward the banquet hall. "Let's go get me a damn drink. You know, Desiree seems kind of okay, actually. In a cheerleader-on-uppers kind of way. I think I may not loathe her quite as much anymore. She amuses me."

"Even though she had readings from *The Prophet* in the ceremony?" Gabe asks him. "And cried while they read them?"

"I appreciate it when people stay true to type." James straightens his waistcoat as we approach our table. "It makes life simpler, don't you think? Human shorthand."

"It was just a damn ceremony." I adjust my dress. The sparkles itch.

"Fine." Gabe eyes me. "So you won't mind if we get married at Boston Trinity Church, then? Because my mother wants us to do the whole high Episcopal ceremony."

I trip over a chair.

"Garrett, oh, my god. You're so bald," James addresses a man in his early forties seated at our table.

"Tell me again how we're related?" Garrett rises to greet us. "Because if it's by blood I'm going to kill myself right now."

"You're our father's brother's wife's sister's child, I think." I offer my unwounded side for his kiss. "You're safe. Garrett, this is Gabriel. Garrett is part of the extended Silverman clan. New Jersey branch. Gabriel is my better half."

A thickening and weary version of the handsome cousin I remember, Garrett shakes Gabe's hand and pretends to throw a punch at James, who is attempting to polish his bald spot.

"That many degrees of separation should have excused you from the wedding, I think." James takes a seat next to him.

"We're Jews, remember? We escape nothing that involves the tribe and food."

"We didn't come to your wedding," James says.

"That's because you weren't invited."

"Right." My brother nods. "You bastard."

"James, shut up. That was five years ago. And the wedding was in New Zealand, right, Garrett?" I look to him for confirmation. "Hey, where *is* your wife? We've never met her."

"Couldn't get the time away from work. Who wants wine? When was the last time we saw one another, anyway?"

"Passover in Princeton." James holds out his glass. "In 1986, I think. That was the year Josh got drunk on Maneschevitz and puked on somebody's date."

"Sounds like fun," Garrett says. "Let's reenact it tonight, shall we?"

As it turns out, it's an emotional rather than a physical upheaval that takes place. By the time dinner is over, Gabe and I have heard a great deal more than we might wish about Garrett's marriage, which, according to him, is a masterpiece of miscommunication and misery. As the floor clears for my father and Desiree's first dance, Garrett actually begins to weep. Gabe hands him a handkerchief.

"I remember our first dance." Garrett blows his nose emphatically. "We danced to 'You're the Tops.' " He takes a deep breath, straightens his shoulders, and wipes his face. "The tops. Well, that's the breaks, I guess. Baby, I'm the bottom." He lets out a sharp laugh.

"What's next, then?" I ask. "Are you going to separate?"

"No. No, no. Why?" Garrett gives me a look of faint surprise.

"Well, I mean. I just thought. If you're both so unhappy. And you don't have any kids, and—" I glance at Gabe, who ignores me. I'm sure he's appalled that I would ask such personal questions at such an inopportune moment. The band strikes up a rendition of "I'm a Believer." My father and Desiree have begun squirming around on the dance floor; James looks from them to me and buries his head into his hands.

"No one in my family has ever been divorced," Garrett says. "No one in hers, either. We didn't vow until one of us gets bored or unhappy. We vowed until death. Do. Us. Part. Commitment's a duty. You do what you say you're going to do, no matter what." He looks fiercely at each of us in turn. "I know it's not a popular line of thinking in our divorce-happy, Paxil-popping age. But I believe that when you make a promise, you keep it." He hangs his head and his eyes well up with tears.

"I know someone else who thinks that way," Gabe murmurs.

"Um," I say.

"Hello, Sheldon," Garrett says to my father, who has just arrived at our table, panting.

"Daughter mine," he gasps, "may I have the honor of this dance?"

I take the sweating hand he proffers and follow him to the dance floor. I glance over my shoulder and Gabe waves.

"I'm a believer," he calls after me. Garrett begins to weep again, and Gabe hands him a fresh napkin.

Saturday, July 28, 200—

"No rest for the wicked," Henry tells me, as we climb out of the car and into the damp, salty summer air of a small town on the far end of Long Island's less fashionable northern fork, where Erica's best friend Melody (whom Henry calls "Peroxide Polly") is getting married this afternoon. "How many is this for you, Joyless?"

"Twelve." Gabe turns from the driver's seat to poke at Delia, who somehow managed to nap through the whole drive out here, and is still curled peacefully in the back seat, humming in her sleep.

"Fourteen," I say. "For me. Thirteen for you."

"Well." Henry tosses her hair as she circles the car. "You all don't even need to have a ceremony. I'm pretty sure you're already married by osmosis. Hey, sugar bear." She leans through the open window into the back seat and touches Delia's cheek. "Dee. Time to get up, baby. We're going to the chapel."

Delia lifts her head and smiles sleepily at Henry. I lean against the car and squint toward the bay, watching the breeze ruffle Gabe's hair. Henry and Delia harmonize "Going to the Chapel" as they collect bags and blankets from the trunk.

"This is okay." Gabe leans back beside me and puts on his sunglasses. "Clambake wedding. Henry said they're cooking lobster and corn for dinner. Digging a big fire pit on the beach. Not bad."

"Also, according to rumor, this is going to be the weirdest extended family reunion ever," Henry says, handing me a beach bag. "Melody's mother has been married five times. Dad six times. Kids and step-kids from pretty much every marriage, so there's all these half- and stepbrothers and sisters, then stepparents remarrying and popping out more kids and step-kids and half-siblings. And most of them are involved in theater and the art world, so of course everybody knows everybody else and they all work together. I think Melody's father's second wife actually married her mother's third husband."

"Erica said Mel's maid of honor is her second stepfather's daughter from his third marriage or something like that," Delia says. "The kids all stay in touch."

"Here. I'll carry the chairs." Gabe pushes his hair out of his eyes and takes several folding beach chairs from Delia. "What about the groom?"

"Freaks." Henry throws an arm over Delia's shoulders. "One sister, younger. Parents were college sweethearts. Still happily married."

"Clearly, they're aliens." Delia gives her a sideways glare.

"Minnesota," Henry says. "Same thing."

We shoulder our burdens and stroll along a narrow road lined with cars. A couple of groups of people pass us, hauling their own bundles of beach paraphernalia. The last house on the left, the base of wedding operations, is a gray-shingled, ramshackle mess belonging to one of Melody's former stepparents. It keels lazily at the center of a broad, lightly browned lawn. Here, amid overgrown flower beds and untended hedges, are an array of mismatched chairs and café tables set with vases of daisies, and shaded by orange parasols. The house and its haphazard surroundings have been lavished with orange, yellow, and white crepe paper and festooned with bunches of matching balloons.

"Those must be the bridesmaids," Gabe nods. On the house's dangerously wobbly looking front porch, which is tangled in flowering vines, a cluster of young women in bright yellow, 1940s-style bathing suits are talking and laughing. Erica, looking like a blonde Esther Williams with a giant orange daisy behind one ear, emerges from the bunch and waves frantically.

"Don't forget your sunscreen," she yells to us. We wave back and follow another group of guests along a weathered plank walk and over a rise to the slender crescent of sand that slopes gently toward the bay. Along the little beach are perhaps two hundred wedding guests, setting up beach chairs and sun umbrellas, shaking out striped towels, unpacking bottles of soda from little coolers. Winding through the crowd is a path lined with large pearly conch shells and bouquets of wildflowers leading to a makeshift gazebo set at the water's very edge. The gazebo's white canopy and silky ribbons flutter on the wind. Beyond, out in the bay, several sailboats rock on the shining blue water.

"Well, shit," Henry says. "This is picturesque." She smiles approvingly at a pair of handsome, tanned, and sun-bleached young men in orange swim trunks standing on either side of what I take to be the aisle. "Hi there, boys."

"Hey," one of them says. "Bride's side or groom's side?"

"Bride," Henry says. "Are you serious?"

"To your left, please." The usher smiles politely. "You'll see there's a place just down there, near the water." He reaches into the lumpy net sack on the ground beside him, pulls out four yellow plastic ducks, and hands them around to us. "Someone will explain how to use these at the end of the ceremony."

"This millennium is getting so complicated," Gabe says, as we pick our way through the crowd to the space our usher indicated. "Since when do rubber duckies require operating instructions?"

"This is *our* spot, kid," Henry tells a very small boy standing nearby, and brandishes her duck at him. "You want to make a sandcastle here, you'll need to purchase a building permit."

"Bride's side or groom's side?" Gabe asks the little boy, who sticks his tongue out at us and runs away.

As we stake our claim and begin to set up, I see Henry's eyes narrow.

"Bitch alert," she hisses, looking across the aisle. "Lock and load."

I follow her gaze to a delicate figure in a nearly nonexistent bikini top and sheer flowing sarong who winds her way through the crowd, her golden, Pre-Raphaelite curls shining in the sun.

"What the fuck is she doing here?" Henry whispers to me, as Ora raises her hand in greeting and comes toward us.

"It's a plot," I whisper back. "Obviously. Hello, Ora."

"Fancy meeting you here." Henry glowers down at her, teeth bared.

"And you," Ora says, all graciousness. "What a pleasant surprise. I'm here with an old friend of the groom's. Gabriel! Hello, darling." She lights up as he moves to kiss her cheek; she offers the second cheek, Eurotrash-style, and, caught off guard, he stumbles before leaning in again, and nearly kisses her mouth. They both laugh, and she puts a hand on his chest. I could swear he's blushing. My stomach lurches.

"Hey." Delia puts her hand out, and Ora takes it.

"Ora Mitelman. You're the lead singer of Mercy Fuck, aren't you?"

"Yup. Delia Banks. Nice to meet you."

"I saw you open for the Apocryphal Angels last year," Ora gushes. "You girls are amazing."

"Thanks, thanks. That's nice of you."

"Do you suppose I could convince you to perform at a private party in a couple of weeks?" Ora still hasn't released Delia's hand. Henry scowls at them, turns away, and flops down in a beach chair.

"It's possible." Delia smiles. "Let me talk with the band and see what their schedules look like."

"Cost is no object, of course," Ora says, letting Delia's fingers slide slowly through hers. "I must have you."

"Dee," Henry says. "Could you please come put some sunscreen on my back?"

"In just a minute, hon," Delia says, not looking away from Ora. "I'm in the book, Ora. Give me a call next week, and I'll let you know."

"Oh, I will. And I'll be seeing *you* there, of course." She beams at Gabriel.

"Seeing her where?" I grab Gabe's arm.

"Joy." Ora stares at my hand. "Is that an engagement ring? Gabe, you didn't tell me you two were engaged!" She has gone gratifyingly pale under her tan. My momentary sensation of triumph is quashed, however, by an unpleasant thought: When would Gabe have had an opportunity to tell Ora about our engagement? And if he had such an opportunity, why would he not have told her? And who installed this *Cosmo* Girl monologue in my brain?

"He surprised me a few weeks ago," I tell Ora, linking my arm through Gabe's. "Though apparently he'd been planning it for some time. He proposed at my thirtieth birthday party. Isn't that romantic?"

Gabe gives me a quizzical look. I don't blame him. I'm acutely conscious of sounding like a complete idiot, but my mouth seems to have developed a mind of its own.

"Well." Ora tosses her hair over her shoulder and smiles coolly. "Congratulations. He certainly is a catch, Joy. You're a lucky girl."

"Funny," I say. "That's just what he said. That I was a catch, I mean. That he was lucky."

"Well. Best wishes to both of you. I should be going, I suppose. My date will be wondering if someone has carried me off! But I'll be seeing you all soon, I'm sure." She turns and sashays off, pausing to flirt with the half-naked ushers. Delia watches her go until Henry throws a bottle of sunscreen, which hits Delia on the back of one leg.

"So," I ask Gabe without looking at him, "what's this party of Ora's you're going to?"

"A launch for the paperback of her novel, I guess. She hired me to be party photographer."

I sneak a glance at Henry, who raises an eyebrow.

"May I come with you?" I ask. "To the party?"

"Joy, you wouldn't have any fun. I'll be working." Gabe shades his eyes with his hand and looks up toward the house. "I see some commotion up there. Ceremony should be starting soon. I'm just going to run down to the water and rinse my hands, okay?" He pats my shoulder and walks away.

"So." Henry squints up at me. "Did you ever get the scoop on that situation?"

"No. I thought it had become a nonissue."

"What situation?" Delia says.

"Nothing." I drop down onto the blanket beside them.

"The wildebeest you were slobbering over five seconds ago, beloved?" Henry glares at Delia. "She's the one Joy tried to beat up last month. With the hots for Gabe."

"Hank, you're not a best friend, you're a human satellite dish. Who else did you tell?"

"Ora?" Delia says at the same time. "She does boys?"

"She'll do any biped in range. If she's that discriminating, even. You never even asked him about it?" Henry shakes her head at me.

"No, I did not. Please shut up now—he's coming back."

"You're a real piece of work, Silverman."

"Thank you so much, Henrietta. You're too kind." I take scrupulously careful note of the instructions on the back of the sunscreen bottle as Gabe sits down beside me. A crowd of children in yellow and orange starts down the aisle, blowing on kazoos and banging tambourines.

THE CEREMONY is interminable. Step-relatives and friends, yoga instructors and voice coaches and Method acting teachers rise to read epic free-verse poems composed exclusively for the occasion, to sing songs accompanied by ukulele, recite ancient Sanskrit blessings, lead the guests in a creative visualization to ensure the couple's happy future. At one point Henry nods off and begins snoring. By the time the bride and groom finally take their vows and are pronounced husband and wife, the sun has begun to set.

"And now," Melody shouts to the guests, raising her arms. "Take up your rubber duckies! We're going to send them out to have an adventure at sea, where they'll always be together!"

We struggle to our feet along with the rest of the crowd, and take our ducks down to the water's edge. Henry and Delia bet on whose duck will go farthest, and hurl them into the bay. Gabe and I follow suit.

"Bon voyage, ducks!" Henry yells. "Good luck and Godspeed!"

Beside us, the little boy we frightened earlier is clutching his duck and crying hysterically as his mother attempts to convince him he should set it free and send it seaward.

"No, no, no!" he shrieks, as she tries to pry it from his fingers. "Mine, mine, mine!"

I know how he feels. I turn and follow Gabe up the beach.

Sunday, August 5, 200—

LATE IN THE AFTERNOON, Henry comes by the apartment to fetch me for a second fitting session with her scary Russian dressmaker. She announces herself by leaning on the buzzer several times in rapid succession and shouting up from the street. When I put my head out the kitchen window to pacify her, she stomps out onto the sidewalk and waves.

"Hurry the fuck up," she yells. "We're running late."

"Nice to see you, too, Hank. Down in a sec." I close the window and skulk through the living room. Laid out on the couch with the dog asleep on his feet, Gabe looks at me over the edge of the *New York Times*.

"We just got back," he says.

"And now I'm going out again."

"Yikes. All right, then." He cowers behind the paper. I ignore him. "When'll you be back?"

"Don't know. Late, maybe. Girls' Night." I pluck sunglasses and keys from the coffee table, and bang the door closed behind me.

"Don't slam!" Gabe yells after me. I skip down the steps two at a time and gallop out to meet Henry, who grabs my hand and drags me toward Seventh Avenue, waving frantically for a taxi. Not until she has flagged one down, installed us in the back seat, and arranged it so that we are heading to the East Side at a highly illegal speed, does she turn to me and smile. She's wearing a battered gray tank top emblazoned with the words *Beer: It's What's for Breakfast*.

"Hi, honey. How was your weekend? How was the wedding?"

"Just great." I shove my sunglasses on and hunch as far down in the seat as I can. "Joan picked another fight with Bix, and then got so drunk she couldn't stand up and I had to baby-sit her. Before dinner I overheard the best man telling the groom that if it didn't work out they could always get divorced. And a world music band played the reception. It was just really marvelous. Thanks for asking."

"Nice." Henry smirks. "Who got hitched?"

"Friend from college. Maybe you remember him—Tom Beggs? He was a junior when we were freshmen. Playwright. Drama department."

"The whole fucking school was a drama department." Henry makes a face.

"He and the bride met at a writers' colony and left their respective spouses for each other. The ex-wife and the new wife will be going into labor just weeks apart."

"Really nice. Very romantic." The cab takes a sharp turn and Henry ends up lying in my lap. "When'd you get back?" She looks up at me.

"Couple of hours ago. Please get off before I scream."

"Oopsie. Here we are." Henry shoves a wad of crumpled bills into the driver's hands, and crawls over me and out the door. "Want to tell me why you're such a big bundle of sweetness and light today?" She offers me her hand and helps me out of the cab onto the dirty street.

"I think I've provided ample justification."

"Yeah, but you haven't answered the question. I can always tell when you're holding out on me, Jo." She rings the dressmaker's buzzer. I sigh and kick at a fire hydrant.

"Ora. Again. She was at the wedding." The door opens, and the dressmaker's assistant waves us in.

"Small white world," Henry says, as we stumble through the dark lobby and into the main shop area.

"She's stalking Gabe. She has spies. She's getting information from the dark forces."

"You are late." Veruka stalks toward us, slashing at the air with her cigarette. "Please to take off your clothing immediately."

"Hi, Veruka. Sorry we're late. How's your summer going?" Henry takes off her shirt and begins to unbutton her jeans.

"You have gained weight," Veruka tells Henry. "Your bosoms are bigger. And you have lost." She stabs her cigarette in my direction. "Go, go. Go to dressing room." She jabs her cigarette out in a coffee cup. Henry and I move to the curtained cubicles at the other end of the room.

"So what happened with Little Miss Mitelman?" Henry says through the partition.

"Nothing. The usual. She kept slinking around. Sharpened her claws on me, flirted with Gabe until I thought I was going to be sick."

"You still haven't talked about it with him, then."

"No."

"And you're not going to?"

"Not a chance."

"You're insane." Henry sticks her head through the curtains of my cubicle. "Hey. You have lost weight. I'm taking you out for milkshakes when we're done. I'm up to four a day." Henry looks down admiringly at herself. "My ass is huge, but my tits are fantastic. What? Don't look at me like that. When I get depressed, I eat."

I step out of the dressing room. The assistant, Magdalena, hands us each a dress made of pale muslin, loosely stitched and pinned together.

"Huh." Henry holds hers at arms' length. "This looks like something by that freako German designer Joan's all into."

"They're dress patterns," Magdalena tells her. "So we don't waste expensive fabric. We'll adjust for size and cut the final dresses off these." She swishes away.

"So, since when are you depressed?" I step back into my cubicle and struggle into my dress.

"Oh, you know," Henry says airily. "Since Delia decided she wasn't sure if she wanted to go through with this wedding."

"What?" I lurch around to her cubicle and part the curtains. "What are you talking about?"

Half in and half out of her dress, Henry looks down at me, grins maniacally, and bursts into tears.

"Out, out, out," Veruka barks. "We have very little time before next client arrives."

I open my mouth to retort, but Henry pushes past me and goes to stand before Veruka, sniffling. I follow her.

"Hank, when did this happen? What's going on?" I raise my arms as Magdalena tugs at my dress's bodice. Veruka shakes her head and clicks her tongue as she inspects the strained fabric over Henry's hindquarters.

"Started about a month ago, I guess." Henry heaves a sigh and wipes her nose on her bare arm. "Delia got a crush on this extreme dyke we met at a dinner party, who started filling her head with all kinds of crap about how marriage is an oppressive patriarchal fascist fuck tradition and she's betraying lesbians worldwide by participating in it. It's all so circa 1970 I can't believe it. Ow! Watch the fucking pins." She glares at Veruka.

"Stop this crazy waving around and you will not be hurt." Veruka yanks at the fabric of Henry's dress.

"Then Dee started getting really weird," Henry continues, "got really moody, developed a total wandering eye. You saw her at Melody's wedding, practically hemorrhaging hormones on Ora. And it was right after that when she told me she was having second thoughts about our wedding."

"She wants to break up?" I feel ill.

"Nah, not break up." Henry shrugs. "She just isn't sure if she wants to do the wedding thing. I don't know what's going on with her. Can we actually not talk about this right now this exact second?" Her eyes fill with tears.

"Okay, girls, we are done." Veruka stands back and examines us, lighting a fresh cigarette. "Please to not add any more weight, my dear. Easier to take in than to let out."

"There's a deeper lesson in that, I'm sure," Henry says, stomping toward the dressing room, "but I'm too goddamn fat to know what it is." She disappears behind the curtain. Veruka puts a hand on my shoulder, and her smoke wafts into my eyes.

"Do not worry too much about your pretty friend," she says. "It will all work out. I know. Ah, and only look. I see you have become engaged, also. Very nice ring. Perhaps when you return for dress, we discuss your plan for wedding gown."

"Sure. Thanks." I walk back to my cubicle. As I take off the flimsy cotton dress, wary of the pins, I hear Henry rummaging around in her bag. Something comes flying over the partition and lands on my head.

"Present for you." Henry's voice is rough with tears. "I got it last time I went home, and I keep forgetting about it." It's a dark red T-shirt printed with black letters that read *My Best Friend Went to Hell and All I Got Was This Stupid T-Shirt*. I put it on, collect my things, and stand in front of her cubicle.

"Hank. Thank you. I'll treasure it forever."

"Just don't let Gabe borrow it," Henry tells me as we

wave to Veruka and make our way out. "Because you know he'll never give it back."

"Milkshake." I hold the door to the street open.

"Tequila shots." She puts an arm around me. "I'm buying."

PANTHEON IS EMPTY when we arrive. The maître d' waves at us from across the room.

"Luke's not on yet," she calls, "but he'll be here soon."

"Thank god for that," the bartender says as we sit down.

"Hi, there." Henry leans her elbows on the bar. "Give me a shot of your highest-octane tequila. With a tequila back. And the same for the lady, please."

"One shot for the lady." I wave at the bartender. "Water back."

Henry punches my arm. The bartender pours the shots, and places them in front of us. Henry raises a glass to me, tosses it back, and slams it down on the bar.

"Okay then," she winces. "Where was I?"

"Your girlfriend was skirt-chasing and having second thoughts about the wedding." I sip my tequila. "And you haven't talked to me about this until now because . . . ?"

"I don't know." Henry sighs. "Don't be mad. For a while I thought I was just jealous and I was embarrassed, I guess, about getting a taste of my own medicine."

"I know how you feel." I have an unworthy moment of feeling pleased that Henry's been humbled, and that I'm not the only one suffering stupid fits of demon possessiveness. It doesn't last.

"That's not it, though." Henry toys with her second shot, dips her fingers into it, and licks them. "Delia can flirt her ass off with all the super-dykes and straight girls in the world, and I don't give a shit, because I know she's coming home to me. But, see, I thought I didn't really care that much about the wedding. It was just an excuse to have a big party and wear a pretty dress and get a lot of presents and have all my friends together in one place. But when Dee said maybe she didn't want to do it I freaked out, and it took me a while to figure out why."

"So. Why?" I wait as Henry kicks back the second shot of tequila.

"I still don't know, exactly," she says. "Our families, kind of. I mean, they're supportive and all, but they don't really get it. I wanted them to see we're a couple the same way they're couples. That we're going to be together and live together and have kids and get old together just like them."

"You wanted your families to see you're just like everybody else."

"Yeah, that's it. But then I realized, I really wanted to prove to *myself* that we were just like everybody else. But we're not." Henry looks over at me. Tears are racing down her cheeks. "*I* want to be like everybody else. But I'm not. I could get married twenty times, and I still won't be. The world is never going to get it, not in this century. I'm tired of them making us different." She snorts wetly and lets out a choked sob.

"Oh, Henry." I hand her a cocktail napkin.

"Married." She sobs. "What a fucking farce. I can't even get really truly married."

"Hey, hey." I lean and put my arms around her, and she buries her face in my neck. "Hen, you know, it's just a ceremony. You and Dee will be together no matter what. You're more married than lots of people are. The ceremony's no big deal."

"Oh, sure, easy for you to say." Henry sniffs. "You're straight. You can take marriage or leave it or get all la-dee-da philosophical about it. Doesn't fucking matter.

People will still see you and Gabe as a real couple, and me and Delia as freaks of nature."

"But *you* know you're a real couple. Since when do you care about what anyone thinks of you? Why does it matter what anyone thinks about you or your marriage?"

"You tell me, friend." Henry sits up and blows her nose loudly on a napkin. "If it's just a ceremony and you don't care what people think, why do you suppose you've made such a fuss about the evils of marriage for all these years?"

"Um." I stare into my shot glass, sensing a trap. "Is that rhetorical?"

"Why haven't you addressed this whole Ora thing with Gabriel?"

"Because. I, uh . . . what's the connection?" I gape at her.

"Coin," Henry says. "Two sides of same. Answer the question."

"Because it's not appropriate. I have no basis for suspecting him, really. And so what if he did flirt with her? Weren't you holding forth recently about flirting as a harmless end in itself?"

"Fancy schmancy," Henry says. "Now, what's the real story?"

"That *is* the real story." I glare at her. She glares back. I sigh. "I don't know, Hank. Of course I want to ask. It's driving me insane. But I want to give him the benefit of the doubt. And bringing it up with him seems like such a typical, stupid, jealous-woman thing to do. I don't want to be such a *girl* about it. I don't want to act like other people do."

"My point. Exactly!" Henry slaps the bar.

"What?" I am now genuinely confused.

"Oh, Christ on a crutch." Henry sighs, and pats my cheek. "I love you, but for such a smart girl, you can be really, deeply fucking dense. Forget it, okay? Never mind."

"Hank. It's going to be okay. Really. Delia's just got pre-wedding jitters. I'll talk to her if you want."

"I know. Thanks. Thanks for the shoulder."

"Yours to dampen any day."

"Hello, ladies." Luke ties on his long white apron and lopes to our end of the bar. "Good to see you. We missed you girls last month."

"Everybody's been honeymooning," Henry tells him. "It's just us tonight, and Joan and Erica. Maud went to visit Tyler's family in Glasgow, and Miel and Max are still in France or some goddamn place."

"Say," Luke says, elaborately casual, "you hear anything from your friend Ora Mitelman?"

I sigh and put my head down on the bar.

"Luke?" Henry lifts her voice sweetly. "If you ever, ever use that name around us again, I will personally detach your testicles, plunge them down your throat, and basket-weave them through every last one of your ribs."

"Sure," Luke says. "You bet. I'll take that as a no."

Monday, August 13, 200—

THE FOLLOWING WEEK, I arrive at the office late for our Monday business meeting. The staff is already assembled around the conference table, faces interred in their morning cups of coffee.

"Ah, Vern." Charles looks up from the job book as I push open the front door. "Thank you for joining us. Children, please scooch around and make room for our laggard leader. Yes. Now. Where were we?"

I pour a cup of coffee and squeeze in between Pete and Tulley.

"We were discussing my sex column," Damon says.

"Which the *Cosmo* client has been led to believe," Myrna says, cutting her eyes at Damon, "is being written by an attractive woman in her early twenties with an array of mild sexual fetishes. Which quite clearly is not the case."

"Dude, it's only half-wrong," Damon says. "Not even half. Anyway, they love it. What's the problem?"

"What?" I choke on my coffee. "*You* submitted to the magazine? Do you know how much trouble this could cause?"

"Oh, come on, lighten up, guy." Damon flips his hair at me. "It expands my range. It's good for my creative juices."

"Joy, it *is* a fashion magazine," Charles says. "The silicone boobs are the least fake things in there."

"Forget it, Damon. This has catastrophe written all over it. No way. Could someone pass the sugar? Please tell me they haven't gone to press yet."

"Calm down, princess." Charles hands me the sugar bowl. "Tulley didn't want to do it, but they wouldn't take no for an answer, they just kept calling. So Damon wrote up a couple of sample columns for fun, and we sent them in with a fake bio. It was a joke."

"Joke's over."

"It's her week to be Bad Cop." Charles pats Damon on the shoulder. Myrna looks pious. "Okay, quickly. Damon is off to Los Angeles for a couple of weeks to visit our movie people. While he's out there he'll meet with the Transgression Enterprise to review our strategy documents, and finalize the contract—the *six-figure* contract. Yes, yes, applause, please." Charles bows as the staff clap and clinks mugs with spoons. "What else? The first round of the *Extreme Romance* series is now in production. They'll evaluate sales and get back to us about it in six months. In the meantime, Joy and her friend Joan at *X Machina* have developed a fabulous proposal for a cross-branded line of erotica, which the Modern Love execs are reviewing, but we probably won't hear anything about that until after Labor Day, and if it goes through we'll be contracting most of the writing out to *X Machina* writers."

"I'm going to miss working on those bloody things." Tulley puts her head on Pete's shoulder and sighs. "I suppose I'll have to start dating again."

"Don't worry, my darlings. I have something very special in mind for you." Charles waves his pen at the staff. "For the last month or two I've been meeting with folks from Talent Agency, which represents all kinds of artists. We've been discussing an initiative called the Medici Project, to broker and manage sponsorship of individual writers, musicians, and visual artists by major brands and corporations. A series of relationships that fall somewhere between the historical artist—patron model and today's sponsored athlete or spokesmodel paradigm. We're assigning Pete and Tulley to work with the Talent Agency reps and creatives from their ad firm." Charles gives me a guilty look.

"Why the long face?" I get up for more coffee. "I signed off on all of this. We deposited their check. Is there a problem?"

"Well, there's good news and bad news." Charles fidgets with the assignment book. "They've already secured three partnerships to launch the program. The good news is the agency picked Delia and Mercy Fuck to partner with Trashy Girl Cosmetics. They want to sponsor an international tour, even. The bad news . . . um. Okay, you know that big fashion guy Obie K.? No, of course you don't. What am I thinking?" Charles shakes his head at me and sighs. "Anyway. He's starting a ready-to-wear collection called Swank or Swish or Swoon or Sway or something like that. And they've signed on as Medici sponsor for Ora Mitelman."

"Mitelman's fucking brilliant," Tulley says.

"That vile nonentity?" Myrna turns on Tulley, eyes wide.

"Who is Ora Mitelman?" Pete bobs his head at me. I could kiss him.

"Vern?" Damon raises his hand and turns to Charles. "I slept with her. Is that a conflict of interest?"

"Overshare," Tulley tells Damon. "Go stand in the corner."

"Joy, you look rather unwell," Myrna says. "Would you like me to open a window?"

"I'm fine." I avoid looking at Charles.

"Well, as we're on the subject of nausea," Myrna says, "I was unfortunate enough to take a call this morning from a certain adulterous, philandering monster—"

"Hector," Pete says. "He called to ask for another letter."

"Two." Myrna twists a strand of her hair around one finger. "One each for lucky wife and mistress. Joy, as a woman whose own ideas about the institution of marriage have recently undergone a surprising reversal, perhaps your position regarding our role in these indiscretions has altered, as well?"

"How'd a smart girl like you get so dumb about this stuff, guy?" Damon turns on her. "Men sleep around and deceive the ladies about it. It's what we've done for millennia. Biological imperative."

"That's enough!" I am on my feet, slamming my hands down on the table. Coffee cups do tiny rattling dances across the pink Formica. The staff stares up at me. "That. Is. Enough. Out of everyone. Pete, do the letters. Myrna, Damon, your opinions are not required. Everybody back to work." I stomp away from the table into the back office, fling myself down on the couch, pick up a section of the newspaper scattered on the floor nearby, and hide behind it as Charles follows me in.

"Good morning, sweetness and light." He sets a fresh cup of coffee down next to me. "Something very strange just happened. My occasionally cranky but generally mild-mannered, conflict-avoiding business partner was just body-snatched. You know anything about this?"

"No idea." I eye my reflection in the coffee cup. "Listen, I'm wondering if maybe we should sit down and talk about the direction the company's taking. We're kind of getting away from Invisible's original mission with all this new stuff. Maybe we need to, you know, reevaluate, get back to basics." I stand up, wander to my desk, wander back to the couch, pick up the paper, put it back down.

"Well." Charles raises an eyebrow. "Sure, we could set aside some time to discuss where we want to take the company in the coming year or two. Never hurts to have a plan."

"Ladies, ladies, lovely ladies!" Miss Trixie hails us from her balcony. She is dressed in immaculate tennis whites. "Come have some coffee with me, darlings," Trixie calls. Charles waves at her, then looks at me. I shrug, and follow him out the window and onto our fire escape.

"Good morning, my little petunias," Trixie greets us. She offers me a delicate china cup balanced perilously on a matching saucer. "Charles, one lump or two?"

"Need you ask?" Charles accepts his cup from Trixie and grins as she plucks two cubes of sugar from a little bowl with tiny silver tongs, and drops them gently into the cup. "You're looking very sporty this morning, dear lady."

"Life is a game, my darlings. One must dress for it." Trixie strikes a pose, then turns to me. "Baby, why ever were you not at that fabulous, fabulous party last week? You missed my performance, and little Delia's girls. And your young man was there into the wee hours."

"The wee fact of which I was abundantly aware, actually. Thanks. I didn't attend because I was not invited."

"What party?" Charles asks.

"Party for the paperback release of Ora Mitelman's novel." I peer down into the alley below us, where a group of children are passing around a cigarette and hacking loudly. "Gabe was there on business. Ora seems to think of him as her personal photographer."

"Ah," Trixie says. "Well. Never mind. I'll be performing in just a few weeks at Henry and Delia's wedding, you know, and I'm sure to see you there."

"Mmm," I tell her, thinking of Henry in tears at the bridal shop.

"And how is everything else, dears?" Trixie asks. "How's your clever little company? Keeping busy?"

Charles shakes his head at her very slightly, and she turns to me.

"How about all those weddings of yours, poor darling? Have you finished the long march?"

"No. Flying to Los Angeles next week. Friend of Gabe's from college is getting married to some actress."

"Well." Trixie gives me a bright smile. "That should be amusing."

"Right. You know, I think I hear my phone ringing," I tell them, and begin to climb back through the window. "Will you excuse me? Thanks for the coffee, Trixie."

"Air kiss," she trills at me, waggling her fingers.

INSIDE, I POKE my head out into the main office, where the staff is hunched at their desks, tapping away at keyboards, chewing disconsolately on pencils. Tulley and Pete are seated at the conference table, going over Medici Project materials; their enthusiasm level for whatever they're reading at the moment appears to be in the deep negative integers. Myrna looks up from her seat beside the window, sees me, and looks away without expression. I retreat to my couch and flip through the newspaper. A few minutes later, Charles climbs back through the window and comes to stand in front of me. I hold up a section of the paper, and point to a photograph of a pleasant-looking man about my age.

"See that guy? He was in law school with me. I knew him, sort of. We went out for dinner once."

"Cute. What happened to him?"

"According to the paper, he's dead."

"I'm so sorry, Joy." Charles sits down on the arm of the couch. "Oh, god. What happened?"

"Paper says he defended a man accused of rape, got the guy acquitted. A week later his client raped and murdered an eleven-year-old girl. So he killed himself."

"Oh, no." Charles strokes my hair. "That's so sad. Are you okay?"

"Suppose Myrna's right, Charles. Should we not be doing these letters? Are we responsible for what happens to Hector's marriage? Are we implicated?"

"Okay, whoa. Take a deep breath, Vern." Charles sets the paper aside. "What your friend's client did and what Hector is doing are not on the same scale."

"That's not what I asked. It's not a question of degrees."

"It's always a question of degrees. And interpretation. And position."

"It's not like I'm some moral absolutist." I swing my legs off the couch and sit facing him. "But let's say, just for the sake of argument, that I personally think sleeping around on one's significant other is wrong. If I facilitate someone else's infidelity, am I or am I not betraying my personal beliefs?"

"Honey, get off the soapbox. You're going to get a nose-bleed up there. This is the grown-up world. Nobody's hands are clean." He moves to sit beside me on the couch. "Your sneakers? Made by tender little Southeast Asian toddlers for pennies a day. Our office is cleaned by an illegal immigrant from South America. That computer on your desk? Running software from a company that violates every antitrust agreement known to man. Forget about moral purity. *Ça n'existe pas.*" Charles snaps his fingers at me. "Here's the thing. I think you're under some personal pressure these days. I think you'd rather chew glass than give any assistance to Ora Mitelman's career. I think you don't want to do those letters for Hector for personal reasons and you're too embarrassed to admit it."

"You are welcome to your opinion," I tell him. "Just don't think the fact that you're correct wins you any points with me."

"Honey. Listen to me. We don't have to do any of this stuff. It's fine. We have plenty of work. We certainly don't have to do those letters. We could even jettison the Medici thing, if you want. I don't really care about being in the right, but I do care about you being happy." Charles looks at me, fond and sincere as a puppy. How can I make him understand that this is about something more than being happy? I kind of know, in a half-in-denial sort of way, that I'd love to take him up on his offer. But I also know I couldn't live with myself if I did.

Let's talk, for a moment, about The Principle of the Thing. The Principle of the Thing is, roughly, the formal standard or rule that ostensibly governs a situation—but it is also a concept that is much abused. When people say it's The Principle of the Thing that concerns them, you can almost invariably be sure it isn't. To invoke The Principle of the Thing is, most often, to claim the moral high ground on a pure technicality. The Principle of the Thing is generally cited only when there exist theoretical but not *actual* grounds for a grievance, or if the actual grounds for a grievance are inconvenient or embarrassing. The Principle of the Thing allows us to be petty, small-minded, vain, self-serving, and righteous without appearing to be so. Because of this, mere mention of The Principle of the Thing immediately arouses suspicion of hypocrisy, and rightly so.

But there really are some people whose conduct is guided by principles, rather than the reverse. For better or worse, I am one of those people. For example: I do want, very much, in no particular order, to run screaming to the phone and tell Hector he can do his own dirty work; to revoke all my wedding RSVPs for the rest of the century; to corner

Gabe and demand to know what the hell is *up*, for god's sake;
to arrange for Ora to be infected with a nonfatal and basically painless but incurable infection that causes the entirety
of the epidermis to be perennially and thickly covered in
oozing, bright pink pustules the size of mini-marshmallows.
I could do these things, all of them. No one would look
askance, there would be no serious repercussions. As Henry
would say, and rightly, to do so would be only human. As
Charles assures me, everyone would understand perfectly.
(Except for the part about disfiguring Ora, and probably only
a few people would object to that.)

But I will not do these things. And why will I not?
Because I believe in the ironclad separation of my personal
and professional life, to the extent that it's possible. I
believe in honoring the promises and commitments I make
to myself and others. I believe that living well is the best
revenge. I believe that if I behave like a girlie girl, like Ora,
like my mother, I will end up becoming like them, and I will
get what they got and what, as far as I can see, they deserve;
and conversely, that if I rise above it, I have a chance to be
and to have something better than what has always been
women's lot in life.

And I believe that if we don't hold true to our beliefs, no
matter how much it might cost us, then we are worth nothing
at all.

It's the principle of the thing.

"Let's just proceed as planned," I tell Charles. "Medici
Project, letters for Hector, everything. Oh, Vern. Please stop
giving me that sympathetic look."

"Joy, things change. People change. We change our
minds about things. A couple of months back you were still
swearing you'd get married over your own dead body. You
can change your mind. It's permitted."

"I can't."

"Because you promised? You gave your word?" Charles makes a face at me.

"I know you think it's odd—"

"And neurotic and uptight and just plain silly—"

"I know, Charles. Listen, I appreciate the offer, I do. Thank you. You're being incredibly thoughtful, and much nicer to me than I deserve. But let's call this the end of discussion. Please." I force a smile. Charles stands up, shakes his head, and goes to sit as his desk.

I snap up a fresh section of the paper and, as luck would have it, open to the wedding announcements. The featured wedding of the week, I read, was held at the New York Aquarium. At the center of the article is a photograph of the bridal pair, taken in the dim grotto that houses one of the aquarium's main exhibits, where a fine-boned, patrician bride and her lanky, goateed groom stand silhouetted, looking into the vast tank. Their hands are clasped, their reflections faint in the thick glass. Beyond, in the bright starry water, two enormous white Beluga whales gaze back at the couple, cherubic smiles on their blunt, mild snouts. The image brings back, with unpleasant clarity, the memory of a grade school field trip I took to that aquarium not long after my parents divorced. I remember the science teacher telling us that Belugas mated for life. The official guide who was with us corrected him sharply: It was a common misconception, she said, but entirely untrue. Mammals rarely mate for life, she added, winking at him. The group of us, a baker's dozen of nine- and ten-year-olds, giggled and blushed without knowing why.

I pull the thin gray pages of the newspaper close to obscure my face so Charles won't see me cry.

GABE AND I ARE RIDING through the Hollywood Hills in the back seat of a hired car, en route to the season's penultimate wedding. Gabe's college friend Theo Kappler, now a television producer, is marrying a starlet in her late twenties known for lively portrayals of popular high school girls, and for naturally ample breasts. We spend the commute doing our level best to ignore the driver; it is not an easy task. Mick is a marginally postadolescent and not-very-recently washed young man who pays far less attention than one might hope to the perilous curves of the road, dedicated as he is to sharing with us a generously detailed synopsis of his screenplay. As we approach a driveway secured by large gates and flanked by a crowd of camera crews, Mick squints at us in the rearview mirror.

"Hey, wow. This is Keller Kappler's place, right? The director dude. You guys are, like, going to Angelina and Theo's wedding? No way!"

"Way," I assure him. Everyone seems to be on a first-name basis in Los Angeles, even with people they don't know personally. Especially, in fact, with people they don't know personally.

A few idle journalists peer in our direction, and Gabe leans out the window and shows our invitation to a guard in mirrored glasses. A leviathan white Mercedes pulls in behind us, and the camera crews spring to life. A manicured hand emerges from car's rear window and waves listlessly.

"Dude," Mick says, contorting his scrawny frame for a better view. "Check it out! That's totally what's-her-name from that show! Who was, like, Angelina's nemesis in that one movie?"

"You will bring your car up through the gate and around the bend to the left," the guard barks at Mick. "You will drop your passengers at the main house and continue on to exit through the service drive. Do not, I repeat, do not turn your car around."

"You got it, bro." Mick gives him a happy thumbs-up and we lurch forward as the gates swing silently open. "Heavy duty, guys. Wow. Wait 'til I tell my roommates about this. Hey, didja know that rapper guy's ex-wife, who he, like, filed restraining orders against and all that, lives in the house across the street? Okeydokey, here we are." He jerks to a stop. A uniformed attendant takes a languid step backward just in time to avoid being mowed down by our car, and moves, unperturbed, to open the door for me. Mick honks musically and waves as he peels out. Gabe tucks the silver-ribbon-entwined box containing our wedding present—a billion-thread-count, twenty-five-foot-long tablecloth from the bridal registry list—under one arm, and offers me his other. We ascend through the milky, eucalyptus-scented air, up a long, low-slung arc of stairs, past a fountain with a hulking abstract sculpture at its center, and up toward an unspeakably big house made almost entirely of glass. Gabe and I exchange glances, and I hear a low laugh rising in his chest.

"No puns," I beg. "I'll get the giggles."

"As you wish." He squeezes my arm. "But clearly you

don't know what you're missing. Oops. There's another res-
olution out the window. I hope it doesn't reflect too badly on
me. I don't mean to cause you any pane."

"I can see right through you," I tell him, as another
attendant directs us through the front door and into a vast,
faux-Japanese-minimalist foyer. A third attendant takes our
gift and deposits it on a long table with a mountain of others,
and a fourth hands us glasses of champagne and waves us on.
The foyer opens onto a slightly sunken and lavishly fur-
nished living room, several times the size of our entire
apartment, where sixty or seventy guests mingle. I am gap-
ing around, entertaining the vague notion that interior
designers are God's way of telling people they're not giving
enough money to charity, when someone calls my name. I
turn to see Christopher Adams, with whom I have very
deliberately had no contact since our contretemps at
Marilyn and Ben's wedding.

"Isn't that . . . Topher?" Gabe asks me, taking a step
forward as Topher comes toward us. I struggle not to blush
or cower or think about anything in particular or at all.

"Gabriel, Joy!" Topher shakes the hand that Gabe
extends to him.

"What are you doing here?" I ask, as he turns to kiss my
cheek.

"Theo was a producer for the first show I worked on out
here—which got canceled after two episodes. Fortunately, he
didn't hold it against me." Topher stuffs his hands into his
pockets. "What are *you* doing here? I didn't know you were
coming to Los Angeles. Why didn't you call to let me know?"

Gabe explains his connection to the wedding party, and
together we observe the requisite round of amusement about
the various ties that bind us and the relative smallness of the
world we inhabit.

"And where is your lovely fiancée?" Gabe asks.

"Evie, yes. I mean, no, she's not here." He looks out toward the patio, then down at his feet. His face is flushed. "Actually, we broke off our engagement. A few weeks ago."

I stare at Topher, feeling a number of things at once, which average out to another case of nausea.

"I'm sorry," Gabe murmurs. I nod assent.

"It's for the best." Topher gives us a stiff smile and clears his throat. He takes his hands out of his pockets, shoves them back in. "Well. It's great to see you guys. This place is really something else, isn't it? Belongs to Theo's uncle. Very strange guy, Keller. I've been up a couple of times for parties. I can show you around a little, if you want. Waiter?" He stops a young man carrying a tray of champagne glasses, and takes one. "Have you been out back yet? You won't believe it. Come on."

Gabe and I follow Topher past the crowd in the living room, through floor-to-ceiling and wall-to-wall sliding glass doors, and out into the area that under normal circumstances would be referred to as the backyard; the term is insufficient to describe this massive tract of expensive landscaping that unfolds before us toward a distant panorama of the smog-swathed city below. Here, serpentine footpaths, paved in some pale green, semiprecious stone, arabesque across a multilevel acre of gray slate patio and around a vast swimming pool. On its surface, thousands of pale lotus blossoms drift like ornate paper boats. At one end of the pool is an odd gazebolike structure covered in gold filigree and draped in long, silky banners; its roof is supported by pillars in the shapes of Buddhas and writhing, multiarmed dancers. It suggests, generally, a pan-Asian temple, and, specifically, very bad taste. Facing this creation, on either side of the pool, are rows of spindly gold chairs adorned with ribbons and set with embroidered cushions.

"That thing," Topher indicates the temple, "was custom-built for the wedding by a woman who won the Oscar for production design a couple of years ago. Angelina converted to Buddhism after she saw that movie about the search for the new Dalai Lama." He kicks back the remainder of his champagne and tosses his glass into the pool. We all watch as it bobs for a moment on the surface, then disappears beneath the floating blanket of flowers.

"Cheers," Topher says. "More bubbly?" He waves at a waiter on the other side of the pool.

"Back in a second," I tell them. "If I don't get lost."

But of course I do. On my search for a bathroom I end up first in a giant kitchen where several people are screaming at one another over trays of canapés, then outside a door at the end of a hallway that I am about to open when I hear the distinct sounds of an illicit quickie. At last, after nearly toppling an attendant whose arms are full of orchid bouquets, I locate the ladies' lounge, conveniently announced as such by an engraved silver plaque on its gleaming cherry-wood door. The lounge decor aesthetic is sort of Bette Davis–boudoir, an opulent shrine to Depression Modern design that would make Charles weep for joy. It is currently occupied by three attenuated, archly pretty young women wearing tiny strappy dresses and tiny strappy shoes, who grace me with bored glances before they return to cutting lines of cocaine on an elegant glass and chrome coffee table. I cross to the rest rooms, my heels sinking perilously into a sea of plush burgundy carpet, and lock myself into the cherry-wood toilet stall.

"This will be a lovely first marriage," I hear one woman say. "You go ahead, honey."

"Oh, it's not her first," another voice says over a series of loud sniffs.

"She had that annulled after three weeks. Doesn't count."

"I give them a year," a third voice says. More sniffing.

"That's optimistic."

"I swear he's gay. My best friend's stylist slept with him last year."

"So did I, honey. Half of the bridesmaids have validated little Theo's parking ticket. He's not gay."

"He's just a hedonist. Like us." The redheaded woman making this pronouncement looks up as I reenter the sitting room. She acknowledges me with a half-nod and a once-over, and proffers a candy-striped straw. "Want to powder your nose before you go? Courtesy of our benevolent host. No? You sure?" She picks up a cut-crystal dish, holds it out. "Percodan? Xanax? Demerol? Ritalin? Stuff'll knock you out quicker than a ghost says boo."

"Keller's so thoughtful like that," one of the other women adds. "No, pain, no pain, that's his motto." As the three of them convulse with laughter, I slip out of the lounge and come face to face with a burly man loitering in the corridor.

"Joy Silverman?" He peers down at me, then strangles out an awkward laugh.

"Hector." I offer him a trembling hand and he shakes it. "I haven't seen you since you came by the office last year . . . Hector *Kappler*. You're related?"

"Groom's uncle. Just waiting for, ah, my wife." He studies his shoes. I inspect the wallpaper. "Think she may be in there. You see her?"

Before I can answer, the feline redhead from the lounge glides through the door and comes to stand beside Hector.

"Anabel," Hector tells her, "this is Joy Silverman. She's a, ah, business associate of mine from New York. Joy, Anabel Kappler, my wife."

"Anabel." I give her my very best blank business face. I try not to picture her with cuckold's horns—or whatever the female equivalent is. Now that I think of it, there probably isn't one. As Damon said the other day, the cultural norm is for men to stray. The term for a man with an adulterous wife is *cuckold*. The term for a woman with an adulterous husband is *wife*.

"Lovely to meet you, Joy." Anabel smiles. "Sorry to keep you waiting, baby. There were such long lines." She winks at me, then takes Hector's arm and leads him away. I watch their backs disappear down the hall and briefly reconsider the candy dish of tranquilizers, before going in search of Gabe.

WITH THIS WINDUP, I'd expected the wedding to include a procession of vestal virgins, ritual smoking of opium in hookahs, and the blood sacrifice of a plastic surgeon or two. In reality, I don't think there was anything like that, but I honestly can't say for sure. I was barely able to take in the details of the ceremony, distracted as I was by the maid of honor: Ora Mitelman. The bride's dearest, oldest friend. Who, after the reception dinner, asked Gabriel to dance, right in front of me, without so much as a blush of shame. And with whom he is currently doing the cha-cha. The two of them are out there on the dance floor, amid the topiary and tiki torches, dancing up a storm with a crowd of tipsy guests, while I sit alone at a table by the pool.

I am throwing sugared almonds at the floating lotus blossoms, and in the advanced stages of a royal sulk, when Topher finds me.

"You don't look like you're having a particularly good time, young lady." He crouches beside my chair. "Where's Gabe?"

"Dancing." I throw another almond.

"Without you?"

"So it would seem, as I'm here discussing it with you, Toph."

"You want to dance?"

"No."

"No. Never mind. I have a better idea." Topher stands and pulls me up. "Let me take you away from all this." He leads me into the house, pausing to coax two bottles of champagne and glasses from a waiter. We wend through the corridors, past the ladies' lounge, and stop outside a set of ominous black double doors. Topher pushes them open and waves me into the pitch-black room. I hear a switch snap, and the lights rise to reveal a private screening room built to look like an old-fashioned movie house. At the front is a half-scale proscenium stage, complete with red velvet curtain and marquee lights. Instead of chairs, the room is filled with rows of love seats upholstered in plush gold fabric. The walls are painted with trompe l'oeil murals depicting luxe balconies and opera boxes.

"When does the next burlesque show start?" I ask.

"Shut up and sit down." Topher nudges me toward a seat in the front row and begins to open a bottle of champagne. "You are wearing an engagement ring, Silverman. We clearly have some catching up to do."

AN HOUR OR MORE slips by as we exchange stories. Topher tells me about breaking his engagement with Evelyn. I tell him about my family's weddings, about the evening Gabe asked me to marry him, about the birthday party proposal, about my fear and loathing for Gabe's family and my anxiety about the engagement party they're planning for us in mid-September, which does not bode well for how much input we'll have in the wedding itself.

As I talk, I realize what a relief it is to get all of this off my chest. I haven't really been able to admit to any of my friends—I haven't, I guess, even admitted to myself—just how psycho I am these days. I'm so weirdly embarrassed about having reversed my stand on marriage, and now that I'm a convert to the honorable estate it feels as though it's somehow not my right to quibble about the particulars. I can't quite follow my own logic, if there is any. I do know that as Topher meets my confessions with sage nods and his trademark lopsided smiles, I begin to feel lighter, easier, grateful to him. He looks so familiar and kind sitting across from me, a friend of my youth, someone I can have faith in.

There's only one hitch. I am unable, try as I might, to answer his query about what affected my change of heart about marriage. This is disturbing, but since both champagne bottles have somehow become empty, I conclude that my vagueness on this point can be explained by garden-variety inebriation, an excuse that Topher accepts.

"Never mind." He grins at me. "Didn't mean to put you on the spot, Silverman. How about a little music? A little night music, please?"

I bob my head and note that the room wobbles rather alarmingly as I do so. Topher weaves up the aisle to the back of the room and into the projection booth; a moment later "I'm a Believer" fills the room at ear-splitting volume for several bars, and then is shut off. Muffled apologies come from the projection booth. I hold my left hand out in front of me and wave it around, wiggling my fingers and looking at my engagement ring. I draw it slowly toward my face, keeping my eyes on it until they cross.

"He certainly is a catch, Joy," I tell myself. "You're a lucky girl." The music recommences at a normal volume, and Topher capers down the aisle to me, singing along to some lovey-dovey-moon-June Frank Sinatra ballad.

"May I have this dance?" He drops to one knee and holds his hand out to me. I nod and take his hand.

"You lead," I tell him, as he puts his arms around me. "I'm wobbly."

"Do you remember when we danced to this song at the prom?"

"No. Uh-uh. Didn't dance to this song."

"We didn't? Are you sure? I think we did." He laughs and twirls me around in a little circle, and we stumble against each other. "Whoops, Silverman. You okay, there?"

"Mmm." I nod, then giggle, then notice that he's looking at me very seriously, and I try to look serious as well. "Right. Okay. What are you looking at me like that for? Wait a minute," I tell him, as he begins to stroke my cheek with the back of his hand, then puts a finger under my chin. "Wait, I've seen this movie."

"Shut up, Silverman," Topher says, and kisses me.

"This movie has a very bad ending," I tell him, and he stops kissing me. Without precisely intending to, I sit back down on the couch. He sits beside me, and puts his arms around me. He gives me the serious look again, and draws me closer. I am attempting to push him away when the door swings open, and a man and woman tumble into the room, laughing. I look up. The couple notices they have company. I shove Topher away, and he falls onto the floor. The woman stares at us. It is, of course, Ora. The young man with her stops laughing. It's Damon. I feel suddenly and extremely sober but not, luckily, for long.

"Joy!"

"Damon."

"Joy?" Topher looks at me slightly cross-eyed.

"Topher!" Ora has gone exceedingly pale.

"Hi," Topher tells her.

"Topher? I mean, Ora?" For some reason this strikes me as funny. "I mean, Topher, you know Ora?"

"What do you mean, do I know Topher? Do *I* know Topher?" Ora goes from white to red with fury. "Oh, I don't *believe* this. This cannot *possibly* be true." She stalks toward the exit. I stare after her.

"You know her?" I ask Topher, who is getting up off the floor.

"I'll explain later," he says, and weavingly follows Ora out. The door slams shut behind them.

"I very much look forward to seeing you attempt that," I call after him, as Damon drops down on the couch beside me. Two shifty, semitransparent doppelgängers of Damon sit down next to him.

"Hello," I tell all three of him, and giggle. "I'm drunk."

"Looks that way," the three Damons agree.

"Are you following me? You're supposed to be at the office. In New York."

"Well, first of all, guy, it's Saturday night." The Damons flip their hair. I close my eyes. "Second, you sent me out here for work, remember? Screenplay, Transgression Enterprise, that stuff."

"Oh. Right."

"Right. And one of the ladies on the Transgression Enterprise just broke up with her man and she asked me to be her escort, and so here I am. Pretty cool, huh?" He studies me for a long moment. "So, what just happened in here?"

"That is an excellent question." I sigh, and slouch into the cushions. "And one to which I'm not at all sure either you or I want an answer."

"Gotcha," Damon says. "Okay. You all right? Do you need anything?"

"I need," I say, "to sleep." And with that, I slip onto the floor, curl up under the love seat, and do so.

3.

You see, I always divide
people into two groups.
Those who live by what
they know to be a lie,
and those who live by what
they believe, falsely,
to be the truth.

—*Christopher Hampton,*
THE PHILANTHROPIST

I MEET HENRY AT PANTHEON for a pre—Girls' Night drink. Since my return from Los Angeles, I have refused to discuss the events that transpired there on the grounds that no events whatsoever transpired. Everything is just fine; that's my story and I've stuck to it.

Alas, Henry knows me too well to believe it for one red-hot second. When I walk into the restaurant, she leaps from her bar stool and gallops to meet me. Her pale pink T-shirt is emblazoned with elegant script that reads *I only date crack whores*. She grabs me by the shoulders, peers down at me, and snorts with annoyance.

"You are such a goddamn liar." Henry throws an arm around my waist and leads me to the bar. "I *knew* it. Your voice has been weird all week. You have some explaining to do."

"Lovely to see you, too, Hank. How's everything? How's Delia? Everything set for the big day?"

Henry and Delia sorted things out a few weeks ago and, several premarital counseling sessions later, their wedding plans are back on track.

"Your diversionary tactics are pathetic, Jo." Henry tosses her head. "Barkeep, a drink for my pathetic best man."

"How was your Labor Day, little gal?" Luke ignores her and leans across the bar to kiss my cheek. My Labor Day, as it happens, was spent in the company of the Winslow family, up in Maine, and I have vowed not to discuss it in polite society. "Hey, I got the invite for your engagement party," Luke says. "Thanks, I'll be there."

"Go away now, barkeep. We're having a girl talk." Henry waves her fingers at Luke, who rolls his eyes and walks, very slowly, to the other end of the bar. "God, he's so annoying. In that annoying sort of way."

"One of these days he's going to eighty-six you from this place and I, for one, will stand up and cheer."

"Are you kidding? He loves it. Luke's one of those men who thrives on abuse. He probably goes to a dominatrix on his nights off and gets whipped."

"He doesn't have to with you around."

"Lucky him. Now what the fuck went down in L.A.?"

"I don't think I want a best friend anymore, Hank. You're fired."

"And don't spare the details—you know I'll know if you leave anything out."

SHE'S RIGHT, of course. So I relate, unexpurgated, what I can remember of Theo and Angelina's wedding. The parts that come after the second bottle of champagne I recall with less than perfect clarity. I do know—not because memory serves but because Gabe told me so—that he spent nearly two hours looking for me, and located me asleep on the screening-room floor only after being tipped off by Damon, who helped him get me into a waiting car and back to the hotel.

Henry starts laughing more or less the instant I begin my tale; by the time I finish, she is convulsed with amusement.

"Thank you for your support," I tell her. "Your compassion rivals the saints'."

"Stop, stop! I have a cramp." She laughs, gasping for air. "Jo, that is *funny*. Gabe must have laughed his ass off when you told him about it." Henry swivels suddenly on her stool, gives me a piercing look, and throws her hands up. "Oh, good grief, Charlie Brown. You didn't tell him?"

"Tell him what?" I raise an eyebrow at Henry. "That I accidentally almost made out with my high school boyfriend while he was dancing with the psycho-tart who appears to be obsessing over both of them? And whom I would mutilate out of unfounded petty jealousy given a quarter of a chance? I'm sure he'd be hugely entertained. So entertained that he'd take this nice diamond everyone admires so much and run screaming. What a good joke."

"Luke!" Henry calls. "Emergency drinks!"

Luke eyes her from the other end of the bar and does not move.

"I'm betting he would find it funny, if *you* told him," Henry says. "I'm thinking he'll find it a hell of a lot less funny when Ora tells him, though."

"When . . . *what*?" I consider fainting.

"Oh, come on. Don't tell me you hadn't already thought of that. It'd be just like her to do it. Jesus, can we get some service?"

"Mind your manners," Luke calls back. "Try asking nicely."

"Lucas, dear, would you be so very kind as to serve us another round? Pretty fucking please?"

Luke sighs and sidles toward us.

"I hadn't thought of it." I push my glass toward Luke and he refills it. "Oh, hell. Of course she would."

"Lucas." Henry turns to him, oozing sweetness. "May I ask you a personal question? If your girlfriend told you that she'd run in to an ex at a party, and that he got drunk and made a pass at her, what would you do?"

"Depends." Luke hands her a fresh martini. "Probably something mature and levelheaded like hunt the guy down and beat him to a pulp."

"Defending her honor." Henry claps her hands together. "That's so macho and adorable of you. Okay, but what if she didn't care, if she just thought the whole thing was funny? Shut up, Joy. Don't interrupt."

"I don't know. Just forget it as best I could, I guess. And dream about beating him to a pulp."

"Right." Henry looks at me triumphantly. "But what if she didn't tell you? What if she kept it secret, and then someone *else* told you? Someone who saw it happen?"

"I guess I'd probably break up with her. If she didn't just tell me herself, seems like she's got something to hide, or something to feel guilty about. Doesn't seem like a trustworthy girl would act that way."

"Objection. Leading." I point at Henry.

"Oh, stop, I was not."

"Were, too."

"Was not."

"Anyway," I say, turning to Luke, "don't you think that's a little extreme? Breaking up with her, just like that? Maybe she had her reasons for not mentioning it, and you'd just—"

"Want to tell me what this is all about?" Luke asks.

"Hey, Henry," says Anabel Kappler, setting her purse on the bar. "Sorry I'm late."

"You're early," Henry tells Anabel.

"I'm confused," I tell Henry.

"Stop the fucking presses," Henry says.

"I think I met you at Theo's wedding last week." Anabel sits next to me. "Right? You work with my husband, Hector?" She smiles and turns to Luke. "A kir royale, please."

"We were just talking about that wedding." Henry kisses Anabel on both cheeks. "What were you doing there?"

"It was my husband's nephew's wedding."

"And your husband works with Invisible Inc.?" Henry plucks an olive from her glass and studies it. "Small white world."

You don't know the half of it, I think to myself.

"Invisible ink?" Anabel frowns.

"My company. We just did an assignment for him." I wave off the questions. "How do you know each other?"

"Love at first sight." Henry flutters her lashes at Anabel. "We met at that lingerie store up near Union Square earlier this summer."

"Bonded over push-up bras," Anabel says.

"Very romantic," I say.

"Joy's the jealous type. So watch out, Bel. And speaking of romance, let me get your opinion on something."

"Hank, please." I put my head down on the bar. "Please drop it."

"Bel, if your husband told you he'd run in to a former girlfriend at a party, and she made the moves on him, what would you do?"

"Nothing. Why?"

"Aha! Now, what if he didn't tell you, but somebody else saw it happen, and they told you. Then what would you do?"

"Nothing, Henry."

"Nothing? Nothing at all? Not even have a little temper tantrum?"

"Nothing at all." Anabel sips her drink.

"Oh, go on." Henry pokes her shoulder. "I don't believe you."

"Believe it, Henry. My husband is having an affair. I couldn't care less. Cheers." Anabel raises her glass to us. I swallow my drink the wrong way, choke on an ice cube, and am taken by a violent coughing fit.

"How do you know? Did he tell you?" Henry asks, slapping my back.

"No, of course not. But it's not hard to figure out." Anabel hands me a napkin.

"And you really don't mind, Bel? Honestly?"

"No. I honestly don't."

"I used to think I wouldn't." Henry looks thoughtful. "How's that work for you?"

"I married Hector for money," Anabel says. "Oh, please, don't look so shocked. I wanted security, Henry. I wanted comfort. That's what I get. Hector does love me, I think. In his way. But it doesn't matter that much. He takes good care of me, and he's kind to me. That's all I care about. I know this may sound very Victorian to you."

"It sounds very wacko to me," Henry tells her. "No offense."

"None taken. But it's not like nobody's ever done it before. Marriage was all about financial security until maybe fifty years ago. And social status. Right? So what's the big deal?" Anabel looks to me for confirmation. I stare back, trying to factor this new twist into my moral dilemma regarding her husband's account with my firm. "Look," she continues, "I've tried the true love thing. I was engaged to a guy I was madly in love with. He broke it off three days before the wedding and ran off with some other woman."

"Oh, god," Henry says. "I'm so sorry. That sucks."

"It was pretty bad. I moped around for a couple of years, and then I met Hector. We dated for a while, and eventually he asked me to marry him. I'd been trying to make it as an actress, and got myself into thousands and thousands of dollars of debt, and Hector made it clear that he'd bail me out, and take care of me." Anabel tucks a strand of bright red hair behind her ear. I notice her engagement ring, which sports a diamond the size of a small dog. "I wasn't hunting for a rich husband," she says. "It just happened that way. I'd decided I wasn't really interested in romance. I don't think I could even feel that way about anyone again. But I want kids. I want a safe life. I just wanted out of the game, you know? Hector offered me all that. And he's a great guy. He's good to me. He'll be a great father. So I thought, why not?"

"And you said yes." Henry gives her a thumbs-up.

"I said yes."

She said yes, I think to myself. She signed on for it. I should be comforted to know that Hector's affair, in which I may or may not be implicated, is causing no grief. Why is it, then, that I feel so unsettled? Am I, after all, as Topher insisted, a romantic—or is it some other discrepancy that is making me feel so weird and cranky?

"I still don't get why you don't care about the affair, though," Henry says.

"Why should I?" Anabel takes a sip of her drink. "I know he won't leave me. I'm the trophy wife." She smiles. Henry laughs. I blanch. I can't tell whether she's joking. "Honestly," Anabel says, "there's no reason it would bother me. He's just as good to me as he ever was. His affairs don't deprive me of anything because, remember, I was never in it for that kind of romance. Although—it's funny, Hector's really not the romantic type anyway. But when he proposed to me, my god. It was the most incredible thing I've ever heard. It was like some angel was speaking through him. I think I was actually in love with him for a day or two just because of the proposal." She stares into space for a few moments, then shakes her head. "I got over it before I accepted him, though."

"Huh," I say. "Wow. Well. Imagine that."

"And anyway," Anabel says, "not that *you* would know,

Henry, since you don't have much experience in this depart-ment. But it's hardly a surprise that Hector's on the prowl. He's a man, after all. No sane woman gets married expecting fidelity." She laughs. I flag Luke down for another drink.

"Ouch!" Henry slaps the bar. "Bel, since you're going to be surrounded by newlyweds tonight, I suggest you keep that opinion to yourself. And I think these husbands may be the exceptions to your rule." She gives my hand a secret squeeze.

"Of course," Anabel says, smoothing back a strand of hair. "Of course they are. There always are exceptions to the rule, of course."

THE GIRLS ARRIVE at Pantheon one by one, crowding up to the bar, exchanging kisses, stories, gossip, photographs of weddings and honeymoons. Miel hands out copies of the picture she took of us in April, our last night together as sin-gle girls, the last time all six of us were here together. As I study mine, she puts a slender little hand on top of my head and gives me a gentle smile.

"Bet you had no idea how much things would change," she whispers. "What a summer it's been for us."

I nod and look into her little pixie face.

"Oh, Jo." Miel sighs and touches the tip of my nose, then turns to Henry, who has joined us. "Can I ask you guys something? Are you, do you . . . have you noticed anything about Joan?"

"Like she's drunk all the goddamn time?" Henry says. "That kind of thing?"

"But I think that's because she's sad. Doesn't she seem sad to you? She's always so worried about Bix. And she's mad at him all the time."

"Think maybe it's just a posthoneymoon thing?" I ask. "A phase? Marriage shock?"

"Maybe. But I mean, she was kind of like this before the wedding, too. I thought maybe it was just because she was nervous about it." Miel glances toward the door. "Do you think maybe we should say something to her about it? Maybe talk to her a little bit when she gets here?"

"I don't think she needs an intervention, honey." Henry laughs. "Joanie's always been a wild one. I wouldn't worry about it."

"Are you sure?" I ask. "She has seemed a little out of hand lately."

"I'm sure she's fine," Henry says. "Just adjusting to marriage or something. She'll get pregnant soon and that'll settle her right down. Hey, speak of the she-devil—there she is. And they've got our table ready. Let's go."

OVER DINNER, my friends embark on a long, wide-ranging discussion about how marriage changes things. I suppose that, as a prospective bride, I should be all ears—and perhaps these observations might hold more weight with me if any of the participants had more than three months' wedded bliss on which to base their findings. As it is, I find myself distracted and slightly miserable for no reason I can identify. Without noticing I'm doing so, I slouch low on the banquette until Henry kicks me under the table and I sit back up. I slide down again, she kicks me again, I sit up. And so it goes. Maud describes how much more at ease she feels when Tyler is out of town now that they're married. Erica, who is cohabitating for the first time, chronicles the anguish of uncapped toothpaste tubes, dishwashing negotiations, dirty socks on the living room floor. Miel, who says her relationship seems to be exactly the same as it always has been, tells us about going with Max to get their names legally changed and how she laughed right through the proceedings until she got hiccups. Joan started the meal with a couple of Xanax and is on her fourth Manhattan by the time dinner arrives; she listens to the girls talk, lets out little ironic snorts, and is uncharacteristically quiet for an hour or so. Then, apparently unprovoked, she bursts into tears and collapses into Miel's lap, weeping and babbling incoherently. It's nearly impossible to make out what she's trying to say, but we're finally made to understand that, at Bix's insistence, she had an abortion a couple of days ago.

"He's been so gone." Joan sobs. "He's been gone since before the wedding. This spring he'd go out without me and stay out until three, four, five in the morning, and wouldn't call, wouldn't say where he'd been, just out. People kept telling me they'd seen him out at clubs and after-hours bars with his little film coterie, with actresses. I thought it was just jitters, that he'd change when the goddamn wedding was over and done with, so I didn't say anything."

"I thought you had such a good time on the honeymoon," Miel says. "You told me you did."

"We did, my sweetheart. We did. It was lovely. I was so relieved. But then we came back, and it was the same. And the couple of times I said anything to him about it, he'd make these hideous arch remarks about the old ball and chain. Someone told me he's been doing heroin again but it could be just idle gossip, I don't know. Then my period was late. I took one of those awful home tests and I went to the doctor and she said I was six weeks pregnant. I was thrilled, and I ran home to Bix, and he didn't miss a beat. He told me flat out he didn't want it, I absolutely shouldn't have it, this isn't a good time for us to start a family because he wasn't ready. What was I supposed to do?"

"Do? Leave the bastard," Henry snarls. "Come live with me and Delia. Fucking hell. I'll kill him, I really will."

"But it's my fault. I didn't tell him I'd stopped taking the pill." Joan begins to weep again. A long silence creeps over us. Anabel, who is seated on Joan's right, puts an arm around her shoulders.

"I'll take her home," Miel whispers.

"I can give you a ride," Anabel says. "My driver's parked outside."

We pay the check, collect our things, and rouse Joan. I am on one side of her, leading her through the front door and out to the sidewalk, with Maud on her other side, when Joan turns and gives me a wondering stare.

"Joy, how do you do it?" She shakes her head and sniffles.

"Do what?" I dig into my bag for a tissue, without success.

"You and Gabe. You make it look so easy."

"Sleight of hand." Maud laughs. "Joy's the man behind the curtain."

"I've never once seen you fight." Joan has begun to cry again. "You come out with us and never worry what he's doing. You let him spend time with Ora, and you probably don't give it a second thought, do you? You're so good."

"I beg your pardon?" I look toward Maud, who raises an eyebrow. "What do you mean, spend time with Ora?"

"Oh, she told me they've been doing a lot of work together." Joan sobs, as Henry holds the door open. "And I saw them at lunch the other day and—that's so great—I could never—you're so good, Joy. You're so strong. I wish I were like you." She hiccups wetly, plants a weepy, strongly bourbon-scented kiss on my cheek, and allows Miel to guide her into Anabel's black town car. The door slams shut. Anabel waves as the car pulls away and the rest of us stand watching.

When they are out of sight, Erica lets out a long, low sigh.

"Pearly girlie." Henry turns to her. "What is it?"

"I'm pregnant." Erica looks around quizzically; it's almost a question.

"Oh, wow." Maud stares. "Oh, honey. That's . . . great?"

Henry crosses to Erica in one giant step, wipes the single tear from her china-doll cheek, bends, and kisses her belly. I sit down on the curb and watch the traffic go by.

HENRY ESCORTS me home. I think we're both in shock, and we don't talk much about the specifics of Joan's dilemma. It is agreed that Henry will take Joan shoe shopping tomorrow, and I will coordinate with Maud and Miel to make sure a Girlfriend Watch is in effect. Then we walk on in stunned silence. The streets still have the empty quiet of late summer: one season over, the next not quite yet begun. At last, as we wait for a streetlight to change, Henry cuts her eyes at me.

"So, how *do* you do it, Joy? How do you keep your magnificent cool while a man-eating memoirist chases your boyfriend all over the city? Inquiring minds want to know. Joan wants to know."

"Hank, be nice."

"Your best friend, on the other hand, knows better," Henry says. "I know you never had any cool to start with. I know you're certifiably insane."

"That'll be our little secret."

"So Gabe is spending a lot of time with Ora?"

"News to me if he is. I guess it's possible. I don't keep track of his schedule." Thinking about this makes me want to shriek obscenities and kick things.

"Maybe you should." Henry makes a ferocious face at me. "Because I'm only allowed to discipline one spoiled rich boy a week, and Bix got in line first. And, by the way, you have a right to know who he spends time with. Anyone would be curious in this situation. It wouldn't be even a little bit girlie-girlie for you to ask him about it, Jo. Hell, it wouldn't be girlie for Charlton Heston to ask him. Or Warren Beatty. Or John Holmes, or—"

"Henry, I appreciate your concern, but can we please talk about something else? My head is going to explode."

"Okay, okay." She shrugs. "New subject. Did you ever find out what the story was between Ora and Topher?"

"No. He's called a couple of times at the office, but I haven't called back. I can't deal with it right now. I can't believe the engagement party is next week. I can't believe any of this." We stop in front of my building.

"Believe it." Henry nods and I follow her gaze across the street to a pair of teenagers pressed against the church's wrought-iron fence, making out like their lives depend on it. Behind them, the blue-plate-special board announces that this morning's sermon was on the steadfast presence of God. The featured passage is from the Song of Solomon: "I will rise and go to the city to seek him whom my heart loves; I sought him, but I found him not." I point it out to Henry.

"Unitarians." She sniffs. "A cousin of mine got married at this Baptist church near Baton Rouge. None of that poetic Old Testament crap for the Baptists. The church had this billboard next to the highway that said 'Accept Christ as the only redeemer or be damned to the fiery blazing pits of hell for all eternity.' Or something. Isn't that charming? We should send Bix down there for a lesson in old-fashioned country manners, don't you think? My cousins would beat the living crap out of him."

"He's actually turning out to be worse than I thought possible. Which really is a feat. But—Henry, what in the hell was Joan thinking going off the pill when he was acting like that? It seems so crazy."

"Oh, no." Henry turns to me, wide-eyed. "No, no, no. Don't you dare make excuses for him."

"Hey, calm down. I'm not. But for her to do it without telling him—that's tantamount to a fairly major lie, don't you think?"

"Little Miss Jojo." Henry points a finger at me. "You of all people are so not allowed to talk about lies of omission."

"That's not fair. It's so different. I'm not lying. I have decided, on principle, not to bring something up because I don't think it's right to do so."

"You know what? I shouldn't talk about this now. I love you and I'm a cranky bitch tonight and I am going home to pick a fight with Delia." Henry makes a face, turns on one heel, and begins to walk away. "I'll give you a call tomorrow," she calls back, and waves without turning around.

"Right. Okay. Sweet dreams to you, too." I stand and watch her go. I glance across the street; the teenagers are gone. I sit down on my front stoop and look up at the windows to my apartment. They, predictably, are dark.

Wednesday, September 12, 200—

IF THERE ARE WORSE WAYS to begin a day, I haven't yet been acquainted with them. At around four this morning I was awakened by the monstrous clatter and roar of garbage trucks. Since then I have been kept from sleep by the unrelenting whir and chatter of my brain; I feel like a ham radio receiving several dozen simultaneous and overenthusiastic broadcasts on the very unpromising subject of my love life. It's like a supernatural version of Chinese water torture.

As bad as things are, they will shortly reach an even more profound low, because at this very moment, I am preparing to commit a truly reprehensible act. Here, in our own home. When my beloved leaves, probably within the next ten minutes, I will toss integrity out the window and engage in a full-frontal violation of the relationship's most sacred principles. Knowing this makes me blush like a nun at a peep show every time Gabe looks my way.

With the bedcovers pulled up to my eyes and the dachshund snoring on my feet, I watch Gabe get dressed, and I consider something Anabel said on Sunday night: If your significant other is having an affair, you can tell. I think, though, that she must use some rare internal radar that gets installed after marriage, because I can't tell a damn thing one way or the other—though I suppose I could attribute that to sheer stupidity. And if Gabe suspects anything of me, if Ora has told him god knows what about our little screening-room scene at Theo's wedding, he's certainly not letting on.

He sits down on the edge of the bed beside me and lays a hand against my cheek.

"You're all flushed. Are you feeling okay?"

"Perfect," I say, blushing furiously.

"Sure? You're kind of warm. And you've seemed a little off the last couple of days. You could be coming down with something. Maybe you should stay home today."

"Nope. I feel fine. Totally fine. Fine, fine."

"Do you want anything before I go? I could make you some tea."

"No, thanks though. I'll get up in a minute." I try a weak smile. Now I really do feel ill, but it's probably just guilt. I met an aunt of Gabe's at his sister's wedding last month, who suffers from some malaise she called "nervous stomach," and which she described in unsolicited and impressive detail; it sounded very familiar.

"Okay then." Gabe kisses my forehead, stands up, and shoulders his bags.

"You going to be out long? Busy day?"

"All day. Couple of different shoots, couple of meetings. I'll leave my cell phone on, though. Call if you need anything." Gabe points a finger at the dog. "Francis, you keep an eye on the lady." He gives me a little wave as he walks out. A moment later I hear the front door close behind him. I stare into space and hold my breath. For the last two days, since Joan's drunken comments about Gabe and Ora ratcheted up my anxiety to an unprecedented level, I've been resisting this impulse. But it's all over now.

"I am a bad person," I tell Francis, and throw the covers

back. "I give up. Let the invasion of privacy begin." I pad to the study and collect Gabe's large appointment book from his desk. The dog follows me, looking suspicious, as I continue on to the kitchen, pour a cup of coffee, and sit down to review the book. I flip back through the weeks to late April and his first known encounter with Ora: a portrait session for the magazine article about hot young writers, the appointment recorded in Gabe's odd cursive scrawl. I note that he misspelled her name. That doesn't happen again—not for the follow-up appointment to review those portraits, in which her name is spelled correctly, not for any of the following sessions, where she is identified only by her first name or her initials—a sitting for new author photos, a review to select prints, a shoot for a fashion magazine that she insisted he do, the paperback party. And there's what must have been the lunch Ora mentioned to Joan, notated by Gabe as an appointment to review the paperback party photos. All of these I knew about. Everything looks above board.

I pour another cup of coffee, return to the study, and commence ransacking Gabe's filing cabinet. Francis waddles in after me, his tail slung low, and watches as I go through folders of Gabe's contact sheets and negatives, beset by a hazy fear that naked photos of the nemesis are in my future. I find none—though I do find prints from several of Gabe's sessions with her, and it takes remarkable will on my part to refrain from reducing them to confetti. Inspired by a faint memory of some old movie, I check his financial files for incriminating evidence on credit card statements and receipts—which turns up only the shocking amount he spent on my engagement ring. There seems to be an invisible force field around the drawer containing his correspondence. Only the pure of heart can enter, apparently, because I can't bring myself to look through it. I run my fingers along the tops of the folders, make myself cringe imagining Ora's prose style applied to the love-letter genre, and close the drawer.

I sit down at Gabe's desk, slide open the top drawer, and recoil in horror from the precise organization therein. Gabe's writing implements are ordered by type, size, and color; he has separate containers for three sizes of paper clips; he owns a staple remover *and* a letter opener, for heaven's sake. I slam the drawer shut.

"Can this marriage be saved?" I ask a photo of Gabe and me, tacked to the bulletin board above his desk. The photo was taken a little more than a year ago at our housewarming party. We're standing in the door between the kitchen and the living room; I'm laughing at the camera, Gabe is laughing at me. It's a nice picture. It was a good party, too; we said then that it was the closest we'd ever get to having a wedding reception. I lean closer and scrutinize our faces, trying to remember what I was thinking at the time. Nothing has really changed since then—I mean our daily lives are the same, how we are together is the same—but somehow everything is different. Thinking about it makes me feel like I do in those dreams where I'm running down a hallway, but as I run the hallway grows longer, stretching out forever, and I run faster and faster, getting farther and farther away from wherever it is that I'm trying to go.

I'm flipping idly through papers stacked on the desktop when I notice a scrap of paper with a large heart drawn on it, carefully shaded in, and pluck it from the pile. My own heart attempts to escape my rib cage in several directions at once.

In Gabe's handwriting are the initials *O.M.* Beside them, slightly smaller, the note reads *P.S.C. 230 PM*; below that are an address and tomorrow's date. P.S.C.? Prehistoric space cadet? Petulant stupid coquette? Please seek counseling? I have just finished copying the information onto my left palm with a felt-tip marker when I hear the front door open, and Gabe's voice greeting Francis. I catapult myself from his desk to mine, crash-landing into my chair just as he enters the office.

"Hey." He waves at me. "You're still here. You decided to stay home after all?"

"Just, um, doing a little work here before I go in. Editing." I pick up a random sheaf of papers from my desk and wave it at him. "Hard to, you know, concentrate at the office and, yes. You're back." I pull the sleeve of my pajama top down over my left hand.

"I forgot a lens I need for my first shoot." He goes to the closet and pulls a padded bag off one of the shelves. "I don't know where my brain is today. I can't focus on anything."

"Huh." I narrow my eyes at him. "Maybe *you* should take a couple of days off. Relax. You're doing too much. We could both, hey, we could leave tonight—we could spend the rest of the week on Nantucket. Your parents aren't there now, are they? You want to?"

"Yes," Gabe says, laughing. "But I have a couple of pretty important appointments. Besides, the engagement party is on Saturday. We can't miss that."

"Right. Well, maybe just take tomorrow off. Reschedule stuff? We can play hooky together. Have a picnic in Central Park."

"I'll take a raincheck on that. Maybe Sunday?" He waves distractedly and walks out. I hear the door close. A moment later Francis snuffles into the study, where I sit trembling in my chair.

When my fight-or-flight shakes have subsided, I call Invisible to let them know I'm on my way, and climb into the shower, vowing that I have learned my lesson. This was an aberration. I will never again stoop as low as I stooped this morning. And I will certainly not make use of the dubious information inked, blue and blurry, on my palm. Absolutely not. Not under any circumstances.

Just in case, though, I copy the information into my Palm Pilot before scrubbing it away. I swear the dog to secrecy and depart for the office.

WHEN I ARRIVE at Invisible, the front room is unnaturally quiet, and the faces of my little scribes are as solemn as gravestones. Pete tiptoes over to me and leans to whisper in my ear.

"Remember how Charles was all excited last night because he was going out to dinner with your brother?"

"Yes."

"To that fancy sushi place downtown?"

"Yes."

"And he thought James was going to propose?"

"Pete. The point." I hear strange noises coming from the back office.

"Well, I, uh. James. Didn't, you know, propose." Pete looks at the floor and scuffs the toe of one sneaker with the heel of the other.

"James dumped him?"

"Shhhhhhh!" Myrna and Tulley shush me at once. I consider turning around, going home, and returning to bed. For several weeks.

"I knew this was going to happen," I say. The Invisibles nod sympathetically and clear their throats.

"Never introduce anybody to anybody," I tell no one in particular. "Is it bad?"

"It's bad," Damon says.

"Really bad," Pete says.

"No suit," Tulley stage-whispers. "No tie. He's wearing jeans. And *sneakers*. And *no hair product*. He's out on the balcony with Our Lady of the Fishnets." Tulley nods in that direction.

"Maybe I should just go home for the day," I suggest to the general assembly. "Seeing me might just upset him more."

"Coward," Damon says.

"So? How'd you like to stand proxy for a war criminal?"

"Get in there," Tulley says. "Remember the Geneva Convention."

"Oh, fine. Hold my calls. If we're not back in a couple of hours, send in a hostage negotiation team, okay?" I slink into the back room and out through the window onto our fire escape, where Charles is blowing his nose energetically and Miss Trixie is making sympathetic noises. When Charles sees me, he tries to smile, bursts into tears again, and throws himself into my arms. I let him stay there and pat his back awkwardly until he pulls himself together. He sits up, takes a breath, looks me in the eye. Then his face crumples and he begins sniffling again.

"Charles. I'm sorry. Are you okay?"

"Oh, Joy! How could he? After all that we had together—how could he? After all the time we spent!"

"It was only three months. You should be—hey, I'm sorry. Don't cry. Hey, come on, it's okay."

"Three and a half months," he sobs. "Four, almost."

"Four months."

"Everyone knows the six-week rule," Charles says, sniffing. "If you don't break up at six weeks, you stay for twelve weeks—that's three months. And if you don't break up at three months, you stay for six months. And so on. So how could he break up with me at *fifteen and a half weeks*?"

"It's statistically impossible, darling." Trixie offers me a Kleenex. I decline.

"Vern, my brother has always defied the odds."

"He said he loved me! How could he love me one week and then just walk away the very next week?"

"I'm sure he did love you, precious." Trixie hands Charles another Kleenex. "How could he *not* love you?"

"Joy." Charles turns on me with big sad eyes, and I brace myself. "What did he tell you? Did he really love me? Was he lying? What did he say? What did I do? Did I do something wrong? Was I too clingy? Was I too distant?"

"We really never discussed it." And for precisely this reason, I want to add.

"Never? He never talked about me? He couldn't have really loved me if he never talked about me with his own sister. I'm such an idiot! How could I have believed him? Never believe anyone when they tell you they love you after six dates."

"That's very sound advice, Vern."

"Oh, my god," Charles says. "Why are you being so unsupportive? Your brother was horrible to me."

"Oh, goodness me. Time to run along," Trixie coos. "Arrivederci, darlings." She dashes inside, and her French doors snap shut. I had no idea anyone could move that fast in stilettos.

"I'm not being unsupportive." I turn back to Charles. "I'm sorry it didn't work out the way you wanted it to, and I'm very sorry you're hurt. But what else can I say? I can't condemn my brother to make you feel better. And I certainly can't explain his behavior—I've never understood him myself. I can tell you not to take it personally. He's never been a long-term kind of guy."

"And you didn't tell me this when we started dating because you're a sadist?" Charles says.

"Okay, stop right there. Halt. Friendship foul. This has *nothing* to do with me. I'm here for you, but I'm not going to take any blame for this."

"Well, you should. Why didn't you warn me? Why didn't you tell him to stay away? How could you have just let me . . . how could you have let him . . . ?"

"Because you're adults, and it's none of my business, and you wouldn't have listened anyway. You didn't listen. I didn't want the two of you to meet, if you'll recall."

Charles starts crying again.

"Joy." Pete leans through the window. "Phone call."

"I said hold my calls."

"VIP." Pete widens his eyes and waggles his eyebrows at me. I glare back, climb through the window, push past Pete, and snatch the phone up.

"Joy Silverman speaking."

"Baby girl? It's me. You sound a little tense."

"Oh, really? I wonder why, James." I wave Pete out and squint at the fire escape, where Charles is weeping over the railing. "What could possibly be happening here at the office, where I work, every day, side by side, with my *business partner*, to make me tense, do you suppose?"

"Oh, honey, I'm sorry. Is he taking it hard?"

"No comment. What the hell happened? Everything was going really well, wasn't it?"

"It was, I guess. He's a sweet guy. It was nice."

"Sweet? Nice? You took him to family weddings. You were together almost every night. You've been inseparable all summer. You let him borrow your shirts. You've never let anyone borrow your shirts. That's not 'nice.' That's *serious*."

"I know. I was. It was. I guess I changed my mind."

"Do you mind telling me why?"

"I don't know, baby." James lets out a dramatic sigh. "Who ever knows why we care, or why we stop caring?"

"Okay, first point, shut up, because you sound ridiculous. And second point, you promised me you wouldn't do this."

"I certainly did not. I take a page from your little book of rules and never make any promises having anything to do with love. Love is absurd. It's totally unpredictable. Anyone who promises anything having anything to do with love is extremely foolish. Weather reports are a great deal more reliable."

"Thank you, Oscar fucking Wilde. You sound just like Daddy."

"Hello, Ms. Pot calling Mr. Kettle black."

"James, you're acting like a *man*. You're crazy about Charles, and it terrifies you. Breaking things off with him is an act of sheer cowardice."

"Again with the stones thrown from the glass house," James says.

"What are you talking about? I'm engaged, if you recall."

"Precisely, baby girl. Are you trying to tell me that surprising little ideological shift of yours wasn't motivated by fear? Does the name Ora Mitelman ring a bell?"

"James, that's the stupidest— She had nothing to do with— Oh, never mind. I'm hanging up now."

"See you at the engagement party," James says, and hangs up first.

"I should have warned Charles," I tell the dead receiver. "Not that it would have done one damn iota of good, but I probably should have." I slam the phone down. It rings again. I pick it up. James probably wants another last word.

"What?" I say.

"Hey, sunshine," Gabe's voice comes over the line. "Having a good day?"

"Oh, Gabe, I'm sorry. I thought you were my brother."

"James on your bad side again?"

"James knows no other side of anyone. That's his inimitable charm. But yeah, he broke up with Charles. Which has caused a little friction here."

"Sorry to hear it. Listen, I've got a bunch of printing to do tonight. I'm going to be at the studio late, so don't wait up for me, okay? Got to run, Red. Have a good day."

"Right," I tell the dead line. "Okay. You, too."

Thursday, September 13, 200—

IT HAS BEEN A DIFFICULT WEEK for my staff, what with both of their so-called superiors going haywire, so as a morale booster I order lunch for everyone from our favorite Chinese restaurant—that is, everyone except Charles, who did not return as planned after his morning meeting. We have just finished gorging ourselves on every variety of Asian noodle and deep-fried vegetable known to man, and now lounge around the conference table, poking at the remains of several dozen white paper containers.

"Postdigestive narcosis." Damon groans. "May I take a nap on the couch, boss?"

"No. Hours to go before we sleep, dear scribe. We need to review the work to date on the Transgression Enterprise today. Lust and Vanity are opening next month."

Pete moans and lies down on the floor behind the table.

"Coffee, extra-strength." Myrna gets up and heads for the coffeemaker.

"Dude, you're a saint," Damon tells her.

"A bloody saint," Tulley says. "Joy, we need you to look over our revisions on the Medici Project proposal. Ora Mitelman's agent called, and he wants to review everything with us next week." Before I can comment on this, Charles bangs the front door open and wobbles into the room.

"HELLO!" he shouts. I can smell the gin on his breath

from way over here. "Hello, my friends! Having a good afternoon, everybody?"

"Not quite as good as yours, I surmise." Myrna pushes Charles away as he tries to embrace her.

"Vern." I reach him just as his knees give way, and he flings his arms around my neck to keep from falling to the ground.

"Hello, you." He rubs his nose tenderly against mine. His breath is all fumes.

"Liquid lunch, Vern?"

"I just stopped by Boîte for a teeny-weeny little cocktail." He giggles into my neck. "And the owner was there and he bought me a couple. A couple. Just a couple."

"That was very nice of him. I'll send a thank-you note. Damon, could you give me a hand? I think Vern gets the couch this afternoon. No, don't lie down here, Vern. Come on, up. Good job. Well done. Here we go."

We half-drag, half-carry Charles to the back office and pour him onto the couch. I get a blanket from the closet, kept there for the occasional late nights required during Invisible's salad days, and cover him with it. As I tuck him in he reaches up and strokes my face.

"Honey, I love you so much," he slurs. "You know I love you, right, Vernie-Vern-Vern? Even if your brother is an absolute heartless monster, I still think you're wonderful. I love you. I'm sorry about yesterday. Bad Charles. I do love you, you know that, right?"

"I love you, too. Okay, let go of my face now. Good boy. Just relax, and we'll see if you can sleep this off, or if we need to have your stomach pumped."

Charles has already passed out.

"Is this Invisible Inc.?" A vaguely familiar female voice echoes loudly in the front room. "Joy Silverman, where the hell are you?"

I whimper, get up, and walk back to the main room. Here I meet with a most unwelcome sight: My staff stare open-mouthed at the front door, where, dressed to kill, gorgeous as the day is long and twice as ferocious, stands Anabel Kappler in a rage.

"Today," she says, marching toward me, brandishing a Gucci purse in one hand and a letter in the other, "I received a letter from my husband. Or so he intended me to believe, since his signature is on it."

I hear a gasp from Myrna.

"However," Anabel continues, opening the envelope and pulling out two sheets of paper, "He also included, and I suspect not entirely by accident, this!" She holds up a piece of paper for inspection, and flourishes it an inch or two from my face. It is unmistakably an invoice, on our letterhead, addressed to Hector Kappler, for two love letters.

"I can explain," I tell her, though it seems unlikely. "Won't you please come back into my office and sit down?" I remember that Charles is passed out on the couch. "Actually, sit down here. Have you had lunch? Would you like some Chinese?"

"I don't need you to explain," Anabel says, hands on her hips and eyes blazing. "I understand perfectly. My husband hired your company to write me this letter. It says right here: *Item Love Letter, Anabel*. Next to *Item Love Letter, Jane*, who I assume is his mistress. Whatever. But he's hired you before, hasn't he, Joy? That proposal I mentioned to you the other night? That was written here, as well. Am I right? By the same person. I can tell."

"I'm not at liberty to disclose the specifics, actually. But listen, Anabel, the fact that Hector didn't *write* it himself doesn't mean he didn't, doesn't, feel those things. We consulted with him, he gave my writer very clear direction."

"Don't give me that," Anabel says. "I was an actress. I did Chekhov. I did Williams. I played practically every ingenue Shakespeare wrote. I was terrible. But I did learn something about words and the people who write them and the people who recite them. And I need to know who wrote this letter. And the proposal. I have to know."

"I can't tell you that. It's confidential."

"I *have* to know. And you *will* tell me. I could sue you for, for . . . something. I'm sure I could sue you for something. Look." Anabel collapses in the chair next to me. "I'm not angry. You already know I couldn't care less about Hector's affairs. And I think it's sweet that he cares enough to commission a love letter for me, for god's sake. Whoever heard of such a thing? It's adorable." She takes a deep breath and closes her eyes, then opens them and smoothes from her forehead a few strands of red hair that have come loose from her French twist. "Just listen to me, please. Do you know what this letter did to me? What it made me feel? I haven't felt anything like that for years—except for Hector's proposal. I didn't think I could feel anything like that ever again. Whoever wrote those—I need to know him. I *must* know him. I think I'm in love with him. You have to tell me who it is."

"Anabel." I touch her hand. "I really can't. It's company policy, and it's protection for our employees. It's in their contracts. I'd tell you if I could, if it were up to me. But I can't. I'm sorry."

"It was me. I wrote them." Pete's face appears suddenly at tabletop level. He has been lying on the floor behind the table throughout this conversation; now his eyes are wide and bright and fixed on Anabel. Everyone in the room stares at him.

"You all, go back to work," I tell them. "No, go to my

office. No, never mind. Go take a walk. Be back in an hour. Oh, boy."

"You wrote them?" Anabel blinks at him. "How *old* are you?"

"Twenty-three. Why? How old are you? Does it matter?"

"Thirty-seven. Does it matter?" They are gazing at each other now with that slightly hysterical rapture you see on the faces of young girls in Beatlemania footage.

"Right." I watch my staff shuffling out the door. "Okay. I'm going for a walk, too. Okay. See you later." Neither Pete nor Anabel acknowledges this. I expect their private soundtrack is turned up too loud for them to hear me. I grab my bag and follow the Invisibles out. On the way downstairs we fall in behind a sullen couple exiting the psychologist's suite, then are tailed by an agent from the real estate company on the second floor, who is making grand promises to another couple about the apartment they are apparently on their way to view. My staff and I stand on the sidewalk in the ochre afternoon sunlight and watch the two groups march off in opposite directions.

"I think I saw this in a play once," I say. Myrna glances at Damon, then looks at the ground. Tulley looks like she might start to cry. I'd often suspected she had a crush on Pete, and now I'm sure.

"I'm hungry again." Damon points at the café across the street. "Desserts are on me. Who's coming with?"

Myrna raises her hand. Tulley snuffles and nods. I look at my watch; it's a little after three. An image of the note on Gabe's desk drifts through my mind.

"You know," I tell them, "I'm going to run some errands. You guys be back by four or so, okay?" I watch as they cut through traffic to cross the street, and tell myself I should go back upstairs and hide under the desk for a couple of hours.

Then I head to Seventh Avenue and turn north. I pass St. Sebastian's Hospital, where outside the emergency room entrance young men and women tricked out in green scrubs and stethoscopes are generating a voluminous cloud of cigarette smoke. I consider checking myself in to the hospital's psychiatric ward. Instead, I check my Palm Pilot for the address I copied down yesterday. It is a beautiful, clear day, a perfect day.

At the building whose address matches my notes, a limp young man in full doorman regalia, his face a riotous constellation of acne, sweats beneath the awning and squints at me.

"Helpyoomiss?"

"Um. Suite Three L?"

"Knowyercomin?" the doorman mutters.

"Yes." I try to sound full of authority and purpose. "I have an . . . appointment?"

"Trewdalobbyantakealef," he instructs, twisting his thumb in that direction.

"Thank you." I enter the revolving door, and complete three full rotations, hoping that I will miraculously acquire the sanity to turn back. The doorman, noticing, shakes his head, and I allow the momentum of my circles to push me out into the air-conditioned chill of the lobby, past the potted palm trees and uninviting couches, and into the south wing, where there be dragons.

As I creep down the hall toward Suite 3L, a door opens. I panic and scurry past, dive around a corner, then peek out to see the hunched back of a very old woman as she hobbles away toward the lobby. She came, I note, from 2L. The door across the hall, which from this vantage point I can't see, should be the dragon's lair. I pause, take a couple of deep breaths, and with no particular plan in mind have begun to ease myself in that direction when the door opens and Gabe walks out. I duck back around the corner and flatten myself against the wall. After this, I think, nothing will be beneath my dignity, as I don't seem to have a shred remaining. It should make my professional life a good deal easier. I hear a woman's voice from within 3L, soft and amused, and Gabe's laugh.

"As did I," he says. "Just wonderful. So, I'll be in touch."

The woman's voice again, lilting, laughing.

"Absolutely. I promise you," Gabe responds. "I look forward to it." I listen to the snap of the door closing, and his footsteps as they retreat down the marble hallway. I consider violence, count to fifty, poke my head around the corner to ensure that the coast is clear, and tiptoe toward the door, wondering whether I should knock and have it out with Ora now, or confront Gabe first, or—

I catch sight of a plaque on the ostensible entrance to Ora's love den, a plaque that announces the offices of the Organization of Medical Practitioners for Social Change. OM. PSC. Right.

I sit down on the floor in the hall and slump against the OMPSC's door. I am a bad person, I tell myself, not to mention ridiculous. Not to mention bad and ridiculous and bad. And ridiculous. And some other things I can't think of right now. But the heart on that note? What about the heart? I am in the midst of attempting to puzzle this out when the office door opens behind me. I fall backward and crack my head on the floor. A very elegant older woman in a white doctor's coat looks down at me.

"May I help you?" she asks.

I fear I am well beyond help, but I appreciate the offer.

"Thanks, I'm okay." I prop myself up on one elbow. The

woman reaches down to assist me off the floor, and I notice the name tag pinned to her coat. It reads: Dr. F. Valentine, St. Sebastian's Hospital, Director of Cardiology. Which would explain the heart on Gabe's note.

"Joy Silverman," Dr. Valentine says. "I don't know if you remember me. I met you at your Aunt Charlotte's wedding."

"Hello," I tell her, and lie down again.

"My granddaughter helped you with your makeup. I'm Frederika Valentine."

"Right. I do recognize you now. Grandma Fred. Nice to see you again. How've you been?"

"We have a couch in here. Why don't you come rest for a minute? It'll be more comfortable than the hallway floor."

"Sure. Good idea. Thank you very much. Listen, may I ask you something?" I struggle to my feet. "That guy who just left. What was he doing here?"

"Photographing me for a story about the organization. I'm one of the founders. Why do you ask?"

Good question, I think to myself. Dr. Valentine gestures toward the sofa, and I sit. A receptionist, seated at the front desk, gives me a curious look.

"He's my boyfriend." A fact which, I realize as soon as I have uttered it, explains nothing, but does manage to make my presence here even more suspect.

"Your boyfriend?" Dr. Valentine lifts an eyebrow. The receptionist pretends to be very busy with something in his top drawer.

"My fiancé, actually."

"Your fiancé."

"Yes."

"And may I ask what *you're* doing here?"

"It's a long story." I inspect the ceiling, then sit up.

"Joy, were you spying on your fiancé?" A smile flickers at the corners of Dr. Valentine's mouth.

"I wouldn't say that. Exactly."

"No? Well, just for the record, he's not having an affair with *me*. Though he is a very charming young man."

"Thanks," I tell her. "You know, I really should be going now."

I BID FAREWELL to Dr. Valentine and walk back through the lobby, past the young doorman, out the revolving glass doors and into the bright day. Dazzled by the sunlight, a little numb, and not a little perplexed by what has just happened, I stand for a moment on the sidewalk, before turning back toward the Invisible office. As I walk, my head rattles like a bingo cage with a horde of stray, strange thoughts: Was the activity I just engaged in actually *spying*, as the good doctor suggested, and not, as I try to convince myself, a perfectly rational, explicable sort of reconnaissance mission? Should I tell Gabe about what I've done? Should I tell him every-thing, since obviously he's perfectly innocent of everything and his presumed dalliance with Ora exists only in my absurd and unreliable brain? Should I forget my stupid vows and confess my secret fears? Or should I stay the course, keep my own counsel, honor the promise I made to myself? I wish, briefly, that I belonged to a religious sect with stern but gentle leaders and very simple rules, and I remember the slogan on Henry's favorite T-shirt, the one she was wearing the day we met: *God is coming, and she's pissed.* Dancing through this crowd of questions like a noisy fool, impossible to ignore, is the memory of my conversation with James yesterday—what he said about my dealings with Ora, his ridiculous intimation that those anxieties had influenced my decision to accept Gabe's marriage proposal. Ridiculous, I tell myself. Ridiculous. It can't possibly be true.

Friday, September 14, 200—

THIS WAS A HISTORICALLY significant morning. I woke
up early again, lay awake and restless, staring through the
bedroom window at the stones and dark arches of the church
across the street. After an hour I slipped out from underneath Gabe's arm, dressed, and wandered through the silent
streets for another hour or so before finding my way to the
office. And thus it was, in an event unprecedented in the
existence of my little company, that I got to the office first. I
managed to arrive even in advance of bright-eyed young
Pete. God only knows where he woke up this morning. I got
to unlock our front door for the first time ever. I got to make
the first pot of coffee as weak as I wanted; everyone else here
takes it like battery acid, black, bitter, and thick as sludge. I
got to choose the music: none. And sitting at my desk in the
alien quiet, going over this week's much-neglected work, I
had that pure, strange feeling I used to get in college, when
I'd stayed up studying so late that there'd seemed no point in
going to sleep; hours and momentum bore me unnoticed
over the edge of the next day. I'd wander from the library
back to my dormitory, across the empty quads, feeling hol-
lowed out or rubbed away, as if I had lost my corporeality or
specificity to the passing night and become transparent,
invisible to anyone who might happen to glance from their

windows into the gray dawn. It was, then and today, an extremely pleasant feeling.

As the morning passed, I returned gradually to the concrete world, but to a suddenly well-mannered and deliberate world in which, as if by mutual tacit agreement of its denizens, nothing was or ever had been amiss. Pete sailed in perhaps an hour after I did; he looked like a canary who'd gotten the better of a cat, but made no comment. The rest of the staff arrived after their fashion, Charles last of all, sheepish and much the worse for wear. No one made reference to yesterday's mayhem; we greeted one another brightly, handed off papers and instructions with brisk, polite efficiency.

By early afternoon, the office has settled into a quiet, steady groove of thorough normalcy. I'm ensconced in the back office with a subdued and industrious Charles, and I couldn't be happier. I'm unabashedly of the "least said, soonest mended" school of thought. I say rugs are for sweeping things under, and I say the hell with it.

"Vern." Charles looks up from his papers. "We should sit down and go over the schedule for the next few months. I think with all the Medici work and the Transgression Enterprise, we may have to bring on another writer or two. Can you do lunch?"

"Not today. I'm leaving in a couple of minutes to meet Henry and pick up our dresses for the wedding."

"Okay, well, maybe we can meet later this afternoon. And listen, take my cell phone with you." Charles slips a phone the size of a lipstick out of his pocket and puts it on my desk. "I may have a question or two about assignments, and since we're a little behind this week—"

"Sure, of course. Just call if you need me." I put the phone into my bag and stand up. "Feel free to pillage my desk. I have notes on all of the projects around here some-where."

"Vern." Charles shakes his head gently. "Finding any-thing in those drawers would require sonar equipment and spelunking gear. I'll just jingle."

"I'll be waiting by the phone." I wave to him and the staff, and head downstairs.

Passing through our building's arched entranceway and onto the street, I am struck with a sudden lightness of heart. The only hint that summer has passed and gone is the utter absence of humidity. The air is soft, the sky bluer than the eyes of angels on a Vatican ceiling, and there's not a cloud in sight. Perhaps everything has set itself right, after all this, I tell myself. Everything will be fine. For one minute, walking east to hail a cab, I feel like Julie Andrews on the mountain-top. And then I see Gabe. And Ora. Together.

I see Gabe and Ora together.

It's interesting that when one's suspicions are con-firmed one's brain somehow simply won't compute the very thing one has been contemplating with such focus and regu-larity for all these hours and days, weeks and months. Ora and Gabe are together. Right there. Standing outside a vin-tage record store about fifty feet ahead of me, peering in the window. I instinctively duck inside the nearest doorway, and find myself in a beauty salon. The woman at the front desk smiles broadly, bobs her head, and asks if I want a manicure. I do not. I lean a couple of inches out the door and watch as Gabe and Ora turn and head north along the street. And without exactly intending to, I begin to follow them.

I do so for what seems like miles. I am forced now and then to duck behind whatever presents itself in a necessary moment. Mailboxes and hot dog carts are especially handy; telephone poles and lampposts will do in a pinch. My followees don't seem to have any particular destination; they wander through the crowded streets of the West Village, stopping on impulse at storefronts, on corners, pointing things out to each other, Ora touching Gabe's shoulder or arm from time to time. The sight of them together crowds everything from my mind; I can't stop and I can't think, my head is tight and reeling and my heart slams like a bionic squash ball against my ribs. At one point, crouching behind a row of newspaper vending boxes, I see a man eyeing me with suspicion and it occurs to me, briefly, that I'm engaged in unusual and perhaps questionable activity. Before I can process this notion any further, I see that Gabe and Ora have moved down the street and almost out of sight, and I flee my hiding place and rush to keep them in view. I lose track of them in Washington Square Park and race through the crowds in the direction I last saw them headed until, several agonizing minutes later, I spot them crossing a street just outside the park. Relieved, I shadow them down the block and around a corner, turning it just in time to see them walk, arm in arm, up the stairs to the entrance of Café Paradiso.

I am following them into the restaurant with my head on fire and no particular plan in the works when the phone in my purse rings, and I stop short. What are you doing? I ask myself, as I grapple for the phone. Are you insane? I know the answers to these questions, and I do not like them.

"What are you doing?" Henry yells when I answer the phone.

"Stalking Gabe." Did I just say that out loud?

"What? You're supposed to be at Veruka's with me right now this second. I think she's going to chew a limb off or something. Are you insane?"

"Apparently."

"*Why* are you stalking *Gabe*?"

"He's with Ora. I saw them and I'm just, you know, following them. To see."

"Well, quit it. Right now. You won't discuss the situation with him on principle, but you'll stalk him? God, this is worse than I thought. Where are you?"

"Near Washington Square Park. How'd you find me?"

"Called the office. Got the number from Charles."

"Henry, Gabe is with Ora."

"I know, honey. You mentioned that. It's going to be okay. Listen to me now. See those yellow cars going by? The ones with the lights on top? Those are cabs. Now raise your hand and wave."

I do so. A cab screeches to a stop in front of me.

"Did it stop?" Henry asks.

"Yes."

"Okay. Get in. Tell the driver to drop you off on Ludlow and Rivington. I'll be waiting outside. Okay?"

"Okay." I hang up the phone, open the cab's rear door, and climb in. I sit, staring into the window of the restaurant until the driver behind us begins honking his horn and my taxi lurches forward.

"Lady, you want to tell me where we're going?" The cabbie scrutinizes me in the rearview mirror.

"Sure. Ludlow and Rivington. Please." I can't see anything anyway.

BEFORE THE TAXI has come to a complete stop on the designated corner, Henry is leaping to open the car door and pull me out. She hands the driver a ten-dollar bill, wraps an arm around my waist, kisses the side of my face, and leads me through the graffiti-covered entrance to Veruka's shop. When we get to the inner sanctum, Veruka gives me an icy stare and gestures brusquely for me to take off my clothes. I begin to walk toward the dressing room.

"No, no," she barks. "No time. You are very late. Clothes off here. Magdalena, the dress."

Henry gently removes my bag from my clutching fingers and sets it down on the floor. I slip off my sandals and stand passive while Henry undresses me as if I were a child. I can hardly breathe.

"Jojo, look at me," Henry says. "Just keep looking at me. It'll just take another minute and then I'll get you out of here. You're going to be okay. Deep breaths. Please don't hyperventilate."

Magdalena holds the dress at knee level and I step in without looking at it, balancing myself with a hand on Henry's shoulder. I hold obediently still as Magdalena zips the dress at the back and steps back to view it.

"Perfect," Veruka says. "Very good. Turn, look. Turn, darling, turn, turn. See yourself."

I shift reluctantly to face the mirror. Wavering there is someone who looks only vaguely familiar, a thin woman with rust-colored hair, pallid skin scattered with freckles, face stamped with doubt and fear. Thirty years old, knowing nothing, possibly crazy, definitely in trouble, heart beating a crazed apoplectic drum solo. And meanwhile, sheathed in the world's most beautiful bridesmaid's dress, which is a deep, soft, midnight blue.

"It's not orange," I tell Henry. "That's so nice." Then I faint.

A HALF HOUR later finds Henry and me at Katz's Delicatessen drinking egg creams, which she tells me are the cure for all ills. I came out of my swoon on the floor of the dress shop with Henry slapping my face and Veruka attempting to get me up and out of the dress so it wouldn't wrinkle. When they were certain I wasn't going to perish or litigate, Magdalena hurried us on our way, but not before Veruka suggested that I make an appointment to consult on my own wedding gown. Henry snarled at her and hustled me out into the bright unforgiving light of the Lower East Side and the September afternoon.

The deli is pleasantly noisy and crowded with an odd assortment of lunch-rush customers: pierced and safety-pinned youths with hair the color and texture of cotton candy, old men wearing pock-marked sweater vests and sad faces, Catholic school girls who dawdle over promontories of corned beef and sneak glances at the crew of handsome black boys at a nearby table, alight with youth and sex, their laughter extravagant, their restless limbs thrusting and flailing into the aisles like carnival rides. A group of husky men with crew cuts came in to the deli just after us; I saw them climbing out of red vans with *Guaranteed Overnight Delivery* emblazoned on the sides. Now they sit stolid and silent at a corner table, confronting the room with a row of hulking shoulders clad in bright red shirts that read G.O.D. in fat white letters. I bet Henry would look great wearing one of those.

In addition to our restorative beverages, Henry has polished off four hot dogs with extra sauerkraut and sweet relish, and a large order of fries. How she's managed to do so while keeping up her monologue is a source of fascination to me; she's talking so rapidly and with such fervor that there should have been no opportunity for her to chew or swallow. I and a half dozen customers at neighboring tables sit in awed silence, transfixed as she holds forth. I'm certain I'd enjoy the whole thing even more if her mesmerizing discourse weren't on the subject of just how very ill-advised are my intended nuptials, and my unsuitability to the institution of marriage in general. I find it vaguely funny that I've spent most of my life defending my right to *not* get married, only to end up on the other side of the debate.

"I know it's a cliché, but baby, you really doth protest too much." Henry slaps the table, heads turn, and the remains of her lunch gain a moment of altitude above the Formica. "If you really just didn't want to get married, you just wouldn't have gotten married. Don't you think all the effort you put into not believing in marriage is an indicator of something? Hey, Jojo! Are you even listening?"

"How could I not? Everyone in the restaurant is listening. Your point, as near as I can figure, is that I believed too strongly that marriage was wrong to just change my mind about it, right?"

"That is *not* my point," Henry says. "I need another egg cream. Okay, look. If you just don't believe in something, if it doesn't mean anything to you, why would you spend so much energy defining yourself in opposition to it?"

"I'm pretty sure there's a long-running tradition of active resistance to dominant paradigms, Hank." I hand her my barely sampled egg cream. "It's called revolution."

"Totally not the same thing." Henry downs half the drink in one noisy pull on the striped straw. "You want a revolution, you have to have something to revolve to. Changing from one thing that you think sucks, to something else you think is better, or at least something that sucks less. Revolution's about the vision thing, not about the suckage. You are all about the suckage. Half-emptiness. Fear. That's not revolutionary. It's reactionary."

"I've quit the resistance party. I'm engaged, remember? I embrace the suckage. I'm not reacting anymore."

"Not in the same way," Henry says. "But you are. Not talking to Gabe about Ora on principle, for example, because you don't want to act like everybody else, you don't want to be a girlie girl."

"And what's so wrong with that?"

"Nothing, per se, except that in this case you think you're being true to yourself, but you're lying to both of you."

"Wrong. I'm being true, trying to be true, to what I *believe*. Just because it happens to be contradictory to what I *feel* at the moment doesn't constitute falseness. Don't you try that Hallmarky, follow-your-heart, emotion-as-barometer-of-the-Real stuff on me."

"And don't pull your Lit Crit 101 schtick on me." Henry balls up a napkin and throws it at me. She misses.

"Anyway, given my current circumstance, all this is beside the point." I sink down in my chair. "My fiancé appears to be having an affair, which seems the strongest argument of all for not getting married. May we discuss that for a moment?"

"Survey says no. BEEEEEP. Wrong. I'm fully certain Gabe is not cheating on you, whatever it looks like. There's just no way. It's not his style. And also, if he'd shown any real inclination to do so, Ora would have made sure, very sure, that you'd find out about it in no uncertain terms. She'd have confessed it," Henry makes quotation marks in the air with her fingers, "with big fat crocodile tears, to Joan or somebody and manipulated them into believing it was their obligation to tell you. Kind of like she already did, right? When she told Joan that she and Gabe were spending time together, which Joan just *happened* to mention to you at dinner the other night."

"Now you're actually making sense. Or is that just wishful thinking on my part?" I watch as the G.O.D. squad ambles out, their red shirts flaring in the dingy beige room.

"Chicks move in mysterious ways, Jojo. Ask any dyke.

I'm totally positive there's an explanation for what you saw this afternoon. But even if he were having an affair with every deadbeat memoirist in the city, there's a better reason for you to not marry him, or anyone else, at least right now. You, young lady, believe in marriage too much. You believe more than any of us—me or Maud or even Erica—otherwise you wouldn't be so opposed to it."

"What?"

"When I was six, a bunch of us kids were picked to be angels in the church Christmas pageant." Henry sees my expression and winks. "Bear with me. I do have a point. We got white robes and gold tinsel halos and really pretty white wings made from real feathers, mounted on these harnesses that went around our shoulders, and they were on some kind of hinge, so they flapped and everything. And one day before rehearsal we were all dressed up and running around in the churchyard flapping our arms and yelling about how we could fly. Then Liza Mack—she'd fallen crazy in love with those wings. She even tried to wear hers to bed one night and I could hear her mother screaming at her from clear down the road—Liza went inside the church and got up into the balcony and opened a window, and she stood on the windowsill waving to all of us. And then she jumped right out. She thought those wings would work. She broke a leg and her collarbone and a couple of ribs and she was in the hospital for the longest time."

"That's adorable, Henry. I'm guessing there's a moral that goes with it."

"Look, there's this story about marriage that we're all told—forever and ever, happily ever after—and you, Joy Naomi Silverman, don't see that particular story coming true in the world, which is why you don't think marriage works. Which it doesn't, for people who have that same idea. I mean, there are other kinds of happy endings. But in some way you really, really want *that* version of the story to be true. Need it to be true. Can't quite *not* believe it. Which is why you had to make so much noise about not believing—to convince yourself that you would never, ever believe such a stupid-ass story."

"Whistling in the dark?"

"Yeah. And if I thought you'd really just changed your damn mind and you were just getting married, I'd give you my blessing and everybody say amen. But I think you *capitulated* to marriage, because you couldn't figure out how to live without a story—or you thought Gabe couldn't—and you got scared, and so now you're hoping the lie is true, you're hoping getting married will do something that it can't possibly do. That's the moral of the story, princess." She makes a grand flourish with her straw. We stare at each other.

"Don't take this as a concession or anything," I say, "but just in case I do think you might have a point, why didn't you bring any of this up earlier? Seeing as how it concerns the rest of my life and everything."

"Because you wouldn't have listened, Jo. You didn't want to hear it."

"And what makes you think I want to hear it now, if I didn't want to hear it before?"

"Nothing. But before you weren't acting like a complete lunatic freak and stalking your boyfriend. Now that you are, I think maybe I have a moral obligation to intervene. Which I know is very dangerous because if you go ahead and get married you may never speak to me again," she leans across the table and stage-whispers, "which I hope makes you realize what a big deal I think this is." She plays a dramatic chord on an imaginary piano. My cell phone rings.

"Saved by the bell," Henry says as I dig into my purse looking for it.

"Charles?" I answer the phone.

"Joy? It's Topher. Hey. Charles gave me this number."

"Oh." I hate Charles. "I really can't talk right now, Topher. I have to go."

"Joy, Joy, don't hang up. Come on, just a minute. Just talk to me. Why haven't you called me back?"

"This really isn't a good time."

"Okay, look, can you meet me tonight for a drink?"

"You're in New York?"

"Yeah, just for a couple of days."

"I don't think it's such a fabulous idea to see each other." I look at Henry, who chews on her straw and watches me through narrowed eyes. She shrugs.

"Joy, please. I need to talk to you. Just talk. I promise."

"Don't promise me anything." All at once, I am exhausted. I consider crawling under the table to take a nap. "You know where Pantheon is?"

"Sure," Topher says. "Meet me there at seven?"

"Okay. Seven." I turn the little phone off and stare at it dumbly.

"Fresh hell!" Henry waves her straw at me like a sorceress with a magic wand. I wait for transfiguration, which is not, apparently, forthcoming. "Want another egg cream?" she asks.

I ARRIVE AT PANTHEON and find Topher seated at the bar talking to Luke. For some indiscernible reason, this strikes terror in my heart. I watch them from the front door, their faces in profile, and briefly consider turning right around and heading back out into the perfectly harmless autumn evening. Then Luke waves, Topher turns and sees me, he says something to Luke, and they both laugh, and I am trapped. I proceed.

"Hey, little gal." Luke comes around the bar and lifts me into a bear hug. "How're you doing?"

"Fine," I tell him, my feet dangling. "Just peachy. Hi, Topher. Want to sit down?"

OVER DRINKS IN a small corner banquette, Topher reveals to me the source of Ora's ire at Theo and Angelina's wedding: Two weeks earlier, she'd arrived in Los Angeles to help the bride with prenuptial arrangements and anxieties. At a dinner party a couple of nights later, she was seated next to a recently disengaged Topher. They went home together that night, and the next, and the next, and most of the nights prior to the wedding. She became somewhat attached to him, as people tend to do when they have ongoing carnal relations with individuals they don't loathe. Naturally, then, she was a touch miffed about finding Topher in the arms of another woman. More than a touch. She had, Topher said, thrown an epic fit, wept and raged, referred to her history of betrayal and abandonment by men, her vulnerability, her deep feelings for him, et cetera. (She did not, as far as I can tell, reveal to him any of her history with me. I leave him unedified.)

As he tells this story, Topher sounds baffled but sympathetic. I am baffled, too—by the fact that any man would fall for such a routine, or that any woman would be shameless, desperate, or stupid enough to stage it. To me it seems totally counterintuitive. I don't have much of an opportunity to indulge my delicious scorn, however; it liquefies into dread as Topher describes how Ora unleashed her fury in my direction, threatening to reveal the indiscretion to Gabe unless Topher promised he would never see me again.

"So did you?" My voice quakes. I can't decide which of

the four of us I dislike most at this particular moment, but I suspect it's me.

"Did I what?" Topher frowns.

"Did you promise?"

"No. Of course not. I told her that I understood how she might feel threatened, but that you and I were old friends, and that if she caused you any trouble, it would be over between her and me."

"Oh. Right. Of course." So I'm probably safe for now, though this puts me in the rather awkward position of wanting Ora to find happiness with Topher. Though if she has or hopes to, why is she still pursuing Gabe? It's not altogether inconceivable that she has a predilection for men I've dated. I fleetingly consider negotiations: the phone numbers of my exes, a list notable for its brevity, in exchange for the surrender of my current beau. "So, Toph. How *are* things between you and Ora? Is it going well?"

"Fine, I guess, for what it is. She's beautiful, she's bright, and she's completely insane, which has its charms. The sex is phenomenal. I don't know how much of my interest has to do simply with how different she is from Evelyn. Very, very different. But I just broke an engagement. I don't want to get serious with anyone, and she obviously does. And I'm in L.A. and she's here."

"Is that why you came to New York, to see her?"

"No, to meet with a producer. I haven't seen her. I didn't even tell her I was coming. I guess I wanted to set things straight with you first, and—I don't know. I'm sorry. What a mess. I'm a mess. Sometimes I wish we were back in high school." Topher gives me a slightly melancholy smile.

"Hey," I say. "This is no time to get nostalgic."

"I'm not." He laughs. "I swear. But—this is all pretty funny, isn't it?"

"Funny ha-ha? Or funny like something's-rotten-in-Denmark funny?"

"Funny like isn't-it-a-crazy-mixed-up-old-world funny." He gives my chin one of those gentle, ironic mock-punches. "What-wacky-stuff-friends-go-through-together funny."

"Well, well. Isn't this cozy?" a female voice coos. We look up. Ora Mitelman is standing at our table, fangs out and fire in her eyes.

"Ora." Topher stands, flustered, reaching for her. "Hi. What are you doing here?"

"I'm here rather often." Ora draws back, gives him a subzero stare. "As your good friend Joy knows perfectly well. So nice of you to let me know you were coming to town, Christopher. We really must stop meeting like this, you know, the three of us. People will talk. Who knows what they might say? You can imagine, though, can't you, Joy?"

"You know what?" I can't look at either of them. "I'm going now. Lovely to see you both. Have a great evening." Getting up from the table, I trip over a chair, steady myself, and depart the restaurant with as much dignity as I can muster, which is approximately none.

WHEN I GET HOME, Gabe is on the sofa with the dog; they are watching a television program about Tibetan monks in exile. I sit between them and stare blankly at the TV.

"Hi." Gabe jostles my knee with his. "You look like you had a rough night. What've you been up to?"

"Aggh." What can I possibly say at this point? Everything. I could say everything, I could tell all, I could clear the air, I could confess, I could tell the truth, I could ask for the truth. I could. Ora will probably be calling to tell him her version anyway.

"What does 'aggh' mean in this particular situation, exactly?"

"It means . . . I had dinner with Henry."

"Henry." Gabe peers into my face, confused, compassionate.

"Yeah. She just kind of wore me out with wedding talk, that's all. I'm going to go to bed, I think."

"Okay." Gabe gives me a forehead kiss. "Sweet dreams. I'll join you in a bit."

"Thanks." I give him a little wave and head for the bedroom. Walking down the hall, I consider the implications of what I have just done. I consider my options, my obligations. I have just, in no uncertain terms, lied. It was a small lie, but there it is, a lie. And I am suddenly, perfectly, and hideously aware that it crowns, like a sad tiara, a season of lies of omission, lies of neglect, silence, misdeeds and deeds undone, willful blindness, denial—lies, damn lies, and so on.

Peekaboo. Where's Joy? Where did Joy go?

Saturday, September 15, 200—

AFTER MANY ICILY GRACIOUS discussions between
Gabe's mother and mine, our engagement party this evening
has been organized to take place at my mother's apartment
on the Upper West Side. So here I am, at ground zero of all
my childhood traumas and delights, surrounded by cher-
ished friends and family who have gathered to celebrate
and sanctify this singular and unexpected occasion of
my betrothal to Gabriel. And I can't think of anywhere I
wouldn't rather be.

It's an unseasonably warm evening and the air-
conditioning in here is prehistoric and there are a hundred
overdressed people crushed into the living room and dining
room, crammed into the den, clustered in the hallway,
sweating and flapping their hands at their faces and drinking vodka tonics like they were going out of style. And almost
everyone seems to have gotten up on the wrong side of bed;
the general mood ranges from imperceptible edginess to
barely contained hysteria. My mother and Mrs. Winslow are
both perched near the front door, vying for hostess-
greeting-guests position, the pretense of cordiality wafer
thin and getting thinner as the evening wears on. Henry and
Delia are in the kitchen conducting a fierce whispered argument that rises every few minutes to shouts that the other

guests pretend not to hear. Josh and Ruth are doing their level best to make conversation with Gabe's youngest sister and her new, incredibly uptight husband, and failing spectacularly. My mother's husband, Howie, has inadvisedly decided to make the acquaintance of Nana and Papa, my father's parents, while Charlotte and Burke attempt to run interference. One of Gabe's old friends, a real estate developer with a taste for much younger women, arrives with his latest arm-charm, a scantily clad coed who turns out to be a maniacal False Gods fan; she corners Tyler and Maud by the fireplace and gushes at them about Tyler's erotic power on stage. Erica and Brian stand fidgeting in the company of postadulterous Vassar playwright Tom Beggs, his new poetess wife, and their infant son, who wails without ceasing. My Gran chats with Charles, the wretch, who brought as his date the owner of Boîte. Gabe's father shrinks in fear beside her as the boys camp it up, Charles putting on a full floor show for the benefit of my brother. James, for his part, oozes jealousy and makes loud, arch remarks to Max and Miel, upon whom his sarcasm is completely lost, and to Myrna and Luke, upon whom it is not. Pete and Anabel canoodle in a corner; when they arrived together, Tulley burst into tears and shut herself in the guest bathroom. It took fifteen minutes of coaxing at the locked door to get her out.

And it's only seven forty-five.

In short, I've had root canals more enjoyable than this evening promises to be. I am standing in the doorway between the foyer and the living room, watching Rome burn and listening to my mother and Mrs. Winslow debate the rate of hors d'oeuvres circulation and placement of the bartender's station, when Maud abandons Tyler to his one-woman fan club and sidles up next to me.

"Having fun?" She knocks her shoulder against mine.

"Oh, sure." I lower my voice. "What could possibly be

more fun than my family and Gabe's trapped together in a stuffy apartment?"

"Just wait 'til the wedding. This, only much more so."

"Thanks, Maud. I can hardly wait."

"What are friends for?" She puts an arm around my waist.

"I'm glad you're here, anyway," I say. "See if you can keep me from insulting anyone, okay?"

"I'll do my best. Hey, look. Joan decided to show up, finally. And—oh, my god. Isn't that—?"

It is, in fact, none other than Ora Mitelman, who stands near the front door with Joan, greeting my mother and Mrs. Winslow. I resist the impulse to begin a horror-movie screaming fit, only because this scenario defies belief. It simply can't be happening.

"That *is* the girl from that awful night at Pantheon, isn't it?" Maud whispers. "You didn't invite her, did you?"

"Yes, and emphatically *no*," I whisper back, watching them come toward us.

"Hello, darlings." Joan gives me a sleepy smile as she approaches, flaps her hands at Maud, and leans against Ora, who returns Maud's murderous gaze with a defiant stare and a raised eyebrow. "Sorry we're so late. I hope you don't mind that I brought a friend, Joy. Bix left town this morning. I don't know where. Or when he's coming back. Isn't that funny? And Ora—do you girls know Ora? Have you met? Ora, this is Joy and Maud." The three of us manage curt nods. "Joy's getting married, too. It's her party." Joan closes her eyes slowly, opens them again, struggles to bring us into focus. She sways a little on her feet. "Anyhow. Ora came over to talk with me because I was feeling a little low, didn't you? She's such a good friend. And I asked her to come along because I didn't want to come all by my lonesome. Are you having a good time, Joy? Is it a nice party? Look. That man is serving drinks. A drink would be nice. Ora, darling, let's go fetch us some drinks, shall we? Girls, we'll be right back, okay? Don't you go anywhere. There's Miel. Hello, Miel!" Joan revolves in slow motion and heads for the living room. Ora moves to follow her, but Maud catches her by the wrist, and pulls her back.

"You're really a piece of work," Maud hisses at her. "How dare you show up here?"

"For heaven's sake, don't make a scene." Ora removes herself from Maud's grip. "Look at her. She's high as a kite on who knows what, and I couldn't convince her to just stay at home. What did you want me to do—leave her by herself in this state? She'd probably take a walk out the penthouse window." Before Maud can reply, Ora turns and hurries to catch up with Joan, who moves through the crowd like a cheerful somnambulist. We watch in silence from the doorway to the living room as Joan accepts a glass of something from the bartender before drifting over to Max and Miel. Gabe, noticing the new guests, moves to greet them.

"Well." Maud looks at me sideways.

"Well," I tell her. "Well, well, well."

An elevation of voices from the kitchen distracts us; after a moment Henry stomps through its swinging doors and marches in the direction of the bedrooms at the rear of the apartment. Delia comes out after her and rolls her eyes at me.

"How are you holding up?" she asks us as she passes. We decline comment, and she continues on into the crowded living room.

"You say the wedding's worse than this?" I ask Maud.

"Maybe you should elope." She shakes her head. "What do we do now? Should we have Ora kicked out?"

"I, myself," I tell her, "have always been a champion of

avoidance and denial. I see no reason to vary that course today."

"Your call." Maud shrugs. "I'm going to go spill a lot of something on her."

"Knock yourself out. Let's keep an eye on Joan, too. Probably best if she doesn't add too much more to whatever chemical mix she's got on at the moment."

"Good thinking, Jojo. Come on, let's go mingle."

I commence to make the rounds, mouthing hellos and waving to people, returning their forceful handshakes, embraces, smiles. After a half hour of awkward introductions, obedient small talk, and discussion of my engagement ring, which seems to go on for an ice age, I hear someone call my name and turn to see Joan swaying toward me, smiling angelically. I smile back and remove from her hand a glass containing the dregs of what I estimate to be her second or third double bourbon. She doesn't notice.

"Darling," she says. "Bathroom?"

"Take a right. Second door on your left. You okay?"

"Mmmmm-hmmmmm." She trails her fingers across my cheek as she continues on.

Across the room, Ora is chatting with Tyler and Gabriel, and as I watch them, I remember what she said to me last night: People will talk. Who knows what they might say? What, indeed. Well, with no further Topher-related incentive to keep silent, they might unfold a sordid tale of my misdeeds to my unsuspecting fiancé, is what. Thereby turning him into my ex-fiancé and Ora's new boyfriend. If he isn't already. I feel a sudden and urgent desire to lie down in the middle of the floor and take a nap, or to burst out laughing, or to gallop out of the party and down the street waving my arms in the air and wailing like an entire Greek chorus.

I decide instead to keep an eye on Joan, and trot through the hall to the guest bathroom.

"Joan?" I tap at the door. "Are you okay?"

"Go away, please," Tulley's voice comes faintly from within.

"Tulley, is that you? I thought you'd decided to come out earlier. Not that I blame you if you've changed your mind. Want company?"

"Go away, please."

"Right. Okay." I lean my head against the wall for a moment, then continue down the hall to the master bedroom, where I suspect Joan has gone in search of an unoccupied lavatory. I push the bedroom door open. It takes me a full five seconds to register that I am not alone; a man and a woman half-on and half-off the window seat opposite the entrance are locked in a very active and very passionate embrace. It takes a bit longer to register that the man and woman in question, who have not yet noticed my presence, are, respectively, Luke and Henry.

"Aggh," I say. They leap apart. We stare at one another. I begin to back out of the room.

"Joy, wait," Henry calls.

"Nope. Bad idea." I lunge backward through the door, race unseeing down the hall toward the party, and run smack into Gabriel.

"Hey, I was just coming to look for you." He catches and steadies me. "Are you okay?"

"In a manner of speaking, no. Not really." I look up at him, feeling suddenly that I have reached critical mass and will spontaneously combust, very soon, if I don't do something about it, if I don't find some way to sort out all these conflicting thoughts that fill my head with this roaring, deafening white noise. "Oh, Gabe. We need to talk."

"Hey. Red." Gabe puts his arm around me. "Take it easy.

We will. Take a deep breath. Whatever's going on, it's going to be fine. I promise."

"You do? You promise?"

"Yes, I do." He laughs. "So relax. Let's try to have some fun here. However unlikely that seems."

"Ah!" Ora is coming down the hall toward us. "There you are. The couple of the hour." She places herself ever so slightly between us. "Gabe, do you have a moment? Joy, you don't mind if I borrow him, do you? We need to talk."

Before I can respond to her—and I have no idea what I'm planning to say anyway, and my heart is in my throat, so it's just as well—my brother Josh appears in the hall, waving at us.

"Joy! Gabe!" he says. "Get in here, you guys. James is going to make a toast." The three of us turn and stare at him. "Come on! They're coming," Josh calls into the living room, and as we walk in, Gabe and I side by side, Ora slightly behind us, the guests stand and applaud. Ora brushes past us into the room, throwing a glance at me over her shoulder. I feel very much like fainting, but two days in a row seems excessive. Someone gives me a glass of champagne. James, standing on an ottoman, whistles for attention.

"Friends, here we are, to celebrate the unimaginable." James holds his glass aloft. "I thank my mother and Mr. and Mrs. Winslow for organizing this event, as Joy and Gabe's nearest and dearest truly need some assistance adjusting to the idea of them getting married. And we'll be holding an engagement party once each month until the wedding, for those who need further acclimation to the concept." The crowd laughs uproariously and I find myself wishing them all swift and painful karmic reprisals. "So." James waves his hands for silence. "To help you along, we're going to try a guided visualization of—"

"Joy! Help!" A scream comes from the hallway. It's Henry. Luke appears in the door to the living room, panting.

"Get an ambulance. Someone call now." He looks wildly around the room.

"What happened? What's wrong?" Gabe asks, as five or six people pull out their cell phones and my mother rushes for a phone on a side table.

"It's Joan." Luke turns to me. "She's out cold. On the floor of the bathroom in that bedroom. We can't wake her up. She's barely breathing."

I run for the master bedroom with Gabe, Ora, Luke, and a handful of other people hot on my heels. I skid into the bathroom to see Henry crouched beside Joan, who is askew on the floor, her face waxy, her eyes half-lidded. Vomit trickles down her cheek and into her dark curls, and forms a pool beside her head.

"What do we do?" Henry sounds hysterical. Her eyes are wild. "What's wrong with her?"

"Oh, for god's sake." Ora pushes past us into the bathroom and looks down at Joan. She suddenly seems unaccountably competent and assured. "She just passed out. Gabe, get those people out of here. Tell them not to bother with the ambulance." She drops to her knees beside Joan and shakes her by the shoulders. "Joanie. Joan, wake up. Wake up. Wake up!" Ora lifts a hand and slaps Joan's face, hard. After a moment, Joan's eyes flutter open, and she struggles to focus on Ora. I slump against the sink, my body weak with relief. Henry lets out a gasping sob and flees.

"Joy." Ora turns to me. "Wet that washcloth for me. Let's clean you up a little," she tells Joan. I have a sudden memory of something from a review of Ora's memoir, something about her brother having died of an overdose while she was in the next room. I pass her a damp washcloth, and very gently, Ora wipes the spray of saliva and bile from Joan's face and hair.

"My head hurts," Joan tells her.

"You probably hit it on something when you fell." Ora stands up and brushes at her skirt. "Think you can move, Joan? I'm sure she's fine," Ora turns to Gabriel, "but I'm going to take her to the emergency room anyway, so they can check her out. Can you help me get her up? Luke, could you run out and hail a taxi for us?"

Gabe and Ora, with Joan between them, make their slow way out; I trail behind. The apartment is deserted except for my mother and her husband, the living room littered with sad half-empty cups and little soiled plates. It seems that the party is over.

At the curb, Luke stands beside a taxi, holding the door open. Ora and Gabe ease Joan into the backseat, and Ora climbs in after her.

"You want me to come with you?" Gabe asks her. "Or meet you at the hospital?"

I catch a pale glimpse of Ora's face; for the briefest of moments her green eyes lock with mine. We are the same, I think to myself. We both want the lie to be true. Ora looks back to Gabe, shakes her head, pulls the taxi's door shut. The car pulls away, and we stand on the curb and watch them disappear down the street.

MUCH LATER, SOMEWHERE ALONG the dark, bleary trajectory between midnight and dawn, I am sitting on the couch, staring into the dim living room. I have been here, sleepless, for an hour or so, when the light in the bedroom goes on. A moment later, Gabe shuffles down the hallway and squints at me from the doorway.

"Hi," he says, his voice thick with sleep.

"Hi."

"Why are you out here?" Gabe pads across the room.

"Couldn't sleep." I move over and he flops down on the couch beside me.

"Was I snoring?"

"No, you weren't. But—"

"Was I drooling?"

"Gabe, did you—would you—are you having an affair with Ora?"

Which is worse, I wonder, as I hear the words slipping from my mouth, to say these things or not to say them? Which represents the deeper betrayal? To betray what I believe, or what I feel?

"What are you talking about?" Gabe laughs, then frowns. "An affair? With Ora? Are you completely insane?"

"Yes. I think we've determined that conclusively. Are you?"

"Am I insane?" He reaches over and turns on the lamp on the side table.

"No. Are you having an affair?"

"No." Gabe shakes his head, genuinely aghast. "Are you serious? I—*no*."

"Were you? Do you want to?"

"No. God, no. What even gave you that idea, Joy?"

"You've been spending so much time with her."

"I have? I guess I have been. But for work. Just work. I mean, she's a pleasant, relatively intelligent, not unattractive woman. She's a good client. But beyond that—"

"What about Friday? I saw you with her. I saw you go into Café Paradiso together."

"I ran into her on the street, between shoots. She was depressed, and she asked me to have lunch with her. She's been very generous about connecting me with new jobs. I had an hour free, and I figured I owed it to her."

"It hasn't occurred to you that she might have some

motive for getting you work, beyond the kindness of her heart?"

"Nope. But if she does, what's that to me?" He looks down, reaches over and touches my engagement ring, looks back up at me. "I'm spoken for, remember?"

I believe him. I am suddenly exhausted and find that I have neither the energy nor the will to not believe him. Doubts are there, waiting to be entertained, but I'm too tired to think about whether he might be lying to me, or himself; to consider how I might have betrayed him, or myself, or anyone else; to confess anything further, to cry anymore, to feel ashamed or even relieved. I decide to just believe, and the tension binding me slackens and the white noise in my head fades to a whisper. I lay my head down on Gabe's knee. He strokes my hair.

"Red, I don't know where you got an idea like that. If I gave you any reason to doubt me, I'm really sorry. But how could you think I'd want anyone else when I have you?" He lifts me up, his hands gentle on my shoulders, and turns me to face him. "We're made for each other, right? We're getting married. Come on, now. No more talk. Let's go to bed. You'll feel better in the morning."

Sunday, September 16, 200—

I'M AT MY DESK in the study with my old friend the laminated six-month calendar spread out in front of me, and many, many scraps of paper (which I continue to accumulate, Palm Pilot notwithstanding) heaped on the desktop and around my feet. Morning light comes slanting across the room, and the voices of departing churchgoers drift in through the window, along with the occasional prematurely yellow leaf.

Years ago, somebody sent me a poem whose opening lines read *"Distrust everything, if you have to / But trust the hours. Haven't they / carried you everywhere, up to now?"* It must have made sense to me at the time, because I copied it out and put it up on the refrigerator, where it eventually disappeared under shifting strata of postcards and *New Yorker* cartoons. But today, there's nothing I trust less than the hours, the weeks unreeling before me. The blank days on my calendar that might erupt into anything, produce any manner of surprise. And as everyone knows, I don't like surprises.

One thing, though, looks blessedly certain: Except for Henry and Delia's wedding next week, I will not be attending a single wedding this season. Unless—it suddenly occurs to me—my mother and future mother-in-law set their hearts on a winter ceremony. It could easily happen. My gorge rises and my stomach jumps.

"Hey, calendar girl. You're up early."

I turn to see Gabe leaning against the doorway. He rubs his eyes, a sleepy child, pajamas rumpled, hair on end. When I woke up the two of us were curled into a knot of limbs at the center of the bed. It took me an age to extricate myself without disturbing his sleep. Gabe doesn't seem to have been adversely affected by my restlessness. He has an irritating in-the-pink look about him that throws my own peevish, restive mood into a deeply unflattering light. I adore him. I ignore him. He laughs and pads away, Francis at his heels. I stare at my calendar's bands of white, am visited by a gruesome vision of myself in a wedding dress, followed by an even more gruesome vision of Joan on my mother's bathroom floor. (She's fine, more or less. She e-mailed me this morning to apologize, and to tell me she was leaving this afternoon for rehab upstate.) I consider returning to bed for the rest of the year, and have nearly convinced myself that this is the wisest of all possible options when Gabe returns with a cup of coffee, which he sets on a few square inches of bare wood that he somehow finds on my desk.

"Drink," he instructs. "In exactly one half hour, we are walking out the front door, and you will escort me to Central Park, as promised. And we will eat pretzels and get heartburn and ride the carousel." He assumes the Olympic victory pose, salutes me, and marches out. Francis sits down among the piles of paper, unwagging, and gives me the eye.

AN HOUR OR SO LATER, Gabe and I push off the little pier of the Central Park lake in a dented rental boat. Gabe rows us out into the murky green water, and I watch the boathouse and the dirty banks of the lake recede. Sun fractures into bright daggers on the water. From the far shore, snatches of music drift toward us, and the singsong voices of people walking the dappled shade of the woods, lolling on the park's wide and trampled lawns.

When we've achieved a respectable distance from the boathouse, Gabe pulls in the oars, runs a hand through his hair, and looks around. Oblongs of reflected light shiver across his face.

"Perfect day," he says. I hold my hand out and he takes it, and we float like that for a long time. We brush through some picturesque canopies of weeping willow, drift into the shadow of a footbridge and out into the main part of the lake. If only it could always be like this, I think, looking over at his still profile. Nothing spectacular, just this. I watch the dark silhouette of the Bethesda Fountain slip into view, its great, grave Angel of the Waters towering at the lake's edge, her wings raised, her arms stretched wide.

I'm staring over the side of the boat at my wavering reflection, when I hear Gabe's voice, ascending in question.

"Sorry. What?" I turn to him.

"A date. I was thinking we need to set a date for the wedding. Most people pick one before they have the engagement party. My mother pointed this out to me *again* last night."

"A date. Oh. Okay." I drag the heels of my shoes around on the bottom of the boat. A small puddle has formed there, and I wonder briefly how deep the lake is.

"Gabe," I say, "I need to tell you something." And without any previous intention of doing so, I do. I make a full confession: all my alarms and speculations regarding Ora, the nights with Topher at the wedding upstate, in Los Angeles, at Pantheon. I confess to the snooping, to the stalking, to the desperation, the anxiety behind my long silences, the justifications, the moments of spectacular failure to my ideals. The words spill from my lips and into the air around us.

At first Gabe tries to interrupt, to stop me. After a while, he gives up and sits motionless, looking out over the lake toward the enormous angel in the distance. When I have lapsed into stammering and then into silence, he turns back to me and nods.

"I know," he says.

"You know?" I feel like the bottom just dropped out of the boat. "You know what?"

"I knew about what happened at Ben and Marilyn's wedding. Topher talked to me when he got back from driving you to the hotel. He was worried about you. And I knew about what happened at Theo and Angelina's wedding. Damon told me when I was trying to find you. He thought it was funny. Which it was. And I figured you were out with Topher the other night. He called looking for you, and he said he was hoping to see you that evening, which is perfectly fine. He's a stand-up guy, you're old friends. Why would I want to interfere with that? I just couldn't figure out why you said you were with Henry."

I stare at him. He reaches out and with one finger lifts my bottom jaw to its full upright position.

"Joy, it's okay. I assumed that if there was anything going on that I needed to know about, you'd tell me. I have faith in you. Some things—there's just no need to discuss them. We don't need to talk about this anymore."

"But—"

"Hush." His hands slice through the air above our knees, smoothing away the ruptures, the stains between us. "Case closed. All right?"

Usually, this would suit me perfectly. I should feel relieved. I do not.

"So?" Gabe tilts his head at me.

"So, what?"

"So how about a date for our wedding?"

I stare at him, lovestruck. I have just tipped my hand, shown the worst of myself—faithless, foolish, weak as any woman has ever been accused of being—and still he wants me.

"Gabe, I can't marry you."

I look around to see who made this pronouncement. Apparently, it was me.

"You . . . what?" Gabe laughs, then frowns. "What?"

"I can't. Marry you."

"I—you're breaking our engagement? Joy, what's going on? Are you leaving me?"

"No! No, no, no. I want to be with you. I do. I just don't want to get married. I don't even not want to. I just can't." I shake my head. We sit staring at each other for a few long, silent seconds. A flock of ducks paddles by, quacking at the top of their little lungs.

"Yes, you can," Gabe says, at last. "Of course you can. Why can't you?"

"Because." Interesting. Why can't I? Oh, yes. Now I get it. Because Henry was right. And my brother was right. How irritating. "Because I believe in marriage too much."

"I don't know what the *hell* you're talking about." Gabe shakes his head.

"It took me a while to understand it, myself. But listen, you said you have faith in me. You're going to have to trust me on this one. I love you. I really do. But we can't get married."

"Joy, I thought we had worked all this out. I want to marry you. I want you to be my wife. I want to be your husband. I want *that*."

"I don't even know how to explain this." I cover my face with my hands. "I think—if we get married, it won't be about you and me and just what we are together. It'll be about Marriage. The idea of it. And about everything I want it to do that it can't possibly do. There's this fear, and it's why I said yes in the first place. But what I have to do is live with the fear instead of letting myself believe there's anything that can keep me safe. Which is what I'll be doing if I marry you."

"This doesn't make any sense."

"Okay." I take a deep breath. "Some part of me believes, deeply believes, that marriage will makes things perfect and keep us safe and in love and happily ever after—it's beautiful, but it's not true. It's a lie. And I don't ever want to lie, to you or to myself. The extent to which I want those lies to be true is exactly how far I should stay away from marriage."

"I just don't get it." Gabe's voice is tight with anger.

"Try. Please. Try harder."

"No, I mean—I understand what you're saying, but it's just a lot of talk. It doesn't have anything to do with you and me. It doesn't make any sense."

"It does, though. It does to me."

"Marry me, Joy."

"No. Live with me." I reach for his hand. He pulls away.

"No." He shakes his head. We stare at each other some more. At last, Gabe picks up the oars and rows us toward the bank by the fountain, where a set of marble steps descends into the water.

"I'm going to go now." He bangs the boat against the steps.

"Wait. That's it? You're just leaving?" I can't believe this. I start to laugh hysterically.

"I'm glad you're amused." Gabe stands up fast and the boat tilts and rocks. "You told me the night I proposed that you believed in me more than anything else you believed in. Obviously *that* was a lie."

"Gabe, please don't leave. It wasn't a lie. At that moment, I truly meant it. But—"

"Look, I'll get out of the apartment for a while, and give you a couple of weeks to move your things out. Maybe you could stay at your mother's until you find something else."

"Gabe. Please. Don't do this." I could burst into tears and cry for the rest of my life. "We don't have to do this now. We don't have to do this ever. I want to be with you. I love you. Why can't we just go on?"

"I don't know." He shakes his head. "I think it's more important for you to be right than to be happy."

I feel as if he's slapped me across the face.

"You know that's not true, Gabe. It's not about being right. It's about being true to myself."

"Oh, right. Your principles. How could I forget?"

"Would you really want me to just toss out everything I believe?" I'm shaking with fear and fury.

"Joy, I wouldn't. I don't want that. I want you to marry me."

"Look, when you proposed, you said it wasn't my place to impose my beliefs on the rest of the world. What about when the rest of the world tries to impose its beliefs upon me?"

"You're in the minority, Red. Maybe the majority of the world disagrees for a good reason."

Who is this man? Is this the same man who just forgave me everything, the man who wasn't afraid to let me lead?

"Maybe," I tell him. "And maybe not."

Gabe doesn't look at me again. He climbs out of the boat and onto the steps. I watch, dizzy with disbelief, as he turns and walks away, disappears into the crowd. For some longish additional period, I stare at the place where he vanished from my sight.

Saturday, September 22, 200—

I'M SITTING ON the porch of a lumbering rustic old hotel in deepest darkest Vermont, in a little town that has been taken over for the week by the friends and families of Henry and Delia. In the chilly morning light, the surrounding hills are already on fire with all the colors of autumn, the air laced with the smell of bruised apples, dry leaves, early frost. It's beautiful, but though we've been here since Wednesday evening I haven't been able to appreciate it, because I haven't been able to stop crying since I arrived on Henry's doorstep Sunday evening. Between then and now, I've cried so much I don't even know when I'm crying anymore. I'll start crying in the middle of a conversation and won't notice until I recognize the concerned expression of the person with whom I'm talking. Henry has taken to calling me The Waterworks. She tells me it's the return of the repressed, and finds it unbearably funny; when she sees me crying she gets the giggles, throws her arms around me, covers my face with kisses, and says things like "The ice queen melteth!" I've humored her. I know she means well. She knows I do, too.

This morning, though, it feels like the deluge may be at an end. My pillow was dry when I woke up, the heavy pressing in my chest had eased, and I clambered out of bed and into the shower feeling something like cheerful—or at least

not crushingly miserable. And now, perched on a phenome-
nally uncomfortable wooden chair with a paper cup of coffee
clutched in one hand, I catch myself humming "My Girl,"
with which Delia serenaded Henry last night at the rehearsal
dinner—a reprise of their early courtship. My musical inter-
lude is cut short by the revving engine and screeching tires
that announce Henry's arrival; she rented a vintage convertible Cadillac for the week, and if the car survives her unique
approach to driving, we'll all count it as a miracle.

"Off your ass and into the vehicle, freak," Henry yells.
"Get a move on." She's wearing a red cowboy hat, a skirt
almost too short to qualify as clothing, and an orange T-shirt
that reads, in neon yellow block letters, *Who's Your Daddy?*

"Good morning to you, Hank." I eschew Henry's pre-
ferred method of hopping the door and get into the Caddy
the traditional way. "You'd better have a good reason for getting me out of bed at six. The wedding doesn't start for at
least twelve hours."

"I do have a good reason." Henry yanks the wheel
around and pulls out of the parking lot, sending a wave of
gravel against the cars of the inn's other guests. "I have the
best goddamn reason ever. I'm getting married today, and I
want to spend some goddamn quality time with my best goddamn man."

"Okay, good reason. Coffee?" I brace myself against the
dashboard to keep from pitching out of the car, and proffer
my cup. Henry accepts, drains the contents, crunches the
cup in her fist, and flings it up into the air.

"Keep America beautiful!" she screams, lets out a war
whoop, and floors the gas pedal as we pass the town limits
and hit a stretch of open road.

"How are you, Henry?" I fasten my seat belt.

"I'm fine. I'm great! Never better!" Henry lifts her
hands off the steering wheel and waves them around. The

trees are whizzing by so fast as to be nothing more than leafy blurs. "I'm fucking terrified, Jojo!"

"Me, too. I don't suppose it would do any good to ask that you slow down?"

"No way. Fucking terrified! What a rush! This marriage stuff is better than skydiving." She laughs, her head thrown back, a crazed movie queen. "And how are you, Waterworks?"

"Fine. I think the waterworks may have shut down, finally."

"Too bad. You look so adorable with your eyes all red and puffy."

"Thanks." I grip the door handle as Henry takes a corner.

"Oh, come on, I'm just kidding. I think it's good for you. That stoic thing you had going just can't be healthy."

"To each her own, as James says."

"That big fag. He's a boy. What does he know?"

"Hen, where are we going?"

"Shut up," Henry tells me, and screeches to a sudden stop at the side of the road, just a couples of inches from where the road's shoulder plunges precipitously into thin air. She points to a sign informing us that this is a scenic outlook. I look. It is. Henry climbs out of the car, reaches into the backseat, pulls out a thermos.

"Come on, Joyless." She tosses her hair, cocks her head at me, and climbs up onto the hood. "Best seats in the house. Get over here and keep me company."

We lean against the windshield, drink coffee straight from the thermos, and stare out at the bright valley below us. After maybe twenty minutes of silence, the longest I've ever known Henry to hold her tongue, she flops her head toward me.

"Jojo?"

"Whatever you're going to ask, the answer is no."

"About that stuff I said at the deli about you getting married—"

"Don't worry about it."

"No, but listen. I'm sorry. I mean, I still think I was right, but I'm sorry if I got you freaked out and that somehow ended up—"

"Hank, really. Don't worry about it." I turn on my side and look her in the eye. "You were right. I didn't know, and you did, so you told me. You get thanked for that, not pardoned."

"Too bad you didn't. Get thanked. Or pardoned."

"Ah. Well. The truth set me free, I guess."

"Funny. You're a funny girl." Henry rolls over and puts her head in my lap. "Maybe he'll come around, Jo."

"Maybe. But probably not. Did I tell you he accused me of caring more about being right than being happy?"

"You know what, freak? Maybe you do." Henry pokes me in the ribs. "So what? That's who you are, and we all know it. It's your blessing and your curse. You always used to tell me there's no point in having principles if you're going to toss them out the window when they become inconvenient, right?"

"Great. My principles are intact, but I'm heartbroken and miserable."

"Jojo, you'd have been miserable if you'd gone ahead and got married. That's the whole point to all this. If you're not doing the right thing, you'll never be happy anyway. That's what I was trying to say the other day."

"I know. I mean, I believe you."

"Hey, there's always Topher." Henry lets out an evil giggle.

"Ora can have him. She should get something for her troubles."

"How about Luke?"

"I thought maybe you were going to keep him. On the side, just for kicks. What was that all about, anyway, that little scene in my parents' bedroom?"

"Hell if I know. I haven't kissed a boy since I was seventeen. I guess I just thought I'd check to see what it felt like."

"And?"

"It felt okay. But I'm in love with somebody else. And I still say Luke's hung up on you. I think maybe he just kissed me because he couldn't kiss you."

"You're delusional, Henry."

"I bet he's a better kisser than Gabe. How about you give it a shot, and find out?"

"How about you shut up and drive me back to civilization so we can get ready for your wedding?" I put my hand over her mouth. She takes it away, flips onto her hands and knees, and puts her face close to mine.

"*Mea mihi conscientia pluris est quam ominum sermo,*" she intones, and kisses my forehead.

"Careful. They don't take kindly to Pentecostals up here."

"That's Cicero, baby. A man among men." Henry slides off the hood and hops over the front door into the driver's seat. "It means 'My own conscience is more to me than what the world says.' And not in a reactionary way, if that's even possible. You should get it tattooed on your ass. Do you want to come back to town with me, or not?"

"Henry?"

"What, freak?" She leans on the horn twice. The noise echoes and ebbs across the valley.

"Henry, I do."

WE RETURN TO THE HOTEL, where we are met by a hysterical entourage who were not informed about our field trip, and in our absence became convinced that Henry had decided to jilt Delia. It takes some doing to calm everyone down, assure them that the wedding is still on, and get caravans started from the hotel out to the nearby country estate where the ceremony and reception will be held. I drive up with Erica, Maud, and Miel, all of us leaning out the windows of the minivan and laughing like lunatics. I am provided with an update on Joan, whom the girls visited at the rehab facility on their drive north yesterday. Maud proposes that we get Joan and Bix a honeymoon suite at Betty Ford; Miel, in a marvelous and uncharacteristically catty moment, suggests his-and-hers restraining orders. When we arrive at the estate, we find the lawns and hallways already swarming with the brides' families: Henry's Louisiana drunks and dropouts, Delia's Chicago Methodists and private school graduates, the Southern white trash and the Northern black elite. I've never seen such a surfeit of aunts, sisters, female cousins, and lady friends as the mob that dances attendance on Hank and Delia. It's amazing that the brides manage to get dressed and make it to the altar at all, with all that well-meant meddling—but they do.

They are married at sunset on the porch of the old mansion, situated on several acres on the top of a hill with a view of the Green Mountains. The brides both wear voluminous white dresses and veils. Henry is given away by her father, Delia by Miss Trixie, who is resplendent in an ornate orange ball gown accessorized with matching tiara and magic wand.

I stand beside Henry, who cries through the whole ceremony, and watch the faces of a hundred guests in the fading light. I am surprised by how much grief I see there, how much sorrow and fearful hope. I find it strangely comforting. Henry's father follows his daughter's lead and weeps his way through the vows while her mother beams and giggles and pats her plump knees over and over, as if inviting a child into her lap; Henry's younger sisters sit on either side of their mother, blushing and shushing her. Delia's mother uses one hand to dab at her eyes with a lace-edged handkerchief, and her other to hold the hand of Delia's stern and poker-faced elder brother who, I am told, still hopes that his sister's preference for women is just a phase. Her father refused to come altogether, about which the girls were initially outraged but eventually philosophic; three out of four parents, they reasoned, was not bad given the circumstances. James and Charles are here, together. James apparently flew into a jealous rage after the engagement party and called Charles every hour on the hour for two days until Charles agreed to see him. I have neither been asked for comment nor offered any. Anabel is here with Hector; she catches my eye and smiles. Aunt Charlotte is here with Burke; her friend Francine, who designed the flowers for Henry after all, is accompanied by her date, a gorgeous boy at least fifteen years her junior; they are seated with my girlfriends and their husbands. An empty chair is held in honor of Joan—like for the prophet Elijah at Passover, Henry said. Not a single one of us makes it through the ceremony without tears. I begin crying as soon as the brides appear, and one after another my friends join me. I suspect we are setting a world record for greatest amount of smeared mascara per capita.

I've never been able to figure out, really, why people cry at weddings, but now I think I understand it. And it's not because they're so happy, which is what people say, and maybe what they want to believe. I think people cry from regret, tenderness, loneliness, helpless bewilderment over how time passes, out of profound, protective, possessive, desperate love, and out of longing—a dangerous, perilous, impossible desire for something we won't lose.

Henry and Delia exchange vows, rings, kisses. The

guests rise to their feet as one and cheer, and I along with
them. The brides run down the aisle holding hands, the tiny
chartreuse lights of fireflies spangling the dusk at their feet.
At the reception, they dance their first dance to a stellar version of Al Green's "Let's Stay Together," arranged and performed by the members of Mercy Fuck. The brides' families
and friends mingle and dance, Henry's giggling mother with
Delia's stern brother, Henry's father, loosened by several
glasses of champagne and still weeping, with Miss Trixie. I
dance with Max and watch Delia's mother whirl by with a
gallant James, and Charles with a tiny niece of Delia's who
has fallen madly in love with him.

Henry cuts in on Max and puts her arms around me.

"Hey, Waterworks." I take her hand.

"The rain, it raineth every day," Henry says. "You want
to lead, or shall I?"

"Hank, let's both lead."

"Good idea." Henry assumes the junior-high-slow-
dance position, her hands on my posterior and her head
lolling on my shoulder. "This is so romantic. Ready to give
your toast, bestest man?"

"No."

"Oh, come on, Jojo. You're going to be great."

"I hate public speaking, Hank. Can't you get someone
else to do it?"

"Joy, you promised." Henry wags her finger at me. "And
I know how you feel about promises." She kisses my cheek.
"Go dance with Delia. You're practically in-laws now."

AFTER DINNER, the guests arrayed around picnic tables
on the lawn, the dance floor lit up by torches and candles,
the speeches begin. I sit between Charles and James and

tremble. After toasts by parents and friends, by Delia's maid of honor, by Miss Trixie, I find that I have stalled all I can.

"Where's my goddamn best man?" Henry yells to the crowd. "Give that girl a hand. Joy, get up here." The guests begin clapping and chanting my name. I turn to James.

"I can't," I tell him.

"You can, baby girl. It's your moment of truth. Make it a good one." He kisses my hand, helps me up, and gives me a push toward the stage. The crowd applauds as I stumble forward and take the microphone, which quivers in my hands. I look at my feet. I look out into the dark. I look for Henry and Delia, who are seated at the front table, beaming at me. And I open my mouth.

"Just before I drove up to Vermont," I can barely manage a whisper, "I was looking through my parents' wedding album, and I found a copy of this poem that someone read for them at their fifteen-year anniversary party. Three years after that my parents were divorced, but that's not the point." The guests roar with laughter at this, which takes me by surprise. "No, really. It isn't. Or, I don't know, maybe it is. At the time, they loved each other. They were as happy together as people can be. And sometimes, as I suspect anyone here married for fifteen years will tell you, that's not very happy." More laughter. I'm beginning to enjoy this. "But they did the best they could, my mother and father, and they had faith that everything would come out right. And it has—not as they expected it to, but in its own way. And I'm beginning to think maybe that's how marriage works. So I have faith, in this, if in nothing else: that no matter what happens for you, Henry and Delia, whether it's just as you wish or beyond what you can foresee here, now, tonight, things will come out right. This is an excerpt from that poem," I tell the brides, raising my glass. "It was written to commemorate the marriage of a couple with whom the writer was friends, and I offer it to you, a poet's benediction and blessing."

> *ideas are obscure and nothing should be obscure*
> > *tonight*
> *you will live half the year in a house by the sea and*
> > *half the year in a house in our arms*
> *we peer into the future and see you happy, and hope it*
> > *is a sign that we will be happy, too, something to*
> > *cling to, happiness*
> *the least and best of human attainments*

I raise my glass and look around the room—at Henry, who is weeping again, and Delia, who clasps Henry's hand against her cheek and looks serious and elated both at once, at my brother, who is kissing my business partner, at all my friends and all the strangers. I think, briefly, of Gabe, and I think that this moment is both identical to all such moments, and also like nothing else that has come before or will be hence, and I think that I am, in my own way, happy.

Acknowledgments

THANKS TO THOSE WITHOUT WHOM: friend and agent nonpareil Elizabeth Sheinkman and the staff of the Elaine Markson Literary Agency; my patient and provocative editor, Kristin Kiser, her assistant, Claudia Gabel, and the staff at Crown Publishing Group; El Staff and fellow members of the NYC Writers Room.

Thanks to dear friends and esteemed colleagues Ingrid Bernstein, Tania Bertsch, Andrea Codrington, Dave Daley, Lisa Grace, Geoff Kloske, Andrew Hultkrans, William Monahan, John Reed, James Sanders (from whom I steal all my best lines), Kevin Slavin, George Stantini, Karen Steen, Rob Tannenbaum, and Chris Weitz, and to generous beta testers Ned Cramer, James Geppner, Jocelyn Mason, Alex McQuilkin, Jules Merson, Jack Murnighan, Julia Murphy, and Molly Ringwald.

For inspiration and encouragement at various junctures, thanks to Elizabeth Bogner, Sarah Burnes, Dawn Davis, Linda Rattner, Sarah Saffian, and Cheryl Willems.

Particular thanks to John Bowe, David Gates, Panio Gianopoulos, Scott Karambis, Bill O'Neil, Pavia Rosati, and Alice Vernon, for invaluable editorial guidance, and for their sustaining enthusiasm when my own flagged.

Finally, thanks to Anthony Steele and to my family—Alice Bradie, Elora Cosper, Skip Cosper, Lenore and Stanley Furman, Steve Johnson, Alex and Ginny, and Mimi Maduro—whose support makes everything possible.

About the Author

DARCY COSPER is a writer and book reviewer. Her work has appeared in publications including *The New York Times Book Review*, *Bookforum*, the *Village Voice*, *Nerve*, and *GQ*, and in the anthologies *Full Frontal Fiction* and the forthcoming *Sex & Sensibility*. She lives in Los Angeles and New York. This is her first novel.